For Anna and Jamie, Indi and Richard, Max and Caroline, M, and Phil xx

Author Note

Each of the stories about Poppy, Sera, Lily, Jess, and their friends at Brides by the Sea can be read on its own. If you like to read consecutively, this is the order:

The Little Wedding Shop by the Sea
Christmas at the Little Wedding Shop
Summer at the Little Wedding Shop

I hope you have as much fun reading the books as I've had writing them, love Jane xx

To plant a garden is to believe in tomorrow.

Audrey Hepburn

Chapter 1

Tuesday, 14th February
At Brides by the Sea: Roving reporters and the
older mindset

'In love with love, on February 14th ...'
It's past six as I pause on the step of Brides by the Sea. As
the warm light shines out into the darkness, the Valentine's
Day motto on the glass of the door catches my eye. Well yes,
I know, that's what it's meant to do. It's only a few white
painted letters and three heart-shaped dots, but there's still a
horrible twist in my chest as I see it.

I know it's stupid. I'm fine with wedding shops because I
come here so often. And wedding dresses still give me a thrill.
It's St blinking Valentine I hate. Every other day of the year
I've learned to be happily single. But February 14th is so
damned coupley. For people like me who once had it all and
blew it, it's hell.

What went wrong? If the wind wasn't howling so hard I'd
tell you more. As it is, a breeze off the bay like today's can
turn the silkiest hair into a haystack in two seconds flat. I

didn't put in an entire hour of straightening earlier to end up with frizz.

Usually I'd spend the day hiding out at home. But today I've come to – excuse the groans – a Valentine's day wedding party. The worst of all worlds then. But before I have the chance to tell myself off for faltering so early, the shop door flies open so fast I almost topple off my new Kurt Geiger platforms.

'Lily, perfect timing. What's the news from Bath? How was your journey? Come on in, Poppy and I are in the White Room, everyone else has gone home to get ready ...'

It's Jess, talking at a hundred miles an hour, and scattering so many air kisses I have time to clamp my wind-blown hair back down, swoon at the snowy suede Jimmy Choo heels on the shoe display *and* get my inner wimp back into line. As I recover my balance, and we finally move off along the hallway, I notice she's humming to herself.

'What a lot of hearts,' I say as I stretch out my hand to touch one of the strings in the window, and set them twirling. It's an understatement. Even if they're sending me to my secret unhappy place, I have to admit the clouds of printed paper shapes suspended in the displays are perfect against the exquisite white drifts of the lace dresses.

'I'll have you know those hearts are up-cycled from abandoned romance novels,' Jess grins. 'On trend, yet subliminally ironic.' She fixes me with her fiercest gaze. 'Flying the flag for all of us *not* in relationships.'

Meaning sad old me and her. The tragic ones. And moving on swiftly, because we're really not that bad, now we're safely inside I'll bring you up to speed. Brides by the Sea is the biggest, most wonderful wedding emporium in Cornwall. Jess, the owner, built the business up using her post-divorce adrenalin burst, hence the heart-shaped irony. In ten years, the shop has grown from a one room shop where I first truly fell in love with flowers, to four storeys of bridal fabulousness, perched above St Aidan Bay. I used to work here as a florist, back when my engagement solitaire sparkled with promise, and my life stretched ahead of me with solid gold certainty. Our wedding, a move to be with Thom in Bath, two years saving up for a house, then we'd head to the country so I could grow the flowers I loved arranging. Just like I used to do with my dad as a child. Needless to say, we didn't get far with those carefully laid plans.

As Jess waves a basket towards me, the scent of cocoa drifts up my nose. 'Truffle?'

'Maybe just one.' We both know I'm joking here. The upside of Valentine's Day at Brides by the Sea is the chocolate-fest. Ignoring my life-long diet, I close my eyes, and take a lucky dip. A second later my mouth explodes with a bitter-sweet mixture of white chocolate, coffee and alcohol. 'Delish ... is that Tia Maria?' I do my best to keep my pleasure moans to a minimum. 'Truly, I've been fantasising about Poppy's truffles since I hit the M5.'

Drooling on the steering wheel is not a good look, but at least it stopped the lairy white-van men in their tracks. They usually have a field day passing my design-your-own Fiat 500, Gucci, which came off the production line so pink my poor boss spent the next two years apologising for it.

'Have a Baileys one, they'll blow your mind.' Jess nods appreciatively as she looks me up and down. As she thrusts the basket at me, she's humming again. 'Fabulous suit by the way. Grey is such a versatile colour.'

Of all my friends, Jess is the only one who will know at a glance how many arms and legs my short jacket and tailored pants cost me. They're my first ever dry-clean only items, bought as a present to myself, to celebrate a pay rise a few months back. Given I'm hopeless with clothes, but still trying to work my massive splurge to the max, I've added a silk shirt and some scarily high heels to party it up for tonight.

'Work still okay?' Jess's question comes with an extra searching stare.

'Brilliant.' I say. Possibly too quickly. My breaking news is that the hotel chain where I was in charge of flowers has been taken over, and my job has dematerialised. But I've promised myself I'll get to grips with that horror once I go back to Bath. Luckily as Jess and I move on through to the White Room the quiet perfection of the white painted floorboards and grey striped chaise longue whisk me straight back to my happy place. My fingers hover over the rail of hanging dresses as I pass, lingering over the most delicate diamanté detail on a lace bodice. It's like a ritual. Every time I come back here I have to go round soaking up all the prettiness, almost touching, and checking out what's come in since my last visit.

'Ready for a pick you up?' Jess grins.

Her familiar war cry goes back to the time when my dad died, and I used to call in here Friday evenings on my way to see my mum in Rose Hill village a few miles away. For months, it was only Jess's straight talking and chocolate that got me through those awful weekends. Although I must admit this is the first time I've heard the not-so-dulcet tones of local radio on in the background in the White Room.

'Lily, you're just in time for the pre-wedding party drinks. Fancy some prosecco?' Poppy, the shop cake maker, smiles as she emerges from the kitchen and drops a glass into my hand and a kiss on my cheek. 'Don't worry about driving, it's taxis all the way from here.' She's the one who made the delectable truffles. Talking of which, I snaffle my next one as Jess comes past me.

'Thanks Poppy,' I laugh, 'I half expected that to be a cupcake, not fizz.' Poppy has a tiny kitchen on the top floor here, and she rushes around the shop with plates of goodies, looking for volunteers to sample her baking. Although she's spent a lot more time this last year working at the local wedding venue at Daisy Hill Farm in Rose Hill, especially since she's been going out with the boss there.

'How's Rafe?' I ask. He's the farmer in question, and every bit as lovely as Poppy deserves.

She grins. 'Hungry as ever, and very busy.'

Given the flurry of romances at Brides by the Sea lately, you'd think someone had been scattering the cupid dust around. First there was Sam who does the dress fittings and alterations, whose wedding party we're heading for this evening. The guy she's marrying is called Sam too, so they're known as Sam squared. Then Poppy and Rafe finally got together just before Christmas. And Sera, the dress designer, who has her studio above the shop, and a room dedicated to her creations, bumped into the love of her life at her sister's Christmas wedding, and got her happy ever after moment too.

As I sink onto my favourite Mother of the Bride Louis Quatorze arm chair, Jess drops the chocolate basket on my knee. Which might be something she regrets later when I've eaten them all. Then, as she bends down to fiddle with the radio, I suddenly get it.

'Brides by the Sea ... You're singing along to your very own jingle Jess!' How could I have forgotten? 'It's the Pirate Radio Valentine's promotion!'

Reading between the lines, Jess was sweet-talked by a cocoa-voiced guy in ad sales. She may have gone all ironic with her shop displays, but when it comes to business opportunities and husky voices she's right on the ball. When the ad sales guy pointed out that every Valentine's romance in Cornwall could end with a bride shopping at Brides by the Sea, Jess agreed to run ads all week. She also had the inspired idea of giving away wedding bouquets and a money-off-the-dress voucher for every bride who is proposed to live on Pirate Radio today.

'We're waiting for a little surprise before we head off to the party.' Jess wiggles her eyebrows at Poppy and me as she turns up the volume on the radio.

'So have there been many on-air proposals yet?' I ask. Personally, I can't think of anything worse. When Thom went down on one knee we were on the empty beach in St Aidan in winter. A rogue wave crashed onto him, and he almost dropped the ring. We both laughed a lot at the time, but looking back that cold water soaking was pretty much a metaphor for where we were heading.

'We've had live proposals from all across the county. They've got roving reporters, and we're trending on Twitter.' Jess's smile is close to ecstatic. 'Someone popped the question on a yacht in Falmouth, the next was on a tandem on the Camel Trail, and someone else took the plunge in a fishing boat off Land's End.' No wonder she's sounding happy, with so many potential wedding dress sales here. 'And I'm pretty sure the next place the Pirate Radio reporters will be going is the fire station ...' Jess reins in her smile, and gives me one of her significant nods.

'Really?' Another friend of ours from Rose Hill is going out with a fireman. 'Is it Immie?' If I'm sounding surprised, it's only because until last summer you'd have said gruff, straight-talking Immie was the last person who'd ever get married.

Poppy's voice is a squeak as she nods. 'It's top secret, but Chas is proposing. Immie's going to pick him up for Sam's wedding party, but he's waiting with his ring. It should be any minute now.'

What was I saying about cupid dust? Immie works with Poppy, and looks after the holiday cottages at Daisy Hill Farm. I've known them forever because we all grew up in Rose Hill village. And Chas is Immie's friendly fireman, who she got to know when his Daisy Hill Farm wedding went all kinds of wrong last summer. Except now things have worked out fine, because he's about to try again. With Immie this time.

'Okay, so are we ready for our next Pirate Radio Valentine's proposal?' As the DJ's voice cuts in, we all lean towards the radio. 'And we're going across to Barbara and David in the biome at the Eden Project ...'

Poppy lets out a wail. 'What happened to Chas and Immie?'

Jess shushes her. 'Don't worry, they must be on next.'

'Barbara and David are our super sixties, a couple of silver surfers who met online ...' The DJ sounds like he's loving the novelty. 'Hello Barbara ...'

As Jess's frown spreads across her forehead, she drops onto the edge of the chaise longue. 'Not being ageist, but I'm not sure we'll pick up a dress order from this one.'

Of all of us, Jess should be most in tune with the older mindset, given she's closer to fifty than twenty. As for me, I'm sizing up the truffles on my knee, deciding which one to go for next. In the end, I go for one that's been rolled in desiccated coconut. It's half way into my mouth, when a peel of laughter comes out of the radio, and stops me dead.

First I go icy cold, then a split second later I break out in a sweat.

The only Barbara I ever met with a laugh like that is my mum. Although obviously it can't be her, because my mum definitely doesn't date. Talking of my mum, growing up, the only thing that saved me was my sensible, down to earth dad. And I miss him like mad. Although from her side it's not all roses either. I was apparently 'this' close to becoming the 'yummy mummy' she wanted me to be when I married Thom. Me messing up on that one was a sackable offence.

Then Barbara chimes in on the radio. 'The Eden Centre's where we had our first date ...' and I almost drop the chocolate basket because from those cut-glass vowels, this could be my mum's twin. It isn't as if this Barbara's even getting the name of the place right. Which is another thing that ties in horribly, because Mum does that all the time.

'Omigod, are you thinking what I am?' My eyes lock onto Poppy and Jess's. It suddenly occurs to me that I did once meet a David on the stairs at my mum's house, changing a light bulb. 'It can't be my mother ...?' *Can it?*

Poppy's face is scrunched in confusion. 'I didn't know your mum had a boyfriend?'

'Me neither.' I'm shaking my head and my stomach's turned to stone. 'But, shit, if she's on Pirate Radio getting proposed to, she must have.'

Barbara – or rather my mum – sounds even more up-beat than usual.

'I can't possibly imagine why David's brought me to the beautiful Mediterranean dome ... on Valentine's Day ...' Her voice is loud, yet breathy. Even on the radio, I can tell she's ready to burst. Although you can excuse her for being excited. It's completely obvious she knows what's about to happen.

Poppy's hand flies over her open mouth. 'Oh shit, it really is her, Lily.' As she listens her puzzled expression softens. 'It's like something off Married at First Sight. I can't believe she's about to get proposed to.'

'Waaaaaaaaaaaaaaaaaahhhhh.' I jam my hands over my ears, because this is so many kinds of wrong. I don't want to hear someone asking my mum to marry them. My mum doesn't want to get married, she isn't even over my dad dying yet. Somewhere along the line my thoughts start rushing out of my mouth. 'And why the hell are they at the Eden Project? My mum's the least green person on the planet. She hates gardening, she never recycles. As far as she's concerned ecology's a virus that gives you the runs. Please tell me this isn't real ...'

Poppy tugs at my sleeve. 'It's over now, you can unblock your ears.'

I shut my eyes tightly and tell myself to breathe. 'How did he sound?' My voice is a croak.

Poppy's treading carefully here. 'Nervous ...'

I open my eyes a crack. 'She said "yes" didn't she?' As if she'd have said anything else.

Poppy nods, although given the background clapping is deafening, I hardly need ask. There's a few more whoops from the radio, then my mum's coming through again, loud and clear.

'A huge thank you to Pirate Radio and everyone here at Eden Valley. David and I are completely delighted, we'll be having a summer wedding, and I *promise* we'll be doing *all* our shopping at Brides by the Sea ...'

I'm biting back my pangs at how word perfect she is.

'A summer wedding?' This is typical Jess, latching on to the practicalities. 'They'll need to get a move on to pull that one off.'

'Unbelievable. Completely unbelievable.' It comes out sounding a lot meaner than I intend, but if your mum springs something like this on you, it's hard not to feel left out.

Poppy raises her eyebrows, and sighs. 'Give yourself time, Lily, it might not seem so bad when you're used to it.'

I know Poppy's only being helpful. But getting used to it is something else.

'I'm very happy for her.' I force out the words, even though I'm not sure I am. Actually, I don't know what to think.

Jess is tugging at her scarf. 'This is definitely a wake-up

call. We need to consider older brides. I can't think how we've overlooked them before.' Then she leaps up, grabs the prosecco bottle, fills my glass to overflowing, and hands it back to me. 'Drink that, it'll help with the shock. I'll go and get the gin.'

As I inhale a huge slug of fizz, the DJ's working the moment for all he's worth. 'So Barbara and David, what's next for you?'

And my mum's off again. Gushing doesn't begin to cover it. 'All the beautiful flowers in the dome here remind me that I was offered a free bouquet, but my daughter will be growing the flowers for mine, so any one else wanting lovely wedding flowers should get in touch too, she'll have plenty for everyone ...'

What? I can't believe what I'm hearing. If she carries on like this they'll have to fade her out. Which luckily for me, they do. I've never been more relieved to reach an ad break. As for which daughter is going to grow her wedding flowers, it isn't like she's got another. I'm her only one.

And almost as if the last three minutes never happened, we're back with the maddeningly up-beat DJ, who obviously has no idea his bloody radio station just turned my whole world upside down.

'And we're moving on with T-rex and *Hot Love*. Because our next Pirate Radio proposal will be coming from ... the fire station in St Aidan.'

'Yay! Go Immie.' Poppy whoops, and punches the air. But by the time she meets my eye, her worried look's back. 'At least Chas let us in on this. One unexpected proposal in a day is quite enough for anyone.'

She's right about that. I'm not sure I'll ever be able to face a coconut truffle again. But what do they say about every cloud? The engagement excitement might eclipse the fact that my own life is in free fall. And after hearing my mother agree to marry a boyfriend I didn't know existed, Sam's Valentine's wedding party is going to be a piece of cake.

Chapter 2

Tuesday, 14th February
The Goose and Duck: Pond life and matching cushions

'I can't believe the party's going so fast, it's eleven already,' I say, as Jess, Poppy and I grab an empty table, and put down our tray of colourful drinks. 'What's more, apart from my killing feet, I'm having a fab time.' Given my heels are at least four inches too ambitious, it's bliss to sink into a chair and kick off my shoes.

Poppy laughs. 'Hey Lily, you match the cushions.'

I glance down at the checked upholstery. 'If I'd remembered the Goose and Duck's wall-to-wall taupe make-over, I might have worn something else.' Although, unlike my mum, who revels in day-glow chrysanthemum prints, I'm happiest blending into the background.

Jess is slurping her electric blue drink with gusto. 'It's been non-stop fun. Supper, speeches, cake cutting, first dance. And now romantic drinks. You have to love a cocktail called *Scarlett O'Hara*.' Although she's possibly losing track. She's rattling through the drinks list so fast she's currently throwing down *Sex on the Driveway*.

Behind us the room is buzzing, full of Sam and Sam's friends and family, who we mostly know because they're from the village.

'Look at that.' Jess nods indulgently through a gap in the crowd towards the snug, where Immie is being twirled around on her high heeled Doc Martens by new fiancé, Chas, watched proudly by Immie's son, Morgan. 'They're doing so well not to upstage the bride and groom.' She's right. Immie's *I'm going to marry a fireman* T-shirt is perfect. Understated, yet says it all. If Chas is choosing engagement gifts like that, she's found herself a gem there. Although we probably knew that already.

Poppy twirls the umbrella from her drink. 'And the engagement ring is a great touch. Very Immie.'

Chunky purple plastic. For now. For a down-to-earth girl. That's Chas playing safe this time around. According to village legend, his ex-fiancée, who dumped him just before their wedding was so super-fussy she swapped the ring he bought *her* four times.

'It's a shame their proposal was mostly beeped out,' I say. Apparently when Chas dropped down the fireman's pole, ring box in hand, Immie was so stunned, all she came out with was a stream of expletives. 'I wasn't taking much in after the shock of my mum, but I'd still have liked to hear it.'

'Have you spoken to your mum yet, Lily?' Five cocktails in, yet Jess is straight on my case.

I search for my happy voice, but don't find it. 'Only for a

few seconds. They were out celebrating at The Harbourside Hotel.'

Jess is straight back at me. 'Gooseberry time. You'd better stay at mine tonight.'

It's an order not an invitation, although knowing how Jess likes to party, it'll most likely be morning by the time we get in.

'When I finish this *Kiss On The Lips*, I'd better go and talk to Rafe.' Poppy raises her fruit filled glass, and sends him a wave as she catches his eye. He's the tallest guy in the group of hunky farmers chatting together at the bar, and he rocks the 'drop-dead gorgeous' cliché with every inch. Although it's Poppy who made him that way. Before he met her, he was grumpy and plain. Which just goes to show what love can do to you.

'These *Chocolate Cherry Cha Chas* are giving me a warm fuzzy feeling.' I say, as I sink my teeth into my umpteenth wedding cupcake of the night. Poppy's finest, with swirls of pink buttercream, and a smattering of sugar hearts. I'm trying not to think of my mum as I take out the decorative 'I do' cards on sticks. It's not as if it even matters if I grow out of my suit trousers, given I won't actually have a job for much longer.

I sigh as I brush the cake crumbs off my boob shelf, then remember to smile. 'It's a change to come to a wedding party in a pub, rather than somewhere bigger.' The Sams just bought their first house, so she made her own dress, the ceremony was just for the family, and the evening guest list was for meaningful friends only. But given Brides by the Sea couldn't work without her, Jess has pulled in favours from all sides too.

Poppy's eyes widen in alarm at what I meant to be a throwaway comment. 'Don't say simple weddings are a new trend. Expanding the business at Daisy Hill Farm is literally scaring the G-string off me.'

Ooops. Talk about sticking my foot in it. Last summer the weddings at Daisy Hill Farm were mostly in marquees and tipis in the fields, but Rafe and Poppy are busy upgrading the buildings, so they can have weddings there all year round.

Jess jumps straight in to smooth things over. 'Don't worry, everyone loves a country wedding.'

I nod at Poppy. 'Most couples want a big day to remember.' Although what I remember about Thom and me getting married is mainly the arguing.

Poppy gives a shudder. 'I just hope we can pull in enough bookings to make it pay.'

It's obvious the next bit's going to be weighty, because Jess puts down her drink. 'You have to be brave to move forward, Poppy.' Her voice is grave as she sits back in her seat, and rests her hands on the carved oak arms. 'Courage is being scared to death, and saddling up anyway.'

'Sorry?' That's a bit profound for this time of night. Poppy and I squint at each other. We might live in the country, but neither of us rides.

A low voice comes from behind me. 'John Wayne said it. He was talking about metaphorical horses.' It's Rafe.

Poppy and I nod furiously. 'We got the pony part.' I can sense the teasing in Rafe's eyes without even looking over my shoulder. Not that I'm comparing, but Thom never twinkled like that.

Rafe carries on. 'Being scared is okay, especially if it means you're pushing yourself. Wouldn't you say, Poppy?'

Poppy's face crumples as she deliberates.

'My point exactly.' Jess nods.

'And we'll all be here to help you make the business a success.' I rush in, remembering too late that I actually won't be.

Poppy's grin is sheepish. 'Okay, my wobble's over. I'll man up.'

'Good to hear.' Rafe reaches across to give her a fake punch on the arm. 'And by the way Lily, Fred by the bar says "Hi". He's the Ryan Gosling look-alikey, waving like his arm's about to drop off. And he thinks it might be love at first sight.'

As we all screw our heads around, we take in a guy with broad shoulders and a beam the width of St Aidan Bay, doing the kind of wave he'd do if he'd been shipwrecked without a distress flare.

'Cool.' Poppy sounds delighted. 'Fred's lovely, he's helping with Rafe's barn conversion. He split up with his long-term girlfriend last year, so I'd say he's over the heartbreak, and ready to go. Funny, kind, exceptionally solvent, likes country pursuits and nice restaurants.' She sends me a playful wink. 'For anyone interested, that is. Not *necessarily* meaning you, Lily.'

I'm gawping at how much background detail she's crammed in there. 'Thanks, but I'm all good here, Poppy.' I grin vaguely in the direction of the bar without actually making eye contact. 'But please say "Hi" back.'

'Will do,' Rafe nods at me. 'I don't mean to interrupt, but Poppy did promise to teach me to dance tonight.' He holds out a hand to her.

Poppy sighs, then begins to wiggle out from behind the table. 'Rafe dancing? Now that *is* a scary thought.' A second later his arm slides around her waist.

They're about to wander off when the best man jumps up on a chair, rattling a spoon against a pint glass. As Poppy and Rafe stop, Jess and I sit up expectantly, to listen.

'Okay, ladies. It's bouquet throwing time.'

Jess and I slump back again, and she points at my glass. 'That's us off the hook. Time for another cocktail?'

The best man goes on. 'Sam wants *every* lady out in the garden, regardless of status. Single, married, divorced, you've all got to come.' There's an undertow of surprised mumbling as the women head for the door.

'That's a new one on me.' I tug on my jacket, and wince as I stuff my appalled toes back into my shoes. 'Looking at all the stilettos, it's probably just the landlord trying a fast fix to get his grass aerated.'

Jess looks at me as she slips on her coat. 'Remember the first ever bridesmaid's bouquet you made for me at the shop?' Jess isn't big on nostalgia, but she often goes back to this one.

As if I could forget. I was so nervous, I was shaking too hard to cut the stems. And I wanted it to be perfect. I grin at her, the same way I do every time she hauls out this story. 'A white and yellow posy. With freesias and daisies, and trailing ribbons. Took me four hours to make.' I was bursting with excitement when I finished it.

She's shaking her head, laughing. 'The look on your face, when I told you we needed five more the same.'

I pull a face. 'Rookie mistake. Lucky for me you went easy on beginners.'

Her smile is indulgent. 'Not at all, I could see your potential, even that first day.' Which is nice of her to say, and reminds me what an appreciative boss she was. As she helps Sam's Granny Kernighan towards the garden, she strikes up a loud running commentary. 'Whoever catches this bouquet is supposed to have romantic good fortune very soon. It goes back to the days when touching a bride brought good luck, and fragments of wedding dress fabric were like charms. Throwing the bouquet was a way of stopping the crowd tearing the bride's dress off as she left.'

I shiver as the wind rushes in from outside. 'That's barbaric. I'm not sure I'm happy with the voyeurs either.' I can't help noticing a lot of the guys are coming out to watch. If they're hoping for a girl fight, there are two here who won't be joining in.

As I hold the door open, I catch Mrs K's eye. 'What are you going to do with Mr Kernighan if you catch the bouquet and find *another* man?'

'I'll think of something,' she laughs back, pulling her collar up against the cold. 'There are lovely white roses and blue anemones in that bunch, so I won't mind if I do catch it.' She gives my arm a prod. 'From the smile that handsome young chap by the bar gave you as we passed, I'd say you're in there, even without the flowers.'

As we move out across the floodlit herringbone brick

paving, I send Jess an eye roll over the top of Mrs K's head, but she's too busy agreeing with Mrs K to notice. Eye rolls to that too.

Now we're outside, I can see there's been a makeover here too. We used to hang out here as teenagers on summer evenings, with our lemonade shandies and cream sodas, but the rough ground has given way to a neat lawn and timber edged borders.

I'm not wasting any time. 'Okay, let's talk avoidance tactics. How about we head for the trees?' Newly planted, in the shadows at the far end.

'Good thinking.' Jess gently passes Mrs K onto one of the women already bouncing on the front line. Talk about pushy. Some of them have even tossed aside their heels. Whatever happened to spiking the grass?

I shudder as I see their toes gripping the mud. 'What a nightmare. It's like school PE class all over again.' My least favourite lesson. Along with maths. And science. As for competitions, I'm the world's *most* disinterested competitor. Although if there was a competition for that, obviously, I'd be completely true to myself, and wouldn't bother to enter.

'Jules, it's great to see you, and just in time for the scrum.' It's Jess, greeting her tamest, most blue eyed, floppy haired photographer. It might be my imagination, but his trademark pricey aftershave cloud seems even stronger in the dark. Jess narrowly misses getting swiped round the face as he flicks back his multi-coloured scarf. Even though she must have seen him already today, she stretches up to give him a peck. This isn't just an air kiss either, it's a maximum effort, lips-to-cheek job. Given how hard she'll have leaned on him to come up with a best moments wedding album for a tiny fee for the Sams, it's the least she can do.

'Happy catching. Watch out for the water.' Jules gives me my own wave, and bounds off to where Sam is positioning herself, flowers in hand, back towards us, by the pub doorway.

'Water?' Jess laughs, and does a funny little purr. 'That boy is such a tease.'

I'm rubbing my arms because they're freezing. I mean whose idea was it to come out here in February, when we could easily have gone through the whole charade on the dance floor?

'Okay, here we go. It's happening.' *At last.* Given we're well to the right, and so far away we're almost in the darkness, I reckon we're entirely out of range. From what I remember from netball at school, Sam's even weedier than me when it comes to throwing.

'One two three ... THROW!' That's Jules. Whatever the wedding situation, he can't resist taking charge.

Sam swings her arms and there's a grunt as she lets go of the flowers. Then the bouquet flies upwards towards the starry sky. In a split second it's already soared way over Mrs K's head. It's a strange spectacle when you're completely detached and disinterested. There's a flurry of disappointed moans as outstretched arms drop, and heads along the entire front row turn to watch. The bouquet rises, tracing an extraordinary arc through the air. If Sam had been a champion hammer thrower, it couldn't be travelling any faster. It's hurtling safely to our left, then at the last moment it veers off like some kind of guided missile. The next thing I know, there's a thump in my solar plexus, and I'm looking down at a bloody bouquet in my stomach.

'Waaaaaaaaahhhhhhh.' Horrified doesn't begin to cover it. I fend off the flowers, flapping my hands, as if I'm shooing away a dog. Bouncing them as if I'm playing beach volleyball. There's the feeling that if I don't actually grasp the bouquet, it doesn't count. I stagger backwards, make a feeble two handed re-launch, and spin it to land on Jess's chest.

'For chrissakes, Lily ...' Jess snaps.

But it's too late. She's put two hands on it. So now it's nothing to do with me – it's hers.

Phew. For a moment, there I thought I might have to go through the whole damned wedding hell again. Talk about near misses.

'There's no denying, you *did* catch it.' Jess is talking at me through gritted teeth. 'Or more importantly, it chose you. It was really quite extraordinary the way it did that.'

'Yeah right.' I don't give a damn, because she's the one holding it now.

Her nostrils flare. 'It's only a bit of fun, Lily. *It's not real, you do know that?*' She runs a critical finger over the edge of a rose petal, reminding me she was the one who put it together this morning, although frankly it's too dim to see much at all. 'I'll give it to Mrs K, she'll be delighted with it.'

'Great, good idea, whatever ...' My one step backwards, into the shadows, is meant to distance me. Metaphorically rather than physically. Like stepping over a line in the sand. Especially as the crowd is moving towards us en masse, all clamouring to see who got the bouquet.

One step, but it feels like I've stepped off the edge of the world. The grass isn't there, and my foot plunges over one of those dratted pieces of timber edging. Platform heels are nothing like as stable as the name makes them sound. When I topple, it's backwards, in a series of staggers. I'm preparing myself to end up flat on my back in a border, with everyone gawping at me. Bad enough, but I'll have to handle it. Then something whacks me on the back of the calves, and tips me over. The toppling I was doing before is nothing compared to this. As I plummet into oblivion, instead of the thumping impact of my backbone on soil, there's a huge splash.

'Waaaaaaaaaaaaaaaaaaaaaaaahhh ...' Every bit of air leaves my lungs as I plunge into freezing liquid. Even my shriek dwindles to nothing. I'm not sure if my skin is burning hot or ice cold. What I am is wedged. Totally stuck. With my bum, head and body in sub-zero water and my knees hooked over some kind of wall.

Jess's voice is a squawk. 'Good heavens, Lily, Jules *did* mean real water. How *could* we miss an above-ground pond?'

'Did someone call me?' A second later, Jules' telephoto lens is pointing down at me.

Spluttering through clenched teeth, I point at his camera. 'Don't you dare!' Seeing a couple of open mouthed faces appearing, I let out a wail. 'Don't just stand there, get me out ...'

Out of nowhere some broad shoulders are blocking the sky, and strong fingers close around my wrist. 'Great attention-grabbing stunt you pulled there. But we'd better get you back on dry land.'

Just my luck to get an ironic one. Where was lovely Chas the fireman when I needed him? Although on second thoughts, as Immie's spectacularly absent too, don't answer that. There's a sudden panic I'll be too heavy for this guy to lift dry, let alone wet. But I needn't have worried. One easy yank later, I'm upright, water sluicing down onto my shoes. Even if I'm giving mental groans at how an LK Bennett dry-clean-only suit will stand up to a soaking, the good news is that somehow my Kurt Geigers stayed out of the water.

Despite my convulsive gasps, and the dimness of the garden up-lighters, when I look up the eyes I meet are smoky grey. They're also disarmingly familiar considering they belong to a stranger. From the way his lips are twitching there's a laugh bursting to get out. And he's right about the audience. Beyond the straggling curtain of my hair, I make out a circle of wedding guests, clapping.

As I scrape the pond weed out of my eyes, my other hand is still clasped in his.

'We might as well get the introductions out of the way.' He gives another tug on my hand, and lets his smile go. 'I'm Kip Penryn. Happy to drag you out of the carp pond.'

Penryn. I'm half way to being dazzled by the charm of it all, when the filing system in my brain catches up, and my stomach sags. Then shrivels. Back in the day Penryn meant rough denim, hot skin, and more brothers you could comfortably count on one hand. A motherless hoard, who descended on their uncle's second – or third – home every summer. They'd roar in to the big house, and disappear just as fast. Wildly unreliable, and between them they covered every kind of bad. Filed under 'B' for 'best forgotten'. At least that explains my racing heartbeat. Sending female pulses soaring off the scale is programmed into the Penryn DNA.

I drag myself back to reality. 'A carp pond? At the Goose and Duck? Aren't carp huge? I could have been eaten.' Bloody Alan Titchmarsh has a lot to answer for.

'Probably only goldfish in there.' He leans closer, examining the leaf he drags out of my hair. 'And water lilies, by the looks of this.' Now that super-smile of his has gone, he's back to the kind of hollow cheeked chic we all know is best avoided.

'So what are you doing here ... Kip, is it?' I'm ransacking my brain, trying to remember all the names. And work out if we've met before. That's the other thing with Penryns. There's no point backing off, you have to face them out.

'Apart from rescuing drowning damsels?' He gives another sardonic laugh. 'I'm from the exclusive local wedding venue, Rose Hill Manor.' Many more laughs like that could get annoying.

'Right.' Two out of ten for an answer that explains zilch. But the Manor's where Sera-the-dress-designer's sister got married at Christmas. They only have about two friends-and-family weddings a year there. Which is a bit of a strange thing to refer to, but whatever. There's something about him that makes me push. 'So how come you know Sam, whose wedding we're at now?'

'I don't.' His shrug is unrepentant. 'I dropped in for supper at the pub, and had to settle for left over hog roast. That's why it's worth paying for an "exclusive use" wedding venue every time.' He *actually does* the finger wiggle speech marks.

And there's that damned laugh again. '*Exclusive use* means you avoid random strangers like me looking for pasties and crashing your wedding party. As you've found out, it's well worth paying for.'

What a disgusting attitude. As for him scoffing the hog roast, I'm so angry I've practically got steam coming out of my suit pockets. I'm opening and closing my mouth like a goldfish – or maybe a carp – because I'm in so much of a rage the words won't come out. But then a knight in shining armour walks in to fill the gap with his smile.

I'm joking here, obviously. It's Rafe's friend who was waving at me earlier. Wearing a three-piece tweed and brogues, not chain mail. As he shoulders Kip out of the way, he's whipped off his jacket. And he's holding it out to me.

'You're shivering. Here, take this.' His Cornish burr is soft after Kip's clipped moneyed vowels. 'We'd better get you inside.'

The jacket's heavy as it wraps around me, but it immediately stops the wind. As for my knight, he's all boy-next-door, and close up his smile is even easier than it was from across the room. Which is way less disconcerting than the Penryn high-wattage version.

'Here, take these ...'

If I'd actually got around to shutting my mouth, I needn't have bothered. The next moment, he's handing me his waist-coat, and what the hell ...? He's pulled his shirt off over his head, and he's handing me that too. I try to make my eyes less wide. Close them even. Not that I'm an expert, but as torsos go, this one's ripped.

'If you wanted a stripper, you only had to say ...' It's Kip, laughing in my ear, before backing off across the grass. 'Catch you later, Water Lily.'

What? I stamp on the shiver that rattles through me. The name thing has to be a coincidence. He *can't* know me.

'He's right, we should go inside.' It's Jess, her hand on my arm. 'Fabulous apps though.' She's not wrong. Apart from the obvious.

'Abs, not apps.' However many times I say it, it doesn't go in. 'Apps are on your phone, Jess, abs are ...' I stop short of drawing any more attention to what's right in front of our noses. Despite the over-powering smell of wet pond, the scent coming up from the jacket wrapped around me is a lot like Jules. Only considerably more subtle.

Jess is steering me back towards the pub. 'We'll dry you off, and get a taxi back to town.'

But Rafe's bare chested friend is on our heels, protesting. 'You *can't* leave now. There's clearly enough clothes here for both of us.'

When I run my fingers through my sopping hair, it's a mass of straggly curls. Worst case scenario. 'I don't know.' What's more, as we come back into the brightness of the pub, the only visible patch of my silk top is completely transparent.

There's another waft of Jules' scent, as Rafe's bare-chested friend leans in close enough to nudge my elbow. 'We all saw you looking gorgeous before. That's what I'll remember when I see the damp version.'

Excuse me while I faint. I can't remember when anyone last paid me this kind of compliment. Although to be honest, I usually manage to fight off attention before it gets to the point of people saying nice stuff to me. Even Jules knows to keep his distance – or else – and he's very huggy. *Has someone sprinkled fairy dust on me? Is this the bouquet effect? Should I be shouting jeez, I'm not marrying anyone?* And then it dawns on me. All that's happened is I let my guard down. Who wouldn't when they were dripping wet and had just been hauled out of a garden pond? So there's no need to panic here. I mean, I really wasn't the one who caught the bouquet anyway. If anyone needs to watch out here it's Jess.

'So what do you think? Stay and party or back to town for cocoa and an early night?' Jess's eyebrows are raised expectantly.

We both know she's bluffing about going to bed. It would be a quick shower for me, then Jaggers until dawn. Jaggers, for those who aren't local, is a cocktail bar in St Aidan, with red perspex tables, a teenage clientele, and a penchant for *Sex on the Beach* happy hours. And if it's a choice between that or this, even if it means letting my wavy hair out in public, there's only one way to go.

Which is how I come to spend the rest of the Sams' wedding in the landlady's Pilates leggings. Wearing an oversized white shirt that smells of algae and photographer, with a tie for a belt. Talking to a farmer wearing only a waistcoat over a bare chest. Who reminds me his name is Fred.

Chapter 3

'Great, now we can get down to proper business.' Jess puts down her coffee, and pulls up a chair at her table in the corner of the White Room.

Considering how late it was when we got back to St Aidan last night, we were up and out startlingly early. I swear I was still comatose as we hit the bakery and the dry cleaners. Not that there was anything dry about my poor suit as I handed it over. The assistant at Iron Maidens promised they'd do what they could. But given her groan as she peered at the sodden fabric in the Tesco bag, I'm not hopeful.

'Right.' As I stare at the stack of pastries towering next to the appointments book my stomach wilts. 'Actually, I might save the pain au raisin for later, thanks.' I have no idea how Jess is dashing around with so much enthusiasm, when I've barely woken up. Although now I come to think about it, her stamina is legendary. At parties *and* in the workplace, she's always the last woman standing.

29

She runs her fingers through her hair. 'When I said working breakfast, I wasn't talking toast, Lily. I want to discuss your job. The one that's disappearing in the company takeover?'

My mouth drops open. Was I talking in my sleep? That would be the lost job I didn't mention to anyone at all last night. The one I'm not even thinking about. 'You know?'

From the way Jess is pursing her lips and clenching her fists, she's building up to something. 'News travels fast in the business community. And I assume your accommodation's going with it?'

Ouch. No messing. Straight for the jugular.

My mouth is so dry, my voice is a croak. 'I've got two weeks to get out. But I get to keep the car.' One tiny compensation in the whole mess of my imploding life. That's the worst part of a live-in job. When they offered me a room in the staff quarters after Thom and I split up, I didn't think it through to the point of takeovers, years down the line. I let out a long sigh, because although I'd meant to keep this secret, it's a relief that Jess knows.

Jess narrows her eyes. 'Did you enjoy the work?'

The question catches me unawares. Being fully responsible for a team, putting fresh flowers in every room in ten boutique hotels was a niche job. It began with flowers for the tables in one restaurant, expanded into front of house and bedrooms, and went exponential as they bought more properties. I'm unlikely to find another job like it. Certainly not in two weeks. But by the end, the job was so large, my assistants were the ones who got to do the fun parts, while I chewed my knuckles into the small hours, over orders and budgets.

'The work was fine. Except I haven't actually touched a flower for ages.' Now I stop to think about it, I miss that. Without realising it, I'd given up the part of the job I loved most. The reason I first came to work with Jess was because I was crazy about flowers, and Jess's tiny shop window showcased the most amazing bridal bouquets. Believe it or not, Brides by the Sea began as Jess selling flowers in one room before it expanded to four floors of loveliness. Every other flower shop I'd seen in Cornwall back then had the same old same old. And the florists where I found a job straight out of college were so old fashioned, the owner made me serve, while she took care of arrangement orders. Doing flowers for Jess was my dream job. And because she pushed me, and the shop expanded so fast, I learned so much about the whole wedding business along the way too.

Jess draws in a breath. 'How would you feel about coming back to Brides by the Sea?'

I'm so surprised for a second I don't reply. 'To do what? You've already got all the florists you need.' There's a crack team, who work out of the lower ground floor of the shop.

She gives a knowing nod. 'I'm thinking so much more for you than just flowers, this time, Lily. It's going to be a super career move. I want you to grow the styling side of the business for us.'

'Styling?' It comes out like an echo.

Jess's eyes are glistening with excitement. 'Whereas planners deal with the nitty gritty bits of weddings, the stylists do the pretty parts. They're the interior designers of the wedding world.' She counts off her fingers. 'Colours, decor, flowers, invitations, furnishings, the setting. A stylist will *perfectly* tailor the look of the wedding for each individual couple.'

I nod. 'I know what you mean. Stylists, as used by celebrities and footballers' wives, and seen in *Hello* magazine.' Surely there can't be enough of those in Cornwall to support a full-time position.

Jess's face breaks into a smile. 'That used to be the case. But not many couples today settle for a bunch of flowers at a local hotel, like you did. Stylists are a crucial part of a lot of weddings now, and Brides by the Sea needs to keep up.' Her significant stare flags up that Thom and I tied the knot long before the word tipi made it into the urban dictionary. 'These days every couple wants a wedding that's totally unique to *them,* that their friends and family will remember *forever.* Making that happen is a whole new growth area.' Those last two words will be the key to Jess's enthusiasm.

'But where do I come in?'

Her eyes narrow. 'A handful of brides are creative enough to know what they want, design their own wedding backdrop, and source every item to make their day spectacularly special. But most newly engaged brides won't know their favours from their fairy lights, and even if they do, they won't have time to organise everything. Which is where they'll turn to you to pull everything together. You might be involved a little or a lot, the budget might be tiny or huge. But basically you'll be here to guide brides towards choosing the right dreams for them. And then you'll make them come true.'

'I will?' My eyes are growing wider with every question.

As she rubs her hands, she's almost purring. 'We'll begin

simply, by sourcing lovely items brides might like to buy or hire to accessorise and personalise their weddings. Then we'll move on to creating a gorgeous department couples can visit for inspiration and guidance.' She's making it sound almost possible.

'Right.' I'm gnawing at the gel coat on my nail.

Her beam is widening. 'It's win win. We'll be helping people get the polished events they want, without necessarily spending any more. You'll get to design the flowers, and so much more too. And we'll offer a set up, and tidy away option. You wait, we'll have a fully-fledged wedding styling service up and running faster than you can say bunting and bouquets.'

That sends my voice high with panic. 'I'll be fine with the flower part. But what about the rest?'

And finally she picks up on my terror. 'There's no need to look so scared, Lily. Trust me, if I didn't know you'd ace this, I wouldn't suggest it.' Her tone has switched from full-on excitement to soothing. 'You've always had a great eye for weddings, you're brilliant with brides, and you're used to spotting trends with your flowers. What's more, you're talented enough to do this in your petticoat. It's the perfect opportunity for you to extend your floral skills and push your creative boundaries at the same time.' She sounds like she's given this a lot of thought.

Not that I'm about to mention it, but apart from my vanishing job, I'm fine with the boundaries I've got. 'But why me, why now?'

Jess gives a low laugh. 'Good business is about seizing opportunities. You're available, you're here, I'd be mad not to tempt you to expand your horizons.' Which all sounds so scary I need to make my excuses. And go.

'I'm not sure I should be running back to St Aidan.' My voice comes out as a croak. I left with such high hopes, and there's not a lot to show for the last five years. Bolting home to the place I worked when I was twenty is like admitting defeat.

Jess gives a rueful smile. 'Which is why I'm adding a sweetener. Poppy barely uses the flat upstairs now she's with Rafe. We could throw that in too.'

'Right.' It's so sudden, my mouth is still catching up. A job *and* somewhere to live. When five minutes ago I had neither. And even if my stomach has disintegrated at the idea of styling weddings, the view of the sea from those little round attic windows upstairs is luring me to think about it. Hard.

'Of course, if you feel St Aidan is a backwards step, why not look at it as temporary? Find your feet, have a go at the styling, and move on elsewhere in your own time if it's not for you. I'm happy with that.'

Jess is so great at making things work for people. That's why she's such a brilliant sales person.

Now she's started, there's no stopping her. 'We don't know what your mum's plans are, but unless she's eloping, I'm guessing she'll be busy with a wedding. This way you'll be around to help.'

What did I say about persuasive powers?

'You might even be able to grow those flowers for her bouquet.'

'Okay.' I hold up my hand before Jess gets completely out

of hand. 'Thank you, and yes. To everything except the last bit. Flower growing was never more than a fantasy.' That dream belongs to a different life. To a girl who took happiness as a given. I'm not that person any more.

Jess draws in a breath. 'We'll see.'

At times, she has a maddening habit of not taking 'no' for an answer. I'm mentally pushing up my sleeves, preparing to argue it out, when the shop door opens, and Poppy dashes in. She's wearing the Barbour jacket Rafe got her for Christmas, and from the way it's done up on the wrong poppers, I'm guessing she left home in a hurry.

Jess pushes the plate towards her. 'You're just in time for our brainstorming breakfast. Cinnamon whirl?'

Looks like this is me off the hook.

Poppy brushes the plate away with a half shake of her head. Without being rude, Poppy eats for England. Refusing breakfast ties in with her face being as white as the walls.

She undoes her coat, and sinks into a chair. 'You'll never guess what's happened.'

Jess and I stare at each other, our jaws locked. Put on the spot like this, it's hard to know which way to jump.

Jess unfreezes first. 'A tiny clue?'

When Poppy speaks, it's not so much of a prompt as a tirade. 'It's the total worst news ever. Never in our wildest nightmares did we imagine this. Talk about saddling up bloody horses. We might as well throw away the damned pony and be done with it. Weddings at Daisy Hill Farm are finished.'

'What?' Jess isn't following any more than I am.

As I go and crouch down beside Poppy, her body is shaking so hard it's making the Louis Quatorze chair creak. 'Okay, take it easy. Whatever it is we'll help you. Now tell us again, but slowly this time, starting at the beginning.'

Poppy takes a shuddering breath. 'Rafe was out early this morning ...'

For those of you who don't know, this particular farmer doesn't seem to go to bed. What with milking, and all things farmerly, as far as Rafe's concerned, getting up at the crack of dawn means a lie in.

I nod my encouragement. 'Go on ...'

'So he saw it first. There's a huge hoarding in the field on the way down to Rose Hill Manor. It must have gone up literally overnight.' Poppy's voice goes so high it's almost a squeak. 'The Manor's setting up as ... as a wedding venue.'

'Surely not ...?' Jess gives a disbelieving shake of her head.

'They absolutely bloody are.' Poppy's talking through clenched teeth now. 'Bloody exclusive use, blissful bloody country weddings. That's what it says on the sign.'

Exclusive use? 'Oh no.' A trickle of cold sweat meanders down my back. Because actually I already know this, and I can't believe I didn't take it seriously at the time. 'Omigod.' I hate myself for saying it, but sometimes nothing else will do. 'The guy who pulled me out of the pond said the same thing, but I took it he was talking through his butt.'

Poppy wrinkles her nose. 'How did Fred know?'

'Not Fred. One of the Penryn brothers was there tucking into the buffet, getting off on acting the hero. I should have warned you.'

Poppy's forehead furrows. 'A Penryn? Not Quinn?'

There's an uneasy twang in my stomach. I can't bring myself to repeat that particular name out loud. 'No, this was ... er ... Kip.'

Poppy is momentarily distracted. 'Quinn was best man at Sera's sister's wedding. Quite a handful. He crashed a van and smashed all the crystal ware.'

Sounds about right.

'Fabulous car though. And charm by the bucketload.' At least Jess stops short of commenting on his apps.

'Out of control? That fits.' An image flashes up in my brain. Me, dripping wet on the shore at the Manor. What is it with Penryns and water? Okay. I'll come clean. I got stranded on an island with that particular Penryn brother as a teenager, and I chose to swim away rather than stay and sleep with him. Perhaps not a great decision given how weak my breast-stroke is but that was the only option for me. 'There's a lake at Rose Hill Manor.' It's out before I can stop it, although luckily I bite my tongue before the rest follows.

'It's not just the lake.' Poppy's voice rises to a wail. 'There's a humungous spectacular house, shedloads of bedrooms stuffed with four posters. And a ballroom. Daisy Hill Farm can't compete with that on any level.'

Jess is tapping her loafer on her chair leg. 'But you have holiday cottages that the Manor doesn't. And you'll soon have the main farmhouse up and running, and the big barn will be done for the autumn.'

Poppy hugs herself. 'But all our financial projections relied on us being the only venue in the area. If we lose any bookings to the Manor, we can't make it pay. And they're going to have everything we offer, only better.'

Jess narrows her eyes. 'Don't underestimate yourself. You've made a lot of friends in the industry. We're all behind you.' Even though she's sitting down she thrusts her hands onto her hips, and her voice drops to a growl. 'If this Penryn wants wedding wars, we'll fight him all the way.'

'If Quinn was anything to go by ...' Poppy's voice trembles.

Jess jumps in. 'Quinn couldn't organise a fire in a coal shed. If he's anything like his brother, this Kip will crash and burn.'

'Every time,' I say, my fist flying through the air. Although that punch isn't only from today. A good proportion of the power is down to past resentments. 'To overthrow Penryns you hit them head on. It's the only way.' Then I shut up, because I don't want to come across as an expert.

Jess's expression softens. 'Strategy is my strong point. And we also have our new secret weapon.' She pauses for effect. 'Brides by the Sea has a *brand-new* manager of a *brand-new* department – Wedding Styling.'

For a second Poppy and I both blink. Then my heart gives a lurch as I catch up. *She means me.*

Jess jumps in to save Poppy's confusion. 'Lily's agreed to take us forward with the designing and accessorising side.' And miraculously she's missed out that I haven't got the first clue how to do this.

'That's brilliant news.' Poppy pulls me into a huge hug, despite her wobbles. 'But what a surprise.'

'For all of us.' I'm not joking. 'I'll fill you in later, Poppy.'

Jess is rubbing her hands. 'It's *very* fortuitous. This way we'll be able to parachute you behind enemy lines, Lily. You can be our under-cover agent.'

'Sorry, you've lost me.' I feel like I blinked and woke up in a James Bond movie.

Jess rolls her eyes in frustration. 'As our wedding stylist you have the perfect excuse to go to Rose Hill Manor. If we can land a styling booking for a wedding there, so much the better.'

If my jaw hadn't instantly locked with fear, I'd be screaming.

Poppy looks unsure. 'I know we're desperate, but doesn't spying sound a bit underhand? You mustn't do anything you aren't happy with, Lily.'

I bite my lip as I weigh up the evidence so far. 'With this Kip Penryn, we're talking about someone who crashed the party *and* ate the Sams' hog roast. His signage appeared in the dark. He's your neighbour, setting up in competition right under your noses, and he hasn't had the decency to call round and discuss it with you. I reckon the combat's already started. If it saves Daisy Hill Farm, I'm happy to come out fighting.' Even if I'm wobbling about the styling part.

Jess rifles through her table drawer so furiously, she could be searching for boxing gloves.

'Right on target, Lily,' she cries, as the contents of her drawer fly across the desk. 'It's survival of the fittest. Do or die, sink or swim. There's no time to lose.' So much for an over enthusiastic imagination. We're back to water again. Eventually she comes up with a pen. 'I'll start with a list of contacts to lean on.'

'Thank you so much.' Poppy gives me a last squeeze. 'Oh

my, you're going to need your lovely suit more than ever for this, is it going to be okay?'

I wrinkle my nose. 'Somehow I doubt it.' But suddenly it doesn't matter any more. Waving goodbye to my LK Bennett is somehow symbolic. As if my ruined suit marks the end of my old life. 'I can always get another. Although I could have done with power dressing for my appointment later.' Hopefully my wink hides how much I'm dreading coming face to face with my mum. I stare down at my jeans and sloppy sweat shirt. Whereas I'm happy to use my all-day pyjamas for exactly that, regardless of destination, my mum always dresses like she's going to Ascot. That's twenty-four seven, whether she's leaving the house or not. My jeans aren't going to cut it, but that's too bad. Life should be about who we are, not what we wear. Maybe my mum needs to learn that.

Jess beams. She's got her mini vac out now, whisking the croissant crumbs off the table, ready for her nine thirty bride. 'Meeting the fiancé is always a big moment.'

True. But when he's your mother's, and you don't know him from Adam, big doesn't begin to cover it. And when your mum is my mum ... Well, anything could happen.

Poppy clasps her hands to her mouth. 'Of course. Blimey. What are you doing?'

'Afternoon tea at Heavenly Heights.'

Which was always my friends' pet name for the modern close at the top of the village where we lived. I'm thanking my lucky stars I've got away with sandwiches and cakes rather than a formal dinner. As for Poppy's wedding wars, not that

I'm a pessimist, but they might not be the only explosions in the Rose Hill area over the next few months.

'Do you need a wingman?'

I shake my head at Poppy's offer. It's great that she understands, but I've got to do this on my own.

Poppy rubs my arm. 'Try to act happy for her. At least for today.'

Which given the way my tummy is twisting, might be difficult.

Chapter 4

Wednesday, 15th February
On the way to Rose Hill Village: Three point turns and
missing rings

BLISSFUL BOUTIQUE COUNTRY
MANOR HOUSE WEDDINGS...

'Not exactly subtle is it, Gucci?'

Okay, I'm talking to my car again. It's easy to slip into the habit when you do a lot of miles on your own together. It goes with singing along to heart break songs very loudly. But enough about that. I'm doing a mini-detour on the way to afternoon tea with my mum, to take in the Rose Hill Manor wedding sign. But the hoarding on the field edge is immense, and the lettering is *so* 'look-at-me', I forget to steer.

'Signs like this should be banned. They're a danger to the public,' I moan, as I veer off the narrow lane and bump along the verge, simply because I can't take my eyes off it. There are so many 'exclusive use' stickers, it's probably visible from outer space.

Pulling to a halt, I grab my phone, and jump out to take a few pics to show Jess later. As I fight my way past the hedge my feet slither on the wet grass. Damn. Hygiene standards at Heavenly Heights are surgical. Arriving with mud smeared boots will put me at a huge disadvantage. But it's too late now.

It's bad news all round then, because the hoarding graphics I'm clicking away at are startlingly professional. Somehow I didn't have the Penryns down as being *this* classy. On the close-up photos it looks like a venue to-die-for. I'm scouring the posters for something to criticise – like anything would do – when there's the roar of an engine on the lane. Next thing I know, there's a Land Rover beside me, with the driver's window open. And when I turn round, I'm staring straight up. At Kip Penryn.

'Speak of the devil.' It's out before I can stop it.

Kip rubs the stubble on his chin. 'Do I know you?' He wrinkles his forehead, then the penny drops. 'Of course, you're the one who caught the bouquet. Dried off, and out looking for a wedding venue? That *was* fast work.'

'More like driving off the road, due to being distracted by your effing great hoarding, you mean. Big can be brash, you know.' I refuse to acknowledge how perfect his promo material is.

'We're doing unmissable introductory offers. I *have* to make this work. Anyone getting married *has* to be interested.'

The words send a chill through me on Poppy's behalf, if only because he sounds so desperate to succeed. 'I'll pass on the offers, thanks.' Although I'm amused that he's got things so wrong with me. 'Unmissable' offers are even more compelling and tasteful than 'special' ones. He's certainly got his act together here.

'We're exquisite and exclusive, but we're also exceptionally negotiable. I can cut you a deal.'

I give a sniff of disgust. 'You do know if you overuse the word "exclusive" to the point of exhaustion, it loses all impact?'

He backs off on the hard sell, and goes back to being persuasive. 'Come for a look around, you'll see for yourself. The offers won't last forever. All those Valentine's proposals, it's a busy time. I've had non-stop viewings since the signs went up.'

Sorry, but his win-win attitude is as annoying as hearing about his rush of punters. 'Except you're here. So I'm guessing you must have stopped.'

'What?'

I'm going to have to spell it out. 'Well you're not doing viewings now, because you're here talking to me, aren't you?' I let that sink in. 'Or do you drag *all* your customers in, kicking and screaming, from the lane?' Saying the word drag, reminds me I should possibly be more grateful for what he did for me last night. But stuff that, given what he's going to do to Poppy and Rafe's business. They're right to be concerned. From what I'm picking up here, they should be very worried indeed.

His lips begin to curl into a slow smile. 'You're not looking for a venue at all, are you? Or you wouldn't be so dismissive. You're not even wearing an engagement ring.'

Dammit. For the first time in years, I wish I was. Just to prove him wrong. And not all engaged women wear rings, but I'm not going to get into that. So maybe he's not quite as in tune with the business of getting married as he thinks.

'I'm not *personally* searching for a venue, but I know people who are. Hence the pic.' At least that's explained. No way do I want him thinking I'm a sad single, taking selfies in front of a wedding sign. Although I'd settle for that, rather than the truth. It's way worse to be caught out spying.

'If there really aren't any takers, you can always give *me* a call,' he says with a wicked smile.

'Sorry?' Now I'm the one who can't work out what he's talking about, it's not so great.

'If you've got a free evening we could go for a drink? I'm new round here, I don't know many people.'

Or more likely, people know him too well, and avoid him like the plague.

What a cheek. 'A pick up on the lane? You *are* joking? You might be desperate, but I'm not.' As I make a dive for my car door, it's total bad planning because it means he gets the last word.

'Your loss.'

Two tiny words which pretty much sum up the arrogance of the guy. As for Weddings at Rose Hill Manor, I suspect this operation is way slicker and more of a threat than any of us imagined.

The only good thing is that for five minutes it took my mind off where I'm going next. As I coax Gucci into a thirty-four-point turn in the lane, and zoom off towards the village for tea with my mum and her new squeeze I feel sick. I would not mind missing the next hour in my life.

Chapter 5

Wednesday, 15th February
At Heavenly Heights: Tangerine jeans and matching
slippers

'Ring the bell? Knock and say "hi"? Or what ...?'
It's the weirdest feeling. Standing in front of the house where I lived since I was eleven. Muttering. Staring at the stonework, not daring to go in, because so much changed in those few minutes' yesterday afternoon. It's not only what I might be interrupting. Walking in on my mum snogging? Don't even go there. It just doesn't have the certainty of home any more.

'Dahling, it's you!'

'Shit.' I jolt as the door opens. And I'm off to a bad start, dammit, given Heavenly Heights is a curse-free cul-de-sac. The language at this altitude is so clean, they don't even need swear boxes. It's also the kind of road where domestic perfection is a competition sport. If home tidying was in the Olympics, they'd have more gold medals than Bradley Wiggins.

'Well, this *is* a lovely surprise. But where did all that dirt come from?' One glance at my feet, and my mum's already got her long-suffering face on. Sad to say, it's pretty much her full-time resting expression when we're together. 'Why are you loitering out here, come on in.' She never looks this disappointed when she's with her friends.

It might be worth flagging up here that of her two kids, she'd *always* rather see my brother, Zac. Eleven months younger than me, he's always been her real dahling. But since he absconded to the job of the century in Silicon Valley in the US, she's been stuck with second best. And what the hell does she mean by 'surprise' when I rang to pre-book eight hours ago? Remembering Poppy's 'act happy' instruction, I wrench my mouth into a smile.

Then as I stumble past a terracotta pot in the porch, I get my lucky break. 'Hey, lovely primroses.' My mum warms to compliments, as much as I'm warming to these flowers. 'Orange ones too.' My dad's favourite. His winter borders in our gardens were always bursting with polyanthus plants. We used to love pouring over the plant catalogues together, planning the colour schemes. I can still remember the thrill of persuading him to try oranges and yellows, when he was still a sucker for blues and reds. Every October, from when I was small, he'd wrap me up in his warmest windcheater, and he'd dig the holes, and I'd hand him the plants. And even though my fingers were burning with the cold, I'd stay out there with him for as long as it took to get every last plant into the borders. It's a relief to find there's still a little bit of that left. Even if it's just one pot.

My mum's pained expression melts with the compliment.

'David helped me do it. He bought the pot when we went for lunch at the Happy Dolphin Garden Centre.'

'David?' From nowhere, there's an iron hand gripping my guts. Although I'm going to have to get used to the name. And he has to be tame, if he's up for traipsing round garden centres. It was a point of honour. My dad preferred nurseries, and he refused point blank to go to places with poncey names, and logos depicting frolicking sea life. Then I do a double take that leaves my heart racing so hard, I almost have a coronary. 'What the hell's that?' I'm pointing at a plastic gnome. And lurid doesn't begin to describe it.

My mum laughs. 'Oh, that's Trevor. He's another of David's gifts. Don't his tangerine trousers go perfectly with the petals?' She lets out a kind of high, spontaneous giggle I haven't heard before. Very unlike her.

'But you don't like gnomes. You think they're tasteless and moronic.' I'm quoting here, and I can't help that my voice has gone all high either. It goes with the 'gobsmacked' territory. That gnome might fit in with my mum's obsession to have her entire life colour matched, but he's a million miles away from her style guide. In full view, on her front doorstep. Where everyone can see him, and judge her. Up to now I was under the impression she'd got engaged, but she appears to have had a personality transplant too.

'Don't be silly, dahling. He's only a joke. Whatever happened your sense of humour?' She's staring at me as if I'm the one with the problem here. 'Hurry up and take off your shoes, there's someone in here I'm dying for you to meet. And please, at least try to look happy for us. Even if you're not.'

My efforts at 'delighted' are falling flat then. But on the up side, this might be the first time in my life my mum has seen me in jeans and not complained. Come to think of it, she's pretty dressed down herself, in button through floral silk, and fluffy sheepskin mules. What's more, as I follow her down the hall, the accent wallpaper hasn't changed since my last visit. Back in January I'd have sworn the yellow and grey geometric print was on its way out. My mum's always been obsessed with redecorating, but since my dad died she does it before the paint has even dried. Although, thinking about it, most of that time since then, she's been away with her bestie, Jenny. Lately, if my mum hasn't been up to her ears in home makeovers, she's been away on a cruise.

As we turn into the living area, I close my eyes. No idea what's coming, but I'll try not to pre-judge. When I open them again, there's a figure standing by the French doors, looking out to the lawn. I have to smother a pang that my dad used to stand in the same spot doing just that. He loved to unwind on the golf course. Then he'd come home for what he called his 'garden gazing'. Whenever I visited I'd stand there beside him, and join in. Nod as he pointed out his latest Tinkerbell primulas, poured out his hopes for his Grandissimo violas. Smile at the promise of sweet peas with dreamy names like Cherub Northern Lights, Berry Kiss, or Cream Eggs.

The funny thing is that arranging my dad's blooms for the village show as a kid was how I discovered I could throw flowers into a jam jar in a way that made them look better than everyone else's. Back then he called me his lucky charm. It's true, he never won when he arranged his own. Better still, somewhere along the line, I found out that picking flowers, and making them look pretty made me happy in a way nothing else did. Dad always claimed his first prize for sweet peas back in nineteen ninety-two was the reason I became a florist. It's one of those family legends we've heard so often, we all believe it now.

But this is no time to drift off into the past. And we certainly won't be talking about it today. I drag myself back to the figure by the window. Force myself to refocus, and begin again. Believe me, 'tight bum' is not the second thought you want to have about any of your mum's mates, least of all her fiancé. But there's no other way to describe what's facing me. This particular backside could give Bruce Springsteen's a run for its money. At least this explains why my mum lost her life-long aversion to denim.

As he turns, I stick out my hand. 'Nice Levis, I'm Lily.' I'm willing the front view to be older than the back. Because, holy crap, I've heard about these young guys who hook up with needy widows on Match dot whatever, and bleed them dry. I'd just never in my wildest nightmares considered it could be happening to my mum.

'And this is David.' My mum's eyes are popping as if she's holding her breath, though I can't see why she'd be doing that.

There's a vague recollection as a blond guy in a sharp Superdry polo-shirt, walks towards me. 'Nice to meet you properly. We met briefly before?' And while he is older than his back view, he still has to be years younger than my mother.

Trying not to gawp at his slippers that match my mum's, I'm going the extra mile here to show I remember, even though it's hazy. 'You're David. *The electrician?*'

His expression is bemused. 'Not quite, I'm a personal trainer.' Which might explain the neat back view.

I throw him a lifeline. 'I was thinking of the lightbulb changing?' One lifeline wasn't enough, so I hurl out another. 'When we met on the stairs at Christmas?'

'Oh that.' From the way his face brightens, he's hugely relieved he's finally caught up. 'Of course. Love at first light. Wasn't it, Barbs?' He winks at my mother, and laughs.

Bad puns, laughing at his own really awful jokes, *and* calling my mum Barbs? All in the space of two seconds? There's only so much assault a person's guts can take. If my mum's waste paper bin hadn't been hand-painted with dragonflies, with a three-figure price tag, I'd have vomited in it. If this David was on three strikes and you're out, he'd already be down the road. And that's before we get onto the winking.

'Anyway, now that's gone so swimmingly, shall we move on with tea, dahling?' My mum's voice is strangely strangled.

The nod she gives David must have conveyed something exceedingly significant I missed. I'm about to offer to help, but he's already in the kitchen. I make a mental note to remember, I'm not the only dahling round here anymore.

My mum skips after him. 'So young, yet *so* well trained.' There might even be a whisper of the word 'toy boy', followed by a muffled shriek. But from the way they both erupt into giggles, I assume that was meant for him not me.

Right now, I'm wishing I'd taken Poppy up on her offer to come too. At least then, when we talked about this afterwards, she could tell me I hadn't imagined it.

My dad always sat in the chair on the right of the fireplace.

The wood burner and the chair have both had an upgrade, but plumping myself down in that position, at least I feel like I'm holding on. Although I'm not quite certain what it is I'm hanging on to. And I'm pretty sure it's futile. Even the thought of the coming cake doesn't cheer me up.

When they finally come back, a whole load of laughing later, my mum's carrying the teapot, and he's pushing her hostess trolley.

'So I've got you your favourite French Fancies, but David's low carb gluten free, because it's Wednesday,' my mum says, as if that explains anything. 'So sandwiches are chicken and pesto, tuna and rocket. Both on special wholemeal, with pine kernels.' Whatever happened to mum's plain old egg and cress?

When it comes to pouring, their moves are so coordinated, they could almost be on *Strictly*. If they're like this serving tea, their first dance is going to rate an off-the-scale 12 across the board. I offer up a silent plea that there won't be any twerking.

I can't stay silent forever, so I accept a pink iced lozenge from the cake plate my mum's holding, and launch. 'So, big congrats, how did you guys get together?' Somehow the word 'engagement' won't come out.

My mum beams at me over her tea. At least she's stayed true to her Gordon Ramsay china. 'We met at the gym. But it was the cruise that really cemented things.'

My cup slams down so hard, most of the tea slurps into the saucer. 'The cruise you went on to New York after Christmas ... with Jenny?' It's high voice time again.

She nods, apparently impervious to any suggestion of deception on her part. Although she makes a lightning change of subject. 'You really should try the gym, Lily. You look as if you could do with the exercise, and who knows, you might meet someone there too. All those miles alone in your car can't be good for your dress size *or* your single status. As Jenny says, it's back to front. You should be the one getting married really, not me.'

I take a second to reel at the insults. On balance, it's best not to count them. At least she missed out her favourite topic, how I could make more of myself if I dressed like her.

My smile is as sweet as the French Fancy I still haven't started yet. 'Except I don't want another husband – whereas, I take it you must, given you just got engaged.'

David puts down his tuna roll, without taking a bite. 'When something's this good, life's too short to mess around wasting time.'

Cliché alert. Did you ever hear so much drivel in one sentence? I'd feel more inclined to believe David if I were certain he meant my mum, rather than her bank account. This early, who can tell? Although when it comes to choosing partners, I'm the last person to talk.

I let my eyes slide towards the garden for a few seconds' respite. Big mistake. How could I have forgotten my mum pegs her washing out all year round as long as it isn't raining? I'm staring straight at the rotary dryer, and the line of under-pants I see hanging there almost brings sick into my mouth. Variations on the Superhero theme. It's *so* not helpful to know your future step-dad wears *Batman* briefs. Although given how many pairs there are hanging there, it's a pretty good indication he's moved in.

'Summer's a fabulous time for a wedding.' It's a squeak, to move my mental image on from flapping boxers. Okay, it doesn't exactly follow on, but I'm talking in the general sense, so I'm not being a hypocrite. 'Lucky I'll be here to help.'

'You will?' My mum can't hide her immediate breathy panic. 'How come?'

I sense I need to back pedal. 'I'll only help if you want me to.' Then I push on to get the next bit over. 'Jess made me an offer I couldn't refuse, so I'll be working at Brides by the Sea in the styling department. Doing flowers, and lots more. As of next week.' Hopefully the spin will make it shine.

My mum's face falls. 'But what about your lovely hotel job?' Believe me, it's never had praise that glowing before.

Saying it out loud is a wake up call. St Aidan is not a consolation prize. It's a safety net I'm choosing to throw myself into. As Jess says, it doesn't have to be forever.

Not every question needs a straight answer. At least this time smiling brightly is easier than it was earlier. 'I'll be living over the shop. Good timing for discounts too.'

'Great.' Her expression doesn't match the word. 'We've decided to stay local for the wedding anyway. Get married in the village.'

'Brilliant.' I couldn't cope with a 'destination'. At least this means a welcome extra booking for Rafe and Poppy. 'The farm house at Daisy Hill will be ready for then too. And weddings there are so fabulous. There's even a grand piano.' Despite myself, I almost feel a flurry of excitement.

'The farm?' My mum sends David a wild-eyed glance. 'Actually we've rather set our heart on ...'

David holds up his hand. 'No Barbs, we haven't decided anything yet. Don't let Lily think it's a *fait accompli*.' He turns to me. 'We're going to have a second look at Rose Hill Manor. We were there this morning. And it ticked a lot of boxes.'

Oh shit. A personal trainer who speaks French too. That's me put in my place. It's already in the bag. 'Lovely.' It comes out as a rasp. So Mr Penryn wasn't lying about his booking rush. Damned ironic that it was my mother though.

My mum's wringing her hands. 'You know me, I was never one for mud.'

Which reminds me, I've been here for what feels like an age, and I still haven't caught a glimpse of the ring yet.

David goes on. 'You could come with us to the Manor next time? As you're in the business now.'

Talk about walking on eggshells. Although it's a surprise he's butting in, when this is between me and my mum.

'I don't want to intrude.' If I had any sense, I'd keep right out of this. Viewing wedding venues with love birds has to be the ultimate gooseberry activity. Although if they're anything like Thom and me, they'll be at each other's throats soon enough. But I'm torn, because for Poppy and Rafe's sake, I should be jumping at the offer. It's the perfect opportunity to check out what that damned Penryn is playing at. 'Actually, yes, thanks for asking me. I'd love to come with you.'

My mum's face crumples in horror, and her mouth opens. She knows all about brides getting railroaded. And wedding interference. She perfected the art when Thom and I married. But before her protest has time to hit the air, a figure appears on the grass outside, and there's a knock on the French window.

'It's only Fred bringing logs.' As she gets up there's a gleam in her eye.

I catch my breath when I hear the name. Which is a complete accident.

'He's from a very nice farm, Lily. And sells the driest wood in the area. You could do a lot worse.' By the time her hand lands on the door handle, she's fixing me with her 'now or never' stare.

Here we go. This is what I have to put up with. 'A "nice" farm? That would be one without mud then?' I say.

But she's not listening, because she's flinging open the door. 'Fred, *do* come in, there's someone here I'm *dying* for you to meet.' That old line. 'No need to take off your boots.'

What? Who gets in *here* in their outdoor shoes? What's more, why has my heart done the tiniest cartwheel in my chest when I'm having no part of this?

She presses a pair of bright blue shoe covers into Fred's hand so fast, she must have had them up her sleeve. Then she seizes a tartan throw from under a cushion, and with one flap it's open, and covering half a sofa. As Fred's blue feet slither across the shiny oak floor, and my mum escorts him to his mud-proofed area, he sends me a grin over the top of her choppy blonde streaks. It's obvious he's done this before.

David has too, given he's arrived at Fred's elbow with a mug of tea, a plate and the tea trolley.

My mum waits until Fred unzips his hoodie and eases back onto his rug, then she launches the Exocet. 'So, this is my daughter Lily, she's currently on her own, and she'd love you to take her out for a drink. Or better still, dinner *and* a drink. Or even ...'

If I cut in rudely, it's to shut her up. 'Or a mini-break in London would work for me. Or even a romantic trip to New York if you're up for that?' I only hope my mum's happy I've been reunited with my sense of humour. And note how she flagged up my status without mentioning the 'D' word. Then I put on my best 'appalled of Rose Hill' face – I get a lot of practice at that with my mum – and shake my head at Fred. 'I'm divorced, by the way. Excuse me while I crawl into a hole and die of embarrassment.'

From the way Fred's choking behind his hand, he has to be laughing. Eventually he stops shaking, and smiles. 'I'm sorry to be the one to break it to you, Barbara. Matchmaking isn't the best look for mums. In any case, you're too late, I'm already taken.'

My insides deflate like a popped balloon. Which really isn't my style. Not that I was interested in Fred. Because I wasn't at all. But whatever.

'B-b-but ...?' My mum's even more confused than my flattened ego.

Fred's lips twitch, and one eye narrows as he catches mine. 'I met a lovely girl last night. Given she went home wearing my shirt, I'd say I'm well in there. Wouldn't you, Lily?' As he holds my gaze, a tiny part of me melts. Then he dips to adjust a foot cover, and slides me a wink.

It takes a few seconds for my ego to brush itself down. Then it does a skip and canters back to where I can't see it. 'Absolutely right, Fred. I'd say the shirt's a clincher.' I'm getting out of my mum's proverbial frying pan here, but who knows what hot place I'm ending up in.

Okay, I know I said winks were tacky. But it does depend on the wink. And who it comes from. And Poppy was so right when she said I could do with a wingman here. Right now, times are desperate. I'll take whatever friendly support I can get.

'So you're saying she'll be up for a mini-break, then, maybe New York?' Fred laughs, and gives me a significant grin.

There's no point leading him on when I've no intention of going. 'That sounds like quite a lot of logs.'

'Good thing I've got a chainsaw then.'

This kind of banter could go on all day. If I don't make a run for it now, my mum will claim her cupid stripes, regardless of women with prior claims. And Fred will be another on her long list of men delivered on plates that got away.

I slide my French Fancy into my bag for later. 'Well I'll leave you guys to your wood delivery. Let me know about the Rose Hill Manor visit.'

Hopefully that gets me off every hook, and leaves the next move up to everyone else.

I'm half way back to St Aidan when I realise. I still haven't seen the ring.

Chapter 6

When I told my mum I'd be back in St Aidan so soon, it didn't feel real. But the up-side of living in a hotel room is there's nothing much to move. My worldly belongings fit into Gucci, and there's still left room for a trip to Ikea to pick up bedding on the way. Less than a week later, I'm clattering down the stairs from the attic flat at Brides by the Sea, to fill in for Jess down in the shop.

'Tuesday morning's our quietest time, as there aren't any appointments. Acclimatise yourself, we'll see you after lunch,' she says, as she rushes off with Sera the dress designer, for an 'at home' appointment with a couture client. As Poppy's not in yet either, I really am 'home alone'.

Creating a new job *and* a new department, it's hard to know where to begin. But given Jess has promised there won't be any customers, I take my laptop over to the table in the White Room. I've decided to start by sourcing storm lanterns to add to the displays, and looking for a dressing table to offer as a cake table for vintage weddings. But I've barely settled into my Louis Quatorze chair, when the shop door rattles. A perfume cloud arrives first, carried on a gust from the sea. Whoever's on their way down the hall, they haven't stinted on the YSL Black Opium. And from the way they're stamping across the boards, they're either wearing tap dancing shoes or dizzy high heels.

'Hello, cooo-ey, surprise ...'

There's a tinkling laugh. Then a clenched fist appears around the door frame. Along with the hugest rock of an engagement ring. In the world. Ever. Like Kardashian size, or bigger. As the diamonds waggle on the arm end, they don't just twinkle in the light from chandeliers. They literally flash. If Jess had warned me, I'd have brought my sunnies down. I tiptoe to the front of the desk, bracing myself for whatever's coming.

'It's soooooo wonderful to be back.'

A figure storms towards me. A second later I'm squeezed into a mega hug, and I'm fighting for breath through fur and a perfume fug.

'Is this real?' I tug on the sleeve. When it comes to wearing animals, I'm a die-hard vegetarian.

'Don't be silly, fox hunting's banned dahling.' The hugger staggers backwards. 'Omigod, where's Jess? And who the hell are *you*?'

Looks like I'm not the only surprised one here. 'Delighted to meet you too.' Crap. Way too sarcastic. My first brush with a client, and it couldn't be a bigger fail. I rush in to smooth things over. 'I'm Lily. I'm working in styling, we're making a brand-new department.' Hopefully the gush will make up for the lack of expertise, and my grimace at almost saying my new job title out loud. 'Sorry, Jess is out.'

'Omigod, you're a stylist? In that case I need to book you. Immediately. Like now.' She's flapping her hands so hard her scarlet nails are a blur.

'Shit.' I wince as something heavy thuds onto my foot. A bloody massive handbag. I bite my tongue, and think of the styling booking as I stoop to move it. 'Oh, it's a Gucci. That's nice. And you are ...?'

As she slides a knife edge of bottom into the chaise longue, and arranges her legs, I get my first proper view. She's pretty much everything my mum wants from me, but doesn't get. Groomed. Glossy as a race horse. Accessories that coordinate. Rocking the red lips and floral silk thing.

'I'm one of Seraphina East's biggest fans, and I'm here for a rematch.' The laugh she lets out is almost a neigh. 'It's my second time around.'

'Fabulous.' Another divorcee. Despite my crushed toes and the horsey giggle, I'm warming to her.

'When I called my wedding off last summer who'd have thought I'd be shopping for a dress again so soon? Or that I'd find my very own James Bond.' A moment later her phone's out, and the proof's under my nose. 'Isn't my fiancé, Miles gorgeous? He's a C.E.O. with his own coatings company.'

Daniel Craig could have made me well jel. Pierce Brosnan with added wrinkles, not so much. Whatever a C.E.O. is – I can never remember – I can see the professional coatings contacts could come in handy.

'Lush.' I sense it's not enough. 'Phwoar ... to die for.' Still more needed. 'What a catch.' Phew to not going on about ex-husbands then, given this one hardly looks first hand. I'm picking my jaw off the floor, and counting on my fingers. 'A new man and a new ring all in six months. Well done you.' You have to admire the tenacity. And the speed. 'Was it a Valentine's proposal?'

She nods, and drops her voice. 'My dress from last year is still in the store. I haven't got an appointment, but we're going for a summer wedding. *This* year. I was hoping for a teensy look at some of Seraphina's dresses. Seeing as Tuesday's your quiet day.'

It's not as quiet as it was, given how her laugh is warming up. No idea why, but my 'tricky customer' alarm bells are ringing. 'It's my first day, and I'm not sure how fast the dresses can be delivered. You might prefer to see Jess later?' I open the appointment book, because I don't want to mess this up. 'She's free from one?' Hopefully my grin will make up for the deferral.

The disapproving sniff is loud. 'I'm one of Jess's most prolific customers, and "now" works for me. I know *all* about Seraphina's range, so if you get the drinks, I'll make a start.' She's scooped up her bag and she's already making a bee-line for the Seraphina East Room, shouting over her shoulder. 'Prosecco's in the kitchen fridge, flutes are on the shelf. And if there's any Valentine's chocolates left, we'll have those too.'

Whatever happened to 'no'? Although, let's face it, not many people buy two wedding dresses in the space of a year. And Jess is big on seizing the moment with customers. By the time I go through with the fizz, there's a row of dresses hanging in the fitting room. And the customer's on her knees, unwrapping a box.

'Last summer I had these darling shoes from White White White Weddings. A total snip, at six hundred. *Do* tell me I'll able to wear them this time.'

That's Bristol's swankiest bridal shop, with prices to match. But I hold in my whistle, because at Brides by the Sea we try not to judge. 'So long as you're comfortable wearing them, go for it.' Although I doubt anyone could be that comfy in the heels she pulls out. 'The bride makes the rules,' I say, then instantly regret it. I'm not sure this bride needs encouragement. As for the emerald beaded flowers snaking over the sandals? Carp ponds and waterweed tangles spring to mind.

'I'm so totally in love with Seraphina's Country Collection, I may need to try *every* dress.' The jewel encrusted watch she glances at as she takes a slug of fizz could almost have dropped off one of her shoes. 'I need to be at the hair salon in four hours. So snip snap! Pass the chocolates, we'd better get started.'

Despite reeling at the Mary Poppins hand claps, I do as I'm told.

Her nose wrinkles as she peers into the basket I offer her. 'You can't fob me off with foil covered hearts, even if they *are* pink. Where's the handmade confectionery?' Disgusted doesn't begin to cover it. 'You do realise White White White give their brides smoked salmon blinis?'

I'm sensing the canape gauntlet is being thrown down here.

'Yes, but do White White White allow casual drop ins?' We

both know they don't. Once I've made the point, I soften, due to guilt. 'Sorry, the truffles went super-fast this year.' In other words, Poppy, Sera and I wolfed them all when we hauled my stuff upstairs. After four flights the calorie deficit was huge. I fire off a customer-is-always-right smile as I head for the door. 'Give me a moment. I'll see what else I can find.'

Lucky for me, there's more 'thank you' confectionery in the kitchen than in a nurses' station on a surgical ward. Given this is approaching an emergency, I grab a rather spectacular Ferrero Rocher tree, complete with taffeta bow, and head back. A lot more dresses have arrived in the fitting room since I left. But I take it from the simper that greets me, I've made an accidental good choice of chocs.

'What a stroke of serendipity.' She wiggles her fingers, and plucks a gold ball on a stick from the Ferrero tree. 'When I marry, I'll actually be Mrs Ferrara. How apt and absolutely fabulous is that?'

Pure fluke. But it reminds me, she still hasn't told me her name yet. Even if I'm about to see her in her underwear, it's somehow too late to ask. At least I know who she's *going* to be.

'Brides by the Sea might not do savoury snacks, but we do our best to have happy brides.' Five years on, and it's all coming back to me as if I'd never been away. 'Which dress would you like to try first?'

The next two hours are so fraught they leave me longing for the calm of fully booked hotels. My worst moment? Discovering the extent of Sera's new capsule 'mix and match range', which Jess has slipped onto the rails to trial. Separate pieces, designed so brides can put them together to create a look that's completely unique. Silk shifts, chiffon tops, lace over dresses. Beaded sashes, ribbons, sequined tulle skirts, diamanté belts. I swear we've tried most of the four million permutations.

'One last chocolate?' I hold out the almost bare tree trunk. Believe me, without the soft praline centres from the Ferrero tree we'd both have collapsed of exhaustion after the first three hundred versions.

The future Mrs Ferrara unwraps it, and pops it into her mouth. 'And only one last dress to try now.' Whatever lippy has held its own crunching through this many hazelnuts, my mum needs to be let in on the secret.

I sink down into the mother-of-the-bride director's chair, and pull the fitting room curtain over my head. 'There's another?' I can't believe we're not done here.

'It's the dress from the Daisy Hill Farm website. From the photo shoot they did there with Poppy's friend. I fell in love with it last year, but it was too late, I'd already bought my other one.' She whisks a dress from the end of the rail, and staggers back into the fitting room. 'Stay there, I can do this.'

If I'd been run over by a tractor I couldn't be more mangled. But the word 'farm' wakes me up. Given they only got engaged last week, the Ferraras will be looking for a venue. There might well be a booking here for Rafe and Poppy.

'Thinking about the styling …' I wait until there's an 'mmmmm' from behind the curtain. 'Have you decided where you're getting married?'

I'm holding my breath, waiting for a reply when the jolt of

the shop door makes me jump. As I reach the hall I come face to face with Poppy.

She frowns and sniffs. 'You've gone wild with the Black Opium today, I can smell it out in the street.' Then she squints at me more closely. 'You look dreadful. Have you been out running again?'

I take it she's talking about my sweat patches, sunken cheeks and haunted eyes.

I gesture frantically towards the striped fitting room curtain behind me. 'I've had *three and a half hours* with a drop-in bride.' Then I tip toe back in to the Seraphina East Room, pulling Poppy with me. I turn up my volume so I can definitely be heard in the fitting room. 'The future Mrs Ferrara is about to show me her wedding dress. And tell me about her venue.'

There's a rustle, as the curtain moves, and from the flash of green I catch under the hem, for the first time, we've got the pricey shoes too.

'Ta-dah ...' Her smile is wide as she shakes her veil and does as much of a twirl as the shoes allow. It's actually more of a standstill with an occasional wobble. 'So much work, but this is definitely "the one".' As she scrapes a nail under her eyelashes, her voice is a whisper. 'Thank you for helping me find it, Lily.'

Brave woman. If I had inch long acrylic nails like hers, there's no way I'd risk poking my eye out. What's more, I can't believe she knew this was the dress she wanted all along, but whatever. That's customers for you. Before I know it, I've grabbed the tissue box, and I'm pushing one into her hand.

'You look beautiful ...' There's a bit of a gap where her

name should be. I stoop to smooth out the hem, and look to Poppy for reassurance that I'm doing it right.

Poppy's brow crumples as she peers beyond the veil. 'Nicole? It is Nicole isn't it?'

The woman blinks. 'Poppy! How lovely to see you again.'

The high speed pecks last a nano second. Then the clenched fist shoots out, and we're back to clustering round first the ring, then the phone.

'You two know each other?' Yes, I know I'm stating the obvious, but it's been a long morning.

Poppy's nod is decided. 'We *certainly* do. And what *brilliant* news about your new fiancé, Nicole.' For Poppy, her voice has taken on a brittle edge.

Nicole runs a finger over the delicate lace covering her arms. 'The best part is, it's not just love where I'm getting another bite of the cherry, I'm getting second chances all round. This time I'm getting everything right, including the dress.'

'You are,' Poppy and I cry together, even though Poppy has no idea how heartfelt that is on my side.

A red nail comes up to quieten us. 'And this time I'm a hundred per cent sure. I definitely want to get married in the farmhouse at Daisy Hill, Poppy. It's what I wanted all along last time. Whatever the size, we'll make the wedding fit the venue. And Lily's already agreed to be my stylist.'

I'm beaming because this is such good news. All round.

'Absolutely not.' Poppy jumps in so firmly, Nicole and I are left gawping. Whatever happened to Poppy grabbing every booking she could?

Poppy senses she's answered too fast. 'What I mean is, I'm so sorry, but that won't be possible. We're fully booked in the farmhouse for this year. But I know you'd love Rose Hill Manor. It's a brand-new venue, just down the road. It's very up-market, and I've heard they're doing fabulous deals on bookings for this year.'

'Up-market?' For the first time all morning, Nicole sounds uncertain. 'I know the cottages were rough and ready, but there can't be anywhere as perfect as your farmhouse.'

Rough and ready? Ouch to that. Maybe that's my clue.

Poppy's nodding furiously at me. 'Seraphina's sister got married at Rose Hill Manor at Christmas. It was magical.'

At least we both know she's sincere about this. She was there. The photos are phenomenal. Who wouldn't want a horse drawn carriage and a white Christmas wedding? Not that Nicole would be expecting snow if she's marrying in summer.

So I chime in. 'It's exclusive use, my mum saw it and she said it was *amazing.*' Okay. I know she didn't say that *exact* word. But she must have *thought* that if she wanted to book it. Even as I throw that in, I'm struck by how like my mum Nicole is. 'And best news of all for your shoes, it's a mud-free zone.'

'Right.' Nicole's expression lightens.

My phone buzzes in my pocket. As if on cue. It's a text from my mum.

Hi Lily, There's a preview day at the Manor on Saturday. If you'd like to come, Mum

As for signing texts with a name, why *do* people do that?

'Excuse me looking at my phone, but I just heard. It's Open House at Rose Hill Manor on Saturday. There's so much scope there for making a truly individual wedding, you should take a look Nicole. And lots of availability for this year too.' I pull a face at Poppy, because I can't believe I'm talking up the opposition. Especially given the way she's slicing her hand across her throat at the mention of the open day. 'And seeing the time, Nicole, we'd better get you out of your dress, and off to the salon.'

There's a glint in Poppy's eye. 'If you do decide to book at Rose Hill Manor, Nicole, don't forget to mention we sent you.'

The sooner I get Nicole out of here and find out what's going on with Poppy, the better.

Chapter 7

Tuesday, 21st February
At Daisy Hill Farm: Ironing piles and storage solutions

In the end, Poppy had to leave the shop before Nicole, so I didn't get to find out why she was turning down her booking. But she did offer us some space in the converted buildings up at Daisy Hill Farm, which is why I zoom over there as soon as Jess gets back to the shop.

'Jess wants us to buy in props to hire out for styling, so we'll need somewhere to store them between weddings,' I explain to Rafe, as we pass him humping some kind of sack up the yard. Jess has decided to invest in things we'll use a lot, and hire in the more unusual items. 'With any luck most of the weddings will be here at the farm anyway, so it would be great to keep them on the spot.' Handy for Rose Hill Manor too, just down the lane, but I skip over that.

'Great, help yourself.' Rafe almost spins on his wellies, but at the last minute he turns back. 'By the way, our friend Fred was asking if I'd seen you. He mentioned a shirt? And a date?'

Crap. 'Tell him no worries, it's on its way to the ironing pile.' Which sounds a whole lot better than, 'It's in the washing bag'. The down side of washing it is that I'll have to get in touch to give it back. As for the date part, I blank that.

As Rafe heads off, Poppy leads the way from the stone built farmhouse, up towards the holiday cottages. By the time we reach a courtyard that's so picturesque it could have come off a vintage biscuit tin, I can see her smile bursting out. 'What's this? Still hanging on to Fred's shirt?' She lets her laugh go. 'Seriously though, have you noticed how much like Jules he smells?'

I shrug, to show how completely not interested I am. 'Except not so over-powering.'

It's amazing how she's completely at home here, in her waxed jacket and a sloppy jumper I suspect belongs to Rafe, with Jet the dog wagging along beside her. Her red spotty wellies are the only hint of her townie past.

As we reach a long low building, and she pushes her way through a grey plank door, a rush of warm air wafts out. 'We've got a couple of spare rooms next to the farm office. See what you think.'

I follow her into a whitewashed space, and gaze up at the high sloping ceilings. 'Nice beams. And it's a lot cleaner than I was expecting.' I'm surprised it smells of fabric conditioner, not cow's bottoms.

'Clean? Why wouldn't it be? My crack team keep the whole farm chuffing spotless.' A throaty voice is coming from behind a mountain of sheets that's wobbling towards us across the cobbles. A glossy black high-heeled Hunter ankle boot comes out and kicks the door open wider. 'You're next to the laundry too, so it's warm and dry.' As the sheets land on the floor, Immie's broad face appears, and she flings a punch at me. 'Great to see you back again, Lily. Let's hope it's for keeps this time.'

I'm rubbing my arm, but I caught a flash of purple along with the left hook. 'You haven't chosen a ring yet then?' Of all our friends, Immie's the one who never left, and who wants us all back in the village. Forever. She won't be happy if she gets the idea that I'm just passing through, which is why I'm moving the subject on.

When she puts her hands on her hips, and rolls her eyes, she looks just like she used to when we were all at infant school. That was in the days before my mum dragged the family up in the world, when we lived in a higgledy-piggledy cottage down in the village. And when the older lads made life hell for me and my brother, because our mum called us 'dahling' very loudly, and insisted on giving us goodbye kisses all the way along the playground over the wall, *and* tooth-brushes to clean our teeth after school lunch, Immie was the one who kicked them into line. Literally.

Immie rubs her knuckles on her jeans, polishing the chunky perspex. 'I'm marrying a fireman, so it's like evacuating a burning building. There's a strict order of priority. Even when organising a wedding. But Poppy had a gap in the farmhouse wedding book in mid-August, so we grabbed that. And we nailed fabulous Jules for the photos. We definitely want it to be different from Chas's last "do".'

The wedding-that-never-happened was a mega bash in a

huge tipi. Legend has it that the bride-from-hell called it off at the eleventh and a half hour. But the party went on regardless, and everyone camped out in the field for a week. Which was when Immie moved in to help Chas mend his broken heart.

'Don't worry, a wedding in the house with dancing in the Orangery won't be at all the same as one in the meadow.' Poppy's obviously used to nursing couples through tricky spots. 'And you can always add a marquee in the walled garden if the numbers grow.'

'The ring's next.' Immie tears at the short spikes of her hair. 'And then there's the whole nightmare of what to wear.' She grabs her throat and makes a strangled scream.

I bite back a smile. 'That bad?'

'Oh yes.' She nods. 'I'm definitely leaving dress shopping until July. At the earliest.'

Poppy rolls her eyes at that, but she's flapping her hands and looking like she's about to burst. 'Which reminds me Immie, something huge happened. I wanted to tell you earlier, but I couldn't find you. Nicole turned up at the shop today.'

Immie's eyes go wide. 'Blazing toad bollocks, you are joking?'

'Nope.' Poppy turns to me. 'I didn't dare tell you when she was there, but Nicole is Chas's ex. That's why I knocked her back with her booking.'

So that explains a lot. 'Not the Bridezilla to end all Bridezillas?' Which is how she's always been referred to, hence me completely missing the significance of who she is. I'm in awe that I spent four hours placating her and came out the other side alive.

'That's the one.' Poppy's groan is heartfelt. 'She was barely warming up today. Demanding and unreasonable doesn't begin to cover it. However desperate we are, I *couldn't* take her booking and go through all that again.'

Immie's face is all screwed up. '*She's* getting married?' For once her husky voice has turned to a squeal.

'To a James Bond look-alikey, after a Valentine's proposal. And she was in to choose a dress.'

Immie's clenching her fists. 'Not Sean Connery? I refuse to let the Franken-bride who wrecked my fiancé marry *him*.'

Poppy's got her soothing voice on. 'Keep your hair on, he's more Pierce than Sean. But getting engaged on the same day as you and Chas? You couldn't make it up, could you?' Poppy bites her lip as she hesitates. When she speaks, her tone has changed from soft to firm. 'But this doesn't need to change anything for you, Immie. Chas loves *you* for yourself.'

Immie changed the habits of a lifetime to go the extra mile for Chas, not that he ever asked her to. But she'd never dallied with make up *or* heels before last summer. You only have to look at her tottering along in those wellies to see the effort she's put in.

I pick up where Poppy's coming from, as well as her wild-eyed calls for back-up. 'It's *you* he wants to marry, Immie. Definitely you. You as you are. Not looking like anyone else.'

'Right.' Immie's nostrils are flaring. 'Ring Brides by the Sea, please. I need an appointment. *Now*.'

'But it's fine to do things your way, Immie.' I say. 'Whatever happened to dress shopping in July?'

Immie's straight back at me. 'Stuff that. I need to get on

the case.' Her eyes narrow, and her voice drops. 'What kind of dress is Nicole having?'

Shit. At Brides by the Sea we're always discreet. And what if there's a new, upgraded confidentiality code I don't know about? 'She was mainly looking in Sera's room,' I say airily. Hopefully that gives Immie the information she wants, without breaking any rules.

'Great.' Her fists are on her hips again. 'That's where I'll have *my* appointment then. Soon as you can, please. But make it a day when you're both there to help.' She blows out her cheeks. 'You might need to tie me down. I'm already hyperventilating.'

I have a feeling she's not kidding. They had their hands full trying to get her into even a bridesmaid's dress for our friend Cate's wedding last summer, which I missed because I couldn't get time off from the hotel in the summer season.

I remember there's a final piece of icing on today's cake. 'And Poppy sent Nicole to see Rose Hill Manor, along with her compliments.'

'Nice move.' Immie's frown melts to a chortle. 'Those Penryns are a laugh in a bar. But they're as likely to deliver on weddings as fly to the moon. That Quinn was like a bull in a china shop when he was best man at Sera's sister's wedding at Christmas.'

I can't help grinning. 'When picky Nicole hits Kip, he'll run for the hills. She's the perfect weapon to see off the opposition, Poppy.'

Even as I'm laughing I'm aware the joke may yet come back to bite me. As Nicole's stylist, I might not be smiling so much if I end up in the middle of them.

Chapter 8

On the way to Rose Hill Manor: Sitting ducks and farmers
on safari

'I'm so excited to see the Manor. But really, I could have driven there myself.'

It's no secret I've been dying for Saturday to arrive to get a sneak peek inside. You have no idea how often I've been pouring over the pictures of Sera's sister's wedding on Jules-the-photographer's website. And how scared shitless I am by the size of the place, and the thought of styling a wedding. If Nicole does decide to have her wedding here, it'll be a huge responsibility for me. It's all very well Jess saying she knows I have the eye and the talent. I'm just not that confident I'll be able to deliver.

I'm definitely not stinting on the 'happy daughter' effort this morning. But as I clamber into the back of David's sporty MPV at Heavenly Heights, I'm regretting it on *so* many levels. And it's not just the close-up view of my mum putting her hand on David's knee as she picks invisible fluff out of his

76

designer stubble. When she leans in for the ear nuzzle she assumes I can't see, I actually get sick in my mouth.

'So have you made a start on growing my bouquet yet, Lily?' It takes a talker like my mum to fire questions through a mouthful of earlobe. She's peering past the head rest at me. 'Why the blank stare? Catch up.'

From where I'm scrunched up on the black leather upholstery in the back seat the PDAs are barely two feet away. Worse, she can put me on the spot about her ridiculous wedding flower plans. Which incidentally, I'm having no part of.

'I thought that was a gimmick to get on the radio,' I say. 'Like saying you do online dating, when you don't even know what the internet is.' My mum doesn't have the first clue how to open a laptop, let alone use one.

There's an amused smile playing around her lips. 'I'll have you know, Jenny and I are entirely computer literate.' At least it's taken her mind off horticulture.

My squawk is high with disbelief. 'Since when?'

'Since we joined our U3A Access course last year. It's Thursdays after Aqua-fit. Once we'd Googled Lonely Hearts, we took to Safari like ducks to water.' She gives a toss of her head. 'David and I are Cornish Casual Computer Couples fifth engagement in a year.'

So that's told me, but my voice is still a squeak. 'Aqua-fit? But you hate to swim.' Talk about the secret life of parents. It could be worse. At least she's not on Tinder.

'When you're all alone, the days are very long.' Her voice has a hard edge. For a moment, she sounds like she might be about to cry. Then it gives way to the giggle that's becoming so familiar. 'But that's *all* over and forgotten now. As for the flowers, it's all arranged. Fred's got a greenhouse for you. By the time they're ready to plant out, he'll have found you a patch of garden to use too.'

'Mum, I don't want to grow flowers. I didn't say I would.' More to the point, I don't actually know how. Doing it with Dad back in the day is way different than doing it myself. I'm protesting through gritted teeth, because there's no way I want to make her argue in front of a stranger. What's more, Fred's been bombarding my phone with messages – unanswered, obviously – and this is the first I've heard of his involvement.

'Lily … how often do I ask *anything* of you?'

Okay, here we go. Whenever I hear that whine in my mum's voice, I brace myself. At times like this I completely understand why my brother chose to live on the other side of the world, and not visit. It's why Bath worked for me. And why St Aidan may not be the best idea, however desperate I am.

She gives a disgusted sniff. 'Quite simply … never.'

'That's not entirely true.' I close out the passing village green as I clamp my eyes shut, although that's not going to save me. This is always how it goes. The times when my mum slips into her martyr-drama-queen persona are not her best.

'I ask you to contribute one thing towards my dream of future happiness, and you refuse. As for *your father* … he'd be *mortified* to know you didn't care.'

Since dad died, she always calls him that. As if he's nothing to do with her any more. And this is nothing to do with me caring about her.

'Leave Dad out of this.' I'm croaking, because my mouth

is dry. It's the ultimate below-the-belt manipulation, because he'd most likely be telling me to stand up to her, and do what was right for me. And we both know that. What's more, if he were here, she wouldn't be needing flowers to get married to another blinking man.

'That's another thing.' She's tapping her fingers on the dash. 'Refusing to go on a date with Fred is foolish. At least if you're in his greenhouse you might warm to him. If you carry on as you are, you're going to be single, old and lonely.'

The 'old and single' chestnut. I heave a big sigh. 'The point is, that will be *my* choice.'

David clears his throat, as he pulls the car around into the lane. 'Why can't we *buy* flowers, like everyone else does?'

If anyone apart from him said that, I'd say good point well made. Although he seems to have missed that I'm the one who'll make up the bouquets. Unless they defect to the opposition again. Which they might do, given their form so far. But this is between Mum and me. He should stay the hell out of it.

'I might give the seeds a try.' As it comes out, I'm as surprised to hear it as anyone. It's something to do with David. And that same feeling I had as a stroppy teenager. If there's a competition between wanting to stand my ground with my mum, and wanting to defy David, there's a clear winner. 'We'll see.' I'm not quite sure what I've let myself in for here.

'Talking of Fred ...' It's my mum again, brightening, as we round the corner.

David joins in, as we swerve to a halt behind a row of waiting cars. 'Watch out, logs in the road.' There's a blast of cold air as he winds down his window.

As Fred saunters up, pushing back his waves, I almost swallow my tongue. He grins at me as he leans his forearm on the car roof. 'We lost our load right outside the Manor entrance. It's taken a while, but it's pretty much clear now. Only blocked the open day for a couple of hours, so we're all good.'

A likely story. 'Fred …?'

He gives a shrug. 'Accidents happen. I don't think he's lost too many customers. The joys of country house weddings, eh?' Just as he's about to go he dips back. 'Do let me know if you think of anywhere my new girlfriend would like to go, Lily. She's proving hard to pin down.'

Then he's gone. Off down the lane, and swinging up into the tractor. And a few minutes later we're driving down a gravelled avenue, between huge oaks, towards tall roofs glinting in the sun. And a country house that's jarringly familiar all these years on, yet completely living up to its build up this time around. As much as I want to hate it, for Poppy and Rafe's sake, somehow I can't.

Chapter 9

Saturday, 25th February
Open Day at Rose Hill Manor: Ice breakers and sharp
claws

'So you see why we like it?'

My mum's suddenly less sure of herself, hanging back as we get out of the car.

It's one of those times when my memory plays tricks with scale. Somehow now we've pulled up on the gravel at the front, Rose Hill Manor's bigger than I remember from the few times I came here as a teenager. Sharper too. But the windows are irregular, and the stone is so mellow, its warmth pulls you in. And the huge front door is open and inviting. Although whoever's organised the parking has scored a mammoth fail, because there's no signage, and there's a jam of cars as drivers try to work out where to go.

'It's lovely.' My hand's on the handle of the car door, when it hits me that my mum's about to commit to something huge here. 'You are sure about this? You don't want to wait a bit?'

She wouldn't be the first woman to sign up for a wedding just because she fell in love with the venue.

She picks up her handbag, and she's missed the point by a mile. 'So long as we're quick, we should beat the stampede. There were a lot of cars in that queue.'

I let out an exasperated sigh. 'I'm not talking about now, I'm asking if you should be waiting longer to get married. You could have the wedding next year instead?' I mean, how would she react if I said I was rushing into marrying someone I barely knew?

My mum's expression is determined, as she catches my eye in the sun visor mirror. 'Time's short. At my age, I have to make the most of the youth I've got left.' As she snaps away her lippy, she glances at a band on her wrist. 'If I skip round the Manor, I should get to ten thousand.'

She's lost me. 'Ten thousand *what?*'

'Steps, silly – on my Fitbit.' She shakes her head at my frown. 'Never mind, we'd better hurry.'

As we arrive at the entrance, David's standing next to a balding potted pine, hitching up skinny jeans that could be borrowed from an eighteen-year-old. Believe me, if I'd picked up on the spray-on denim earlier, I'd never have left Heavenly Heights. But as we go into the lofty hallway, I take Poppy's advice, to pick out the positives.

'Fabulous staircase, and it's lovely and cosy.'

There's a flash of dayglow lycra as my mum unzips her jacket. 'What a crowd. And it's positively tropical. Lucky I'm wearing my technical top.' She picks up my blank look. 'Special exercise fabric – it wicks away the sweat, darling.'

On a need-to-know basis, that's way too much. Whatever happened to her love affair with Phase Eight and a sedentary lifestyle? But she's not joking about the crush. Despite Fred's delaying tactics, the place is rammed. As we thread our way through the wide-open plan reception rooms that flow from one into the next there are couples hugging the walls.

'Any idea which way we go?' I ask, as I squeeze my way into a room with polished boards, and linen covered sofas. Even though it could have dropped straight from a Country Living magazine, there's no hint of weddings at all. And there's a thrumming sound track, that sounds like it came from a Driving Rock CD. As Meatloaf gives way to Led Zeppelin, at least the chaos is eclipsing David's embarrassing trouser situation. It's not like you can see anyone's legs.

A girl rolls her eyes at me over her glass of fizz. 'Bubbly's in the study. We served ourselves, but we haven't got a clue where to go next.'

When it comes to listening in, my mum's a pro. 'Don't worry, we know our way around, we've been before. Follow us.' As she begins her running commentary, more people start to tag along. 'The winter garden's where the ceremonies take place, then the ballroom's the party space.'

David's right behind her. 'You can have marquees by the terrace, or even a lakeside tipi.'

Not that I've landed a styling commission yet, but at least soaking up the spaces and the atmosphere makes me feel less like a spare part. Although it would make me a traitor to Poppy, a job here would be a dream if I had the courage to do it.

'And upstairs there are masses of luxury bedrooms, and a bridal suite.' My mum can't hold in her enthusiasm. 'We'd better head up there now, if we're going to get to spinning.'

'Spinning?' As I puff up the stairs, trying to keep up with her, I get my first clear view of her state-of-the-art Nike trainers. Given how pink they are, I can't think how I missed them earlier. What's more, it's the first time I've ever known her leave the house without four inch heels.

She laughs over her shoulder. 'It's all go. The hazards of having a fiancé who's a personal trainer. As soon as you see the four poster you'll understand why I want to marry him here.'

The thought of my mum on her wedding night makes me shudder. 'Maybe I'll check out the other rooms. Give you two some "couple" time in the bridal suite.'

Linking arms with David, she heads for an elegant panelled door. 'We're in here then, you'll need to be on the next floor. The single rooms are up under the eaves.'

There's no point taking the truth as a jibe, but it still stings. 'With your insider knowledge, they should be employing you as a guide.' As I back down the landing, I'm visualising cupcakes. 'I'll wait for you by the refreshments.'

It's a fight to reach the study, but I know I'm there when I spot a hand-written sign blu-tacked on the door. *Drinks and Bookings*. Kip Penryn is obviously an optimist then. The bad news is there's not a crumb of cake in sight. It's an indication of the entire event. I'd give ten out of ten for venue, zero for effort. But on the plus side, the study's delightfully empty, with an array of bottles and ice buckets on a long oak desk.

I'm helping myself to apple juice, when I hear a voice in the corridor outside.

'If the fizz is as good as the rest of the place, they'll be splashing round the Bolly. Fingers crossed for smoked salmon blinis.'

Someone blagging smoked salmon blinis? How's that familiar? My stomach wilts, although it's all my own fault. I'm the one who was shouting about the open day.

It's a good thing I've put down my juice, because the next moment the door pushes open, and an apparition in white fur is storming towards me, arms out-stretched.

'L-i-l-eeeeeeeee ...' Someone elongates my name as they drag me into a strangle-hold. 'I was *soooo* hoping you'd be here.'

'Nicole ...?' I haven't totally seen her face, but the haze of Black Opium, and the faceful of fur are the giveaways.

'And this is Miles ... Miles, this is *amazing* Lily from Brides by the Sea, who found me my dress, and who's going to be our wedding stylist.'

As Nicole relaxes her grip, I make a mental note to keep my toes well away from her bag.

'Hello Miles, lovely to meet you.' However big my smile, it's going to be hard to live up to the build up.

'You too, Lily.' As he raises an ironic eyebrow and grasps my hand, he's every bit as 007 as Nicole promised. A little bit older in real life than on his photo, but an impeccably cut suit lifts his 'phwoar' factor to a solid eight point five. Speaking impartially here, obviously.

'Bolly for both of you?' I'm joking, but when I pick up the bottle to fill their glasses, I'm spot on. Which is a teensy bit crazy, when Prosecco would have done the job. And in no way makes up for the cupcake deficit. As I hand them their flutes, I can't help thinking it's like Nicole and my mum got their men mixed up. But that's entirely up to them.

'Did someone say Bolly?' This time it's my mum's head coming around the door, so they must have fast forwarded on the bedrooms.

'You were quick.' I manage a smile as they shuffle in.

'There's no time to lose, we need to do this.' The corners of her mouth are white with excitement.

'Have we met?' Nicole butts in, staring at me expectantly.

'Sorry, Nicole, Miles, David, and Barbara is my mum ...' I rattle off the names, and throw in an ice breaker. 'You all got engaged on Valentine's Day.' I skip the Pirate FM bit. The sooner we forget that, the better.

When Nicole's fist comes forward, surprisingly – or maybe, not – it's not for a hand shake. 'I'm so lucky, and isn't this the most fabulous engagement ring?' She's waggling her rocks on her left hand, and seeking out my mum's ring hand with the other.

I'm bracing myself, because if this is a bling competition there can only be one winner.

'Ooooh, very Beyoncé.' My mum's smile freezes, as she pulls her hand away. 'Actually, mine's still being re-sized.'

So that explains why I haven't seen it. More surprising still, now they're closer, I can't help notice her lips match Nicole's. Bright pink Chanel Mighty. I'm still reeling at my mum's bitchy return, trying to think of some way to move the conversation on when the door swings again.

86

'So Bolly and bookings? Have we got any takers? Everything's half price today.'

Okay, it had to happen. Kip *does* live here. I'd just hoped to avoid him. Less ridiculous than it sounds, seeing as he was doing such a good job of making himself scarce.

As he strides in his smile's wide, and he's rubbing his hands. Literally and metaphorically, no doubt. And if Penryns in denim are dangerous, in a dark jacket this one's incendiary. Not that it matters to me though, because I know to keep a country mile away. At least.

'So ... we meet again. You really *couldn't* resist my exclusive venue?'

Seeing he's whizzed straight past four potential customers, to home in on me, I'm guessing his business sense isn't as sharp as he pretends.

My mum jumps forward. 'This is Lily, she's my daughter ...'

If she asks him for a date on my behalf I'm going to expire. But I'm saved because Nicole's straight in there.

'But *much* more importantly, Lily's from Brides by the Sea, and she's *my* wedding stylist.' If she lost out in the ring tussle, she's not backing off now. And professional trumps family every time. 'We're here to make a booking, and as we were in here first, it's only right we get first go.' She's powered past us, plonked herself in the swivel chair, and she's tapping an acrylic nail on the polished desk. 'Although we will be looking for assurances of up-grades. Complimentary cocktails, snacks in the Bridal Suite, a hot tub on the lawn. You could do with having a wedding fair too.'

And that's just for starters. Exactly why Poppy ran a mile. And Nicole's barely begun. I must be mad thinking I'll work for her.

'Great.' Kip sounds less excited then he might. 'If I can get to my seat, we'll see what we can do.' He shepherds Nicole back around to the front of the desk.

'Saturday August 12th, it'll be our six-month anniversary, and we want two days before thrown in too, for styling.'

I should be grateful for the extra preparation time she's grabbed, but instead my knees are actually knocking with nerves that it's real. I'm sure that's when Immie and Chas are tying the knot too. What are the chances of that?

Nicole dips into her bag. 'Here's the deposit.' A shower of notes slithers across the desk. At least that explains why she needed such a humungous bag.

My mum's low moan is so heartfelt, it almost has me looking for a wounded dog.

I turn to her. 'You didn't want that day too?'

She bunches up her mouth, and nods.

'Too late, it's taken.' Nicole's air punch is gloating. 'Second best gets second place. Suck it up.'

I know I'm not ecstatic about my mum getting married. But right now I'd like to knock Nicole's lights out. Or smother her. Or anything else that would silence her. What's more, I can't understand why any couple who've only been together a few months would put themselves under the pressure of organising a wedding. At such short notice too. It's not as if they don't know any better. They've all been there before.

From the way my mum's mouth bunches, she's not taking

that lying down. 'Lily's never actually styled weddings before. So good luck with that one, Nicole.' Ouch. With friends like my mum, who needs enemies? Although I'm probably the first ammunition that came to hand.

'It always rains in August. September's much sunnier,' I say, momentarily putting to one side that my mum's just dropped me in the shit, *and* wrecked my chance of a job. Am I a bitch for wishing torrential storms for Nicole? With any luck my mum will see this as a sign. Leave it until next year. By which time she might have come to her senses.

'Whatever.' Kip counts the cash and tries three drawers to find a pen. The way he reaches for an A4 ruled pad to write out a receipt sets my alarm bells ringing.

'So what about corkage?' I blurt it out before I can stop myself.

I'm no expert. But it's to do with costs for opening wine, and every venue has a policy. It's not exactly my business, but it is the perfect test question to see if he knows what he's doing here.

'Corkage?' As soon as Kip repeats the word, he gives himself away. It's obvious from the wiggles on his forehead he hasn't the first clue what I'm talking about. A definite fail.

'A list of approved caterers and suppliers? Price lists? Agreements?' I watch his eyes widen as I screw him down, and his throat bulges as he swallows.

But a second later, he holds up his hand. 'Not *quite* in place. *Yet*. Hence the stonking early bird discount.' Talk about thinking on his feet.

'So what else don't you know about?' I'm not the one

making bookings here, but his don't-give-a-damn attitude's left me fuming. My voice soars. 'These people are trusting you. You can't mess around. We're talking about the biggest days of their lives here.'

The smile's vapourised, and his scowl is directed straight at me. 'What exactly *is* your point?'

In other words, butt the hell out. But if he thinks I'll back down, he's wrong.

I make my eyes as cold as his. 'If you can't take a whole lot of heat, you really shouldn't be messing around in this *particular* kitchen. Is what I'm saying.' I suspect he hasn't got any idea what he's getting himself into here. And he could ruin a whole lot of hopes and dreams, as he claws his way up the learning curve. 'Running a wedding venue is about a whole lot more than collecting the money, you know.'

Although, I might be talking to myself here, given my mum's entirely engrossed flicking through a tiny diary, and David's nodding wildly.

'Right, that's settled. We'll take the third Saturday in September.' My mum's missed the whole altercation, and she's hurtling towards the metaphorical cliff edge like a happy lemming.

'What date's that?' Kip dips to scramble through the desk drawers, presumably searching for a calendar, but comes up empty handed. He drums his fingers expectantly.

'16th September,' my mum says, helpfully.

If I were a tiger, I'd be roaring. 'An appointment book might work here?' I'm spitting the words out. 'Or is it too early for something so rudimentary?' There's no point telling him most venues have dedicated files, for years ahead.

He rips a sheet of paper off the pad, and scribbles the date. 'Got you.'

Nicole's pointy nail pokes Kip on the chest. 'And don't forget us. You haven't written us down yet.' Just this once I forgive her for being so unbearably pushy.

'You might need to add names and phone numbers to those dates, you know.' It's not my place, but someone has to tell him. And maybe staple the paper to his head to stop him losing it. As for what it's going to take to pull a wedding out of this? We're about to find out, because David's already tearing his cheque off.

My mum's scribbling her details next to her date. 'Sorry, we've got to dash. We'll be in touch. Fifty per cent off, we can't go wrong,' she's saying as she heads for the door.

In my head, I'm screaming, 'oh yes you can, don't bloody do it, for *every* reason' at the top of my voice. But somehow the words never make it into the air.

We're barely two steps out of the door when my mum lets rip instead. 'Who *was* that awful woman? Someone should tell her pink doesn't work on brunettes. You must be mad leaving that nice hotel to work with hideous people like that, Lily.'

At least she still thinks I had a choice. Although seriously, I'm quaking at the thought of taking on Nicole. We're outside getting into the car when I remember what I've got away with.

'So much excitement, you forgot to try to fix me up with a date with Kip Penryn. That has to be a first.' If there's one good thing about my mum getting married, that was it. Unless she had the good sense to see this is the one guy in the world best avoided.

The sun visor's already down and she's getting to work with the Chanel Mighty. 'There's no point either of us wasting time there, Lily. He's *way* out of your league.' Her lips are popping as she launches into her favourite mantra. 'You could do *so* much better for yourself, if only you'd make the effort.' She looks at my trousers, and winces.

Black jeggings. A size too big. Very practical for the shop. Not that someone in fitness bottoms like my mum's is in any position to dish out fashion advice.

David gives his own jeans a wrench as he slides behind the wheel. 'As a guy I'd say old Kip was *way* more interested in Lily than he was in us, *or* his bookings. Seriously Lily, he couldn't take his eyes off you.'

There he goes again. Butting in. And talking the usual bollocks. As for my mum, the criticisms' been raining down since nineteen eighty-four. Mostly I shrug it off.

'Part of the Penryn empire went to the wall recently.' David's rubbing his chin, musing as he waits for my mum to finish. 'It was all over the FT, as I remember.'

My mum raises a querying eyebrow. 'The what?'

'The Financial Times.'

As my frown meets David's in the driving mirror, his is worried, while mine is disbelieving. I suppose he has to read something when he's on his exercise bike. Or he might be making it up.

My mum brushes away his concerns, as she flips the sun visor up again. 'You mustn't believe everything you read in the tabloids, dahling.'

Meanwhile I file that information snippet safely in my 'good to know for a later date' box, because it's always useful to have something to hold over a Penryn. And as the tyres scrunch along the gravel drive, I'm horrified to find I'm scanning the horizon for logs and tractors. But thankfully they've all gone.

'Let's just hope "old Kip" pulls his finger out, and stays solvent here until September.' I say, as we roar off up the lane towards the village. Because if he fails on either count we're all in trouble.

Chapter 10

At Brides by the Sea: Gold paper and personalised T-shirts

Despite Immie's desperation to get started immediately, we'd deferred her appointment until today. If she's going to play the reluctant bride, it's best she does it in an empty shop. When Immie was a bridesmaid last summer, despite softening her with alcohol, they practically had to winch her into the fitting room for the first trying-on session. But as we hit the kitchen to sort the Prosecco, she's not hanging back.

As I get the glasses off the shelf, she frowns. 'Forget champagne flutes, I need a proper glass. Give me the biggest you've got.'

I hand her a tumbler, and fill it with fizzy wine. But before Poppy comes in half a minute later, I'm already topping it up.

'What the hell are those?' Immie wrinkles her nose at the dainty biscuits on the plate Poppy's carrying.

'Amaretti cookies, just out of the oven. They're great when you're trying on, because they're tasty, but very light.' Poppy's coaxing is falling on deaf ears.

'Stuff light. I'm going to need cupcakes at the very least.

Big ones too, not those piddling bite sized things. What the hell's the point of those?'

Poppy grins as she reaches for the box under the plate. 'I thought you might say that. Vanilla okay for you? With heart sprinkles to get you in the mood.'

If I thought Nicole was demanding, a nervous Immie is leaving her standing.

'You'll feel better once you have a calorie hit, Immie,' I say, trying to encourage her. As I snaffle one too, I can tell from the weight they're XXL specials. By the time I'm peeling down the gold paper case, and dipping my finger into the buttercream on mine, Immie's sinking her teeth into her second.

Poppy bites into her own. 'And your *We're getting married at Daisy Hill Farm* T-shirt is looking fab too.' It's one of the first of a new line, with personalised happy-couple names, as masterminded by Rafe. Eat your heart out, *Not On The High Street*.

'The king of the chest-front slogan gets full marks for these.' I'm wiping the crumbs off my hands, bracing myself for what's coming. 'I love the glittery print.'

Not that I'm mentioning it to her, but Immie's curves are in all the right places once she loses her baggy sweat shirts. It's just that at five feet nothing, with an appetite that would put a lumberjack to shame, she's never going to pull off Nicole's long-legged race-horse look. Until shin extensions are invented, she's always going to be a good foot shorter. But that's the thing. At Brides by the Sea we help each individual bride find the perfect dress *for her*. Every one of our brides looks beautiful.

Seeing Poppy dishing out the wet wipes as Immie produces another empty paper case, I grab a couple of extra bottles of wine. 'Shall we go through?'

Immie gives a sniff as she passes the window display. 'What's with the newspaper hearts then?'

'It's up-cycling,' I begin, then decide not to push on with the full story.

Poppy's got my back. 'Very on trend.'

'Trend my arse. If you ask me, they look like rubbish. Total shite.' It could be worse. At least she's not slagging off the dresses. But the sugar rush hasn't kicked in as spectacularly as we were hoping.

Poppy's treading as gently as if she were humouring a toddler. 'You don't have to get a dress Immie. You could go for something completely different. Why not get married in a tux?' Which would be a great way to side step this morning's problem. We could pass her on to groomswear.

'Eff that.'

That's told Poppy, then.

By the time we reach the Seraphina East Room, Immie's scowl is so deep her eyebrows are practically on her chin. Her mouth is a straight line as her fists clamp on her hips. 'Right. What happens next then?'

Poppy's voice is as light as the Amaretti biscuits we passed over. 'So we usually go along the rails, and pick out any dresses you might like the look of.' Not that we're expecting many of those.

Immie nods her head at the rail, then grunts. 'You know bloody Nicole's picked the same day as us.'

Poppy broke that news to Chas and Immie as soon as I'd found out, but since then we've been trying to play it down.

'Chas reckons she was desperate to have the dress off the Daisy Hill Farm website.' Immie's frown eases a fraction. 'Is that dress here?'

Here, exactly as ordered by Nicole, although she's having a ton of extra diamonds sewn on. Which gets me off the hook. At least I haven't got into trouble over that secret. But for someone reluctant, Immie's suddenly sounding amazingly focused and proactive.

There's a whoosh of lace skirt, as Poppy pulls a dress off the rails with a flourish. 'This is the dress from the photo shoot we did at the farm, remember?' She fingers the delicate lace cuff.

'Bollocks, that's no good.' Immie blows out her cheeks, and takes another glug of wine. 'I'm way too sweaty for sleeves.' Which is a relief, because Immie getting married on the same day, in the same dress as Nicole would just have been plain weird.

I pick up the baton. 'Any dresses you like the look of, we'll hang in the fitting room.'

Seeing the face Immie's pulling I don't bother to broach the undressing part. But there is something I can dangle. 'As for Nicole, she tried on *every one* before she chose.'

The noise Immie lets out is close to a growl, as she slams down her glass. 'I refuse to be outdone by that bloody Nicole. Bring it on. Show me the lot.'

'Here we go then.' I can't believe how we've turned this around. 'What have you got, Poppy?'

The dress Poppy swishes out is slinky cream satin, with hand sewn beading.

Immie chokes. 'Wouldn't be seen dead in it. I hate sequins.'

'Except you've got them on your T-shirt. And they look great on there.' Sorry to be the one to point it out, but...

'Okay.'

I blink in surprise. 'Sorry?'

'Good point.' Immie nods, as she pops the cork on the next bottle of fizz. 'Stick it on the pile. Next?'

The fairytale tulle Poppy's holding up gets a nod too. Although Immie was possibly taking more notice of me topping up her glass than of the dress.

'Yup ... yup ... yup ... yup ...' That's for the chiffon covered silk, two more with fluttery tulle skirts, and a lovely dress with a lace overlay.

Admittedly there were as many glugs as there were 'yups'. But talk about a sea change. Poppy and I can't believe our luck here. When we're on a roll we're not going to stop just because the fitting room rail is groaning.

An hour later, there are only three dresses left on the rails in the showroom. They got the thumbs down from Immie, or more accurately, the 'full-blown vomit' impression. The rest of the dresses are in the fitting room, waiting.

'Are you coming in then, Immie?' I'm tugging at the stripy curtain in readiness.

Immie tucks up her legs behind her on the chaise longue where she's lying. Her chin's propped on her elbow, and she screws up her eyes. 'I think that's as much as I can stomach for one day.'

'Sorry?' Poppy shoots me a 'what-the-hell?' look.

'Jeez, all that choosing. I'm totally knackered.' Immie's eyes are closed, but her mumble is decided. 'Make me another appointment. I'll have to come back for the next bit.'

I'm not sure what Jess is going to think, but I'm about to find out, because we can hear the clip-clop of her loafers on the floorboards. As she comes striding through, Immie gives a hiccup.

Jess gives one of her beatific smiles. 'Great progress, Immie. We never rush our brides.' The diary's wedged under her elbow. 'Same time next week?' As Immie topples back and lets out what sounds horribly like a snore, Jess shoots a searching frown at Poppy and me. 'And next Tuesday, we'll go easier on the Prosecco on an empty stomach, won't we?'

She's wrong about empty, but whatever. I'm definitely getting the blame for this because it's me Jess is homing in on.

'And Lily, there's a customer waiting for you in the White Room.'

My curiosity stops my quaking. 'But I don't have any ...?' Apart from the dreaded Nicole, who I'm damned sure wouldn't wait anywhere she was told to.

'He's specifically asking for you.' As she drops her voice there's a smile twisting her lips.

'Really?' I ignore that my stomach did a somersault when she said the word 'he'. As to why my mind's fast forwarding to Fred...

The way she peeps at me over the top of the appointment book, tells me she's playing games here. 'Enough teasing. It's your Prince Charming from the pub. Lovely boy. Definitely not stinting on the charm either.'

So, Fred's calling in to say thanks for the chocolate saw I left at the farm as a 'thank you', along with his clean shirt. How sweet is that? Except on second thoughts it's not any kind of sweet *I* want. And for the future I'm going to have to be firm that work's strictly out of bounds for casual visits. It also reminded me I'm going to have to up my ironing standard too, now I'm back in the shop.

'You seem to have made a big impression.' Jess purrs, as I follow her across the hall.

Although from where I'm standing she seems to be the one who's most impressed. I'm checking round my hair for rogue waves as I hurry, and kind of pre-preparing my completely casual 'Hi Fred' smile. But when I catch sight of the gaunt figure waiting beyond the shoe display, you could knock me over with a Jimmy Choo. Talk about Jess confusing her royals.

Just in time, I manage *not* to make Immie's full blown vomit noise. From somewhere in my deflated chest, I drag out some words.

'Kip? What the flip ...?' Rolling straight into a cough gives me time to recover. 'Er, what can we *possibly* do for you?' Whoah. For the first time in my entire life, I sound just like my mother.

As for thinking my second customer encounter of the day couldn't be any more of a spectacular fail than my first? Wrong, wrong, wrong. And it's barely begun.

Chapter 11

Tuesday, 28th February
At Brides by the Sea: Cock ups and royal waves

'I Googled wedding fairs ...' Kip's sauntering around the White Room, hands in the pockets of his parka. And he couldn't look any more chilled if he owned the place.

'Whoop-di-do. Well done for that.' It comes out as a bit of a sneer. But it's the politest I can manage. Any guy in charge of bridal arrangements at an exclusive use venue who says that has to be winding me up.

'As suggested by the lovely Nicole.' He's staring at me as if I should be reacting. 'She can stick her demands for a hot tub right up her fur coat. But now I've done my research, another promotion event could be great for business. It's something I'll be running with.'

Me erupting with laughter at the stuffed-up hot tub image isn't professional, so it's lucky he's not a real customer. Anyone other than Nicole, I promise I wouldn't be choking on my shirt cuff.

'Still not understanding why you're here though?' I say, as soon as I can speak again.

There's a flash of a rip in the front of his cashmere jumper as he turns. And I'm pretty horrified to see he's back to rocking the Penryn ragged-jeans thing too.

He rubs a thumb across his jaw. 'Google also tells me Brides by the Sea is a one-stop wedding shop. It's a no-brainer. You're my answer to an instant event. How does mid-March sound to you?'

He's staring at me as if he's expecting me to jump up and down. Whereas I'm inwardly cursing. How bad would a wedding fair at the Manor be for Poppy and Rafe? Especially one that would be unlikely to go ahead if we didn't join in. I need to shut this down now.

I make a big effort to get reunited with my best grovelling customer-service voice, and toss in a suitably sickly smile. 'A fabulous wedding fair takes mahoosive planning.' Can you imagine him putting in the work? Because, seriously, I can't. 'What's more, we couldn't possibly pay to appear at a half-cocked mess-up like your Open Day.' Now I say it, he's mad even to be asking us.

When he bites his lip, his teeth are slightly uneven. 'Who said anything about paying? Wouldn't I be the one to pay *you* – for organising it?'

There's the noise of a plate crashing down in the kitchen. From the hammering of loafers on floor boards, I'd say Jess is running to reach us like she just left the starting gate. Even though we're all of ten feet away, when she arrives she's breathless, with her chiffon scarf streaming behind her. And her smile is dazzling enough to make up for every one I've held back.

'I'm liking what I'm hearing, Kip, tell me more.' There's no trace of embarrassment about her eavesdropping either. For a second she looks as if she's going to link arms with him, but thankfully she limits herself to a pat on his hand.

Dammit. Who'd have thought she'd be so taken in by hollow cheeks and threadbare chic, when the guy's such a pretender?

Kip clears his throat, and starts again. 'I want to showcase the whole venue package, with the focus on ultimate inspiration for big days. Clothes, flowers, photography, cakes.' The man's clearly got all this from his search engine.

'Ye-e-e-e-s ...' Jess really should think before she lets out that purr. She shouldn't be encouraging him.

'I'd like Brides by the Sea to handle the lot. Stage set the Manor. Organise other exhibitors. How are you fixed for two weeks' time?'

He has to be joking. I'm looking from Kip to Jess in silent horror. Not only because this shows how little grasp of the wedding business he has. But whatever happened to chasing him off the premises? Where's our solidarity with Weddings at Daisy Hill Farm?

'We might need at least three?' Jess's smile has been replaced with the peculiar hungry stare she slips into when she's negotiating. 'Free exhibiting for us, all expenses, an hourly rate for staff, five per cent off for you on whatever you spend with the shop?' Although I suspect Kip's such a numpty, he'd have jumped at it, without that last reduction.

Kip's hand comes out of his pocket to shake Jess's. 'Great,

you got yourself a deal.' Which is ridiculous to say, when he's the one who wants it. 'You stand to pick up a lot of business here. Do I get a cut on orders you take?' Put in a wishy-washy way like that, Jess'll wipe the floor with him.

She's straight down his throat. 'No you damn well don't. You're a beggar not a chooser. And you do realise my stylist doesn't come cheap?' That's Jess clawing back what she just gave away, as she practically wrenches his arm off with her hand shake.

The sideways glance Kip sends me has a payback lip-curl. 'I'm sure she's worth every penny.'

Which is a lot more than I am, given I can't even get my voice to work. If I could I'd be yelling, telling them to stop. Immediately. Because Poppy and Rafe are suddenly a minor concern. It's finally dawning on me, conjuring this wedding fair out of thin air is going to be completely down to me.

'Do you have a maximum budget?' Note how she's firing the questions once the job's in the bag.

Kip shrugs. 'Whatever it takes. I need to get this off the ground with a bang.' Ouch to how he's mixing his metaphors there, as well as to his complete lack of financial planning. Which doesn't bode well for someone whose previous business just crashed and burned. Allegedly. 'And leave the publicity to me.' Given how many punters he pulled out of nowhere for the Open Day, that's one area he might be on top of.

Jess's expression still hasn't relaxed. 'Obviously with a job as tricky as this we'll need a "hooray handshake" too.'

What's more, she's completely ignoring my violent head

shaking, and the not-so-silent "no's" I'm mouthing at her. I could possibly do this if I had three months. Three weeks is setting me up for a fall. And it's her reputation that will come crashing down along with me.

And there's no point Kip turning to me to explain what she means, because I haven't got a clue either.

Jess rolls her eyes. 'The "hooray handshake" is the incentive bonus. Index linked to the difficulty of the task. Twenty-five per cent on top, if we pull off the impossible. Agreed?'

Kip's face cracks into a grin. 'Now I've heard it all. Let's see how amenable and talented your stylist is first.' He lets out a low laugh, and as he backs towards the door he's still shaking his head and chortling with amusement. 'Remind me to introduce you to my uncle. Talk about two of a kind. You'll meet your match with him.'

Over the years, there's not many times I've seen anyone stand up to Jess and get away with it. Come to think of it, she's rarely speechless either. But she is now.

'That's the Penryns for you, all over.' I say, trying to explain, as well as to fill the silence. 'Nothing princely *or* charming about them.' They do you down every time. Which is why it's best not to go anywhere near them, or their damned Manor.

This is not going to be easy. For any of us. The way things are panning out, I want to point Gucci towards Bath, and not stop driving until I get there.

Chapter 12

Saturday, 4th March
At Daisy Hill Farm: Men's work and little slips

There are times in life when you just have to stop grumbling, and get on with it. Four days later, after a lot of phone calls, I've enlisted an array of exhibitors for the wedding fair, and the date's set for April 1st. Fingers crossed we aren't tempting fate with that. The good part is I've done most of it from the comfort of the sofa in the attic, and I haven't been anywhere near the Manor. What's better still, I've reached the prize that was spurring me on. This particular Saturday morning I don't mind at all getting up when the little porthole window in my bedroom is still black, and the lights of the boats are glistening across the water. Because today, to ease me into my stylist's role, I'm helping set up the flowers for a wedding in the farmhouse at Daisy Hill Farm. Woohoo to that.

'You have to love a bride who goes for wall to wall properly dazzling pink,' Poppy says as she comes across the wide reception room with a coffee tray.

My mouth waters as I catch sight of a stack of cupcakes with bright fuchsia icing. On a normal day, this would count as an early breakfast, but we already had crusty bacon cobs what seems like hours ago.

Clambering down from the step ladder where I've been fixing cerise carnations from a batten suspended over the top table, I grab a drink and a cake. 'They're so pretty, it's a shame to eat them.' I nibble the edge so I don't spoil the deep curls of buttercream rose petals.

Poppy grins. 'These were my practice ones.' There's also a spectacular three-tier cake sized version in the kitchen. 'They're so "look-at-me", they might work well for April Fools' at the Manor. Talking of which, have you drummed up any more interest in the fair?'

When the news of Kip's big event broke, we considered all the options, including putting on a rival day at the farm. But in the end there weren't enough suppliers to go round two, so Poppy decided it was more practical to capitalise on the Brides by the Sea free pass. At least that way she can pick up some cake orders, and we'll have all the contacts for the Daisy Hill event in the autumn.

'We've got everything from gazebos to microbreweries. Even the vicar's coming.' I'm catching my crumbs in a piece of kitchen roll, given Poppy's already buffed the scrubbed oak floor to perfection. 'Someone's bringing a bridal camper van. More importantly, there'll be a hand cart giving out free ice creams.'

'Yay to that.' Poppy picks up a carnation I've dropped, and twirls it in the air.

I reach for a box and start to get out the table flowers. 'I've also blagged a whole load of jars of confectionery to create our own sweetie table.' Not that we're shallow, but it's going to be a long day. And can *you* resist a flying saucer or a sherbet lemon?

'More pretty pink here.' Poppy swoops on the ruby bunches of tulips, bound up with their own leaves. 'I'm so looking forward to having more weddings here once we've got the extra rooms done. The farmhouse looks so beautiful when the rooms are filled with flowers.'

Rafe and Poppy live in the side wing, but the main Georgian farmhouse is a rambling work-in-progress they're just starting to use for weddings. So far they use the light airy reception rooms, and the orangery, but they're working on a bridal suite and more of the upstairs bedrooms. Although it's a similar age to Rose Hill Manor, the rooms here are much more intimate. They might not have the stately home grandeur, but they're beautiful and more relaxed.

'It's lovely to be working with flowers again.' As I slip three bunches into each long glass tub, adding water from a watering can as I go, I can't help smiling because it feels so good. 'I'm not so happy about growing them for my mum though.'

From the wicked glint in Poppy's eyes, she's not about to talk floristry. 'Fred mentioned it when he dropped round to pick up his shirt. He's hell bent on luring you into his greenhouse.' It's fine for her to laugh.

'My mum is too.' The corners of my mouth drop in horror that it's gone further. 'No way I'm falling for that. But I really need somewhere to start the seeds off.'

Poppy's tone is teasing. 'We haven't got any weddings here until the refurbishment is finished upstairs. If you're sure you don't want an excuse to hang out at Fred's house, you could always use the orangery?'

If my arms weren't full with tulips, I'd hug her. 'That would be *so* great. If I don't get them started soon, they won't grow in time. I'm not even sure I can do it at all.'

Poppy grins. 'Don't worry. Once you've got your plants going a lot of them will go on forever. We can make confetti every year with the left-over flowers.'

I let out a groan. 'Hang on, I'm trying for a bunch, not a field full. And I haven't even found a garden yet.' That's the thing with plants. They're a lot more long term than I am. As soon as something better comes along, I'll be on my way.

Poppy laughs. 'Fred'll find you a patch of soil at his place, even if it means digging up his lawn. Something tells me he's very taken with you and determined to make you stay around. I mean, dropping by at this time of morning is *keen*.' She nods at a figure passing the window.

'You are joking?' I've no idea why my stomach's melted to liquid fudge. As for the panic gripping my chest, I shouldn't even give a damn. It's just no way was my bed-head pony tail meant for public viewing. 'But why's he so enthusiastic?' It can't be me. Looking down at my extra baggy working shirt, frankly I'd look more glam wearing a supermarket bag for life.

Poppy purses her lips as she considers. 'Strictly between us, after spending so long in a relationship that didn't work out, I think Fred feels time is running out. We all already know you're great, so you're like a fast-track safe bet.' Her grin breaks free. 'And, perish the thought, but given how banging you are, it's not inconceivable he's actually got the hots for you. The great part is, Rafe says you're definitely the only woman on Fred's horizon right now.'

Which isn't good news at all, from where I'm standing. I slam down the flowers, and make a lunge for my watering can. 'I'd better fetch some ...'

But Poppy's too quick for me. 'I'll get the water, Lily.' She snatches the can out of my hand.

I'm hissing at her through gritted teeth. 'I accidentally borrowed the guy's shirt, that's all; I didn't sign up for coupledom. For jeez sake, stay here.'

'Fred's fun. And moving on is good too, I can definitely recommend it.' She grins, and from the way she turns and walks out, she's ignoring my plea.

As she skitters away a different scent engulfs the flowers I'm clutching. Clean man, with an extra-large helping of Paco Rabane. What's softly subtle in a late-night pub comes across as overkill at eight in the morning.

'Fred, what are you doing here?' Swishing across the room, hands in the pockets of a Barbour isn't the answer I'm looking for. Whatever they say about certain notes in men's body spray making you more susceptible, I'm determined to fight it all the way.

The hair he pushes back is nut brown and silky clean. 'You're a hard one to track down.' His mouth curves into a soft smile. 'Now I've found you, how about a drink tonight? Dinner if you'd rather.'

If this is what he's coming out with, I regret giving him an opening at all.

'St Aidan, London, New York?' He's working those soft brown eyes to the max here. 'It's your choice, my tractor's waiting.'

Somehow now he's in front of me, my melty insides have set like treacle toffee. Let's face it, I'm not my mum. I don't fall into bed with the first person who tells me how to use a cross trainer. Even if I was looking for a guy, there's no point starting anything here, when I'll be gone before I know it.

I clear my throat, to make sure my voice is going to work. 'I'm going to have to take a rain check on that.' I cringe because I hate the phrase, but just this once it's suitably innocuous as a knock back. 'I've actually got a rule not to go out with guys until I've known them at least six months. It saves me a lot of problems in the long run.' It's a brain wave that's just hit me, and I'm liking how plausible it sounds.

Fred grins as he counts on his fingers. 'So I'll have to wait until August 14th for an "official" date? Fair enough, I can work with that. We'll see each other around in the meantime.'

I'm feeling proud of myself for that coup, and move on swiftly with the excuses. 'We're throwing a last-minute wedding fair together for the Manor, working round the clock to make it happen. So I won't be around much.' No need to feel guilty either when it's the truth.

'What's this? Defecting to the opposition?' He gives me a playful nudge, prompting another power-packed waft of body spray.

If he knew how uncomfortable I am with this, he wouldn't

be pushing it. 'Sometimes there's no choice. And hopefully we'll spin it so Rafe and Poppy come out ahead in the long run.' Who knows, if the Manor goes up to full price, there could be a lot of priced-out customers happy to book at the farm instead. I'm hoping that it works that way, rather than the other.

'Don't worry.' Fred sends me a wink. 'We'll do coffee at mine when you come to see about your seeds. I told Poppy and your mum. Nothing official. Just as friends. But the glazed section off my living room's all yours.'

Since when did a greenhouse down the garden become a conservatory annexed to his sofa? Talk about lucky escapes. I'm taking a deep breath, bracing myself to reply, when Poppy breezes back in, and hands me back the watering can with exactly the same amount of water in as before.

'Actually, Lily's going to use the orangery here for her seeds. She can call in every day on her way to the Manor.'

Good thing she was listening in the hall then. That's a true friend for you. Making sure she didn't get in the way of romance, but on hand to come to my rescue.

'Very convenient.' My smile hides that my heart's sunk. Surely I won't really need to visit the Manor that often?

Fred's beaming. 'That's great, I'll still see you here, Lily. I'm doing the renovations upstairs.'

I'm frowning. 'But I thought you were a farmer, helping with Rafe's barn conversion?'

Poppy laughs. 'It's diversification. When he's not ploughing, he does property development and heads up a building team. That swanky quayside development in St Aidan is Fred's too.'

Seems like I have some catching up to do. 'So what about the logs?'

Now it's Fred's turn to laugh. 'Being a lumberjack's my way of keeping fit.' As he stretches his arms, and his T-shirt lifts there's the teensiest flash of tanned six pack.

Not that I'm not impressed, but I think we'll move this on before he reveals any more.

'Well, I'm almost done here.' I get hold of the steps, hoping that will be the cue for him to leave.

But instead of leaving he jumps forward. 'Those ladders have to be way too heavy for a slip of a girl like you. I'll handle this, it's a man job ...'

Okay, it's my fault I don't react more quickly. If I'm honest, I'm spending a moment revelling. No-one ever called me small before. As for the weight, sure, the step ladders are tall, but they're aluminium, and it's just a matter of knowing how to handle them. Dropping them, grabbing them close to the centre, and taking corners carefully works a treat.

As for Fred, when I come back to reality, he's not doing any of the above. He's charging across the room, with the steps at full height. Higher even, because being extra manly here, he's hoisted them up on his shoulder.

Poppy and I both yell the same words at the same time. 'St-o-p Fred! Stop!'

But he doesn't. If anything, he goes faster. Charging straight towards the flowers suspended above his head.

As the steps hit the batten of dangling carnations the crack echoes off the walls. Then the whole caboodle comes crashing down. Onto the steps, onto Fred, onto the top table.

'Crap ...' Poppy and I are muttering under our breath. 'What an arsehole ...'

'Oooops.' Fred's biting his lip, staring in disbelief, flowers sticking out around his head in all directions. 'Jeez, that wasn't supposed to happen.'

I jump forwards. 'Are you okay? Did you bump your head?'

He's disentangling himself, pulling stems out of his hair, doing a fine wounded puppy impression. 'No, fine, great, not hurt at all.' Except for his pride maybe. 'Shit, I'm so sorry, I was only trying to help and I've wrecked it. Talk about demolition man.' He said it.

From the way Poppy is shaking, I can see she's holding in her laughter. 'Maybe not so much of a guy's job after all?'

He's hanging on in there. 'No, really, I insist. Let me put it up again.'

I cross the room, and get hold of the steps. 'It's okay, Fred, we'll take it from here.' I should never have let go in the first place. 'Actually, we need to get on, there's a wedding happening in here very soon.'

That shocks him into action. This one's a church ceremony at two with the reception here afterwards, so there's a few hours' breathing space. But it's a relief when he concedes defeat, and shakes the last of the pink petals out of his hair. As he backs out of the room Poppy and I are giving each other oh-my-god stares.

'Is he accident prone?' I ask, as I climb back up the steps to fix the damage. 'The last time I saw him, he was clearing up a log spill.' The batten fixing here was pretty robust, but it wasn't strong enough to stand up to a hunky guy testing it to destruction.

Poppy's shaking her head, and grinning. 'Just exceptionally eager to impress you.' She laughs, and raises an eyebrow. 'At least he kept his clothes on this time.'

I just hope he's more careful with her en-suite.

As for me, it looks like I've found an ideal place to start growing my seeds. I'll just have to make sure Fred and his team of builders stay well away from them.

Chapter 13

Monday, 6th March
At Rose Hill Manor: Ice weasels and frozen trunks

'I can't put it off forever, and at least we've got a lovely day for it.'

Sorry. I'm talking to Gucci again. It's Monday morning, and as we bump along the country lanes, heading for guess-where-we'd-rather-not-be-going, the early March sunshine is dazzling as it bounces off the fields. There are fluffy clouds racing across a sky so blue it could almost have come from a picture. Add in the sheep grazing down by the lake, and the morning's so perfect I'm almost floating. But when I arrive and knock hard on the front door of Rose Hill Manor for a good two minutes, and there's still no reply, I come back down to earth with a bump.

'You can always count on a Penryn to wreck your day,' I mutter. I'm at the point of thinking I should have found something more professional than a shopping bag with Frenchies on for my papers, and I've got to 'd' for diablo in my alphabet of curses, when a regular thumping breaks my train of thought. As it's hell on earth finding a swear word beginning with 'e', I stop and listen. *Bump, bump, bump.* Still there. Tentatively, I wander around the end of the house, following the sound. And what do you know, there's Kip, completely oblivious. Soaking up the rays. Bashing hell out of a swing ball.

Unreliable, lazy, unprofessional? All of the above. I rest my case.

I take a second to gulp at the sweat patches on his skimpy T-shirt. Then I re-set my expression to mildly exasperated, and wander onto the lawn. 'Sorry to interrupt your work out, Kip, but it's ten o' clock.'

Although he frowns, he doesn't miss a hit. 'Great to see you too. And your point is?' He still hasn't taken his eye off the ball.

'We're *supposed* to be having a meeting.' I have a sudden vision of his dates scrawled on scraps of paper. 'If you've actually managed to write me in your appointments book that is?'

Ten hits later he catches the ball. 'Obviously, I haven't forgotten. I'm here aren't I? I even brought you a bat.' He dips down, and next thing, he's holding it out to me. 'Want a go? It's way more fun with two.'

I send him a 'what the eff?' stare. 'Absolutely not. I'm here to work.' If it comes out stronger than I intended, it's because I'm not just horrified. I'm appalled. My hand-eye coordination is fine so long as I'm doing pretty stuff with flowers. But if we're talking slamming a moving object with a bat, I've got more chance of winning *Strictly*. Quite apart from the fact

I'm being rushed off my proverbial feet. If he wants his damned wedding fair, someone's got to put the work in, even if it isn't him.

'Your loss.' He shrugs, and puts the bats together. 'You need to loosen up Water Lily. Pretty much the only up-side of working at a wedding venue is there's time to play.'

'Excuse me?' Quite apart from the prickles on my neck at what he's calling me, I can't believe he's taking the job so lightly. Or that he's sounding so negative about it. As for working, there's not much evidence of that on his part yet.

'Keep your veil on. I mean playing *between* ceremonies, not during.' As if that makes it any better. He's making no attempt to hide his laugh either.

'Elephant balls.' Out of nowhere it pops into my head for 'e'. It's one of Immie's curses, and it wasn't meant to get anywhere near my mouth, let alone be blurted out, and echo across the grass. Although seeing Kip's wide-eyed shock, I'm happy about the slip.

'That's one way of putting it.' So he did hear. 'And where *do* you stand on cursing in front of customers?'

As I fold my arms across my carrier bag, I'm kicking myself. A briefcase would look so much weightier. And not every question gets an answer, especially if it's a Penryn asking.

'Shall we make a start?' As I march off towards the open French windows I catch sight of the muddy patches around the swing ball post. 'And you do know you shouldn't be tearing up the lawn here? It's not an extreme mud run. You're going to need this area in pristine condition for wedding photographs.' I'm cringing at my snappy tone. When it comes to

Kip, I sound like an irate head mistress every time. But it's only because he's constantly behaving like a naughty school boy. There's fields and fields where he could play ball, but he just doesn't join the dots enough to use them. And what makes me more irate still, is that I'm pushed into being the bad guy here. When he really should have worked it out for himself.

'So, I'll run you through where we're up to,' I say, as we wander into the house, and end up in the airy white and blue living area. As I pull the folder out of my bag and pass it over, I can't help feeling slightly smug.

I take it from his grimace as he's flicking through the sheets that he's surprised.

'So, the marquee on the lawn ...?' he says.

I nod, slightly taken aback that he's already read enough to be homing in on individual items. 'It might be a tipi. I'm waiting for confirmation.' When we get back to doing things in the order I planned, I'll share that I've tracked down a hundred miles of liberty bunting to deck it out.

'How exactly does people tramping around a tent on the lawn fit with the "pristine" you were talking about earlier?' From his delighted grin, it's obvious he's playing for points here.

Forgetting the bunting, I draw in a breath and smile serenely. 'You manage the location. Keeping it perfect is down to you.' One all. And happily that part is nothing to do with me.

He's straight back at me, with a bark. 'And you're managing this event, so I say that particular ball is in *your* court.' His face cracks into a bemused smile. 'Seriously though, how *do* you stop the mud? Because I don't have the first idea.'

Oh, crap. This is not good news. It was better when we were fighting. I sniff. 'I'm a wedding stylist, not a ground engineer. But as far as I know the tents have floors, and you put matting on the pathways.'

He coughs, and tilts his head on one side. 'Except you aren't actually a wedding stylist, are you?' His words come slowly, as if he's trying to screw the truth out of me. 'Not according to what your mum said. In the office. On open day. And let's face it, a mum should know.' He raises his eyebrows triumphantly, and waits for my reply.

Bugger. I'm opening and closing my mouth, working out the best way to handle this. I have to hide how nervous I am about the styling. If I show any sign of weakness, he'll eat me for breakfast. Although I need to stay away from the mum snipes, because as far as I remember, he lost his when he was young.

He jumps straight in to capitalise on the gaping space I leave. 'Exactly how many country house weddings *have* you styled?'

Okay. Put like that, he's got me. I have to hold my hands up. 'Actually, none.' The way his face instantly splits into a grin somehow makes me so annoyed, the cogs in my brain spring back into action. 'But I was fully responsible for floral arrangements in ten hotels, on a daily basis, for every eventuality including weddings. Reception areas, conference suites, restaurants and close to two hundred bedrooms.' I'm so furious he's implying I'm as hopeless as him, I'm hopping up and down on his hand hewn Persian rug, hissing like a snake. 'What's more I worked in a wedding shop for years before that. Believe me, styling a wedding after that lot will be a piece of piss.' Dammit. The second it's out, I know I should have said 'cake' instead. What's more, I know he's got me. Serves me right for sounding over confident. Because truly, I'm a million miles away from that. But I'm not about to admit it to the likes of Kip.

He gives a low laugh. 'There you go again. Delighted to hear you've got the styling covered, but there's still a lot to work on with your swearing.'

If I had a custard pie in my hand, right now, I'd like to slap it onto his face and rub. Long and hard. But seeing as I don't happen to have one with me, I visualise it instead. And while I'm doing that, I take a few long slow inhalations. I'm so lost in the moment it comes as a shock to open my eyes and see he isn't scraping squirty cream out of his stubble.

'Right. Moving on.' I make my voice bright, and this time I go at top speed, leaving no gaps for argument, counting the rooms off on my fingers. 'We'll put the exhibitors in the marquee, the winter garden will be set out for a ceremony, we can put a "top table" in the ballroom, and have examples of table settings there too.' Up to this point he's been nodding benignly. 'And maybe some of your approved caterers could serve snacks in there too.'

His face freezes in mid nod. 'Approved *what*?'

'You said you'd make a list of approved suppliers? In the office on the open day?' If he was staring at me coldly before, now's my chance for pay back. 'Seems like you can quote my mum word for word. Is your memory more selective when it comes to your own obligations?' If he was freezing me out before, this is the start of the ice age.

There it is again. The 'whatever' shrug. 'I don't remember promising anything of the kind.' And a point blank denial.

I get out my best line of office-speak, polish it up, and throw it in. 'I'm not here to discuss semantics.' Hopefully it's weighty enough to make up for my missing briefcase. I pause for it to sink in, and hurry on. 'Fancy balustrades and a massive lake are the tip of the wedding iceberg. The rest is down to *you*. You damn well need to get your act together. And fast.'

'So you keep telling me.' He's got his hands in the pockets of his jeans and his tanned forearms are glistening in the sunlight. What's more, it's obvious he doesn't give a flying fig.

I shouldn't have to be saying this. If my mum hadn't backed this loser of a pony, believe me, I wouldn't be. But at the same time his throwaway attitude is making me want to fight him. Hard.

'That's your family all over, Kip – only interested in plundering the good bits.' As I spit out the words, my eyes are wide with surprise at what I'm daring to say, and how bitterly it comes out. Not that I meant to drag up the past, because it's the last place I want to re-visit. I force myself back to the present. 'After all, why work when you can play on the terrace instead?'

For a second the corners of his mouth pull down, but then as he leafs through my lists again, his eyes dull. 'Great to know you've got such a high opinion of us.'

As he lets out a long sigh, suddenly I realise the truth. The guy is completely bored. Worse still, he has no interest at all. I'm trying to cover up my horror, because the penny's just dropped.

'You don't know the first thing about weddings, do you? And I'm not sure you even care. Am I right?' If I make a huge effort not to sound judgmental, I'm more likely to discover the truth here.

He folds his arms, and scrunches up his face as if he's thinking hard, although it might just be because the sun's in his eyes. 'You might be closer than you think with that. Guilty as charged. I admit the whole bridal thing is a bit of a mystery. But ...' The lines on his forehead melt away. 'On the up side, I've already got my first approved supplier on board.'

'You have?' Who'd have thought? That's taken the wind out of my wedding dress. 'And?' I tilt my head expectantly, because I can't wait to hear this.

'Yep, my wedding style expert is all lined up. A complete rookie, but she more than compensates for that with her bossiness. Welcome to the team.' He's sticking out his right hand, waving the sheaf of papers in his other. 'As for the rest, this remarkably comprehensive exhibitor list you've put together should provide everything I need. Thank you for that too.'

Damn. That's a scumbag move if ever I saw one. But there's no point protesting. It's game set and bloody match to Kip Penryn. And I'm the fool here for handing over the names. If I hadn't been so eager to show off, I'd have kept them to myself. What's worse, a lot of those names came from Poppy. I've just leaked him a whole lot more ammunition to use to beat the opposition. How did I need reminding he was going to play dirty?

'Well done yet again, Kip, for achieving maximum results

with zero effort.' A perfect example of what I was talking about two sentences ago. There's no point in complaining, but this way at least we both know I've got him worked out – as a complete and utter lowlife.

From his laugh, he couldn't be enjoying this more. 'There's no such thing as a free lunch, Water Lily. Brides by the Sea are getting a damned good deal out of this fair. By the time Jess sends me her bill, I'll be paying for your work ten times over.'

If it's really that bad, I've no idea why he finds it so funny.

'Great. If there's nothing else you want to talk about, I'll let you get back to your swing ball.' More fool me for expecting a more productive discussion. If I thought Kip was going to be difficult to work with, he's just proved he's bloody impossible. At least this way I get to make a fast getaway. By the time I pass the linen sofas and reach the door to the garden, I'm practically running.

Kip's voice stops me in my tracks. 'Leaving so soon?'

From the warmth of the wind blowing through my hair, it could almost be summer. 'There's more to say?' I hate the way I've jolted to a halt on the step. And that he's got me hanging here, like a puppet.

'If you're in too much of a hurry forget it.' He's tossed the folder I gave him down on a chunky oak coffee table. 'But if you want to save us both some work, there's something outside in the Coach House that might be the answer to all our problems.'

I'm not sure I want to be included in a collective problem with anyone, even in a throwaway comment, least of all with

Kip. Didn't he just tell me, there's no such thing as a free lunch? I should know better than to be drawn in. But before I know it I'm following him. Sometimes I'm my own worst enemy.

Chapter 14

Monday, 6th March
In the Coach House at Rose Hill Manor: Frogs and
demolition experts

Did I expect to be following Kip around to the stable block? Am I comfortable being led on yet another wild goose chase, by the biggest weasel in Rose Hill? It's a big fat 'no' to all of the above. But at least it moves us on from the testosterone spillage by the sofas. As I follow Kip around the end of the house, and into the shelter of the stable yard, the half round windows, and the tall doors under the triangular gables take me right back. Years ago, we always took the route past the stables to reach the lake.

'Still just as beautiful.' I kick my feet on the stone sets, and make my next comment louder to cover my slip. 'If I were a bride, I'd insist on getting married here rather than in the house.' Although given I ended up at The Harbourside Hotel for my wedding, I'm clearly a lot more easily pushed around than I'm pretending.

Kip gives my comment the bemused stare it deserves.

'There's no pleasing some people. Lucky you're not a customer then.'

I hesitate by the old mounting block. When I slide onto the dip where the step has worn, the stone is warm under my bottom. It's only for a second. But it's so familiar it might only have been yesterday I was sitting here. Before we go wherever we're going, there's one thing I have to ask, so I prop my chin on my hand. 'So remind me why you're doing weddings again?' I suspect we both know it's a random choice for Kip. And now we're outside, with luck and a following wind I can pass off the interrogation as casual conversation.

As Kip rests his shoulder against the stone doorway the shadows under his eyes darken. 'You don't always get your first choices in life. There are times when you end up doing stuff you never thought you would.' He rolls, and leans his back against the wall. 'But you have to get on and make the best of it.'

If anyone knows about life not going to plan, it's me. Even so, I can't quite believe what I'm hearing. 'But weddings are so full on.' Even though he's a Penryn, my heart's sinking on his behalf. Not to mention my mum's. 'So why not do stag parties? Or hens? Or Airbnb instead?' If I'm sounding like a careers officer on amphetamines, it's only because I suspect he's so far out of his comfort zone.

'We can hardly let stags loose here, let alone hens. Whereas weddings work well. Or so Quinn assures me.'

'Quinn?' My gulp is so huge, I almost fall off the step.

Kip's explaining. 'My younger brother. Wild and outrageous. Everyone knows Quinn.' As if that was necessary.

Another gulp at the name, and I feel like I swallowed a balloon. 'I know the one. Best man at Sera's sister's wedding. The pictures are mega. But that wedding didn't happen by itself. A lot of people moved heaven and earth to pull that biggie together.' Mahoosive doesn't begin to cover it.

'So, there's a lot to pick up. Quinn's photos sold it to me, and until something better comes along, this is me.' Kip gives a shrug. 'According to Quinn, it'll be a piece of ...' He hesitates momentarily, before filling in his own blank. 'Cake.'

'Right.' I decide to skip over the bull and china shop allegations, even though my sources are reliable. If Quinn was my brother, I'd know not to believe a thing he said.

Kip almost lets a smile go. 'That's my surprise.'

Quinn? In the Coach House? You hear of people who are so shocked their hearts stop beating. From the bang on my chest wall, for a second I think that's me. I jump off the steps, hoping to hide my shock.

This time Kip's smile breaks. 'No need to look so terrified. The good news is, we can plunder what's left from that Christmas wedding to use for the fair. Fairy lights. Candles. Jam jars. I'll show you.' Now Kip's talking about a wedding he wasn't involved in, he's a lot more enthusiastic. Or maybe he just likes free stuff.

I grin, relieved it's left-over wedding accessories and not actually Quinn that he wants to show me. 'So long as you only take bookings from brides who want twigs and white lights we're all good for the future then.' The photos are full of them, but I'm joking, obviously. Then my stomach sinks, because from Kip's earnest expression, he thinks I'm serious.

He's suddenly fired up. 'Like Quinn says, armed with the Penryn charm, weddings should be easy as falling off a log.' Somehow the imagery is muddling. And Kip can't rely on any legendary charisma either. From where I'm standing, the so-called Penryn charm's not exactly gushing. It's not even a dribble.

As I follow him into the Coach House, my jaw drops when I see the wall of boxes marked fragile. 'Wow, are those *all* fairy lights?'

Kip gives a cough. 'No, those are *all* full of broken glass. Left over from one of Quinn's more significant accidents.'

Luckily, the dimness in the Coach House hides how gobsmacked I am. When Poppy mentioned Quinn's smashed crystal, I imagined a trayful. Forget a bull in a teensy china shop. This is more like totalling the entire glassware department of Johnny Loulous.

'Looks like Quinn's not your best role model then.' Although some of us knew that anyway. 'Maybe you need to visit another venue to see how weddings actually work, and get on top of the job. Choose one with good reviews on Trip Advisor, and pick their brains.' Under the circumstances, it seems a sensible suggestion.

Kip's interest perks. 'Like Daisy Hill Farm, you mean?' As if he'd be welcome next door at the venue he's driving out of business.

What the hell do I do with someone so clueless? 'Definitely *not* Daisy Hill. Best choose one a few counties away. At least.' As I move further, and come to the next humungous pile of boxes, I peep into one. 'Here we go. Enough fairy lights to light up most of Cornwall. From what I gather, the Christmas wedding had branches and twinkly lights suspended over the whole ballroom.'

Kip gives a nod. 'Apparently the fire brigade came to put up that twiggy ceiling.' For any normal person that would set their alarm bells ringing, but Kip looks delighted.

'I heard that too.' When Quinn failed to come through on that one, Chas and his fire-fighter work mates came to the rescue. 'But you do know you can't ring 999 every time you have a booking, Kip?' Somehow it would be funnier if I didn't have to say this. I'm prodding at the next pile of boxes. 'Ooo, chair covers. They'll be useful. Do you have tables and seats, or do I need to hire them in?'

There's his familiar shrug. 'Who knows? I haven't seen any yet.'

I'll take that as a 'no' then. 'They'd be a good investment – in the long term.' As, I sense him flinch, I understand exactly where he's coming from. I won't necessarily be making a big commitment to St Aidan either. Moving on to another box, I crouch, then pull out a glass jar to see if it's anything we could use. When I realise he's watching me, I look up.

His brow furrows as he meets my gaze. 'So how about you, Water Lily? Are you in this for the long haul? Whatever happened to all your hotels?'

The question is so unexpected it makes me jump. Literally. As I lurch, and wobble on my haunches, the mug slips out of my hands. It skitters away across the cobbled floor, and comes to rest next to the toe of one of Kip's ragged Converses.

He stoops, picks it up, and hands it back, still in one piece.

'No damage. Toughened jars are a popular choice when the best man's big on demolition.' Then he gives a low laugh. 'Sorry, did I hit a nerve there asking about your old job?'

I sniff as I slide the jam jar back into the box. 'As you say, opportunities come in all shapes and sizes. I'm where I need to be to help with my mum's wedding, and after that I'll ...' I slam the brakes on just in time. It's one thing shutting Kip up, quite another spilling my guts. The first rule of dealing with the Penryns is never to over-share. The less they know the better.

Even though it's almost dark, his eyes are narrowing. 'What I'm picking up is you're here, but not here. Maybe wishing you were in another place entirely, doing something very different?' It's as if he's dissecting a frog. He's sliced his scalpel through the skin, and he's poking round to see what's inside.

I need to stamp on this here and now. 'Absolutely not. I love weddings. I'm about to love styling. Who wouldn't love living in St Aidan?' All almost true. If there are other nuances, he's being damned perceptive to pick them up. And whoever heard of a guy being *that* sensitive? Although maybe he's just downright sneaky. 'I suspect my problem is *you* projecting *your* problems onto me. You might have screwed your life up, but I damn well haven't.'

After all that, he's laughing. 'Deny it all you like, but it takes one to know one, Water Lily. Sounds like we're both in a similar place. Washed up somewhere we'd maybe rather not be. We should stick together.'

Me like him? I'd rather eat my own parka than admit there are *any* similarities. As for sticking together, how about NO

NO NO? With the caps lock on. I'm still shuddering with horror when I literally have one of those moments of clarity about why Kip's here. Seeing the amount of fairy light bulbs around here, *and* David flagging it up, I must be dense not to have realised before. And obviously this makes our situations completely different, which is why I'm going to have to bring it up.

'But of course, I've got it now. You're actually only here because ...' So what is the etiquette when someone's company has gone bust? I'm struggling for the best way to put it when Kip jumps in.

'Because the London division of Penryn Trading went broke?' His shrug is diffident. 'Great deduction, Sherlock. It's no secret. It's been splashed all over the nationals. In case you missed the details, I was at the helm at the time.'

'Oh shit.' It comes out as a croak.

He takes a deep breath, and slams his shoulder against the wall again by the door. 'Six brothers, the other five all busy being super successful elsewhere. I was the one left holding the proverbial family baby. And I broke it. It's as simple as that.' He drums his fingers on his arm, and blows out his cheeks. 'Believe me, I couldn't have screwed up any worse. There's a lot of ground to make up. I need to come good.'

Wherever I meant to go with this, it wasn't here. 'But to try and come good with *weddings*?' If the word comes out as a shriek it's because I'm incredulous. He's so obviously unsuited to the job, he can't seriously be pinning his hopes on such a precarious career move.

'It could hardly be worse, could it?' He lets out a hollow

laugh. 'But this is the lifeline Bart's thrown me. I've got to turn it into a success. I can't run out on this one.'

For a second I think of Poppy and Rafe and how much easier it would be for them if Kip wasn't in competition with them. 'But if you're hating it, isn't it better to walk away?' It's worth a try. For all of us.

He shakes his head hard. 'Totally out of the question.' A bitter smile spreads across his face. 'We Penryns are a damned determined lot at the best of times. When we've failed, it's a thousand times more important to win next time around. That's why it's non-negotiable. I've got one chance to redeem myself here, and the family reputation too. It's "do or die". I *have* to make this business work.' With so much public shame to live down, he couldn't be more driven.

'Great.' I couldn't be hugging my Frenchie bag any harder to my body if it were a lifebuoy. 'Good luck with that, then. I hope it all goes swimmingly for you.' Despite trying to sound light and airy, I end up sounding like my mother. On a bad day. Again. There's something about his dry desperation that's making me fight for air too. Let's face it, as news goes, for Team Daisy Hill, this couldn't be worse.

His smile has gone now, and his cheekbones are in sharp definition as he swallows hard. 'This won't be about luck, Water Lily. This is about guts, and sheer determination. If I have to fight to the death to succeed here, I damned well will.'

This is exactly what I *didn't* want to hear. There are some situations in life where you need to get the hell out fast. And this is one of them.

'Great.' I try it again, because that was the part that worked before. Only this time it comes out as a squeak. 'Thanks for that insight, Kip. And thanks for showing me the freebies. I'm sure they'll be very useful.' My voice has dwindled to a whisper, and my back's to the wall as I edge towards the front of the house. 'But if that's all your good news for today ...' I'm tiptoeing backwards now, and I can't remember when I last took a breath. 'I really should be getting on ...'

As I finally make it back to Gucci it takes a few minutes before I recover enough to turn the key. And just before I do, I'm damned sure I can hear the thump of a swing ball again. And although it's already spring, the end of summer seems a very long way off. How the hell am I going to put up with Kip for all that time? And is he going to make it through to September and mangle the opposition in the process? Or will he crash and burn, and leave my mum without a wedding?

Chapter 15

Tuesday, 7th March
At the Happy Dolphin Garden Centre: Team spirit and
hungry fish

'Marigolds, nasturtiums, cosmos, larkspur ...'
In any spare moments while I've been sorting out
the wedding fair, I've been hitting Google myself. I've pretty
much read everything there is to read about growing your
own wedding flowers. What's more, I've been totally seduced
by the images. Endless views of tangled blooms. Country
meadows in soft focus. Close ups of Queen Anne's Lace.
Somehow they take me right back to the first pack of seeds
I ever grew for myself, on the little patch of garden next to
my dad's greenhouse. Seeing the pictures now, it's all rushing
back. The anticipation that had me holding my breath for
days before I scattered the seeds. Then the anticlimax when
nothing happened, even though I watered them every day
with my pint-sized watering can. My dad laughing as I almost
had my nose in the mud, as he watched me search for

sprouting. Then that whoosh of excitement as I finally spotted the tiny green threads of shoots in the soil. The thrill as weeks later, the mass of poppies and cornflowers and daisies burst into a chaos of red and blue and pink blooms.

I was only six, but that sunny summer was where my love for flowers began. And it's like I'm falling in love all over again now. Reminding myself why I stood up to my mum and insisted I did floristry at college, not the beautician's course she was pushing me towards with the force of a motorway-building earth shifter. All the way to the day I tiptoed into Jess's newly opened flower shop, because the window display was so spectacular. How somehow I dared to ask if she needed any help. And how when she said 'yes' I ran all the way back to my friends on the beach, waving my arms and whooping so hard, I only noticed I'd lost a flip flop when I got onto the sand and grazed my foot on a rock.

Right now, I'm a hundred per cent hooked on growing my mum's bouquet. So enthusiastic, my flower list covers two sheets of A4. Ready to take the plunge, even. This morning when Immie rang the shop at the last minute to call off her trying-on session – no surprise there – I jumped into Gucci, to put the time to good use.

Which is why I'm putting my cringing to one side, pushing a trolley past rows of blue and pink primroses, and miniature daffodils in pots, and heading into The Happy Dolphin Garden Centre. Okay, I admit this is one of the top places I would rather *not* be seen. It's just not a good look to be caught hanging out where your mum buys her garden trugs and blue tit supplies. But given there's no-one here remotely in my age bracket, I reckon I'm safe. And at least inside the conservatories as large as football pitches, it's warm.

'Two bags of compost ... twenty seed trays ...' As I tick off my shopping list, the tingle in my tummy is half the expectation I remember from being a child, half pure fear that I'm going to fail. However tantalising the anticipation is, I'll do this at the speed of light, and get out of here. As I push my trolley past bird tables, calendars, pottery badgers and thermometers, the overpowering smell of gravy from the cafe completely wrecks the garden ambience. As I cross the first expansive showroom full of garden furniture, I'm marvelling at the variety, and the size of the place. By the third, I'm losing the will to live. And I'm also getting a bit panicky that I might never find my way out again.

When I finally spot an assistant in a padded jacket, I dash up behind him, tap him on the shoulder and clear my throat. 'Excuse me, could you possibly point me to the seed packets?'

As soon as he turns, I know I've stuffed up. For a start, there's no sign of a grinning dolphin logo. And second there's a chest full of cashmere, with horribly familiar rips.

'Kip? What the hell are you doing in here?' I have no idea how I missed the trademark jeans from the back.

If he's surprised to see me, he doesn't let on. 'You told me to up my game. So here I am. Doing as I'm told.' His shrug is so laid back, you'd almost think he hung out at the Happy Dolphin every day. And thankfully yesterday's desperation has gone overnight too.

'You're shopping?' *And* upping his game? All on the same day? I'm doing the metaphorical jaw on the floor thing.

Although why anyone with a house as big as his should look that pleased with two miniature box balls in pots, I don't know.

His grin is as euphoric as the name of the place. 'I'm sorting the planting for either side of the front door. I thought it would be one less thing for you to do.'

I bite my lip as I look at his miniature plants, and work out how to break the news. 'I was thinking of something bigger. Perhaps. Say standard bays, maybe in lead planters?' Okay, it's not very original, but we're talking fast fixes here. Six foot ones rather than a six-inch version. Bought from a wholesaler so we wouldn't be paying 'grey pound' prices. But now we're here, I don't want to be too discouraging.

'Whatever you say.' He's being unnaturally compliant. 'Tree's are back this way.' A flash of orange as he turns, draws my eye to the basket on the trolley handle.

'You've got a gnome?' Even though I'm stating the obvious, and trying to play down my horror, it comes out as a shriek of disbelief. A dead ringer for the one on the front porch at Heavenly Heights too. 'What is it with men and gnomes?'

As he leads the way to the outdoor planting, his frown is puzzled. Like he's having a 'women are from Venus' moment. 'A gnome seemed like a great way to liven up a dreary entrance. He's ironic, obviously.'

As if that's any excuse.

'And he was on offer.'

Worse and worse. If we're talking about irony, this must be it. 'And we all know how irresistible fifty per cent off is.' I can't keep the bitterness out of my voice. 'It's what makes people sign up for a wedding when they didn't even know they wanted to get married.'

Just when you think you can't hear anything more unbelievable, the guy tops it. What's worse, how can anyone in his position be so out of touch with the up-market wedding aesthetic? I shiver as the automatic doors swish us out into the cold, but on the up side it won't be for long, given we're facing a line of tall bays.

'There you go. Classy and understated, perfect for the job. Ideal for customising with bows.' Could have been made for the back of his Land Rover.

As he picks up the price ticket he lets out a long whistle. 'Forget ribbon. If that's what they cost, no-one's going near them.' But despite the grouching, a couple of seconds later, he's thrown two on board, along with a couple of planters that luckily look as expensive as their price tag. And he's off again at speed.

'You might like to put the gnome back on your way to the tills.' I'm running to keep up with him. 'If you're on a budget.'

Kip wrinkles his nose. 'He can go by the back door. Or on my private terrace.' Wherever that is. Then he takes note of my shaking head. 'What? Every guy needs a friend. It's damned lonely rattling around in that house on my own.'

Now I've heard it all. Talking about it as a 'him' not an 'it' too. 'I'll save the violins for later.' I'm busy muttering when he stops so suddenly I crash my trolley into the back of his ankles.

'Seeds – you were asking for seeds?' We've come to a halt next to a row of rotating displays, and he's staring at my bags of compost. 'Are you growing veggies?' The fascination in his voice isn't healthy.

That's the trouble with meeting someone out shopping. It should be like when you meet someone in the doctors. There's an etiquette. The last thing you do is to start quizzing them about why they're there. It's actually well rude to look too hard at what's in someone's trolley. As for firing questions…

I might as well get this over with. 'I'm growing a few flowers for my mum's wedding. That's all.' Although that sounds like I'm taking it for granted it's going to work. Knowing me, I'll kill the lot.

His brow wrinkles. 'On the window sill? I thought you lived in a flat?'

Who knows where he got that from, or what's sparked the interrogation. I think I preferred it when he was acting clueless about weddings.

I clutch my list to my chest so he'll back off before latching onto that too. 'Not in the attic, I'll be looking for a bit of ground outdoors once the seeds have sprouted in Poppy's orangery.'

His face slides into a grin. 'Lucky you've asked the right guy. You can use the kitchen garden at the Manor. It needs digging over, but there's plenty of space, and it's sunny. You'll be company too, when we're quiet.'

I shuffle, stick my foot on my trolley, and try to twist my face to look grateful rather than appalled. 'I'm not sure.' Except I am. Completely sure. I can't think of *anything* worse. And I'm not bloody rent-a-crowd. Quite apart from it meaning I'd have to spend even more time hanging round the Manor, I'd be indebted to a Penryn. That's one place you shouldn't ever go. We all know that.

He's straight back at me. 'So that's a deal, then. I get to keep my gnome, you get to use the garden.'

From where I'm standing that's a 'no' on every side. I'm just getting my head around how to break it to him when a familiar squealing laugh leaves me rigid. *My mother?* Although I shouldn't be shocked if my mum's here. It's one of her favourite hang outs. If anyone should be gobsmacked and astonished, it should be her when she sees me. As I turn, sure as eggs is eggs, two crimson track suits are storming towards us.

'My mum and David, in matching gym wear?' It comes out as a low moan. 'Could it be any worse?'

Kip gives a shrug. 'For anyone who's red-green colour blind they probably blend nicely with the foliage.'

Mum covers the last ten metres faster than an Olympic sprinter, and her shriek is a thousand times bigger than the one I let out when I saw the orange-trousered traveller who'd hitched a ride in Kip's trolley.

'Lileeeeeeeeeeeeeeeeeeeeey! Dahling!? Whatever happened to that job of yours?' She gives the sleeve of my parka a disparaging poke. 'Please tell me you're not lunching at the Happy Dolphin in that dreary old anorak.' Considering the humming discord between her Mighty pink lippy and the tomato-red of her top, she's in no position to judge.

I skip the bit about working, and my astonishment there's a dress code at the cafe, because some jibes call for retaliation. 'At least I'm not trying to colour coordinate with the ketchup.'

David grins, and pulls a face as he flexes his thigh muscles. 'Or a traffic light. I told your mum if we chose these we'd need to give out sunglasses.' There he goes again, butting in with a stupid joke.

I sniff. 'Last time I looked traffic lights were three colours.' Just saying. Because someone has to. And what's wrong with calling them sunnies?

For a second my mum's glare is furious enough to torch me, but then it mellows.

'Kip, you're here too!' The way she's scrutinising his bay trees, no-one told *her* about shopping manners either. Her squeal rises an octave. 'And *look*, you've got *our* gnome. Have you seen, David?' Her beam sweeps across each guy in turn. 'Ours is by the front door. What are the chances of *that*?' Excited doesn't begin to cover it.

Given most of the gnomes scattered randomly amongst the displays are out of the same mould, I'd say it's no surprise at all. So long as you're one of the crazy few who'd buy one, that is.

Kip gives David a 'team-gnome' nod of acknowledgement. 'We're here buying seeds. Lily's taking over the kitchen garden at the Manor.'

'Really?' My mum's eyes are wide. 'But what about ...?'

I rap out a reply, before my mum gets to splurge about Fred's offer to use his place. 'Thanks for mentioning that, Kip.' Hopefully the withering look I'm firing will shut him up too. There's no time for denials, because I need to wrap this up, and fast. One visit to the Happy Dolphin is enough for anyone. I won't be coming again. *Marigolds, sweet rocket, aquilegia, delphiniums*. I'm scanning my list, whirling round the displays. As I snatch at seed packets I can't help thinking that Dad and I took the whole winter to buy flower seeds. How we'd buy a couple of packets a week, then sit by the open fire in our cottage, him in his arm chair, me on the little stool he'd made me out of an orange box, fanning out the packs, pouring over the pictures. I learned to read stumbling through the long words on the descriptions. We'd cross check with last year's successes, consult our wish list, decide what else we needed. If I'd somehow imagined savouring the moment today, lovingly deliberating over every pack, pouring over the descriptions like Dad and I used to, it's just too bad. *Dill, cornflowers, lobelia, phlox...*

'Can anyone see love-in-a-mist, or borage?' I grab the packets Kip's holding out, throwing the lot into the trolley. 'Okay, that's me done, we mustn't keep you two gym bunnies from your food.' I grab the trolley handle and run. If I'm feeling short changed, I've only got myself to blame for stuffing this up. As I manoeuvre past the birthday cards, I spot an entire wall of gnome clones. As I hurtle towards the checkout, my main concern is to get Kip out before he tries to buy the whole consignment.

As for the deal, I'll have to wriggle out of that one later. After ten minutes of Kip in a garden centre, one thing's clear. I can't possibly stand being around him for an entire growing season.

Chapter 16

'For someone who doesn't know what they're doing, you're very organised.'

It's Poppy, her pumps tapping on the lovely old black and white tiles of the orangery floor later in the day, bringing tea to help me along with my seed planting.

Even though my head is so full it's bursting, I've nipped away from the shop early today to get the job done. Ideally I'd wait until after the wedding fair, but that'll be too late. So Poppy's set up a trestle table, with plastic to protect the floor. And I'm basking in the golden afternoon sun shafts coming through the small paned windows, listening to faraway snatches of music from the builders' radio upstairs. There's also the occasional very loud crash, of course. Given Demolition Fred's up there helping, anything could be happening.

'If every day is as warm as today, the seeds will come

through in no time,' I say to Poppy, as I look up from my potting compost. 'How are the drip cakes going?'

Let's get our priorities right here. Sometimes food comes before gardening, and my mouth is watering in anticipation of what Poppy's bringing. She's been working on some practice cakes for the fair. And I'm very happy to help her eat them, even though my mum is telling me if I don't lose two stones, I'll be a blot on her wedding pictures. How ridiculous is that? Everyone knows a wider bridesmaid is very flattering for a bride.

Poppy puts down two steaming mugs, and two extra large pieces of cake. 'I reckon I've mastered the drip thing. Once I got the main cake cool enough, the ganache worked a treat. See what you think?'

'Remind me what ganache is?' I say, as I hurtle to the cloakroom.

'A glaze made from chocolate and cream which is perfect for dripping.' The words drifting from a room away remind me how hungry I am. 'Last summer everyone went crazy for nude cakes, but ombré and drizzled icing are the next big things.'

It takes approximately two seconds flat to wash my hands. Then I'm back, perched next to Poppy on the low windowsill, and my fork is hovering over crumbly sponge, coated with vanilla buttercream that would be delicious on its own. Add in a cocoa topping, drooling down the sides. And a random pile of chocolate Oreo's welded together with more sticky icing...

'Too good to eat,' I say, then laugh, because from the way saliva is running down my chin, obviously, I'm kidding. There's enough calories here to put two inches on my hips in one sitting. If she could see me now, cake fork at the ready, my mum would have a heart attack. It's always the same with Poppy's cakes. They bring instant bliss. One forkful, and I reach dark chocolate Nirvana.

'Fabulous.' It comes out as a little moan. Three forkfuls later, I take a conversation break to make it last. 'And with the seeds, it's all coming back. I used to help Dad grow bedding plants when I was little.' Our cottage in the village had a ramshackle greenhouse at the end of the garden where Dad and I would hide for hours. Needless to say my mum wouldn't hear of anything as unsightly as a greenhouse spoiling the manicured perfection when we moved up to Heavenly Heights.

'It's funny how things stick from when you're young. Your dad and your flowers, my mum and my cake icing.' Poppy slides an arm round my shoulders and gives me a squeeze.

Her mum died just after my dad, so she knows about that empty ache in my chest that won't go away, even though it's five years later. It was sudden for both of us too. Her mum was ill but hadn't told her. Whereas my poor dad was completely well, but was struck by lightning playing golf. At the eighteenth hole, he was so close to finishing. If only he'd been at the nineteenth, and in the bar, he'd still be here.

'That's the funny thing.' I frown at the weirdness. 'As soon as I started, I knew how deeply to fill the trays, and how much compost to sprinkle on top for the different flowers. And to tuck the seed packet in the end of the tray so I know what I've planted.' Just like Dad always taught me. Although somehow I'd forgotten how much I enjoyed it.

Poppy was the year above me at school, but their cottage always smelled of her mum's baking. And there were always fairy cakes for tea, and icing sugar dusting the table, and fabulous birthday cakes.

'They look very neat.' She takes in the row of trays on the table in front of the small paned floor to ceiling windows as she munches. 'And full of promise.'

I smile at the last word because I can feel the anticipation too. 'When I was really small, my dad used to hold my hand to make holes in the compost for the nasturtium seeds. My finger was just the right size.' And suddenly my mouth is full of saliva. Not because of the cake. Just because I'm thinking of my dad, and how lovely he was. And because I can't believe I'm never going to see him again. As my mouth stretches, and I turn to bury my face in Poppy's jumper, I can feel her shoulder shuddering too.

'Sorry.' I scramble in my pocket, hand Poppy a tissue, and we both blow our noses loudly. 'Crying over nasturtium seeds. How silly is that?'

That's the awful thing about losing someone. It doesn't go away. And you can't ever predict when something's going to tip you over the edge, or what it will be. You can go for months and be fine. Then something completely ridiculous will have you in bits. Forget birthday badges. Badges would be way more useful for broken people like me. Lost my dad, prone to wobbles, would cover it. Or maybe they should make T-shirts.

It's why I can't understand how my mum's forgotten Dad enough to marry someone else. When it happened, it was awful. She didn't get dressed, and she wouldn't leave the house. For three whole months, she walked round in Dad's pyjamas. Then one weekend I came home, and she was in the kitchen in her lippy and her heels. I can't tell you how much of a relief that was. Next thing, she was cruising in the med with Jenny. Also good. But I never imagined she'd get to this point, when I'm still welling up over seed packets.

Another big bang from the depths of the farmhouse drags me back to the orangery.

'Ouch.' Poppy and I are still exchanging grimaces, when there's a clattering of boots on the stairs, and the echo of footsteps crossing the drawing room.

There's a throaty laugh too. 'Lily, I saw your car from the bathroom window ...'

When your car's bright pink, the bad news is there's no place to hide. As for Poppy and me being interrupted in mid-snivel, hopefully Fred'll be oblivious.

I swallow hard, and scrape my finger under my lashes. 'Fred, how's it going? Sounds like you're having a smashing time up there.' As an impartial observer, I have to admit, the checked shirt and dust streaked forearms are cheering me up.

He grins, and pushes a lock of hair out of his eye. 'That's what building work's like. It gets worse before it gets better.' Then he turns to Poppy. 'Actually, I'm here to complain. First Lily's too busy to come out with me, and now Barbara tells me she doesn't want my garden either.'

As he puts his hands on his hips and sticks his leg out, the rip in his jeans separates. Who knew tanned knees could be so attractive? As for my mum spreading the word, for one time only, I don't mind.

Poppy gives her nose a dab, and manages a half laugh. 'You didn't have any space in your garden, Fred. That's the whole point. It's good Lily's found somewhere else.'

If it was anyone but Fred, I'd insist that nothing's decided. I'm still reluctant to spend time at the Manor if there's any other garden on offer. I'm agonising, when I notice Fred peering first at Poppy, then at me.

'What's up with you two and your red noses? Been chopping onions?'

So maybe we haven't got away with it. 'It's just that cold that's going around.' I use the excuse to give my nose a last noisy blow.

Fred couldn't have leaped back faster if I'd told him I'd got the plague.

'Whoa, don't sneeze on me. I've got way too much going on here to catch man 'flu.' Given the orangery roof is glass, his upwards nod is directed at the sky not the bathroom, but we get what he's meaning. 'I was going to whizz you over to see my development, Lily, but maybe we'll leave that for another day.'

Phew. Sounds like I made a lucky escape. 'What's this?' Now I'm off the hook, I can ask.

Poppy's grinning. 'Fred's quayside conversions. I was telling you about them, remember?' For some reason she thinks this is hilarious.

Fred joins in 'Rock Quay. Executive flats with sea views across the harbour. One foot in the door, you'll be out of that pokey little attic in a shot. There's a prime two-bedroom one ready now. Say the word and it's yours to rent.'

I'm not sure if it's a sales pitch or a take-over bid on my life. 'That's very kind, but I love the flat I've got, thanks. It's very convenient living over the shop.'

Fred watches me tugging on my tissue, and retreats another step. 'Don't worry. As soon as you see it, you'll want it. I'll do it at the right price.' He sends me a wink, before he goes on. 'There's a load of manure with your name on too. I'll drop it over at the Manor.'

First a flat and now cow shit. Maybe Poppy's right about Fred being eager to please. He's certainly not holding back on the gifts.

'Brilliant.' Then a vision of a lane filled with logs flashes into my brain. 'Actually, there's no rush. Mid-April will be great.' If I haven't decided on anywhere else by then. I give an involuntary shudder. The closer it gets, the more I go rigid every time I think about what's happening in April.

The inward whistle and derogatory head shake Fred gives is the same one builders give when they're preparing you for a monstrous estimate. 'There's a lot of digging to make that Manor garden anything like suitable.'

I stand my ground. 'I'm ready for hard work.' Which I'm not at all. But I'm sensing it's important not to back down here. 'Or I will be as soon as my cold's better.' I grin as Fred flinches.

Now all I need to do is make sure the wedding fair isn't derailed by a mis-delivered muck heap.

Chapter 17

'**D**id someone order fertiliser?'

It's over three weeks later, and Kip's leaning on the doorway, calling to where I'm hard at work, stage setting the winter garden.

As I break off to answer, I grab the chance to fix my flagging pony tail. 'That's a very random question to ask someone who's mid-way through tying bows onto chair backs, with a wedding fair careering towards them at a hundred miles an hour.' Every time I remember it's less than twenty-four hours away, I can't help letting out a strangled squeak. Somehow I stop the hyperventilating, and yank my voice lower. 'We're expecting hay bales, a bar in a horse box, a bicycle cart full of gin, a van load of suits and wedding dresses, and two pianos. But definitely not fertiliser. Why?' If I'm sounding stressed, it's only because I am. To the power of sixty-four.

Kip scratches his head absently. 'The farmer who has the

grazing here is outside with a trailer load of cow muck asking for you. That's all.'

'Oh crap.' I turn to Poppy, who's currently stringing fairy lights and putting a thousand candles into jars. 'If this is Fred, I might just have to throttle him.'

As I scurry through the house, I'm not expecting Kip to come too, but he's at my heel like a lap dog.

He sounds relieved. 'Just checking it wasn't malicious. Like those mass pizza deliveries you hear about.'

The idea of so much stuffed crust is making my tummy rumble. 'I'd settle for a food mountain over a muck heap any day.' And I'm not suggesting malice, but if I was pushed I'd say manure arriving at this particular moment smacks of mischief. Although I'm not quite sure who it's aimed at.

We go out into the bright sun, and sure enough there's Fred's second biggest tractor, blocking the drive. Nothing new there then. Bright blue, he's in it most days at Poppy and Rafe's. And the man himself is leaning against a back wheel massively taller than he is. If my mouth was watering at the thought of food, despite my better judgement it waters a little bit more when I take in that easy smile, and his scruffy Barbour.

'So long as you're loaded up with either straw, or pepperoni pizzas, I'm happy to see you, Fred.' When it comes to toppings and bacon sarnies, I suspend my veggie tendencies every time.

Fred twitches his mouth. 'Don't worry, the bales are coming on the next trip.' The wind sweeps through his hair, and his Paco Rabanne cloud reaches us before he does. 'But seeing how well our seeds are coming along in the orangery, I've brought a load of manure. It's April tomorrow. You'll need to dig it in, pronto.'

Talk about fabulous timing. It's true the seeds have sprouted brilliantly. The nasturtiums have already got four leaves. If Fred's becoming over invested, it's only because he's on the spot every day when I call in to water them.

'Great, bring it this way, you can pull alongside the gateway.' Kip's leaping across the gravel, towards the stables. 'Come on Water Lily, I'll show you too while you're out here.'

What is it about guys? They don't multitask. But the first chance they get to switch, they'll happily drop whatever they're doing, and hurl themselves into the next job.

I'm protesting as I run to keep up. 'This probably isn't even the garden I'll be using.'

Kip's laughing over his shoulder. 'I'd say a ton of manure is the decider, wouldn't you? Bagged and well-rotted too. You must be in his good books.'

I should be laying up top tables, and making bridesmaids' posies, not chasing around after a farmer who won't do as he's asked, and a wedding venue manager who's too easily distracted. As for being rail-roaded by Kip, if I wasn't completely out of breath, I'd be blowing my top. When I finally catch up with him, it's only because he's stopped by a doorway in a high stone wall. I open my mouth to let rip. 'I haven't got time for this and I don't even ...'

Before I get any more words out, he holds up his hand. 'You're here now. See it first, then decide.' He grasps the knob, and pushes the plank door open.

'Whatever.' As I follow him, I'm so busy huffing, shaking

my head and staring at my feet, at first I don't register anything.

'So ...?' Kip's waiting for a reaction.

As he says, I'm here now. When I swallow back my rage, and finally force myself to look up, every bit of anger melts away. Because we're in a square space, surrounded by mellow, coursed stone walls. There are grass paths, criss-crossing between empty borders, and what look like fruit trees along one end.

I'm blinking with surprise. 'It's like something out of a picture book.'

Kip's laugh is low. 'The original secret garden. Just waiting for you. Unless you can find somewhere better, of course.'

For once only, that awful confidence of his is justified. If I scoured the country, I wouldn't find many gardens as secluded.

'No, it's beautiful.' I'm standing staring, taking in the space. 'But it's huge. I doubt I'll be able to fill a corner.' Even if all my plants grow, they probably wouldn't take up a tiny bit.

He shrugs. 'Use as much as you need. The maintenance guys keep the weeds down, but they never grow anything.' He glances at his watch. 'We'll unload here. Wedding fairs don't organise themselves. You'd better get on.' He's almost shooing me out again.

Despite the waiting work, I'm hanging back. Strangely reluctant to leave.

'Glad you came?' he asks, as I tear myself away, and we step back through the wall again, and out into the world.

But before I can answer, Fred's tractor roars along, gravel spitting up from the wheels. So I leave them to it, hug my cardigan more tightly around me, and make a dash for the house.

Penryn traps come in all shapes and sizes. But for one time only, this enchanted garden might be worth the risk. And much as I wanted to limit my trips to the Manor, if I'm coming to spend time in that garden, I know I won't mind at all. I'll just have to make sure I come when Kip's not around.

Chapter 18

Saturday, 1st April
Rose Hill Manor: Knitting and Shakespeare

'Well, wasn't this a wonderful idea of mine for a wedding fair? And I've decided on diamonds for my wedding theme, so we can begin whenever you're ready, Lily. Only one question – where the hell's the hot tub? And why the frig aren't there any anchovies?'

You guessed right. It's Nicole. With the volume, and the Princess Anne accent turned up to full strength for the benefit of the not inconsiderable crowds. And from where I'm standing next to the Brides by the Sea competition table – our not-so-sneaky way of getting people's email addresses – that's two questions, not one. As for diamonds, who'd have guessed that?

Luckily it's afternoon by the time she rocks up, so I've already had a morning's worth of sugar from the sweet cart. I reckon I've consumed enough rhubarb and custard bonbons to be able to withstand a nuclear winter. As for whether that's enough to come through ten minutes with Nicole, watch this space. I slip in a last sour worm from my under-table store, just to be on the safe side.

'So sorry Nicole, but Kip held off on the hot tub, to avoid scorch marks on the grass. And there's a worldwide shortage of teensy fish due to a plankton virus in Portugal.' Can you tell I made that up on the spot? Even worse than the white lies, my attempt at one of Jess's customer-soothing purrs, sounds more like I've got a caterpillar stuck in my throat. 'But Kip's come through in spades on the smoked salmon canapés.' Nicole's downing those faster than Immie's necking Poppy's multi-coloured mini cupcakes. 'And he's onto a winner with the weather, too.' Another instance of the guy falling on his feet. Like a cat, it seems like he just can't help it.

The good news for all of us is it's one of those balmy April days that make you think that summer's already arrived. The sun's splashing across the south facing terrace in front of the house, and making the lake shimmer blue with the reflection of the sky. Best of all, it's warm enough to throw open the French windows. So couples are drifting from the ballroom, out onto the grass, and back in to where we've set up our Brides by the Sea area beyond the sofas.

David and my mum have finally arrived, after their morning spinning session. And along with all the other guys, he made a beeline for the microbrewery stall in the gazebo. From where she's standing next to him out on the lawn, my mum's perfectly placed to send Nicole dead eyes. For one day only Mum's dumped her Adidas gear, and reverted to type, and she and Nicole are vying for whose chrysanthemums are most vibrant. My mum's edging ahead with acid yellow blooms on fuchsia.

But at dinner plate diameter, Nicole's white on black definitely get the prize for size.

'And we're thinking four tiers, and an ombré dribble for the cake, Poppy. And every kind of cupcake tower.' Nicole's making an expansive hand sweep that includes *all* the cakes. On the cake table. And in the world too. 'All with huge amounts of diamond clusters on, obviously.' She blinds us with another dazzle of her ring, just in case we'd missed it last time out.

Poppy taps her flowery cake book. 'You're pencilled in, Nicole. I'll search out some serious sparkle, and we'll finalise the design at our private consultation.' Poppy's been racking up the orders, because her cakes look stunning. As well as the drip cakes, everyone's been drooling over her sugar dusted nude three tier, with raspberries and roses. And we've had a lot of takers for the Daisy Hill Farm Holiday Cottage cards. Given they've erected a nice new Weddings at Daisy Hill Farm sign, and most people visiting the wedding fair will drive past, we're hoping that people will put two and two together. Then make their wedding booking at the farm.

From the way her brows knit, I can't help thinking Nicole wanted more than pencilling in. Writing in in indelible marker perhaps? But at least she's got her dress sorted, and her shoes, and her ring, which is more than I can say for Immie or my mum. Immie's still sporting purple perspex, and my mum's ring finger is bare.

Nicole hoicks Miles by the arm. 'Right, we'll see you later, we're off for a wander by the water.'

Poppy waits until they're outside, then she leans across to

me. 'I swear poor Miles got through the door without his feet touching the floor there.'

I grin back. 'He might as well get used to it. And he doesn't look as if he minds.'

As soon as Nicole's safely outside, my mum tiptoes into the space she's left, which is strange. Usually she's way more expansive when she arrives.

'The jewellery's beautiful, isn't it?' I say. When did my mum ever need drawing into conversation? The very swish local designer jewellers jumped at the chance to exhibit, and I noticed Mum and David hovering round their cabinet earlier. 'Did you see anything exciting?'

She rubs her bare ring finger thoughtfully. 'The venue was easy. Nothing feels quite right yet for the ring.'

Poppy smiles. 'How about the dress? Is there anything here you'd like?' She walks over to the Brides by the Sea rail, and my mum goes too and nods at the mannequins.

'It's hard to decide which way to go,' my mum says, in a hesitant way that's very unlike her.

Let's face it, red track suits and electric pink Nikes are hardly indecisive.

'You could have a pastel linen dress and jacket?' Despite her penchant for dayglo florals, I throw that in to see where she stands. 'Jerry Hall looked fab in pale grey Vivienne Westwood chiffon.' Although somehow I don't see my mum in anything *that* understated.

'Per-lease dah-ling, we don't *all* want your brand of dowdy. All over sequins are the new satin. I'm a *bride*, not a bride's *mother*. Although there's precious little hope of that ever happening either if you don't lose that puppy fat.' The despairing shake of her head directed straight at my singledom doesn't last long, and she carries on. 'Beyoncé's mum had bare shoulders, and snow-white slinky satin with a gold belt when she got married. I can carry that off, even if *you* can't.'

So even though that's put me in my place, it's a relief she's back to her bitey old self. At least we know when it comes to dresses she's taking Destiny's Child and mermaids as her starting points.

She drops her voice again, and raises an eyebrow, which for anyone who knows her, is her full blown 'matchmaker' mode. 'By the way, Fred's looking for you.' Dammit, even at a coupley event like a wedding fair, I thought I'd escaped her trying to glue me to anyone.

'Are you sure?' My heart sinks. He brought enough manure to fertilise the entire village yesterday. And there's no other reason for him to be here today.

She nods. 'David and I met him when we went for a romantic lakeside stroll.'

I ignore the sick feeling in my stomach at the thought of their stroll. 'Shouldn't you be getting back to David? See what you think of the table settings and the flowers in the ballroom. There are even some menus too.'

The way my mum struts off, those few snipes have rebooted her mojo.

Poppy sighs. 'She doesn't get any better, does she?'

'Nope.' I'm completely used to shrugging off my mum's extreme bitching. At the same time I'm beyond grateful Poppy didn't remark on how loved up she was looking. 'Time for vanilla fudge before the next rush of customers?' As I sidle over to deliver one to Poppy, I give a nod to where Kip's giving out glasses of Bucks Fizz in the ballroom. 'So how do you think he's doing?'

Poppy untwists the paper, and pops the fudge into her mouth. 'Pulling you in to organise today was a genius move. But he's a lot less worrying in the flesh than his über professional signs suggest, that's for sure.'

I like that Poppy's so perceptive. 'He's clinging onto that new clipboard like it's a life raft, serving drinks one handed. There's still no appointment book either.'

Poppy frowns. 'That's a recipe for disaster. When I took over at the farm, weddings were in all kinds of a mess. On the bright side, if Kip's in chaos we might get to pick up his double bookings.' Somehow that sounds way too defeatist.

I wave the list of email addresses we've already collected. 'We have ammunition here, but there has to be more we can do. Give me a few days, I'll put my mind to it.'

As the notes of a piano come drifting through from the ballroom, I peep forward so I can catch a glimpse of the clusters of candles and daffodil bunches in jars along the top table. 'However much of an amateur Kip is, he's got a fabulous house to work with.' Just for a second, the refrain on Adele's *Someone Like You* makes my heart squish. Maybe I should see if I can spot Fred, if only to see what he's up to. 'Are you okay here if I pop outside for a second?' Don't read anything into it, by the way. It's a well-known fact. Adele does that to us all.

On the lawn it's even warmer than inside. Kip's installed his latest idea of a romantic play list at the microbrewery tent, and the beat of *Addicted to Love* is thumping across the grass. I'm padding across the turf, scanning the milling couples, and sniffing to see if I can catch that familiar scent of farmer drenched in body spray, when a rugged guy with dusky grey hair and a tan as deep as a pirate's steps towards me, with his arms outstretched.

'I hear today's all down to you, Lily. Congratulations, you should be very proud.'

I send him a bemused grin. 'Thanks for that, I hope you found the day useful.' Even though I don't know who the hell he is, my chest is still swelling with the praise.

'I do have a *special* interest.' For some unknown reason his eyebrows are rising expectantly. If he'd been wearing a suit instead of a crumpled linen shirt, his smile would have looked vaguely regal. 'I'm Bart, Kip's uncle.'

Oh crap. No wonder he looks like he could own the place, when he does. Major respect called for then. 'I'm very honoured to meet you. If someone –' That's *someone*, as in Kip. '– had let me know you were coming we could have given you a special welcome, and a VIP tour.' Of his own house? Even I know I'm sounding ridiculous here.

His laugh is even huskier than Kip's. 'Not at all, I dropped in incognito. It's almost impressive enough to tempt me to do it all over again.'

I'm staring beyond him, to someone waving their arms over the hedge in the distance, when I hear Jess's purr behind me.

'Lily's done a fabulous job.'

I leap to make the introductions, before Jess has a chance

to make a fool of herself like I almost did. 'Jess, the force behind Brides by the Sea ... meet Kip's Uncle Bart.'

This time his laugh is even more gravelly. 'I saw you looking at the rings earlier, Jess. So *you're* taking the plunge then?'

Jess's eyes widen in horror. 'Hell no. The shop's strictly for customers, I'd sooner jump in the lake than take on another husband.' For some reason when her laugh breaks, it's extra husky today too. 'I buy my own perfume, choose my own jewellery and my life's bullshit free. What's not to like?'

For some unknown reason, this cracks Uncle Bart up. Eventually he stops slapping his thigh for long enough to reply. 'Maybe the lady doth protest too much?'

Whatever he's getting at, someone needs to tell him talking in ye olde Englishe is very aging. On closer inspection, he's got some serious wrinkles.

Jess must have seen those too, because instead of her normal flirty purr, her nose shoots into the air. 'Methinks Sir is talking total cobblers.'

I have to say, I'm with her on that one.

Uncle Bart claps his hands, apparently delighted. 'By George. She be but little, but she is fierce.'

I'm opening and closing my mouth, because no-one would dare to diminish Jess by referring to her as small. What's more, I seem to have landed in the middle of a slanging match that could have come straight off a stage in Stratford-upon-Avon.

Jess, hands on her hips, is straight back at him. 'Excuse me, but loathsome toads spring to mind here.'

And since when did Jess curse like Immie? I'm raising my hands, trying to work out how to stop the spat, when I spot

Kip waving back at me beyond the cluster of guys clinging to micro-brewery plastic glasses.

'Lily ... sheep ... loose ...' is all I catch of his frantic yell.

For a nanosecond I think he's joining in with the family insults. Then I hear the baaaa-ing and my heart skips a beat. Next thing, there's a clatter of hooves coming around the end of the house, and what seems like hundreds of sheep are stampeding onto the lawn.

Country lesson one: never confuse fully grown sheep with fluffy lambs. They're about a thousand times huger and when they're galloping at forty miles an hour, they have the momentum of small tanks. First they take out the corner leg of the gazebo, then they topple the beer table, sending barrels bouncing. As the beer tasters scatter, their flying beer makes golden arcs in the sunlight. The indignant cries of protest are all about spilled drinks. They're largely ignoring the livestock.

Uncle Bart's hand lands on my shoulder. 'Come on, Lily, we'll head them off.' He hurls himself across the grass, scattering couples as he goes.

As I dash after him, Jess is yelling breathlessly as she follows. 'The ballroom, for chrissakes keep them out of the bloody ballroom ...'

She diverts right like a sprinter, and reaches the wide-open doors at exactly the same time as the sheep. 'Oh no you don't ...' She's lashing out with her loafers, beating the woolly faces with her fists.

That's the thing with sheep. They definitely have that flock mentality they're so legendary for. When the lead sheep decides

Jess is more trouble than she's worth and veers away, the rest follow.

'Near miss, or what?' Uncle Bart's blowing, exactly as you would if you almost had a flock of sheep rampaging around your own personal dance floor.

We let out a collective 'phew' as we watch the shaggy bottoms bouncing, as they bolt off around the end of the house.

Kip hurries up, and puts his arm around Jess. 'Well done, Jess, I always suspected you were a superwoman, now I know for sure.'

Behind us, the brewery chaps are rounding up kegs and collecting the shredded plastic glasses. The only trace of sheep remaining are the hoof prints between the grass blades, and clumps of sheep dottles.

As I leave Jess to her congratulations, and hurry after the sheep, it's only to be sure they aren't going to turn and come back on a return trip. Somehow I don't think we can pull off Operation Wool Stop a second time. Once was enough of a fluke. Beyond the ballroom, I join the path that leads round to the stable yard. You don't have to be Sherlock Holmes to see they've headed past the coach house. But as I round the corner, I'm stopped in my tracks, when I come face to face with a radiator grill and some huge wheels. There's a tractor blocking the way. And it's perfectly positioned to drive the sheep through an open gate, into one of the fields that run down towards the lake. Bright blue can only mean one person.

'Fred. You've come to the rescue again.'

Shooing the last sheep into the field, he swings the gate

closed. 'Pleasure to help.' He grins as he checks the closing catch. 'Lucky I had my tractor here. All these towny customers, leaving gates open on their way down to the lake. You can't blame the sheep.'

Somehow there seem to be a lot fewer woolly backs now they're spread out in the field than when they were careering over the lawn.

'You're a hero, Fred, however we look at it.' The funny thing is, the footpath down to the shore was so clearly marked, even a townie couldn't miss it. Knowing how crap Kip is at signage, I triple-checked it myself.

Fred swings up into the cab. 'The joys of country house weddings, eh? Any time for a break?'

I've heard that somewhere before too, but I can't place where. 'Sorry, I've got two more hours of wedding fair waiting – which is still all in one piece. Thanks to you.'

He gives another 'it was nothing' shrug, then hesitates on the top step. 'A little bird told me Kip's got some big features coming up in wedding magazines. Can I count on *you* to neutralise those?'

Trust a guy to make real life sound like Call of Duty. But he's right. My heart's sinking at the thought of what Kip's nationwide publicity exposé could do to Rafe and Poppy's business. And if I 'accidentally' discover what's in Kip's pipe-line, at least it makes the proverbial playing field more level. If we know what they're up against, we can make a counter attack, and sort some similarly spectacular pieces.

'Leave it with me.' I back away. 'And thanks again for "neutralising" the livestock.' I send him a wink. 'A hundred sheep loose in the house could have wrecked a lot more than just the day.'

He laughs. 'There were only five, Lily.'

'Right.' This is why I'm a florist, not a farmer. As for the challenges from the Manor, I'm bracing myself. Something tells me magazine articles are the start of the war, not the end.

Chapter 19

Friday, 21st April
In the walled garden at Rose Hill Manor: Blisters and bad hair days

'So how's it going Water Lily? Long time no see.' It's Kip, in the walled garden, over by the door in the wall.

I take a moment to get over the tummy lurch. For a minute there I thought it might be Fred. Whereas Kip on a Friday tea time is just what I don't need, even if it is three weeks since I last saw him at the wedding fair. Although on the plus side one look at him is enough to kill anyone's butterflies. Staying out of his way has pretty much been my only achievement in April. Whereas Fred has dropped by most times I've been here. He claims he's checking on his sheep, but he's actually overseeing, and looking decorative in equal amounts. And he usually wafts in approximately ten minutes after I arrive, whatever time of day or evening I get here. It's not as if I can exactly be discreet about where I'm hanging out when I drive a car as pink as Gucci. But despite spending hours in the garden over the last couple of weeks, you can barely see where I've been. When Dad and I gardened, he did the digging, while I carried weeds to the compost heap in child-sized buckets. And sometimes I raked the stones away with my kiddy rake. We all agree with feminism and equality, but when they gave out the muscles, I didn't get any. So sadly, when it comes to exertion, I let down womankind every time, because I'm crap. The patch of border I've turned over today is tiny, and my legs and arms have already turned to jelly. At this moment I couldn't be missing my lovely dad more.

I grunt, and ram my fork into the soil so I can lean on it and still look like I'm working. 'I'm having a ball, Kip. I'd have thought that was obvious.' I can't help the sour worm sarcasm. 'Digging's excruciating, the blisters are agony, my back's killing. What's not to like?'

Gardening has turned out to be *so* much worse than I anticipated. Anyone who tells you it gets easier is talking bull. For someone like me who hates exercise, it's hell on earth. You've no idea how much effort it takes to get one teensy patch of hard mud to the consistency of raw crumble mix. When I push back my hair, it sticks to my forehead. How disgusting is that?

Kip's squinting at me like he's examining exhibit one. 'When did you get curls?'

He could have commented on anything in the damned garden. The leaves coming out on the fruit trees, the robin on the wall, the yellow forsythia flowers bursting out by the water butt. Just my luck he homes in on my wavy and wild sweat drenched pony tail.

'Remember eighties perms?' I pull a face at the image, even though I'm not old enough myself. 'It's a try out for a party.'

169

That's a bluff and a half, given I haven't been out in weeks, but whatever.

Kip's hands are in the pockets of his jeans, and as he wanders along by the trees at the garden end, he's kicking the grass with his bashed up Converse. 'At least you look less like a bossy headmistress today.'

What the heck? 'If it wasn't your garden, I'd tell you where to stick your rake.'

He ignores that, and rubs his chin. 'More like the girl off Dirty Dancing?' Trust Kip not to let a subject drop once he's running with it.

Bleughhh. Worse and worse. I shake my head and try to hide my horror. 'You're old enough to remember Baby? Who'd have thought?'

'Still no apple blossom then.' Nice change of subject there from Kip.

Although talking about the weather, it's one of those years when the buds have stayed at the same point for ages. Despite the smattering of sunny days, there's always been a chilly breeze from the coast. I'm wondering what he's been up to, although I'm not about to ask.

'Have you had any more animals rampaging round the place since the fair?' It's a neutral place to start.

Kip gives a dismissive sniff. 'The sheep have un-learned the knack of opening their own gate if that's what you mean. And Bart's disappeared to Antigua.'

I sense ambivalence in both comments. 'Jess will be delighted to hear that.' I've never seen anyone ruffle her feathers quite as much as Uncle Bart.

Kip pulls a face. 'She's not the only one. Thanks to him meddling with the wedding prices, my big "hello" discounts went out the window. The bookings won't be flooding in to an unproven venue without those.'

Despite how this might hit the styling, I'm still cheering inside on Poppy's behalf. I turn my grin into a grimace. 'Oh dear, what a pain.' Although when did Kip ever use words like unproven?

His nod is very knowing for a rank amateur. 'In the wedding business you make your name by reputation. The serious cash comes later.' As he takes in my look of astonishment, a smile spreads across his face. Smug doesn't begin to cover it. 'I've been visiting venues to see how it's done. There's a lot to pick up.'

Shit. Who'd have thought he'd go and do that? I try for sincere, and end up with super-bright. 'Great. Anything you're dying to share?' I finally abandon my fork. I'm disconcerted that I'm desperate to know where he's been.

Kip bends down and tweaks out a weed. 'There's a country house hotel in Yorkshire where they run four weddings simultaneously. And a converted mill in Manchester, where they've already exceeded two hundred exclusive-use bookings in their first year. I'm cherry picking from both business models.'

Which explains why he hasn't been hanging round the borders. As it sinks in, my horror grows. 'You're thinking big then?'

He can't keep the excitement out of his voice. 'I'm thinking wall to wall weddings. It's going to take a huge team of coordinators, and we'll have to show people round in the early mornings. But the income figures are phenomenal. Three six five weddings a year is the target.'

This is all my fault. I was the one who told him to check out other venues. And to think that five minutes ago, my biggest problem was my bolting nasturtiums. 'Bloody hell Kip, this is Rose Hill not Vegas.' Is it bad that my tone's so downbeat, when he's embracing two startling new concepts – wedding planners and staff?

He jumps forward. 'But people *love* Vegas.'

How is he not getting this? 'Are they the same people who love Cornwall?' I can see by his bemused expression he's hell bent on the stateside vibe.

'It's all about attention to detail,' he's saying, moving on like he's on a crusading mission.

At least we're back to understanding each other. I can't resist chipping in. 'Attention and detail are two more areas where you'll need to raise the bar then.' Currently he's failing by a country mile on both counts. It strikes me as an ideal time to slip in my undercover media question. 'But the magazine coverage will tie in brilliantly. Who's running it again?'

He closes his eyes as he thinks. '*London Brides*, and *Perfect Wedding*. And there's a *Cornish Guardian* supplement too.'

Kerching. Result. 'Fabulous.' I file them in my brain for later, and realise I'm sounding way too enthusiastic. 'I mean, they'll really help with the three six five thing.' Which gets scarier every time I think about it.

Kip forges on. 'So, I'd like us to get a few off-the-peg styling ideas together, so we can offer some ready-made themed packages.'

I may need to take a vomit break. I try not to pull a face at how gross it sounds. 'Fine. I'll coordinate that with my planting visits.' The 'us' part sounds ominous.

'Great, let me know when you're coming, and I'll put you in the diary.' He's rubbing his hands like he's ready to go.

My jaw drops open. 'Excuse me while I pick myself up off the floor. You finally succumbed?' I have to laugh. The only good news I've heard all morning. Maybe the boy's coming good after all.

'Which reminds me, I forgot to mention the booking.' He couldn't sound more nonchalant if he were talking about forgetting to pick up Weetabix.

I take back everything I said. 'The what?'

'It came in the morning of the wedding fair, which is why it got overlooked. Some friends of friends from London. They've got a special licence for a ceremony and lunch here on May 1st, before they fly off to a bigger celebration abroad. They're sorting the caterers, and we're looking after all the props and the floral stuff.'

I can't believe what I'm hearing. 'You've known for three weeks, and you're telling me with ten days to go?'

'Isn't that loads of notice?' His expression is miffed. 'You *could* be more excited. It's the Manor's first wedding – with me at the helm anyway.'

But that's the scary thing. I'm not so sure anyone's in control here. It's as if I'm standing on a drifting ship. And no idea why, but it feels like we're heading straight for the rocks. It's just my bad luck I'm stuck with this garden. After all this work, I'm not backing out now. So long as my flowers grow,

I'll have to suck it up, and stay on board until summer.

'Great.' I say. 'Couldn't be better.' I'm hoping he picks up on my scathing tone. 'Aye aye, Captain. Let's hope we don't have to call out the life boat.'

As he folds his arms he's frowning. 'Are you managing here? With the digging I mean?'

I grit my teeth. 'Why wouldn't I be?'

He takes a second to consider. 'You're still in the same corner of the garden where you started. And you sound a bit wound up. That's all.'

That's all? 'I'm growing enough for a bouquet, not a flower festival.' The patch of earth I'm staring down at is at least the size of a small sofa. It has to be almost big enough. And dealing with an idiot would be stressful. An ignorant, conceited idiot is ten times worse. I round on him. 'And your point is?'

Even though his brow furrows, he's sounding expectant. 'I can always give you a hand if you need one?'

Mr Quick-buck-profiteer? Helping in the garden? I'd rather pull my own teeth. 'Thanks, but it really won't be necessary. I've totally got this covered.'

From the 'yeah right' look he shoots over his shoulder as he sidles towards the door, he's not buying my bullshit any more than I am. And by the way, me watching his exit has nothing to do with admiring the rear view. I mean, someone's got to make sure he leaves, don't they?

Just before he gets there he stoops to pick something out of the grass.

'Hey Water Lily, which way up do you hang your horse-shoes?' He sends me a grin as he waves one in the air. 'Ends up, and you catch all the luck and keep it safe. Ends down and the luck flows out to anyone around. Win, win, very like me. It's your choice ...'

Yet another example of Kip wasting time. 'As if I even give a damn.' I heave my fork out of the ground, then stab it in again.

He's laughing now. 'I know zilch about weddings and yet I'm running them. And you're in exactly the same boat with gardens.' He leans across the border, and props the horse shoe in a little alcove in the wall. 'Let's go ends up. Something tells me we *both* need all the luck we can get.'

As his laughter floats up over the top of the wall as he walks away, I make a mental note to get my hands on every available horseshoe in Rose Hill.

Chapter 20

Sunday, 23rd April
Rose Hill Manor: Cold shoulders and muscle tone

Okay, I come clean. I haven't really got time to be in the garden, with a wedding careering towards me. But at the same time, according to what I've read about 'growing your own' on the Up the Garden Path Weddings blog, I have to get the seedlings hardened off before they go in the ground. So I'm spending half an hour on a Sunday afternoon to bring over the seed trays with their bright green seedlings, and pop them into the cold frame in the Manor garden to acclimatise. And now I'm doing it, it's all coming back. Me trundling seed trays along the brick path of our garden in the hand cart my dad had made for me out of an old push chair. From the greenhouse with the paraffin heater the colour of melted chocolate – how did I ever forget that fumey smell that was so disgusting it made me bury my nose in my cardigan sleeve every time I went near? – to the rickety cold frames, made from mismatched windows, discarded from houses all around the village. My dad was such a magpie in that garden. No wonder he drove my neat-freak mum to seek refuge in the razor precision lawns of Heavenly Heights.

'Cooo-eeeeee ... Lily ...'

Even though I didn't hear the roar of a tractor, I still know it's Fred. I'm actually surprised I've managed to make three trips between here and the farm with trays of seedlings before he arrives and pops his head around the garden door.

'Fred, what a surprise.' Okay, it's only a tiny lie. The surprise is he wasn't here sooner. 'If you've come to congratulate me on my magnificent zinnia plants, they're over here.'

He knocks the mud off his boots, then wanders down the grassy path. As he leans across the cold frame by the tool shed he's grinning. 'Three inches tall, and bushy too. Haven't we done well with those?'

'We?' I give him a little punch on his rolled up sleeve for that, and note that he's wearing my favourite blue checked shirt, that almost goes with his eyes. 'Just because you were in the orangery when I found the first seed shooting, doesn't mean they're yours.' Even though the most he's done is watch me water them, he still seems very interested.

He gives me a wink. 'You *know* I'm backing you all the way. It's called vicarious flower growing.'

Which is another thing I want to talk to him about. 'Have you noticed I've done quite a lot more digging than before?'

He laughs. 'You *have* been busy. Two whole borders, and you're still standing up?'

I half close my eyes. 'My point entirely.' Every time I come back, more ground has been turned over. If I'd had to do that lot myself, I'd be on my knees. I lean in towards him, and drop my voice. 'So is there anything you'd like to tell me about the secret spade fairy?' I reckon there has to be, seeing it must be him.

That makes him laugh. 'If I did it wouldn't be a secret, would it?'

Okay, if that's how he wants to play it, I'm happy to go along. 'Well let's say it's fabulously kind of you. And I'm very grateful.' You might think I'm over doing it, but believe me, it would have taken me years to get that done.

He gives a self-effacing shrug. 'Really, it's nothing.'

'You're sure you don't mind?' If he's looking like he's expecting a thank you hug, I'm sorry, but I draw the line at that.

There's another chortle, and he pats his six pack. 'It certainly beats going to the gym.'

I rub my hands on my thighs. 'I'm with you on that. Who'd have thought gardening would tone up your legs?' My arms too. And my bum. Although I know better than to get into comparing biceps with a lumberjack. Or drawing attention to my butt. It might be a teensy bit tighter, but it's still a major item. And definitely not for scrutiny.

Fred's beaming expectantly and gives me a little shove with his shoulder. 'So what have you got planned for the rest of the afternoon?'

Shit, I didn't think this through. 'Maybe more digging?'

There's another shoulder shove from Fred. 'Although as you say, you are unexpectedly ahead of the game in that area now.' If the shoves get any stronger someone's going to end up in the cold frame along with the cosmos. 'If you've got a spare half hour, seeing you're so well on the way with the garden work, why not come down and see Rock Quay?'

'I'm not sure ...' Even as I open my mouth, I know I *can't* say 'no' here. Not when he's put in so much effort for me with the digging. No idea how he fitted it in between all his building and his animals either, which makes it even more special.

'Come on.' Luckily for me *and* the cold frame, he's now just nudging my elbow with his, and he's upping the persuasion. 'I've been admiring your seeds for weeks. Now it's your turn to croon over my apartments. And I could throw in a cream tea?'

I think this guy just found the cheat sheet to my heart. 'Put like that ...'

Anybody's for a piece of cake? Guilty as charged. And dammit that I'm wearing my third best black jeggings and not my second-best pair.

Five minutes later, we're in his pick up, zooming towards St Aidan.

Chapter 21

Sunday, 23rd April
At Rock Quay: Succulents and triangular bread

'You've done a great job here, Fred.' I have to hand it to him. He's nailed every detail at Rock Quay, from the etched glass door numbers, to the lemons on the hewn wood platters and the cacti on the coffee tables. And I'm very pleased I came, because looking around's made me see Fred in a whole new light.

We're in our third apartment now, and because they're in a converted warehouse, they're all slightly different. In this one, with the floor to ceiling windows rolled back, the immense living kitchen runs straight out to the balcony. I'm leaning on the stainless steel hand rail, looking out across the harbour, to the twinkling sea beyond. We're talking high ceilings, and vast living areas, with a fabulous blend of old and new, and wall to wall luxury.

'Are you sure I can't tempt you to move in?' Fred's working his wounded puppy look to the max here. 'Or go out with me properly.'

I've been making my excuses since the moment we walked through the first monumental front door. Although I have to admit, that more than once I've had a brain flash, imagining how it would be if I were tucked up in a chunky king sized bed, watching Fred coming out of the slate clad shower, in nothing but a low slung towel.

'If I were grown up enough to want to settle down, it would be my first choice. And I've told you already, I never go out with anyone I haven't known for at least six months.' My trouble is, once I'd unpacked my stuff into Fred's wall of wardrobes, I might never want to move again. As it is, Jess's attic, with my shirts hanging on a piece of plumbing pipe, feels comfortingly temporary. Which is exactly what I need. Once autumn's here, I can up and go as soon as the right job comes along, and I won't feel the wrench. Apart from missing the views from my tiny porthole windows obviously, which I'm making a big effort not to get too attached to.

After a couple of hours of pushing, he appears to be taking my rejection with a shrug and moving on. 'So how does the Harbourside Hotel sound for afternoon tea?'

And finally. He's so quick to latch onto things, I can't think why he's taken so long to get the message about me not going out with him or wanting one of his flats.

To bring you up to speed, the HH is the ultimate in five star luxury, sits on top of the hill behind the harbour, and takes its name from its view. It's where Thom and I had our wedding do. Fred's definitely pulling out all the stops with that choice. Everyone knows the teas by the beach at the Surf Shack are to die for. Whereas if you were looking for sophistication rather than downright deliciousness, mostly you'd head for the Yellow Daisy Cafe, or the Sugar Stop up in town. The Harbourside not so much. It's the local equivalent of going for tea at The Ritz.

'Have you won the lottery?' I'm asking because it's seriously pricey. Like it costs arms and legs. At least.

He's sitting on the polished concrete work surface, kicking the heels of his Timberlands on the dark oak island unit. 'It's where I take all my prospective clients. I've sealed many a deal over cucumber sandwiches in the Harbourside Terrace Room.' He pulls down the corners of his mouth. 'Although I promise today is totally without ties.'

Now he's cleared that up, I'm more enthusiastic. 'After all that gardening, I'm starving.' I'm momentarily forgetting I haven't actually done any work yet, but whatever. A stand stacked full of sandwiches and sausage rolls and fancy cakes? Who gives a damn where we eat, my mouth's already watering. Big time.

Fred's arms are folded. 'Actually, I took your mum and David there earlier this week.'

A sudden gust of cold air off the sea blows right inside my padded jacket and makes me shiver. 'Really, whatever for?' Although given the rate David throws logs on my mum's fire, it's not really a surprise. They probably won the outing for being Fred's most massive wood consumers.

He's staring at me as if I'm dense. 'We went there after I showed them around the penthouse here, of course.'

My frown has nothing to do with keeping the sun out of my eyes. 'Why did you do that?' I'm guessing it's Fred showing off again. I get that he's proud of his achievement, but you'd think he'd have better things to do with his time. All this fruitless running around, no wonder he's behind schedule with his work at the farm. And if I'm a teensy bit disappointed it isn't just me he wants to show off his flats to, I'm not going to admit it.

'The penthouse would be the perfect place for them to move on to.'

Hang on? If he doesn't stop kicking his feet, I'm going to have to tell him to stop. I turn to face Fred, and lean my back on the rail. 'Why would my mum move on? She's got everything she needs in Rose Hill, and David's milking it to the max.' The words are so high and hoarse, they almost get blown away. My mind is whirling. 'Anyway this development is exclusively for young professionals. You said so. It's way too stylish for *old* people.'

Fred shrugs. 'Obviously I told *you* that, because you're young. But it works equally well for a more senior demographic. The over sixties love their funky interiors.' He waits a few seconds for that to sink in.

'And were my mum and David *interested*?' Saying their names together in a sentence has me swallowing back the sick. Living in a flat by the coast? Where the hell would they put their garden gnome? And the tiniest last thought, I barely dare let loose. *What the hell would happen to Heavenly Heights if they came to St Aidan?*

Fred's biting his lip. 'That's where you come in, Lily. Now you've seen Rock Quay for yourself, I hoped you'd have a persuasive chat with them. Throw in some positive reinforcement?' He pushes his hair back. 'Shifting that penthouse would transform my finances.'

I can't believe what I'm hearing. If my eyes were wide before, they just turned to saucers. 'Like my mum listens to *me*. In any case, I *really* can't see her moving.'

Fred's smile tells me he knows better. 'They're very keen. The thumbs up from you will be all the encouragement they need. It happens a lot. Fresh starts by the sea. New beginnings without the baggage.'

I want to scream that it bloody doesn't happen where we live. Not that I've ever heard of anyway. We're not talking about leaving city grime. Rose Hill's the kind of desirable village where people fight tooth and nail to get a house. Once they move in, they stay there forever. At least. The way my stomach just dematerialised, I may have to make a dash for the travertine-clad wet room.

I clear my throat. 'We'll see.' I say it through gritted teeth. Over my dead body, in other words.

'What's wrong? You look like you swallowed a sour apple.' As Fred jumps to the floor, he's rubbing his hands, and laughing. 'I assumed you'd want the best for them. You're not a teensy bit jealous they're happy are you?'

Despite the blue and brown checks of his shirt looking fab with his tan, for once the combination isn't making my knees weak at all. To be honest, my knees already feel as if they're going to give way for every other reason.

'Bollocks to jealous, I can't believe you're exploiting them, Fred.' There's no point not saying what I feel here.

As he shakes his head, he turns the 'wounded puppy' to

full strength. 'You should be thanking me for flagging up what your mum and David want. If they've fallen in love with Rock Quay, it's only because it's so right for them.' He comes over to the balcony, slides his arm around my back, and squeezes. 'Don't worry, Lily pad, after a couple of scones with clotted cream, you'll be loving the idea as much as they do.'

'Tea?' I squirm away from his arm. Then as his warmth ebbs away, part of me wishes I hadn't.

He grins. 'Catch up, slow coach. Isn't that where we're heading?'

He has to be joking. The way my insides feel right now, I may never eat again.

Chapter 22

Tuesday, 25th April
In the attic kitchen at Brides by the Sea: Iced gems and
other sprinkles

I might be flat out pulling together the flowers and the props
for the short notice wedding at the Manor that's only a week
away now, but some appointments can't be shuffled. Two days
after my trip to Rock Quay, Immie's finally coming to try on
dresses this morning, and Poppy and I agree this is happening,
regardless. And this time we're filling our stomachs before we
hit the showroom. Which is why Immie and Poppy are sitting
at the tiny table in the attic kitchen, watching me as I conjure
up breakfast. I'm peeping out of my porthole window, watching
the cloud shadows move across the deep green sea. As I wait
for my phone timer to buzz, I can see the people along the
shoreline are wrapped up against the chill of the early morning.

'Croissants and pain au chocolat don't come any hotter
than straight from the oven,' I say as my handset vibrates
across the work surface. Okay, I come clean, I got the dough
out of a packet, but we can't all cook like Poppy. 'And here's

your hot chocolate.' The milk in the two tall mugs I slide across to them has been frothed within an inch of its life.

'Phwoar, squirty cream.' Immie seizes the can and squeezes caterpillars on every finger, then sucks them in turn. Which is great. After our last trying on session, lining her stomach in advance of this one is a great move.

'We've got all the fave toppings, plus Baileys, marshmallow fluff, coffee ice cream, and mini chocolate donuts.' I drop them onto the table, along with some spoons. 'Dig in.'

'Bliss.' Poppy sighs, as she zig zags golden dribbles of salted caramel on top of her whipped cream, and sprinkles on some grated dark chocolate. 'For once it's lovely to have breakfast without the noise of builders banging up and down the yard.'

I pull up a stool and wave my croissant in the air to cool it. 'How's the barn work coming on Pops?' I deliberately don't mention Fred, but I still throw ten times more marshmallows into my hot chocolate than I mean to.

'You know the thing about it getting worse before it gets better?' Poppy pulls a face. 'That. And talking of Fred, is Barbara really serious about buying that penthouse of his?'

Damn. How did we get onto him? 'When I asked her she went horribly quiet, so I'm still no wiser.' I let out a long sigh. 'What *is* she doing marrying a jerk like David? I keep hoping she'll come to her senses.'

Immie frowns. 'Love literally does make people blind. It's the chemicals in the brain giving you time to build a family unit before reality catches up.' She's giving us the benefit of her part time psychology degree here. 'Give her eighteen months, *then* she'll see he's a prize dickhead.'

My heart slides down as far as the toes of my sensible black pumps as I groan. 'But the wedding's in *four*.'

Immie blows out her cheeks. 'Sorry Lils, being sensible by September is a physical impossibility for your mum.' As if to prove the futility, she goes back to the donuts.

Poppy's pursing her lips. 'Cheer me up, Lily, tell me about your short-notice wedding instead.'

I dunk my croissant, and take a bite. As I chew, I try to wipe David and his spray-on jeans out of my brain. By the time I swallow, his Levis are barely a shadow on my mind's eye retina. 'The bride's called Vee, short for Viola, and she's marrying a gorgeous Spanish guy called Salvador. They're having a small ceremony at the Manor, then everyone's flying on to Madrid for the main party. And she's taking her name as the theme.' Not all brides will be as easy as Vee. But I've been amazed at how we've got so far fast-tracking with phone calls and emails.

Poppy's talking excitedly through a mouthful of pain au chocolat. 'Violas are *so* pretty.'

'Vee wants to keep things natural. She's having box planters for the tables with herbs, and violas and pansies. And tall pots by the entrance, with tumbling violas and daisies. And a posy of pansies rather than a bouquet.' I send Immie a wink. 'Best of all she's having an extra large donut table. Scattered with pansy flowers, obviously.'

'Talking of which ...' Immie scoops up another handful of mini donuts, and uses them to scrape up her cream. 'Try one Pops, they're delish.'

Poppy takes one from Immie. 'Well done for nailing it, Lily.

You've pulled something completely unique and fabulous together here. We all *knew* you'd be a natural at styling weddings.'

Now we've started, I can't hold in my excitement. 'She's ordered lots of the signs I've had made up too. And she chose the dressing table I bought in for her cake display, along with some initials with light bulbs in.'

Immie's eating marshmallow fluff straight from the spoon. 'Yay! Light up initials? Chas and I *must* have those. What signs did she choose?' She moves back to her pain au chocolat.

I know this without thinking. '*And they lived happily ever after*, *So I can kiss you any time I want?* and *Te adoro*, which is I adore you, in Spanish.'

'How romantic.' Poppy's gone all dreamy, but I'm not sure if it's down to the Spanish, or the Baileys slug. 'Sounds like the work's being done just in time.'

I'm confused. 'What work?'

Poppy's hand flies to her mouth. 'The builders in the basement next to the flower prep area. That has to be for you. Let's face it, when did Jess ever hold back on what she wants?'

I chew my thumb nail and wish I'd taken more notice. 'No, they were definitely only jet washing the yard.' My chest tightens so much, my voice turns to a squeak. 'Weren't they?'

Poppy laughs as she pops the last piece of pain au chocolat into her mouth. 'Keep your petticoat on, Lily. If Jess has got plans for you, we all know there's no point fighting her. And we're all here to help.' She scoops the froth out of the bottom of her cup. 'Meanwhile, on to the job in hand. We've sorted some key dresses for you to try Immie, whenever you're ready.'

I get that Poppy's using distraction tactics, but it's moved me on like a dream. There's no point panicking about a rumour with no foundation whatsoever. So on to today's strategy, we've made a shortlist from Immie's very, very, long longlist. And we'll take it from there.

Immie leans back on her chair, and rubs her stomach. 'One more croissant, and I might be ready.'

'Only one?' As I grin at Immie and grab another myself, my phone beeps, and as I pick it up I can't help smiling. 'It's only Nicole, she insists on tagging me in all her Instagram posts.'

Immie shoots upright. 'She's on Instagram?'

'With bits of wedding news, that's all.' Given it's several times an hour, I'll play it down.

A second later, the stools are flying as Immie bolts around the table, and grabs my arm. '@TheFutureMrsForeverDiamonds? What kind of a ponced-up up-her-arse name is that?' Her nose is two inches away from my screen. 'Where's her pictures?'

As I send Poppy a wild-eyed plea, the question of client confidentiality is racing through my head. 'I'm not sure ... what do you think, Poppy?'

Poppy bites her lip as she gets out her own phone. 'Nothing interesting. Currently a thousand options for napkins.' She flicks through a few pictures. 'Lily's tagged because she's Nicole's stylist.'

'Pass it over.' Immie grasps Poppy's phone, pours over it, then flings it back a few seconds later. 'Right, Lily. You're hired.' Immie's jaw couldn't be more rigid if she were a Staffy whose teeth were locked onto a bone.

'To do what?' From the expression on her face she might be looking for a hit woman.

'Style the wedding for Chas and me.' She's blowing out her upper lip as if she's playing the trumpet, prodding the air with her finger. 'And to set me up on Instagram. Like, now this minute.'

'Fine.' I say, blithely, because I'm not sure I'd risk doing anything other than agree with Immie in this mood. 'Pass me your phone. What name would you like then?'

Poppy chimes in. 'The eBay person who bought my wedding dress was called Glitter-knickers. If that's any help?'

'Not a lot.' Immie sniffs. 'This is Instagram, I don't want to attract a load of pervs.'

'Very true.' I say the next thing that comes into my head. 'A wing and a song?'

Immie rounds on me. 'Hell Lily, I've heard better wimp farts. Good thing I've hired you for your styling not your snappy handles.' She stops to sniff. 'I want something spangly. Bright, but not diamonds. With a ton of irony.'

Poppy laughs. 'Off the top of my head, sequins ... sparkling ... rubies ...?'

Shucks. I'm being employed for this. 'Er ... sparkling ... gems ... Bride-to-be ...?'

Immie scratches her head. 'I'm liking sparkle. But it needs to sound *way* bigger than Nicole's if I'm going to wipe the floor with her.'

This is what we're doing here? How did I miss that before? I rack my brain for huge words. 'Mahoosive ... humungous ... whopping ... monstrous sparkle ...'

'Monster sparkle. That's it! And this is why a stylist's worth her weight, every time.' Immie punches the air. 'Fucking brilliant, Lily. Or even better @SparkleMonsterBridetobe. Suits me down to the ground.' She's the one who said it.

'Woohoo, go Instagram Immie,' I shout. 'We'll take lots of photos while you're here, and you can post them later.'

Poppy's grinning. 'Breakfast before shopping for your dress is a great place to begin.' Although given the crumbs and chocolate rings, it's hardly going to be super-aspirational.

The stylist in me is frantically dabbing the table with kitchen roll. 'Shouldn't we clear up? Or prettify?'

Immie grabs a mug with one hand, and waves a croissant in the other. 'Bollocks to that, stick some squirty cream on this, and we're good to go.'

Double chins? No problem. Turning sideways to get her best side? Not worried. If I said muffin tops, I suspect Immie would salivate rather than grab her hips.

Poppy's dashing round the kitchen as much as you can when it's only five feet wide, waving Immie's phone at all angles, snapping away. 'Got you.'

We lean in, and pour over results that are less than flattering. Fifty takes of Immie, grinning behind a breakfast that looks like it was hit by a hurricane and a cream storm. 'Do you want to go again, Immie?'

'Hell no.' Immie laughs, as she grabs her phone. 'They're a hundred times more interesting than Nicole simpering over a bloody napkin ring.'

I feel I have to point it out. 'Instagram's about making

everything look extra fabulous and upmarket. Smoke and mirrors, filters and faking it. That kind of thing.'

'Stuff that, I'm staying real.' Immie's staring from me to her phone, like I've lost my mind. 'Right, tell me some hash tags.'

'Try #weddings, #bridetobe, #bridesofinstagram, #weddingstyle—' I have to say that one.

'All done.' Immie grins. 'So what happens now?'

Poppy's glance is apprehensive. 'People who like your posts will start to follow you. Nicole's already got forty people following her.'

At a guess, they'll only be her mates from the singles club. With Immie as competitive as she is, I'm not sure I'd have advertised that, but it's too late.

Immie looks aghast. 'Holy crap. Forty's a shitload.' She knocks back the last of her hot chocolate, and wipes out the mug with her croissant stump, then slams it down on the table. 'So what are we waiting for? There's a whole bridal shop waiting downstairs. If I'm going to get more followers we need to pull our fingers out.'

Poppy and I are staring at each other in horror as we clatter down the stairs after Immie. What *have* we unleashed here?

Chapter 23

At Brides by the Sea: Floor boards and flat beds

'How about one of me here? I could caption it, *Me waiting to try on the dresses.*'

Immie's standing, shoulder wedged against the hanging compartment in the Seraphina East Room. With her crossed legs and folded arms, she looks more as if she's propping up the wall on a building site than shopping for her wedding. And considering up to an hour ago this woman refused point blank to have her picture taken, saying there's been a sea change in her attitude would be an understatement. Let's just say, when it comes to her big day, Jules' job will be ten times easier than it once might have been. In fact, he might find her directions a complete nightmare.

'Get on the chair, Pops, so you can take the photo looking down.' Immie grins up at Poppy. 'Got me?'

I'm not sure how pleased Jess would be about Poppy clambering over her best mother of the bride Louis Quatorze chairs. Or that we've been rampaging through groomswear,

194

taking shots of everything from velvet lapels to *Here comes the groom* socks. And a million items between. As for the Bridesmaid's Beach Hut, we'll have a lot of tidying up to do in there too. The candy stripe decor was a perfect backdrop for in-front-of-mirror selfies. Poppy and I held up every dress, while Immie took up increasingly wild photo-bombing poses behind us. If Jess hears the screams, she'll assume we've downed more Prosecco than at Immie's last appointment. Whereas thanks to the breakfast, we haven't even started yet.

'We mustn't forget the fizz.' On the basis that we might as well make the most of every photo opportunity now we've come this far, I pop through to the kitchen, and grab some glasses and a bottle.

When I reappear, Immie's over like a shot. 'Would you like to take me popping the cork?'

I hand her the bottle. 'Now you're relaxed and stripped down to your T-shirt, you're looking *so* good in the photos.' Somehow before today it was hard to see beyond her oversized jeans and hoodie. 'Truly, you've got the most fabulous cheek-bones.' Although I suppose there could be a lesson here for all us baggy clothes wearers.

Immie rolls her eyes. 'They talked the same bollocks last time, when Jules had his camera out at the farm.' She takes her phone back from Poppy. 'I'll just send something to Instagram then we'll crack open the wine.'

As I take my first break since they arrived, I remember what I need to tell Poppy.

'Pops, I found out Kip's nabbed an advertising feature on Rose Hill Manor for the next Cornish Guardian supplement.'

Not that I want to tell Poppy, but it's a massive spread at newbie concessionary rates. 'We should try to get the farm in there too, but we need a hook to get them interested.'

Immie looks up from her phone. 'Isn't it a year since your first wedding there, Pops? Maybe they'd go for that?'

'Brilliant idea. They could do a resume of some of your high points, Pops. Like when the bride gave birth on her wedding night.' Given I'm flapping about a few signs and some seating hire, I can't think how Poppy coped with that at one of her first weddings as manager, but she did. 'I can ring the paper and pitch the idea? The features editor was in my class at school.' With Kip grabbing coverage right, left and centre, Daisy Hill Farm needs all the press exposure it can get. Fight fire with fire, and all that.

'Cool,' Poppy says. She's playing it down, but I can tell from the flush of her cheeks and the way her eyes have lit up that she's thrilled. 'Let me know when they're coming to interview us, and I'll have the cupcakes ready.'

As my phone beeps, I look at it and grin. 'Hey, Immie, you tagged me in your post.' When I click the link, the picture's of her lounging on the chaise, re-enacting her drunken slumber from the first abortive appointment.

She lets out a gruff laugh. 'Why wouldn't I tag my stylist? I've got three followers already. Eat your heart out Future Mrs Diamanté Knickers.'

As my phone gives another buzz, I frown and sigh. 'Talk of the devil, it's Nicole *again*.' You can see why phones are banned in the workplace, this is a full-time job. As I open her link I come close to barfing. 'Bleurgh. Yet another shot of her wedding shoes.' As if we hadn't seen enough of them. 'This time she's upside down, waving her feet against a sunrise.' I know she's my client, but the swaggering #sixhundred tag has me retching. As for three posts a day, every day, of the same old shoes, bleurgh to that too.

Immie, perching on the chaise edge, goes rigid. 'Shoes?' As she lets out the shout, she's beating her head with her fists. 'Hell's teeth, I've been so busy covering random stuff like *Property of the bride* boxer shorts, I've missed the bleeding obvious.'

I scan the waiting rail of dresses Poppy and I spent so long picking out yesterday evening. 'How about we do shoes at the very end?'

Immie's hands are already on her hips. 'Out of the question.' As she takes in Poppy's shocked expression, Immie mellows. 'Humour me, Pops. Just one "feet in the air" shot. In the sparkliest, most extreme heels you've got.'

As I turn to Poppy for instructions, I'm thanking my lucky stars I'm not the senior assistant here.

Poppy's pursing her lips again. 'Bring the Jimmy Choo Crystal Crossovers. In a 7 please, Lily.' As she turns to Immie I can hear the grit in her tone. 'And then you're straight into that fitting room, okay?'

I scamper up the flights of stairs, and belt across groomswear into shoes. By the time I get back panting and breathless, Immie's shed her high heeled trainers, and rolled up her jeans.

I pass the box to Poppy. As she takes off the lid, and slides out the bootie, we all give a collective gasp.

'So glittery.' I grin. 'These will give Mrs Bling Pants a run for her money.'

Immie's groaning as she negotiates the straps which are every bit as crossed as their name suggests.

'Lie on the chaise, and leave the fastenings to me.' Poppy deftly tweaks the straps through the buckles, then swings Immie's ankles up, and arranges her feet.

I'm letting out silent 'wows' at the towering heels as I circle with the phone. 'Okay, hold it there.' I push the shoot button half a dozen times to be sure and change my angle. 'This time I should pick up the reflection in the mirror too.' Three more seconds, I've checked the pictures, and it's a wrap. 'Okay, brilliant.'

Immie revolves, and next minute, she's back on the edge of the chaise. 'Could I actually walk in these?' She's staring down at her twinkling feet like they belong to an alien.

I laugh. 'It takes a dedicated heel-wearer like Nicole to manage spikes like those.' Even as I say it I realise my mistake. Immie pottering round in her platform wellies is hardly in the same league as seven inchers.

Immie's brow wrinkles. 'Beyoncé wasn't built in a day. It's not as if I'm a complete heel virgin. Come here, let me give them a go.'

Before I can stop her, she's hauled herself up on my elbow and she's staggering across the white painted floor boards.

She lets out a cheer. 'Yay, I'm a natural. How do I look?'

I wouldn't have come clean if she hadn't asked. 'The gap between your feet's big enough to drive a double decker bus through. Otherwise, great.'

'Woohoo, you've done it.' Poppy's biting her lip anxiously. 'For chrissakes sit down.'

Now she's in the centre of the floor, despite her outstretched arms, Immie's wobbling worse than a tight rope walker about to plummet. '*Trying out the Jimmy Choos* … What are you waiting for? Take the damned picture before I …'

I grab her phone, take a couple of snaps, and then watch, helpless, as she begins to totter backwards.

'Ooooo, careful, Immie.' Poppy's shout is way too little, way too late.

There's a roar from Immie, then a crash as she topples straight backwards into the main dress hanging area, taking a mannequin with her.

Immie's voice is muffled, coming through layers of lace skirts. 'Toad buttocks, what the hell happened there?'

Call me hard hearted, but this is too good not to capture in pixels for posterity. 'At a guess, you fell off your platforms.'

Poppy and I are pulling agonised faces at each other as I put the phone down, but as we spring forward to help, there's the distant clip clop of loafers.

Poppy's muttering under her breath. 'Talk about bad timing. We could do without an audience for this bit.' Especially a spectator as invested as Jess.

Where do you start when there's a solid weight of woman, helpless on her back, in a tangled heap of wedding dresses? By the time Jess arrives, we haven't got any further than gawping.

Jess's eyes are rolling so much they've practically disappeared. 'I thought today was going to be alcohol free?' Her sniff comes out with such force we can feel the breeze across the room. 'Leave this to me.' She grabs a Jimmy Choo-clad ankle in each hand. Her tug is so hard Immie shoots out across the floorboards, and ends up staring straight up into Jess's face.

Jess looks at her watch, turns to me, and raises an eyebrow. 'Lily, as you're obviously done here for today, I'd like a word.' She spins back to Immie. 'I take it we'll be trying this again once we're sober. Any day so long as it's Tuesday, please Poppy.'

A second later, she's marching out, and I'm skipping behind her into the hallway, trying to keep up. And quaking. Everyone knows 'a word' can be diddly squit. Or it can be Jess-code for something mahoosive. I'm aching that I'm up to whatever's flying my way.

Chapter 24

'So how can I help?'
I was expecting either a bollocking from Jess, or to hold pins for a bride in the White Room. But instead we're winding our way downstairs to the flower prep area. And when Jess doesn't reply immediately, my heart's beating faster with every step.

My throat's dry. 'Am I making up a last minute hand tied?' I know for a fact there's nothing in the book for today, because I double checked.

Jess smiles over her shoulder as we reach the bottom landing. 'No orders.' Jess isn't one to have twinkles in her eye, but right at this moment she almost does. 'There's a little surprise down here.'

The flower prep room is in the basement under the shop. It's below street level at the front, but above ground at the back, where the hillside falls away towards the beach. Instead of turning to where we make up all the bouquets and arrangements, she's turning the other way, pushing open the door to the cellar no-one ever goes in. Until now.

'So what do you think?' As she strides in, Jess's beam is as bright as the sunlight that's illuminating the whole space.

Instead of the darkness and cobwebs I'm expecting, the light's flooding in through the line of small paned windows, and bouncing up off a red brick floor that's scrubbed and clean.

I narrow my eyes as I take in a long room, with lime washed brickwork walls. 'It's fabulous. I thought it was a grimy cellar.'

She laughs. 'It was until a few weeks ago. Fred's men have been coming in and out in secret through the back door.'

'Fred?' I could do without the tummy flutter when I hear his name. Especially given he gets everywhere.

Jess goes into her croon mode. 'He's a lovely boy, very accommodating. Once he knew you were involved, *nothing* was too much trouble.'

Me? I move on from whatever her one raised eyebrow is implying, and look towards broad glass doors in the centre of the room. My eyes widen as I catch a glimpse of the tide racing up the distant beach below. 'Oh my, there's even a sea view in here.' I have to ask. 'But what's it for?' Whatever Poppy hinted at before – and thank goodness she waved a warning flag – I can't believe it's the truth.

Jess's lips are twitching. 'This is our new styling area. We might just call it The Style File. It's yours to play with.'

It takes a second for the words to sink in, and when they do my legs feel as if they're too weak to hold up my weight. I can't help my yelp. 'I've styled a couple of items at one mini wedding that's not even happened yet, I'm not ready for a whole department.'

Jess comes across and her hand lands on my arm. 'I've wanted a dedicated room at the shop for ages. You're letting me live the dream. I wouldn't ask you if I didn't know you could do it.'

Even though I'm lost for words, there's one question I can't keep in. 'How are you so sure?'

She takes a breath. 'I picked you out as special years ago, when you first started doing flowers. It was one lucky day for me when you dropped in and offered to help. As soon as you started you were just so tuned in to everything about weddings. If you hadn't upped sticks to be with Thom, we could have done this years ago.'

This is the amazing thing about Jess. If she backs you, she'll push you all the way. You only have to look at how she's supported Poppy and Sera. 'It's a huge compliment, but I'm still not certain I'm up to it.'

She goes across and flicks on a light switch, which activates a whole series of spot lights and hanging bulbs. Then she clicks her tongue. 'That's the trouble. Between them, your mum and Thom robbed you of every bit of your confidence. And we're here to put it back. You're up to this, and a whole lot more too. I believe in you, Lily, I always have. Wait and see – in a few months, you'll believe in yourself too.'

Just for a minute, my nose goes all achey, and I think I'm going to cry. 'I don't know what to say.' I sniff into my sleeve. 'I'll try my hardest. And thank you ...' I swallow hard. I'm hardened to taking criticism. Hearing nice things, not so much.

Jess whisks across the room, and comes back with a carrier. 'There are strings ... a couple of things I'm insisting on.'

My heart sinks. 'Yes?'

'As our super stylist I want you to stand out from all the other staff, so you'll have to drop the all over black. Get yourself some good clothes, with a splash of colour. There'll be an allowance, obviously.'

I stare at Jess's classy charcoal flannels and cream sweater. 'I'm not sure I can ...' When you've got a mum like mine, dark clothes are a refuge. They also make you conveniently invisible.

She snaps straight back. 'Sorry, it's a deal breaker. That bit's definitely non-negotiable.' Although somehow it sounds like she's making this up as she goes along. 'And you have to accept this as your "hello" gift too.' There's a wide paper carrier dangling from her finger.

As I reach out and peer in, my eyes almost pop as I take in the LK Bennett logo on the side. 'A suit? Jess, this is way too much.' Anything from there would be.

'Not at all. It's an unashamed bribe to get you to work wonders in my basement.' She eyes me sternly. 'You're totally worth it.'

'So what do you have in mind?' My voice wavers as the weight of the responsibility sinks in.

'I simply want you to showcase a few ideas here. There won't be room for everything we offer. But if you inspire brides to bring us on board, tempt them to add pretty things from here to their day, you'll have done your job.' She pushes the door open, to a tiny terrace. 'We can spill onto here too, with some outdoor tables and quirky outdoor lighting ideas.'

'Right.' My frightened mouse squeak doesn't begin to cover it.

She's pulling away a dust sheet that's hanging against the wall. 'And look what came while you were with Immie.'

The cover falls away, and leaves four waist-high letters, with light bulbs embedded.

I let out a shriek of excitement. 'My L-O-V-E sign's arrived.' I'm flapping my hands because it looks so fabulous, especially against the rough brick wall.

As Jess nods, she looks proud enough to burst. 'See, you've proved me right already. It's a great call having that made up, Lily. It'll clinch a lot of deals.'

I get where she's coming from about the clinching. 'It's *very* cool. I'd *so* want that at my wedding if I were a bride.' Okay, we all know I had my go, and it crashed and burned. But this sign is so fab, it almost makes me want to risk it all over again. Whatever I vowed to the contrary.

Jess is frowning. 'Me too. How absurd is that? I *never* imagine being a bride. Not myself.' She lets out a low laugh. 'That's how I know what a huge winner that sign is.'

'Exactly.' Swinging my suit bag on my finger spins me back to the night Jess caught Sam's bouquet. Not that her massive change of heart would be anything to do with that. Because we all know stuff like that is complete balderdash.

The way she's rubbing her hands, she's already moved on. 'So it's over to you, Lily. Less is more. Anything goes, so long as it's completely beautiful. Relax, be yourself, I know it'll be wonderful. Okay?'

Jeez. No pressure there, then. No idea how the hell I'm

going to manage. I shut out that in my head I'm screaming waaaaaaaaaaaaaaaaahhhh, and concentrate on the weight of the LK Bennett bag. Try not to hyperventilate. 'Now I've got my suit, I have to pull it off.'

Jess laughs. 'So long as you promise me not to go falling in any ponds in this one, we're all good.'

Much as I hated falling in the water that night, I reckon that was the easy bit, compared to what's coming.

Chapter 25

Getting in shape for the wedding ... NOT ... #selfiebride #bridezilla

You have to hand it to Immie, she's really going for it on Instagram. A bathroom selfie, on the scales, swathed in a towel, while eating a cupcake, calls for advanced camera skills. Given she's already got ninety-three followers, I'm not the only one LOL-ing at her posts either. This photo has me laughing so hard, when Kip creeps up behind me, I only hear him tutting at the last second.

'It's the first wedding at the Manor, and you're out here on your *phone*? That's really *not* the kind of professional image we want to portray.'

He sounds apoplectic, whereas I'm just delighted I found some signal. Given I finally got hold of the reporter from the Cornish Guardian, I could hardly persuade her that Daisy Hill Farm Weddings would make a great story, with Kip listening in.

Vee and Salvador just got married in the Winter Garden in the sweetest early morning ceremony ever. The pansy posy was perfect against her simple embroidered silk dress. In the end she had a matching head piece too. Pretty didn't begin to cover it. And the sun stayed out all the time the outside photographs were being taken. But Kip's obviously moved on from that now.

Looking at his grave expression and his 'I don't believe this' tone, it crosses my mind to share Immie's picture to help him lighten up. On balance, I decide against it. But he's not the only one who can act outraged.

I put on my own shocked screech. 'Excuse me? Get real, Kip. Thirty guests are currently up to their ears in a six-course lunch. They'll be tied up in the ballroom for hours. So it's hardly likely they'll fall over me when I'm hiding round the side of the house for all of ten seconds.' As for the guy who didn't know the customer's names, and forgot he'd taken the booking? How are standards suddenly so important, when a week ago he didn't know the word existed? Although from the point of view of future couples, this is no bad thing.

His voice is all low and implacable. 'I'm the one making the rules here, and I did ask you to stay in, or around the office.' Since when did laid back Kip get so kick-ass?

I sigh loudly, because I learned long ago you can't argue with idiots. 'Fine.' Although it isn't at all. On a lovely day like today, even if there is a tiny office terrace to sit on, being cooped up on it with Kip and his bloody gnome is my all-time nightmare.

As for why I'm at the Manor at all, so many guests are dropping in to Vee and Salvador's wedding in helicopters, they've engaged me for the day to sort out the damage to the outside floral decorations caused by the down draft. How unbelievable is that? You can see the blades sticking up where they're parked down in the field.

'Shall we go then?' Kip's propping his shoulder on the house wall as he waits. And for those wanting a fashion update, for one time only he's dropped the ubiquitous faded jeans. Dropped as in left them in the wardrobe, obviously. Not in the other sense. If anything shows he's got serious, it's that. As for how he's looking in his suit, if it was anyone other than him I'd say smoking. But luckily for all of us, his pain-in-the-butt mix of arrogance and hypocrisy takes away every bit of heat.

As I follow him round to the front of the house, I nod at the cars lined up along the gravel. 'Jeez, it's like stumbling into the parking area for Top Gear.' They're the kind of sleek vehicles that slide past you on motorways and make you feel like you're not moving. What's more, now I've got a better measure of the clients, I'm cringing at some of the stuff I said to the bride. 'If I'd known Vee's family were gazillionaires, I'd have been way less chatty in my emails. And I'd never have suggested pansies either.' In truth, I'd have been scared so rigid, I wouldn't have been able to type a word. Let alone talk to her on her mobile, or sort out her flowers.

Kip pulls a face. 'People who are loaded have more noughts on their bank balances, but otherwise they're only like the rest of us.'

Gucci might be way shinier than his bashed up Landy, both parked around by the stables, but this is the guy who lives on his own in a manor house with twenty plus bedrooms. So I have to call him on this. 'Us?' Even the word makes me shudder. 'Sorry Kip, but no way can you and me be lumped in the same affluence bracket.'

He gives a shrug. 'These are Quinn's friends not mine. And whatever flowers you've given her, she's ecstatic about them.'

'That's pure luck.' I jump in to point it out. 'This could have gone *so* wrong.'

As he pushes the front door, and holds it open for me, the hard line of his mouth softens. 'Or maybe you *are* up to the new job after all, Water Lily. Had that occurred to you?' This is Kip. If there's a half smile, it just has to be sardonic.

And if we're back to that, I need to move on as fast as I just skipped past him. 'As for today, so far I've replaced two roses that dropped out of the rustic arch I decorated for photos down in the garden. It's hardly a lot.' And one reason I'm resorting to looking at Instagram.

He gives a low laugh. 'And I've shown one confused caterer to the kitchen. But the point is we're here, and we're available. We're willing, yet invisible. As far as customer service goes, now we're off our phones ...' He pauses to send me a pointed glare '... we're nailing it.'

'Right.' Holy crap. Who'd have thought he'd be taking this so seriously? I'm having a 'pick me up off the floor, because I've just fainted' moment here. And then I remember. 'This wouldn't, by any chance, be part of your Vegas Three Six Five initiative?' How stupid am I? Of course it bloody would. This has nothing to do with making sure people have a wonderful day. It's all about drumming up more bookings. And more importantly, racking up those noughts on that bottom line Kip was talking about.

By the time we reach the office he's whooshed past to open the door again. 'Got it in one. They certainly know what they're doing in Yorkshire and Lancashire. And I'll be following them all the way. So long as no-one lets the side down.' He ushers me out onto the terrace. From the way he nods and points to the Adirondack chairs, he's expecting us to sit down. 'I see it dried out okay then?'

I choose the chair furthest from the gnome – not that it's possible to get very far away from anything when the terrace is this tiny – and roll my eyes. Quite apart from his ethos-from-hell, three hours of random questions like this from Kip were what drove me round the end of the house in the first place. Is he talking soil structure here, or leaks from champagne buckets?

'Sorry? You'll have to give me more clues than that.'

Now he's the one looking like he's dealing with an idiot. 'Your suit. Isn't that the one you were wearing that night at the pub, when you caught the bouquet, then chucked yourself in the pond?'

Damn. When I asked for clues, I definitely didn't mean that kind of detail. No idea why, but I'd rather he hadn't raked up the bouquet. 'Actually, let's get this straight. Jess caught those flowers, not me, okay?' Somehow I can't go on until it's clear. 'And this is a different suit.'

He's back to the mocking. 'So many expensive suits, who's the affluent one round here now? So what *did* happen to your other one?' At least he's moved on from bouquet flinging.

For eff's sake. 'When it dried it was a total write off, even though I tried dry cleaning it. It went in the bin, okay?'

The way he's pursuing this, you'd think he was in dry cleaning not weddings. At least that shuts him up for a few seconds. 'Ouch, that's awful. I'm sorry I didn't catch you sooner. Clothes like that cost an arm and a leg. You should be taking care of them, not trashing them.'

There we go again. Typical of the guy to make it all about him, then turn it into a lecture.

If I had any hope of changing and catching up on some digging in the garden today, while keeping one eye on the sky, I can obviously forget that. But maybe if I get out my laptop and bury my head in more style research, at least it'll stop Kip's inane chatter.

I push myself up from my chair. 'Actually, I think I'll go and work in the office.' Losing the sun is a small price to pay for getting away from Kip. 'Do we know how many more choppers we're expecting?'

As he shrugs there's a hint of disappointment on his face. The kind you see on a cat when they've had a mouse taken away. 'There's already four parked down in the field.' As he tilts his head and stares up at the sky I try not to notice how vulnerable his neck looks. Or how often he makes me want to metaphorically wring it.

'Keep a look out, and call me if any more come?' As I pass him, I see the mark on his jacket shoulder, where he was leaning against the wall earlier. Before I can stop myself, I'm stretching out my hand, and brushing off the dust. 'Hey, didn't you say to look after expensive clothes? And stay smart for the customers.' And waaaaaaaaahhhhh to accidentally touching him when it was the last thing I intended. If this was the other way round, I could be had up for sexual harassment in the work place.

He pulls a face, and swallows. 'It's really not attractive being a smart arse, Water Lily.'

Like I care about either of those things. 'Straight back at you, Kip.' And if my stomach flipped in complete unison with the lurch of his Adam's apple there, it's only because I'm squeamish like that. 'Not that I give a damn personally, obviously. This is purely on an FYI basis.' FYI? For your information. Or in this case, for his.

He looks suitably appalled that I just inadvertently implied he claimed an interest in me. 'And back at *you* for that last bit Water Lily ... with knobs on.'

Okay, we all knew he wasn't attracted to me from the start anyway, so we just squared the circle. As for handing me ammunition, that's plain stupid. 'Knobs? Yes you are, Kip. Thank you for reminding me.' Shit. I can't believe I just said that. Scrapping like seven year olds? How embarrassing is that? I drag in a breath, and bolt.

Once I'm in the office I go for the best available seat. Kip's. Behind the desk. On the basis that he's the one insisting I stay here. And there's no point not being comfy, because this is going to be a damned long afternoon. On the up side, not many people have helicopters. And fewer still are worried about them wrecking their wedding flowers. There won't be a repeat of this. So with any luck I'll never have to spend this long with Kip ever again.

Chapter 26

Monday, 1st May
At Rose Hill Manor: Irrigation and mistaken identity

'So, there aren't any more helicopters coming. There were only ever four.'

Kip doesn't even have the grace to look apologetic as he delivers the news. As chief liaison guy, it was his job to find this out. The last one arrived hours ago.

Gobsmacked about covers how I feel. 'So you're saying I've spent the last six hours waiting for helicopters that didn't exist?' If there wasn't a bride in the building, I'd really let rip. As it is, I'm keeping my voice to a low growl. 'Right now, all that's saving you is your chair, Kip. Lucky for you, I've had a damned comfy afternoon.' It's amazing how much work you can get done when you cut out distractions and interruptions. But I'm not about to tell him I've got through shedloads of the stuff, even if I have sorted out floral designs and sourced props for four of the off-the-peg style packages he was wanting.

'The bridal party will be leaving soon. I'm happy for you to stay to see them off with me, but it's also okay for you to slip away if you'd rather.' Although he's got his hands in his jacket pockets, like he's completely chilled, he's a lot paler, and gaunt around the cheekbones than he was this morning.

'Great.' As I push myself out of the most luxurious swivel chair in the world, I'm thinking more of watering my plants than rushing away. 'I'll leave by the terrace then.' And there's no reason at all for Kip to stand open mouthed like I've left him in the lurch. If he'd been in any way flexible, I'd have done my watering already. Just to show him I don't give a fig, I get out my phone, and inadvertently flick straight onto Nicole's pics of bridal lingerie tossed on a silk covered bed.

'Bleurgh ...' It comes out before I can stop it.

Kip's sigh is long suffering. 'What's wrong this time?'

Although I'm not happy at the drama queen implication, I can't help smiling as I think what's coming Kip's way in August. 'Nicole's wedding-night underwear. Want a look?'

'Hell, no.' Result. His 'appalled of Rose Hill' face is all the compensation I need for my own shudder.

I'm also musing over Nicole's previous shot. Captioned *Bride-to-be shaping up*, it's a selfie with a tape measure pulled tight around her waist with a disgustingly teensy measurement on. And an unnerving similarity to Immie's shape-up post. That *has* to be a coincidence. Doesn't it?

'If I can't tempt you to a flash of Nicole's stockings and suspenders, I'll be on my way then.' I grin as he winces again.

A few seconds later, I'm a free woman, hurrying towards the door into the walled garden. I know I'm in my suit, but so long as I'm careful, I can easily do the watering without getting dirty. We all know I detest the digging. And I'm growing seeds under extreme duress. If I've spent most of the day wishing I could be in the garden, it's only a sign of the afternoon from hell. And a double dose of nostalgia due to the flower growing stirring up all my childhood memories. Aside from the astonishing work rate, on a scale of one to ten, where ten is worst, being a prisoner in Kip's office ranks fifteen at least.

There's something very calming about a view of seed trays in orderly rows, filled with tiny, bright green plants. When I stop to look across at the cold frames today, I can literally feel my blood pressure easing. As the seedlings get bigger, I've been pricking them out into new trays too, to grow them on. Both sorts of marigolds are doing really well. The nasturtiums took ages to get going, but now they're almost ready to be planted out. As I turn on the tap by the shed, fill the can, and lug it across to the cold frames, the late afternoon sun is golden on the empty borders. Did you ever feel the weight of a full watering can? This is why I'm getting muscles. As for getting excited about cosmos plants, I used to as a seven-year-old. And I remember my dad literally whooping the day his hard to germinate oriental poppy seeds came through. But me, the sensible adult from Bath, who checked the accounts every evening, and always kept the noise down because I lived in a hotel? Well, I can't understand it either. And thinking about the plants like children really isn't healthy, but that's another story.

After the sunny day, the soil's quite dry so the watering takes a while. I work my way along and I'm onto my last few trays. But when I get to my sweet peas, there has to be a mistake, because the soil in the trays is bare, and the plants are gone.

'If this is Fred's idea of a joke ...' As I bend down to examine them, I can't hold in my scream.

'Waaaaaaaaaaaaaahhhhhhh ...'

All that's left of my four trays of beautiful baby plants are a few stalks. If you'd put in the huge effort I have to get to this point, and found your plants destroyed, I promise you'd be wailing too.

I'm still prodding at the holes in the compost, when I hear running feet on the gravel outside, and the scrape of the garden door.

'Lily, are you okay?' A second later Kip arrives at my elbow, breathless, suit flapping.

Damn. I wasn't expecting an audience. 'My sweet peas have completely dematerialised. Apart from that, I've never been better.' Gutted doesn't begin to cover it.

The way he tugs his fingers through his hair, he looks almost as over-wrought as I am. As he slides down beside me, one bent knee arrives right next to mine.

Suit fabric stretched tight over a guy's thigh? And the scent that's been tantalising my nose from a distance all day? Both zooming into my personal space, in the equivalent of big screen technicolour close up. If I had any breath left, I'd scream all over again.

He purses his lips. 'It has to be mice.'

How on earth does he know that? His face is so close I'm not only seeing the slices down his cheeks where he's starting to smile. I can see every pore too.

'Mice?' My voice is so high, I'm squeaking like one.

'Field mice love any peas. They're very cute, but they'll eat the seeds and graze on the leaves every time.' He doesn't need to sound so triumphant about it. 'At least you've still got your others. You'll need to be planting out soon.'

Nothing that chomps my plants is 'cute'. And when exactly did Kip turn into Monty Don? 'If it hadn't been for a wedding dropped on me with zero notice, I'd already have planted out. As you can see, Fred's been hard at work in the meantime.'

Kip's eyebrows shoot up. 'Who?'

Sometimes he has so little idea. I remind him. 'Fred. With the runaway sheep and the blue tractor. Surely you didn't think I dug all this lot on my own?'

He's shaking his head, laughing. 'I obviously overestimated you. In more ways than one.'

I scan the darker soil on the newly dug borders. 'The amount Fred's dug since yesterday, he must have been here for hours. I'm surprised you didn't see him.' Although Kip's so self-absorbed, seriously, I doubt he'd notice if Fred dug up the lawn in front of the house. 'You know what Fred's like, he plays it down. Apparently digging saves him going to the gym.'

'Brilliant. No doubt it does.' When Kip really laughs, like he's doing now, the corners of his eyes go all crinkly. He's pushing himself up to standing when the door scrapes again, and he turns.

'Vee, I'm sorry for dashing away. Lily wasn't being murdered after all. It was only mice devastating her sweet pea crop.'

Only? I shouldn't be surprised. It's typical Kip, to diminish what's happened.

I stagger to my feet, as the newlyweds make their way down the path towards us, hand in hand. 'Are you heading off?'

Vee smiles up at Salvador beside her. 'We're driving back to London for the night, then we're flying on to Spain tomorrow.' She's changed into a faded cotton midi dress, but she's still wearing the flower crown in her hair.

'*So* exciting.' I can't help being infected with the thrill. 'And *so* great to think you'll be getting married all over again.'

As she comes forward and hugs me, her eyes are shining with tears. 'Thank you both so much for this part. We've had the most amazing day, and we're so proud to be your first wedding. It's been perfect to be looked after by such a wonderful couple.'

Couple? My eyes bulge. Surely she can't think …? I'm about to let out a squawk of protest, when Kip's glare closes me down. A second later his brogue lands squarely on my pump.

'It's been our pleasure. Hasn't it, Lily?' He's beaming, and crushing my toes at the same time.

It's almost a squeal. 'Absolutely.' I squirm my foot out from under his.

Vee pushes an envelope into Kip's hand. 'Here's a little extra thank you for going the extra mile to fit us in. Treat yourselves. A mini break somewhere luxurious, or something special for the house. And best of luck to both of you with your fabulous venue.' She drops a kiss on each of our cheeks, and then she steps back. 'Okay, we'd better be off.'

As we watch them wandering off hand in hand, my first thought is *Eewwwww*. If she's serious about the mini break, that must be *some* tip she's left. But even if it was enough to pay for a cruise to New York first class, it couldn't ever make up for the agony of being mistaken for an item with the awful Kip. How the hell that happened, I've no idea.

That's the thing with walled gardens. You've got to be very careful what you say when you're in them, because you never know who's on the other side of the wall. From the way we stand in rigid silence, Kip's clearly as appalled as I am.

Eventually it's Kip who breaks the silence. 'All this digging Fred's doing, you don't have enough plants to fill it.'

The area of waiting ground is huge. 'I've got even less now.' Sad but true, and I can't help pouting.

Kip's looking thoughtful. 'How would you feel about planting flower mix seeds in the spare borders? I found them on Google. They give you fast-fix flower fests. I could buy industrial quantities of seed, and you could sow it.'

As I imagine the whole garden filled with flowers, instead of just a corner there's a flutter of excitement in my chest. As I think of my own very first border I had as a child, but garden-wide, the flutter expands to a wild flapping. 'A garden bursting with flowers would be amazing for wedding photos too. It's such a special place, it's a shame to keep it hidden.'

Kip laughs. 'Why didn't I think of that?'

I have to be honest. 'Because you still have zero idea about weddings. You're only interested in the bottom line.'

That makes him smile. 'Which brings us neatly on to my next suggestion – selling the crop. Home-grown flowers are in great demand for weddings. It's another win win.' He's making it sound feasible. And attractive. Which is the Penryn way every time.

Although realistically, considering my sweet peas failed completely, I can't be trusted to grow anything. I suspect he's had one good wedding today, and he's getting carried away.

'So what's the catch?' Even as I ask, I already know. If using a border in a Penryn garden was bad enough, this is way worse.

That seems to amuse him. 'No catches. So you'd better tell Fred to hurry up and get that digging finished.'

Beyond the wall, an engine turns over. As Vee and Salvador's car roars away up the drive, Kip's grin widens. 'Great result there for both of us, Water Lily.' He slides the envelope into his jacket, and taps his pocket. 'I'll look after this for now. At least until we book that mini break.' As he wanders off along the path he's laughing to himself all the way to the door. And for a second, after today's performance, I can believe he might have it in him to pull off his wedding business after all.

Although from where I'm standing, with my hard-earned tip disappearing into the distance, I can't see the funny side at all. As for the flower growing, something tells me this is lots more work for me, with the Penryns reaping the benefit. Same old story there then too.

Chapter 27

Tuesday, 30th May
At Brides by the Sea: Brambles and pricks

The series of tipis and marquees appearing in the fields as I drive past Daisy Hill Farm in the next few weeks are a sure sign that the wedding season is underway. Summer in the wedding shop is always frantic, and it's often late by the time I get out to spend a couple of hours in the garden at the Manor. But luckily the days are long, and even though it's only May, the weather is mild, and the evening air is balmy. Somehow I get all my seedlings planted out into the ground, even though by the end I feel like my body's aching in places I didn't know I had. And Kip was good as his word on the flowers. The day after Vee's wedding he turned up with seeds by the sack load. When the instructions say scatter, and water regularly, it really is that simple. Especially if your soil is already warmed, because it's in an idyllic and sheltered south facing walled garden, as it is here. A few days later, there were tiny seedlings, pushing their way out into the soil.

Alongside helping with flower orders and dresses in the

shop, I've also been making the basement every bit as beautiful as Jess ordered. And Jess being Jess, she loses no time in showing it off with a cork popping event.

'Very Berry Pimp Your Prosecco? What do you recommend?' Fred's arrived early, and he's pouring over the frosted glasses, and dishes of berries. Even though he was mainly involved at the start of the project, he's happily taking the credit for the entire department. And in his faded chinos and light tweed waistcoat, he's certainly rocking the style thing.

I push a liqueur bottle towards him. 'Raspberry and limoncello's delicious. Or watermelon and mint. Unless with your green fingers, you'd rather go for hibiscus flowers?'

It's a Tuesday evening, because that's when wedding business people are most likely to be free. But we've also invited brides, and anyone likely to use our styling, or spread the word. And my mum's pushed the 'friends and family' thing to extremes, and invited practically the whole village, on the basis that everyone there knows someone who's getting married.

Fred ignores my gardening tease, and pops a cherry into his mouth. 'I might kick off with a dash of kirsch. And then I'll head straight off and schmooze, Barbara's just arrived.'

'So early?' My heart sinks as I catch a flash of emerald green parrot print silk by the door. As for Fred, he can lay off the persuasion, because my mum hasn't mentioned Rock Quay for weeks. I reckon she's come to her senses on that one.

Poppy sidles up. 'Mini raspberry and vanilla cupcake? And your dress looks fab, Lily. I love the geometric pattern of the lace.'

'Saving my life again, Pops.' I sink my teeth into the soft icing and brush the crumbs off my new black and white shift as I watch my mum. She passes by the Country Terracotta table, with its plant pots and daisies, skirts the Boho Beautiful area with its random jars of cosmos, roses and larkspur, whips by the vintage blush roses and mismatched china. When she reaches the eucalyptus swags and white roses, she finally comes to a halt, and gazes at the flickering candles in straight sided jars.

Fred's back at my elbow. 'We're filling up nicely now, I'll take two fizzy waters with lime slices. David and Barbara are on a detox. And by the way, they both say "hi".'

I can't help pulling a face. 'You'd think people who obsess about getting their ten thousand steps in would walk across the room to get their own drinks.' What's more, I seriously doubt that particular greeting came from David. Lately when he's not saying 'Watcha' he's developed a horrible 'Namaste' habit.

Fred leans in and hisses in my ear as he whisks up their glasses. 'Just giving you space, sweets. They don't want to get in the way of your big moment.'

'Right.' Not that it ever bothered my mum before, but whatever. My phone beeps, and as I have a peep I see Nicole's upstairs and uploading to Instagram. Caption: *Arriving for my big night with my stylist #happybride*. The happy bit might be because she's currently got three more followers than Immie. When I look up again, my mum's bestie, Jenny, is heading straight towards me, with old Mrs Kernighan from the village hanging onto her arm.

Mrs K beams at me. 'Aren't you doing well, Lily? Your mum told us you were.'

It's funny how whenever my mum's involved, I can never quite believe what I'm hearing.

'Wonderful, Lily. And you're looking gorgeous. Sun kissed definitely suits you.' Lovely Jenny gives my hand a squeeze, and comes in for a peck. 'What would you like in your Prosecco, Mrs K?'

Mrs K studies the board on the easel. I'm glad about this, because Jess insisted on a cocktail list with some truly hideous names, and it took me the entire afternoon to master the chalk markers and the italic writing.

She wrinkles her nose, and points at the blackberries. 'I'll have Foragers Fizz, thanks but not too much sloe gin. But first you'll have to tell me what that For Sale board's doing up at your mum's house. You're not leaving us, are you?'

I know I've spent most of the afternoon dashing to the toilet, due to nerves. That was between bouts of triangular writing, obviously. But this sends my stomach into a new kind of free fall. I swear it comes to rest somewhere around my kneecaps.

'Sorry?' The rasp that comes out is like nails scraping down a blackboard. 'Are you sure?'

Jenny's agonised grimace beyond Mrs K's ear should be all the confirmation I need, but somehow I need to hear the words.

'I couldn't believe it either. But it's there all right, on the front lawn by all accounts. The whole village has seen it now. One of them dark blue Bradleys' ones.' Mrs K's tapping my arm, urgently. 'But why'd she want to go and move?'

Jenny shakes her head. 'Sorry, Lily. Come on, Mrs K, Barbara's the one you need to see about this.' She's propelling Mrs K across the room from behind, driving her towards my mother and the White White White table.

I'm just deciding if I'm going to cry or be sick, when someone grabs me from behind, and sweeps me into a bear hug.

'Bloody hell, Lily, putting the house on the market and not telling you? What total toad bollocks is that?'

Somehow the tears win, and before I know it, I'm snivelling all down the shoulder of Immie's *I'm on fire* T-shirt.

'Bastards. Let's get you outside.' Her voice is gruff, as she shoves me towards the door to the terrace. Seconds later, the cool breeze from the sea is drying my tears to salt smears. Above our heads the suspended candle jars are swinging on their strings where they zig zag over the space.

I'm catching my breath as I collapse onto one of the heavy wrought iron chairs. 'If I wasn't so upset, I'd be ... be ... really angry.'

I might not live there anymore, but somehow everything that's left of Dad is in that house. If it's sold, it'll be like losing the last part of him. And so much for Fred's claiming they're giving me space. My mother doing things behind my back is no surprise, given the way she got engaged. What's way worse is Fred playing me too, just because he wants the sale.

Immie drops down beside me. 'Classic avoidance tactics. They're anxious about how you'll react. And now they've ballsed it up completely, and the cow pats are hitting the fan and splattering everywhere.'

At least Immie's gruff analysis and graphic imagery has me giving a watery smile as I sniff. 'I'll be okay in a moment.'

Immie pulls out her phone. 'Meanwhile, Mrs Glitter Bum's doing so many selfies en route, I doubt she'll ever make it as far as the Prosecco.' The picture she flashes is Nicole descending the basement stairs like royalty arriving at the Oscars. 'And then there's the sparkle monster alternative version ...'

I bite my lip to hold in my laughter, as I take in Immie lying upside down on the stairs, arms flung outwards. Something tells me I shouldn't be encouraging her. 'Shit, Immie. So this *is* bride eat bride on Instagram?'

She's straight back at me. 'Too bloody right.' Her laugh is low and very wicked for someone so straight forward. She squints at me. 'You're a better colour now. Back there you went so pale under your tan, I thought you were going to chuck up.'

I wrinkle my nose. 'I've got a tan?' Jenny said so too.

She's grinning. 'You and Kip both. Suits you both too. It's all the gardening.'

Both? I let out a grunt of disgust at being lumped in the same sentence as him. 'Kip's is nothing to do with Rose Hill, it's one of those rich-guy year-round tans.' As for the garden, I doubt he'd recognise a hoe if it hit him in the petunias.

Immie smirks. 'Well we can examine it for ourselves now. Here comes the man himself.' She gives a chortle. 'On the war path, Kip? How's the flower growing going?'

Given he's had zero involvement since he flung the seed at me, I decide to answer this one. 'There's a massive area, so the watering takes ages. But luckily my spade-fairy Fred is also great with a garden hose, and thanks to him the seeds are doing brilliantly.'

Kip's laugh is sarcastic. 'You don't say.' It's typical of him to belittle other people's efforts.

Immie pulls a face. 'This is the same Fred who's pushed Barbara into selling her house without telling you?'

Hmm, am I sure that's what's happened? 'But Fred's been so helpful. Would he put pressure on my mum like that?'

As Immie stares straight at Kip and me, there's a growl in her voice. 'If you ask me, it's time for some straight talking.'

'Too damn right it is.' Kip throws himself into the third seat, and tosses a newspaper down on the table. 'What the hell's going on with the *Cornish Guardian?* I shell out for four pages of coverage in the wedding section, and it's totally eclipsed by a front-page spread about the venue next door.'

So much for talking Kip through the styling, which is what he's meant to be here for. As for the article, I'm as shocked as he is. With the stakes as high as they are for him, I can kind of see why he's jumping up and down here.

As I lean in to see the supplement, my stomach disintegrates again. '*Love grows with the weddings, in the meadows at Daisy Hill Farm.* How Rafe and Poppy got together? Why the hell did they write that and put it in this bit? It was meant to be fizz for a first year, in the main paper.' This is all my fault. When I suggested it, I had no idea it would pan out like this.

Immie's laughing again. 'Wow, great shot of Pops and Rafie.' They're practically life size, faces glued together on the front page. 'The perils of letting a reporter loose on your farm. You never know what the angle will be.'

Oh shit. 'Where's Poppy? She needs to see this.' And I need another cupcake. Or six. As I stare at Kip, part of me wants to tell him Poppy's going to be as apoplectic as he is about this. But the words coming out are something else entirely. 'You came to this party second, Kip, so grow some balls and stop bleating. As I said before, if you can't take the heat, stay out of the goddamned kitchen.' And oops to how venomous I sound. If Fred's not being straight with me, I shouldn't be taking it out on Kip. But if Kip hadn't bumped me into looking after his whole garden while he sits back and reaps the benefit, I might have felt less snappy. I guess everyone's getting what they deserve here. I also can't pretend I'm not happy about who's come out on top in the publicity race here, regardless of the content of the article. Kip knew about the opposition when he set up his business. Despite him giving me work, I know where my loyalties lie.

Kip picks up the paper, and pulls down the corners of his mouth as he gets up again. 'Well lucky for me I've got a lake and a mansion. When it comes to the *Wedding Venue of the Year Awards*, that'll count for way more than a loved-up farmer with a tent in a field.'

'Did someone call me?' Poppy appears in the doorway, and the good news is she's carrying a tray. 'What's this about awards?'

Kip's laugh is bitter. 'The *Cornish Guardian's* announcing them next week. I'd have thought you'd already know, given how pally you are with them. Front page on the supplement mean anything to you?'

Poppy's face drops as she sees the headline. 'Shit.' To her credit she recovers fast. A nano second later, she's wafting confectionery under Kip's nose. 'Cupcake anyone?'

Kip looks as if he'd rather eat his own head. 'You *have* to be joking.' He juts out his chin, and narrows his eyes to a scowl as he gets to his feet. 'If you want to fight dirty, Poppy, bring it on. I'm here to stay, and if we're competing head to head, I'll make sure I take you down. Every time.'

He marches back into the basement, leaving Poppy, Immie and I staring at each other, our jaws sagging.

'Holy fucking crap.' Immie's muttered curses speak for all of us.

'Ouch.' The cupcake I grab slides straight into my open mouth. I'm mumbling through the sponge. 'What a night, and it's barely begun.' The vanilla buttercream melting onto my tongue delivers the surge of deliciousness I'm desperate for.

Poppy blows her fringe up. 'On the up side, if it's any consolation, your mum says she's sorry. The sign only went up as they left the house today, a lot sooner than they expected.' She scrunches up her face. 'We all know what estate agents are like.'

Immie gives a rueful grunt. 'The joys of living in Rose Hill village. Everyone knows what you're doing before you've even done it.' She sniffs. 'Still a bastard though.'

'It's definitely a shock. But so long as my mum's in lust with David and Rock Quay, there's not a lot I can do.'

Poppy nods at the three bubbling glasses on the tray. 'Down this, and you'll feel better, Lily. Special recipe. I pimped the Prosecco with Jess's Rescue Remedy.'

That makes me smile. 'Like Jess ever needs rescuing.'

Poppy grins at me. 'Shows how well it works then, doesn't it? With Kip on the war path, we're all going to need it.' She gives me a hug, and hands me a glass. 'Come on, sweetie, bottoms up. Then you're going to go out there, and sparkle.'

'And be awesomely stylish ...' Immie's got an evil glint in her eye. 'I just heard a noise like a donkey, so I take it Nicole's here. Bags I get the first selfie with the stylist.'

So it's wedding wars all round then.

Chapter 28

Thursday, 8th June
At Brides by the Sea: Quick changes and waves on the
shore

My mum's idea of making amends for the untimely appear-ance of the 'For Sale' sign at Heavenly Heights is a cream tea at the Happy Dolphin Garden Centre, followed by a dress trying session at the shop. Part one of the plan goes on the skids as soon as we hit the cafe, when my mum declines solids, and downgrades her skinny latte to a black tea in mid-order. Cream tea eating isn't any kind of spectator sport, especially when the chief viewer is abstaining to the point of being nil by mouth, so I downsize to an espresso and Jaffa Cakes in cellophane faster than you can say tray bake. Which means instead of the planned two-hour heart-to-heart calorie-fest, we enjoy a full seven-minute silence before my mum finishes her drink and puts her teaspoon back on her saucer.

'You know we're not *definitely* selling, don't you dahling?' This is her latest line on the agent's board. However often she says it, the only person she's fooling here is herself.

I stop peeling the chocolate off my Jaffa Cake. 'Like you said, you're simply dipping your toe in the water, to see if the boat floats.' You can tell from the mixed metaphors that I'm quoting her. And I'm despairing at the pretence. We both know the minute a buyer bites, she'll be off to Fred's penthouse faster than you can say Pickfords Removals.

She beams. 'See, dahling, so you do listen sometimes.' Half closing an eye, she leans across the table. 'Fred's only helping us to get in your good books. He's a lovely boy, and so keen, I can't understand why you haven't snapped him up already.'

Not that I'm admitting it, but there's actually something my mum and I agree on – I can't understand my reluctance on this one either. And I also agree, at times, he's practically edible too. I've been so close to leaning in to those flirty nudges of his, and not leaning out again. But for some inexplicable reason, I always pull back.

'I've got a lot going on right now; there isn't space to add a guy in too.' It's how I explain it to myself. The other biggie is I want to stay free to move on myself when the time comes. Once I've saved up enough to afford a flat. And found a new job. Which realistically, thanks to the extra wedding styling at the Manor, is a lot closer now at the end of May than it was back in February.

My mum purses her lips. 'I know what Thom did was awful, but you can't let it define you forever.'

'Excuse me?' Not that it's any of her business. But when someone I trusted and built a life with turns round and says they don't want to be with me anymore, I'm hardly going to risk a repeat. I'm better off on my own.

She wrinkles her forehead. 'When tragedy strikes you have to pick yourself up and move on. Where would I be now if I hadn't done that?'

Not that I'm going to say it, but I know she'd be in a better place. Not going out with a dickhead for one, and the house wouldn't be on the market either. 'You'd probably be having a lovely time with Jenny.' I'm not being bitchy either. I'm only saying what's true.

She conveniently ignores that. 'We only want you to be happy, dahling.' Back to that old mantra.

'We?' I hate it when she includes David as if they're surgically attached, when he patently doesn't give a damn. Come to think of it, I haven't seen her on her own for months. It's taken a trip to a wedding shop fitting room to shake him off.

When I meet her eye again, she's back to wiggling her eyebrows. 'Fred's *very* taken with your new image. It's why he's going the extra mile for us.'

Dammit. It's obvious my mum's blanking my side of the conversation entirely. Sometimes I have to resort to extremes to shut her up.

'That's total bollocks. And you know it.' It comes out so loud the bright pink gerbera vibrate in their vase next to the salt and the ketchup bottle. And if I were a look-at-me person, who wanted every eye in the cafe trained on her, I'd have done the job. But however snazzy it is, my mum can't hang this one on my latest houndstooth shell top.

Her pink lips part in a mortified gasp. 'Lily! That's *not* Happy Dolphin appropriate language.' If I'd emptied the water jug over her head she couldn't look more horrified. She finishes the running repairs to her lippy, and jumps up onto her pink suede courts. 'Come on. You might be losing your puppy fat, but you've still got a lot to learn in the manners department.'

She's out of the cafe, and back into garden gnomes so fast, there's no time to answer back. I scurry behind her as she stomps out to the car park. Then we head for the Brides by the Sea in silence.

As soon as we arrive at the shop Jess shepherds us into the Seraphina East Room. Then she sets about breaking the chill. Who'd have thought one teensy swear word could turn a fun afternoon so glacial?

'Barbara, it's *so* lovely of you to come. And we'll definitely be able to redeem your Pirate Radio Bridal Bouquet prize against the dress, as well as offering you ten per cent off.' When it comes to financial detail, Jess has the memory of an elephant. She turns on her purr. 'And we'll obviously do an additional close-family discount too.'

I'm not sure my mum wants to be reminded of any link to me right now, even if it does mean saving herself a fortune. As for finding a wedding dress, the hunt couldn't feel less auspicious.

Poppy skips in behind us, drops a plate of pale pink home-made macaroons onto the table, and shoves me firmly down into the mother-of-the-bride chair. 'Would you like Prosecco, Barbara?'

I eyeball Poppy. 'Some *special zero calorie* Fentiman's lemonade would be fab. All round.' There's no such thing, but I think we'd both benefit from a sneaky sugar hit here.

Poppy puts a finger on her lips. 'I'll bring the extra healthy version we serve in glasses not bottles.' Great, she's got me. Since she hooked up with David, Mum's a devil for examining labels.

'So we're aiming to turn heads here, Barbara?' Jess gets straight to the point, obviously primed by Poppy. 'Well done for that.'

My mum softens faster than ice cream in a microwave. 'As David says, if you've got it, go for it.' She smooths her hands over the rose garden silk of her skirt, and rubs a shell pink nail. 'That's the up side of being over sixty – you can be "banging" without looking like you're on the pull.'

I grab a macaroon to save myself expiring on the spot. As a mission statement, it couldn't be clearer.

'So definitely not these then?' Jess's mini parade of the muted grey and cream linens and chiffons she's brought down specially from upstairs are all dismissed in a single head shake.

'And not lace either, because it's aging. I'm thinking slinky rather than blingy, and I'm not ruling out backless.'

Jess is listening intently, thinking on her loafers, working out her next move.

As Poppy hands me my drink I suck on my straw. 'What did you wear last time then, Mum?' I'm curious rather than stirring here. My mum's interior makeovers banished family snaps to the loft years ago, and she was too out of it to get them down when my dad died. It's the kind of thing I think I know, but always forget to ask.

My mum has a faraway look in her eye as she laughs. 'Back then every bride wanted huge skirts, cream silk and puffed sleeves so she could look like Lady Di when she married

Charles. But we'd spent so much buying the cottage, I ended up in a shift from C&A. It was all a bit of a rush.'

'Was your hair darker then?' Do I remember a brunette on a photo?

She pushes at her carefully styled waves. 'We're all a lot blonder than we used to be, dahling.' She makes it sound as if it's down to climate change, rather than L'Oreal. 'Except for you, obviously.'

I squint down at my dark brown hair, and ignore the dig. She's been pushing me to have highlights since I was fourteen. Well over half my life then.

Jess pulls a couple of silky dresses off the rails. 'Seraphina's designs can be sexy and very flattering. We could start by trying these?'

'Lovely.' My mum perks up as Jess drops in the 'x' word, and zooms into the fitting room.

When she appears through a gap in the white striped curtains five minutes later, she's looking totally amazing.

'Wow. So gorgeous. Bias silk and traces of beading.' Sera's dresses have a tendency to bring out the best in a woman, and they've certainly worked their magic on my mum, which is why we're all crooning.

My mum stands in front of the full-length mirror, tutting as she twists. 'It's a bit demure. More meek than I was hoping for.'

'Okay,' we chorus, because in dress trying, it's the bride who takes the lead. 'Next!'

Every dress she comes out in, it's the same story. Sedate ... boring ... modest ... plain ... Even though to us they're anything but. The sixth has a back that plunges to the waist, and a front slashed almost as low, and still gets a 'matronly' thumbs down.

It's not often we see Jess perplexed. She wrinkles her nose as she leans on the mirror. 'So what do you feel we're missing here, Barbara?'

My mum scrunches up her face, as she thinks. 'Actually I was hoping for sequins. A lot more sequins.' She hesitates. 'Maybe even sequins all over.'

As I ram down my fifth macaroon, I'm truly regretting backing off on the afternoon tea.

Poppy smiles. 'That's very helpful, Barbara.'

Encouraged, my mum goes on. 'It's so wonderful with the sun pouring through into the Winter Garden at the Manor where we're having the ceremony. I really want to shimmer.'

Jess nods. 'If shimmering is what you're after, that's what we'll do.' She turns to Poppy. 'Pop up to bridesmaids. Let's try Ariel and Andrina. In moonshine and pearlescent.'

There's a clatter of footsteps on the stairs, and when Poppy bursts in again, her armful of sequined dresses are rustling like the tide rushing up the beach.

Despite all her face-firming yoga gymnastics, my mum's chin is wobbling. 'Ah ... They're *exactly* what I was hoping for.' She scrapes under her lashes with her finger nail.

As she heads behind the curtain, Poppy and I are grinning at each other in sheer relief, and biting our lips in anticipation.

'Okay?' Poppy asks, after what seems like forever.

There's a mumble. When my mum appears in her cream

sequined sheath, she's taking teensy steps, because she can't move her legs. And she's tugging at the top.

Jess steps back to assess. 'The nice thing about these pearly white sequins is they only shine when the light catches them.'

'I'm not sure about this one after all.' My mum's frowning at herself in the mirror. 'It's quite clingy.'

'It's pretty much a floor length boob tube.' I'm bracing myself to accept that my mum's hell bent on getting married in a skin-tight mermaid's tail.

Jess nods. 'It's snug. But then you've got the figure for it.'

Poppy scratches her head. 'It's definitely banging.'

My mum gives a groan. 'I love the shimmer, but I feel a bit exposed. And a tiny bit slutty.'

I sit up in my mother of the bride chair, because I can't believe what I'm hearing. Wonders never cease. Excuse the cliché, but this is the last thing I expected from this 'out-there' version of my mum. 'Maybe you've got to the edge of your comfort zone?' And maybe there is a fairy godmother of embarrassed daughters after all.

'Okay. Next.' Jess's war cry hurries her back into the fitting room.

When the curtains part again, we're all holding our breath. But after the last big build up and crashing disappointment, we're not expecting too much. So when my mum swishes into view, it's like she's walking onto a blank canvas, and we've got completely open minds. And we watch in silence as the fabric flows around her body in fluid waves as she moves.

Jess's whisper is hoarse. 'This is the pearlescent one. It shines across the pastel blue and pink spectrum.'

The straps sweep down to a simple low neck at the front, and plunge at the back. But because of the way the fabric hangs and skims and swings, the effect is classy, not brassy, in a way I wouldn't have thought possible.

My mum's flapping her hands in front of her face like she just escaped from an American teen soap. Turning backwards and forwards in front of the mirror. I think she might be mouthing silent omigods, but nothing's coming out.

I know I should wait for her to find her voice, but I can't hold back. 'I didn't think I'd say this, but truly, it's lovely, Mum. You look seriously shiny, and totally fabulous.' Who'd have thought we'd stick my mum in a head to toe sequined brides-maid dress and it would work. This is why Jess is so clever. She matches the bride to the dress every time.

When it comes my mum's voice is all strangled too. 'The shape's everything I imagined. And more. But just tell me ... am I shimmering?'

Poppy and I are laughing through our tears. As I stagger out of my chair I grab a handful of tissues from the mother of the bride box, and swab the slick from my nose.

Then before I know what I'm doing, I throw my arms around my mum. And I'm squeezing her tighter than I ever remember. 'You're looking amazing. And yes, you're damn well shimmering. You couldn't be more shimmery, or more beau-tiful if you tried.'

Just at this moment, I forget she's engaged to a knob-head who thinks he's a teenager and is after her cash, and that I'd rather she wasn't getting married. Because when a bride finds her perfect dress, for a few seconds of her life, none of the rest matters. All that's important is her. And how happy she is.

As our hug loosens her hands are patting up and down my back. And then they stop, and she pushes me to arm's length. 'Lily, have you been secretly working out?' Her expression is accusing.

No-one wrecks a moment like my mum.

I stare back at her. 'You know I'd rather listen to your Barry Manilow CD while having my tonsils removed with a rusty spoon than go to the gym.'

Her nostrils flare. 'But you've got traps and lats to die for under that little top of yours.' You can tell she's engaged to a fitness instructor. Who knew there were muscles called that?

Maybe my aching shoulder muscles from all that watering were worth it after all. 'Don't worry. It's probably the gardening.' Or hurtling up and down five flights of stairs between the basement and the attic.

She's beaming with delight, and her extra loud laugh's back. 'Carry on like this and we'll be back here choosing a wedding dress for you soon.'

I'm about to swear. But Poppy's behind her, doing throat cutting signs.

Then Jess joins in. 'The wine merchants are having an event next week. We'll make sure we grab her a tall dark and handsome businessman while we're there, Barbara.'

I know Jess goes the extra mile to be a customer pleaser, but this is too much. Jess and I are united by our disinterest in men. But since Rafe came on the scene she's developed an unhealthy interest in farmers and landowners. But when she says tall and dark, I can't help thinking that Fred's more on the sandy side.

So a day of surprises all round. I'm happy my mum's marrying in sequins, and she gave me a compliment. What's not to like? Times as good as this can't go on forever.

Chapter 29

Friday, 16th June
At Rose Hill Manor: Rust and a fuchsia bloom

'So for the ceremony room we'll go with an archway of tall blossom trees, all the way down the aisle, with rectangular chrome vases, bursting with white hydrangeas at floor level.'

Nicole and I are in the Winter Garden at Rose Hill Manor, which frankly needs to be re-named for summer ceremonies. The sun's streaming in as we stand waving our arms, and finalising ideas. Although I say finalise in the loosest sense. Can you believe we've been styling and restyling Nicole's wedding since March? And so far we've agreed four full schemes. Then hours later Nicole's dumped each one, and seamlessly moved on to the next. I'm beginning to think our design consultations are simply an excuse to hang out at the Manor for Instagram opportunities.

Nicole twirls on a blush patent stiletto. 'That's white with the tiniest hint of pink this time. And remember, the strings of diamonds draped through the branches are non-negotiable.'

I smile. 'As if I'd forget.' Trailing diamanté is the one constant in our schemes. We're shipping it in by the mile from the USA as we speak.

'And tell Jess, I swear on my rock, no more changes. Every minute's spoken for from now on.' There's a flash as Nicole sweeps her engagement finger through the air, then she brushes an invisible speck of dust off the sleeve of her white leather jacket. As she takes a step forward, and one elegant knee appears through the slit on the front of her pencil skirt, she doesn't exactly look like she's rushed off her Jimmy Choo's.

'Jess doesn't mind.' We can put together as many schemes as Nicole wants, so long as Miles is willing to pay. Jess's tip for Nicole – say yes to everything, and she'll eventually burn herself out. All good so far, in that we haven't had any fights. But I've no idea how close to the end game we are.

Nicole gives her donkey guffaw. 'We'll *have* to stop when the wedding happens.'

There's another lower laugh, coming in through the open window. 'Indoor trees? I hope you know you can't call 999 to get those installed, Lily. Not long now, Mrs Ferrara-to-be.'

Despite my cotton dress, I'm already sticky with sweat due to the baking June day. But the thought of how close the wedding is, has rivulets running down my back.

Nicole laughs, as Kip wanders in from the garden. 'Still no hot tub though, Mr Penryn?'

'Not yet.' He's unperturbed. 'But I'm going to an event at the wine merchants soon. I promise I'll look out for a special on champagne to fill a bath for you.'

Damn. I only hope that's not the same jolly we're going to.

There has to be more than one booze company having a promotional knees-up in Cornwall.

Kip's the same with all Nicole's demands. If he wants what she's shouting for he jumps straight onto it. Otherwise he brushes it off with a joke, and she sucks it up. Faster than Immie with squirty cream. So much for Poppy's plan for Nicole to drive Kip round the bend. These two are like new besties.

Nicole's silvery nail lands on his chest, and pokes hard enough to make an indentation in the faded fabric of his T-shirt. 'You need to talk to your hot tub installer fast, or you'll be missing a few stars when my review goes up on Trip Adviser.'

Yay. One – nil to Nicole. That wipes the smile right off Kip's face. He knows reviews can make or break a wedding business, which is why he's so jumpy. But there are times when we women need to stick together, and for now I can overlook Nicole's ability to give it out like a true bitch queen from hell. And all the work she's dumped on me. Come to think of it, if we were likening Nicole's wedding to Monopoly, I'm the one who landed on Mayfair with hotels on, while Kip grabbed the Get Out of Jail Free card. Yet again.

Kip pulls out his phone, and stares at it. 'Three hours discussing crystals. Again. If you're all done then Nicole, I'll show you out.' He raises an eyebrow. 'Lily and I have other urgent business to discuss.'

'We do?' This is news to me.

He nods. 'In the office first, and then the garden.'

A few minutes later, we've dropped Nicole off at her impossibly shiny Mercedes convertible, and he's burrowing in a parcel under the desk.

'This is for you.' A folder slides towards me, and the fact it travels across the polished oak at a hundred miles an hour, then shoots off to land in my hand shows exactly how glossy it is. 'Feel free to show it to the competition, I'd like them to know what they're up against.'

If my eyes are popping out as I take in what I'm opening here, I can't help it. 'A full colour brochure ... with package options and prices?' Okay, I'd be picking my jaw up off the floor at that alone, but there's more. Lots and lots more. As I leaf through the pages, I can't find anything he's not covered.

Two more folders whizz across the desk. 'And a welcome pack for couples who book, and another for the day itself.' He's looking steely, rather than pleased with himself. 'You'll find we've pretty much nailed the communications and information.'

I'm opening and closing my mouth, but nothing's coming out. Holy crap would do. Or toad bollocks, thank you, Immie. 'But why now?' I rasp, when I finally find my voice. As my eyes slide to the wall to my left, they get wider still when they land on year planners for the next three years, complete with colour coded booking stickers. And a startlingly large number of them too. This guy is hitting the top of his game, and is so far away from being the Kip who didn't used to give a damn that I practically don't recognise him.

Kip's cheeks flex as he digs his hands into the pockets of his denims. 'Just ensuring we're unbeatable, for when the Awards team visit.' If he's still clinging onto the faded jeans, at a guess it won't be for long. 'I wasn't sure weddings were for me, but now we've had a couple, I'm damned grateful to

Quinn for suggesting them.' Implacable doesn't begin to describe the determined line of his mouth.

'You did this all on your own?' He always says we, so it's hard to tell.

He gives a shrug. 'Uncle Bart dropped in for a brainstorm.'

'I thought he was somewhere exotic?'

Kip laughs. 'It's a flying visit. His carbon footprint's a disaster, but his air miles are ace. As was his input. My dad might be a financial disaster area, but Bart makes up for it tenfold. And luckily he treats me and my brothers like his adopted children. Let's face it, if he didn't I wouldn't be here in the first place.' This is the first Kip's mentioned of his dad. Since that day in the stables he's been pretty guarded about his family.

Talking of Uncle Bart, I'm wondering if he's worked his magic with the wedding magazine. 'Has the Manor been featured in *Perfect Brides* yet?' I flick through all the big magazines Jess gets, but I haven't spotted it yet.

The shadow of a frown crossing Kip's face suggests that particular bubble isn't floating into happy land in quite the same way as all his others. 'That's been delayed until November, because the photos they took are wall to wall snow. But this business is all about taking the long view. I'm confident the Ferraras' wedding will get picked up for next summer's edition too.' He gives me a significant nod. 'You'll get a shout out, and a shed load of commissions from that one.'

'Great.' I say, trying to look the right amount of excited. Next year sounds like a lifetime away. With any luck, I'll be long gone, making a fresh start where no-one knows me.

From the way he wrinkles his nose, he's not pleased with my reaction. 'Don't knock me over with your enthusiasm. Maybe you'll look happier when I tell you the flower news.'

Now it's my turn to frown. 'There are roses cascading in front of the windows, lilac in the distance, irises, carnations and forget-me-nots by the door. You need to be more specific, Kip.' He might have his wedding communication under control, but he hasn't got a clue about the rest.

He's biting back a smile. 'Cosmos ring any bells?'

'I planted some chocolate cosmos, which reminds me how long it's been since breakfast. And some pink ones.' I screw up my face to drive away the hunger pangs. 'Have you been on Google again?' It's the only place Kip would come across them.

He tugs on a handful of hair. 'Yes, but only for identification purposes. Sorry, I've got to tell you, there's a cosmos flower out in our garden, Water Lily. How amazing is that?' His voice is high as he lets his grin go.

'*Our* garden?' Of course he'd say that. 'You went in?' More fool me for pretending it belonged to Fred and me.

For a second Kip's smile falters, then it's back. 'The guys came to cut the grass. I was showing them which bits to mow when I found it.' He's already round the desk, and over by the door. 'Aren't you coming to see?'

His strides are so long as he speeds across the gravel, I have to run to keep up. By the time I go through the door into the walled garden I'm gasping, and he's already down by the apple trees.

When I finally catch up with him he's standing by one of

the big borders where we – or rather I – sowed the mixed seed.

'This is the sunniest corner, which is why it's come out here first. Isn't it amazing?' He's pointing down at a tiny pink scrap of a bloom, with straggly petals, all of two centimetres across.

'It's fabulous.' I stagger backwards, smacking my hand into his as a high five comes out of nowhere and knocks me off balance. And at the same time, it isn't fab. Because the flower's so small, I'd have needed a step ladder and binoculars to have noticed it from across the garden where I planted out my seedlings. I'm actually ashamed to admit, Fred's the one who's been watering this part.

Kip's almost as breathless as me even though he's only been walking. 'It's the start of our crop. Better still, it means your mum's going to get her homegrown bouquet.' His beam couldn't be broader, and he's looking scarily as if he'd like to hug someone.

To me that sounds like wild optimism. I edge back, putting the corner of the border between us. 'I hope so.' Just like with weddings, gardening needs patience, and a long-term view. 'Everything's still very small.' Worryingly so from where I'm standing. There's a long way to go from one tiny flower to a whole bouquet.

The skin on Kip's arm is dark beside mine, as he gives me a gentle bump with his shoulder. 'Trust me on this. The next couple of weeks is the time of year when the garden goes whoosh.'

Excuse me? He comes into the garden for the first time in

weeks, and suddenly he knows it all? If there's one certainty in Rose Hill, it's that Kip is the last guy to be trusted. Even on something as insignificant as gardening bullshit. Although when I think hard, I can still hear my dad and his mates from the allotment club laughing about June, busting out all over. 'Going whoosh' is the up-market, Penryn view of that early summer growth rush that astonishes me every time. I just hope it happens again this year.

I give a sniff. 'One bunch of flowers is all I need from here. Anything else is a bonus.' I'm not being deliberately downbeat, or tetchy. I'm being realistic. Even though the plants are mostly ankle high, they're nothing like the bloom studded internet pictures on the site Kip ordered the seed from. It will be just my luck if this is the one time in his life when a Penryn gets taken for a ride. As for the way he's swooped in and taken ownership, that's what I feared all along. This garden comes with strings, and I need to keep that in mind as much as I need to remember Nicole's trailing diamonds.

He's laughing now. 'Relax, Water Lily. Who knows, by September you might even start to enjoy yourself.' Which just goes to show it's true what they say about laughter being good for you, even if it is sarcastic. Because the tension lines have gone from his face, and for once he's lost the gaunt shadows under his cheekbones.

I back away down the path. 'Trust me on this – I won't ever have a great time anywhere that makes my muscles ache as much as this particular garden.' It's only when I reach the door I find I'm laughing too.

Chapter 30

At Huntley and Handsome Wines: Ice buckets and passing trade

'Coming to a complimentary wine event, and refusing to drink, Lily?' Drinks are being served by the glass, by waiters in pristine white shirts with dark red Huntley and Handsome logo aprons, weaving skilfully among the guests. But Jess is storming across the stone cobbles a champers bucket in each hand. 'Quick, grab us some more glasses.'

The wine merchant trades out of a range of converted barns half a mile along the coast from St Aidan. The doors from the showrooms have been opened up, and guests are spilling out into the courtyard, where there's a fabulous view across the beach, to the ocean beyond. We've been catching the last of the sun as it slides down towards the horizon. Jess gets through gallons of Prosecco entertaining brides, so she's one of the local wine merchant's most consistent customers outside the restaurant trade. And if I was under the impression this was a tasting event where drinks would be sipped and

251

savoured I couldn't be more wrong. From the way guests are throwing down the alcohol, it seems more like they're trying to drink the place dry.

I do as I'm told, and lift some flutes off a passing tray. 'Nicole's in at nine to finalise favours, so I'll need a clear head for that. She's going for the monogrammed solid silver key fobs after all.' Given I'm here as Jess's plus one, supposedly to spread the word about Brides by the Sea's new department, I reckon my excuse is watertight. I'm also so knackered after an early start, if I drink too much I'm liable to end up in a heap.

Jess props the bottles on our cafe table, knocks back the contents of both glasses, pops a cork, and pours. 'Special delivery, all for us. Moet first, then a spot of Bolly to compare.' She tips my orange juice into a potted palm, and rams the bubbly into my hand. 'There's no such thing as a champagne hangover, remember.'

'Is Fred coming this evening?' I'd sworn I wouldn't ask. And since Heavenly Heights went up for sale, even though he's been watering plants like it's going out of fashion, bless his cotton socks, I've barely set eyes on him in person. But if it's a choice between saying his name, or drinking my own weight in champagne, I'll risk Jess jumping in to match make every time.

Jess sends me a knowing smile. 'He was invited, but a Rock Quay viewing came up at short notice.' She couldn't have better information on the whereabouts of eligible Y chromosomes, if she looked after their personal diaries. 'If he's close to a bite, he'll be wining them and dining them to close the deal.'

Dammit. On the excess alcohol front, not the romance front obviously. I scan the throng of summer dresses and chinos trying to locate Poppy and Rafe instead, so they can come over and help us out here. The best Poppy can offer for now is an eyebrow wiggle and a wave of a handful of cards from the edge of a very involved discussion. The cards she's giving out are Daisy Hill's fight back to Kip's latest forward surge. Jules the photographer took some amazing pictures of a bride and groom in the dark, in front of a huge tree at the farm with fairy lights stretching to the ends of every branch. We're all hoping the promise of that one iconic shot will be a clincher for bookings. I'm just picking up my own card from the table, and waving it back at her, when a hand lands on my shoulder, and there's a familiar laugh.

'Nice picture, great idea. Daisy Hill in a spin because of my new brochures? Remind me to organise an illuminated tree at the Manor first thing tomorrow.'

So Kip is here after all, dammit. Disgustingly blatant too. He grins at Jess. 'Uncle Bart's over at the barbecue hitting the Hunter's Chicken. Fuelling up for another argument, and dying to see you, Jess.'

Jess waves the bottle at Kip. 'And I love you too, sweetie. If you want some Moet you'll need a glass.'

Kip shakes his head. 'I'm designated driver. It's alcohol-free sauvignon blanc all night for me.' He raises an eyebrow at the empty chairs at our table. 'Okay if we join you?'

I pull out a special sparkly customer smile. 'I'd rather have my teeth pulled.' No point not being truthful is there? It's only the kind of thing Kip would say to Nicole.

Kip grins back. 'Good to see Ms Happy's not venturing out of her comfort zone by being upbeat. I'll take that as a "yes" then.'

The next second he lands on the cafe chair next to mine. 'Fabulous.' I say. 'Not.' Although there's a plus side. If Jess was planning to keep her promise to my mum on the tall dark and handsome front, I couldn't ask for a better space blocker than Kip. In which case, I'd better get busy with some scintillating conversation. I glance up at the light bulbs threaded above the courtyard. They're glowing against the fading sky as they swing above our heads in the warm breeze from the sea. 'Did Nicole mention illuminating the jetty down by the lake?' As an attention grabbing strategy it works a treat.

Kip sits up straight away. 'We thought you could do us a scheme for the terrace as well as the lakeside. Let's face it, everyone loves candles and lanterns and strings of lamps, especially award judges. They beat floodlights any day.'

'You want me to do both places?' Damn. This isn't where this was supposed to be heading.

'Tea lights in dangly jars are your big thing aren't they? Make it a priority, and we'll do some pictures at dusk before the end of the week.' Talk about bish bash bosh. Kip's turning into a whirlwind decision maker with tyrant traits.

Jess gives me a nod. 'Fabulous, Kip. Exactly why Lily's here. All the best deals are done over champagne.' Her purr drops to a gentle groan. 'Don't look now, but the original crumple zone's coming our way. Someone should show your uncle a trouser press, Kip.'

As I look over my shoulder, sure enough, Bart is heading

over, rocking head-to-toe Caribbean chic, with a cheesecloth shirt and baggy trousers.

'Ahoy there, me hearties.' He sets down a plate piled high with food, and beams. 'Anyone for grog and grub?'

Jess snaps at him, with a tight-lipped glare. 'If you're on a rum raid, Uncle Bart, forget it. Every drop of our champers is spoken for.'

I lean across to Kip. 'Pirate talk?' It's like that day on Facebook when the emoticons all got eye patches.

Kip rolls his eyes. 'Cornwall collides with the Caribbean. He's channelling his inner Jack Sparrow.'

Bart chortles. 'Don't get your knickerbockers in a twist, Jess, I'm not here to plunder, I'm sailing with my own supplies.' The champagne bucket he whips out from behind his back contains two bottles. As he slams it onto the table I can't help smiling to see the Bolly and Moet labels are identical to Jess's.

Jess snorts. 'That's rich coming from someone whose drawstring pants appear to have more wrinkles than an octogenarian's bottom. Have you never heard of a travel iron?'

'Creases are the new smooth, although you're not entirely wrinkle free yourself.' Bart sends a wink in the direction of Jess's slightly rumpled linen slacks, then grasps a bottle, and twists off a cork. He splashes fizz into Jess's glass, then fills mine too. 'That should scrape the barnacles off. Bottoms up, wenches.'

Kip pulls a face. 'Okay, less of the cutlass wielding you lot. Try a hot dog, they're venison.' He pushes one each at Jess and Bart.

As Jess gets up and tugs the folds out of her trousers, she's staring daggers at Bart. 'Don't let him in our bucket, Lily, I'm off to mingle in a pirate-free zone. Give me a shout when the coast's clear again.' She turns an especially steely scowl onto Bart. 'When Captain Pugwash has buggered off, in other words.' From the speed she grabs a bottle and her glass and disappears into the crowd, she can't wait to get away.

Bart's tanned face lights up as he leans over. 'Isn't she fun? So easy to ruffle her feathers too.'

Kip sends Bart a stern frown. 'Jess does a lot of work for us, we can't afford to upset her. If you don't behave I'll take you home.'

I can't tell if he's joking or not, but Jess is bomb proof. Nothing fazes her. She keeps her cool when the rest of us are reduced to wrecks, so I've no idea why Bart gets under her skin so easily.

Bart tucks a bottle under his arm as he gets to his feet. 'Aye aye, Cap'n.' Somehow his unrepentant grin isn't reassuring.

With Jess circulating and likely to bump into eligible hunks at any moment, there's all the more reason for me to keep Kip talking, so I fill my glass again to keep my strength up. 'Bart's still here then?' Stating the obvious, but at the same time something tells me there's a lot of mileage in this one.

Kip lets out a long breath. 'He left and came back again. He's perpetually on the move working his deals, although he might be happier if he wasn't.'

'It's great if he's helpful. Not wanting to overdo the nautical thing, but he looks like a bit of a loose cannon.'

Kip scratches his head. 'He's like a second dad to me, and he's not usually this excitable. When our mum died, and our dad went to pieces, Bart had us at the Manor whenever we weren't at boarding school. It can't have been easy keeping tabs on six of us.'

I pull a face. 'Teenage boys on the rampage. You did have a bit of a reputation in the village.' To put it mildly.

Kip laughs. 'With so many of us, we all took the rap for every screw up. Singly we were only a sixth as bad.'

Nice way of looking at it. 'That sounds like a great disclaimer.'

Kip looks hurt. 'We had rules.'

That's hard to believe. 'What, like you weren't allowed to kill each other?' Pretty much anything else was up for grabs as far as I remember.

He pulls a face. 'Mostly with girls. If one of us expressed an interest in anyone, the rest had to back off forever. A strict code of conduct was the only way to make sure we didn't murder each other.'

'And?' All these years on, it's a strange privilege being given an insider view into the Penryn code of ethics.

He laughs. 'That was about it. Uncle Bart had standards, but he let us stick to them in our own ways, so we developed as individuals. Like most brothers, we're all very different.'

That's not something that really struck me before. 'All wild, all in faded denim. Not many people got beyond that.'

His elbow's on the table, propping his chin in his hand. 'Fascinating. And horrifying at the same time.' He laughs. 'Thanks for the enlightenment, Water Lily. That explains a lot. No-one's put it like that before.'

A few minutes of honesty, and he's back to being sarcastic.

'I definitely think of you as Penryn first, and yourself second.' I hesitate, and take another glug and empty my glass. That's the weird thing with champagne, sometimes the more I drink, the thirstier it makes me. I doubt I'd have said that before I drank the last four glasses. 'Does Kip come from Christopher, then?' Can you tell I'm back to keeping him in his seat? Although it's a slog, and this morning's five o'clock start is making my eyelids droop.

That brings on the crinkles at the edge of his eyes, and his extra low confessional tone. 'No, Kip's short for Kipling.'

I should have known it would have to be something super-posh. 'Nice to be called after an author though. Didn't he write *The Jungle Book*?'

Kip laughs again. 'He did, but I'm named after the other Mr Kipling. The one who bakes the cakes.'

'Now you're kidding me?' I wouldn't usually find that funny, but for some reason it makes me giggle. A lot. Eventually I hiccup to a stop. 'How come?'

He gives a shamefaced grin. 'My mum ate a lot of his apple pies when she was pregnant with me. I was one of the eldest too, so it wasn't even as if she was running out of boys' names.'

'How sweet is that?' There are worse things to be named after. One of my friends in Bath was called Charlotte, after some writing her mum had read in a toilet.

'It might have fitted better if she'd been eating his Manor Cake.'

Which reminds me. 'Mmmm. I love his Cherry Bakewells. And the Mini Battenbergs and the Viennese Whirls. Not forgetting Almond Slices ...' Once I start I can't stop, and the mouth-watering reminds me I haven't eaten since lunch. Call me squeamish, but I can't ever bring myself to eat a deer, even if it's wrapped up as a sausage.

Kip smiles. 'Anyway, that's enough about me, how about you and your family?'

Such a direct question is enough to make me down two glasses straight off, which means Jess's bottle is empty, and I'm almost at the bottom of Bart's. As for whether they're Bolly or Moet, right now I don't give a damn. I'm trawling through my brain, failing to find a non-incriminating, throwaway comment when a shout goes up across the courtyard.

'Hey, everyone down the beach – time for volleyball.'

I'm beaming at Kip, because this gets me right off the hook. 'Great, I think this might be our cue to go home.' Right now, I can't think of anything more comfy than snuggling into my bed under the sloping ceiling. Although given my legs feel like lead, I'm less keen on the four flights of stairs I've got to climb to get there. As Jess comes dashing over, I'm expecting her to be right with me on the disgusted of St Aidan thing. 'Time to leave?'

'Leave?' From her shocked tone she's appalled. 'Huntley and Handsome's sunset volleyball is one of St Aidan's finest after-drink traditions. We play until we can't see any more. It's unmissable. Nothing else would get me into sand shoes, believe me.' As she nods at her feet I notice she's swapped her thousand-variations-on-a-loafer theme for some slip-on snake-skin trainers with silver stripes. Although given there's a Gucci logo on the back, she's not selling out completely.

My heart plummets so far I can't help my screech of disbelief. 'We're actually joining in?' Since when did a civilised wine evening turn into a drunken scramble on the sand? I'm practically wearing a mini skirt too. That's a mistake I won't make again, either.

'Absolutely. Come on, what are you waiting for?' As one of the waiters bounces a ball at her, Jess pounces on it like a tiger on raw meat. She starts patting the ball, and following the throng of guests down the steps, and beyond the courtyard.

As I turn to Kip in desperation, he's pursing his lips. 'I can run you back to town?'

Jess hears and jerks back towards us. 'Don't you dare, Kip. If you won't join in, Lily, at least come and cheer. If I'm going to smash that Bart into the ground, I want witnesses.'

Kip's laughing at me. 'Looks like you're here for the long haul. I'll grab something from the Landy for you to sit on.'

If anyone told me I'd spend the evening talking to Kip, I'd probably have stayed at home. If they'd said I'd end up watching ball games on the beach, I'd have expired. But when the alternative is joining in, you can find yourself getting a long way out of your comfort zone very fast.

Chapter 31

Tuesday, 27th June
On the beach at Huntley and Handsome Wines: Under a
starry sky

'You are playing, aren't you?'
        As Kip kicks his way across the soft sand to where
I'm standing watching the players warm up, he bats an
escaping ball back into the melee. In front of us women have
hitched up their frocks and are leaping and whooping, and
the guys are shouldering each other out of the way either side
of a head-high net which was already waiting as we wandered
down the sand.

'Definitely not,' Kip laughs. 'Unlike Jess, I'll be taking the
opposition down in business, not on the beach.'

Great. Just what I didn't want to hear. For Poppy in the long
term. And for me getting stuck spending yet more time with Kip
this evening. I go for a bit of persuasion. 'It's a shame to miss
out on the – whoah ...' I stagger as Kip suddenly drags me
sideways, and a stocky guy making a wild lunge thumps down
full length onto the exact piece of sand I was standing on.

'C'mon, Water Lily.' He grabs my wrist and hauls me back up the beach. 'Unless you want to get well and truly squished here, this is when we run like hell to a safe distance.' Twenty yards up the sand, he throws out the tartan blanket that's under his arm, drops down onto it, then stares up at me expectantly. 'There's no point waiting for half time, you can sit down now.'

'Fine.' Even if he's comfortable cosying up, I'm not, so I kneel as close to the edge as I can. You know when your skirt is practically knee length standing up, then you sit on the floor, and find it's barely the length of a T-shirt? That's what I'm struggling with as I tug my hem as far down as it'll go – a pitiful amount – and tuck my legs sideways.

Ideally the rug would be twice the size, but at least Kip's keeping to his side. Knees bent, chin propped on his fist. Watching the game, rather than my legs. Other than his white cotton shirt pulling out of his chinos at the back, where he's stretching forward, he's looking remarkably neat for a Penryn. And at least we're out of the firing line of the volleyball game, which is getting louder and rougher by the minute.

He gathers a pile of pebbles, and throws them at a smooth rock, stone by stone. When they run out at last he turns to look at me. 'So with the weddings, I've noticed it's always the women taking the lead.' At least he's chosen a neutral subject there. And stopped the stone clicking which was starting to get annoying.

The handful of sand I grab is silky as it runs through my fingers. 'The guys do the asking, then often it tends to be the girls with the ideas and the imagination. Some of them know exactly what they want years before they meet the guy they end up marrying.'

'Really?' The fact Kip's eyes go wide show he's still got a lot to learn. 'So you've already worked out what you're doing then?' He sounds fascinated and appalled in equal amounts.

Who'd have thought we'd get here so fast, when I never intended to talk about it. Suddenly there's nowhere else to go. I clear my throat and take the plunge. 'Actually I've been there, got the T-shirt, and come out the other side.' I'd almost rather be playing volleyball. If I let myself get backed into this particular corner, it's only because it's the end of a very long day.

'What?' He's blinking and screwing up his face.

I shrug. 'I had my own big day ages ago. The marriage barely lasted a year.'

'Shit, what the hell happened there?' Kip shakes his head, and bangs his fist on his skull. 'Sorry, no, you don't have to answer that. I shouldn't have asked. It's none of my business.'

Do you ever find drinking champagne makes you a hundred times more likely to bare your soul? In the same way it makes you more bouncy. Like when the world takes on that amber tinge and feels all warm and sun bathed. Although that bit might be down to the glow in the sky where the sun's sliding down past the horizon.

I take a deep breath. 'We had a long distance relationship that always left us wanting more. But when we moved in with each other full time after the wedding, we found out there wasn't much we agreed on.' A fast forward view of our marriage. Thom was the one to come out and say it. Just like that. He'd made a mistake, I wasn't what he wanted. He was right, of course. But it was still devastating to face what a big mistake I'd made. And worse still when all our plans for the future fell away, and I was left with nothing.

Kip takes a deep breath. 'Awful. So it doesn't upset you working with brides?'

I scrunch up my face. 'It's fine with people I don't know.' That's true. I'm concentrating on the details, not the emotions. 'With close friends' weddings it's harder. We all remember mine, and how hopeful I was, and how it all came crashing down.' Although looking back, it's easy to see the cracks were there all along. I was too in love with the idea of my happy-ever-after to see them. What's more, I can't think why I'm sitting here, spilling all this to Kip, when I could have shut up.

He's staring at me with the fascination of a scientist examining a specimen. 'I'm so far away from it I can't begin to imagine what it must have felt like. Although for what it's worth, I'm sorry you went through it.'

Seeing how frank I've been, I figure I'm entitled to ask. 'So you've never been close to taking the plunge yourself then?' Although as soon as the words are out, I know how ridiculous they are. We're talking to a serial sleep-around Penryn here, after all. But at least I get to see him squirm at the thought.

He tugs his fingers through his hair as he pales. 'I've been far too busy for a serious commitment. More importantly, I'm entirely happy as I am.'

The last bit sounds like perfect sense to me. 'Good point. Since the divorce, I'm pretty much the same. On my own and loving every minute.' Sitting on the sand, agreeing with Kip? How unnerving is that?

He's still staring at me like his eyes are boring into my soul. 'So this explains why you ended up here doing a job you aren't trained for, living in a matchbox over the shop?'

I sigh. It's a typical view of a guy who lives in a house with twenty bedrooms. 'In a roundabout way. It's a bit more complicated than that.' There's no point sharing how much I love my attic, because he wouldn't have the first clue how to understand. I see his eyebrows rising expectantly. But dammit, I've spilled enough here. 'But actually, it's your turn now.'

'Right.' From the way he blinks I've caught him by surprise. And given what I've just shared, to even things up, I need to go in for the kill. 'So, how did you break your company?' Now it's out there, it sounds horribly bleak. I throw in a few metaphors to soften it. 'I mean, there are six in your family, so how come you were the only brother working on the ship that sank? And why the hell did they leave you to steer it in the first place, if you were going to run it onto the rocks?'

Kip's eyes widen as he hesitates. 'I take it you don't read the financial papers then?'

'Not unless I want to go to sleep.'

Kip sighs. 'In that case I'll give you the short version. All six of us tried the family business at one time or another, but my dad wasn't easy to work with. I was the only one who stayed.'

'You got on with your dad then?'

Kip pulls a face. 'I was less hot headed than the others, so I was better at dealing with his moods, and taking the flack. I understood how badly he coped without our mother, because I missed her too. Then after three generations of success, one bad decision brought the company down. We were finished in one failed deal. The others had trusted me to look after things, and I let them down, big time. That's why it's so good of them to give me another chance at The Manor.'

'Oh my.' So I'm not the only one here with a complicated back story.

'As soon as Quinn mentioned weddings at Rose Hill, the rest of them couldn't wait to come on board.'

'So they're all backing you with your brand-new business?' I'm starting to see why he's so keen to push the Vegas model as far as he can go.

He nods. 'It's my first time away from Penryn Trading. I'm very lucky they've got my back on this.' So he's got every reason to try and make this huge.

I bite my lip, and think of how comfortable I am with the work I do. And how like a jelly fish stranded on the sand he is, when it comes to all things bridal. 'It's a shame it's not an area you enjoy more.'

He wrinkles his nose. 'I have to work with what I've been given. But I've got our flowers too. That's the first project I've done without Penryn involvement.'

Mostly I try to blank out those flowers. Although to be realistic, they are in a Penryn garden, so they aren't completely outside the Penryn domain. 'I can't imagine being so tied in with family. Don't you ever ache to be free?' If I was a hundredth as beholden to my mother, my life would be hell.

The furrows in his brow deepen. 'Being tied to the family company is all I've ever known. And it was a great life, while it lasted. If I ever manage to make up for my epic fail, I can take the chance to move on then.'

The way he's talking that will be when he's run Rafe and Poppy out of business, grabbed every wedding ceremony in the south west for the Manor, and put in a manager.

'So what will you do then?' It may sound nosey. But it never struck me that Kip might have dreams. Or that I'd ever be interested in hearing them. I can only blame the champagne. And the volleyball.

Kip swallows hard, then there's a growl in his throat that turns out to be a laugh. 'Signing up to hear the Kip Penryn life plan? I didn't know you were planning on sticking around all night.'

What? 'Absolutely not. I'm heading off at the first opportunity.' Which neatly lets him off the interrogation hook. And will hopefully be a.s.a.p. As I'm scanning the sky, I see the spot of light, like a diamond in the smoky orange blue of the dusk. 'Hey, look, the first star. That means it'll be dark in no time, and the game will be over.'

As I lean backwards on my elbows, hoping for more evidence of nightfall, I let myself flop onto my back. As the sand beneath the rug moulds to my back I'm trying hard to wrench my gaze away from Kip's throat as he stares up at the sky too. When my eyeballs refuse to be unglued, the only alternative is to shut them. It's only for a second. Then because it's so comfy, I roll over onto my side, and cup my cheek in my hand. This shift dress wasn't meant for curling up in, but as the noise of the volleyball drifts further away, I haul the hem as far down as it'll go.

Kip's hand lands on my shoulder. 'Hey, Water Lily are you going to sleep? See, I did bore you with my business talk.'

Sleep? I give a long sigh. 'Definitely not.' I'm only closing my eyes for a moment, but the denial comes out as a mumble. I'm too tired to talk, but my eyes are open again, so I'm one hundred per cent awake. And I'm listening to the sound of the waves lapping up the shore.

The next time I open my eyes, if anything the sky is paler not darker. But the blanket I was lying on is tucked around me and as I put my hand onto my shoulder, I feel the silky lining, and the structure of a jacket.

'Kip, where are the stars?' I know he's here, because I've got a view of his rolled up chinos, and his deck shoes next to his bare feet. What I'm less happy about is the sudden cloud cover. A view of the Milky Way against a blue velvet sky was the one compensation for having to stay here until way past bed time.

He responds with a yawn. 'Sorry, Water Lily, the stars have been and gone.' He has to be joking.

As I lift my head the crick in my neck is killing me. 'So the volleyball's finished?' That's my first concern.

He pulls out his phone, and glances at it. 'Approximately four hours ago. Jess and Uncle Bart went on to town. I managed to bore you to sleep, but I promised we'd join them as soon as you woke up.' He lets out a low laugh. 'Unless you'd rather have an early morning swim?'

Worse and worse. 'Hell no.' Waking up on a beach with a Penryn? Talk about sleeping with the enemy. Even if I'm the only one who ever knows about this, I'll never live it down. I sniff, and grab my head. 'How's my hair?' As I drag my fingers through the tangles, it's feeling horribly wavy.

He rubs his chin and frowns slightly. 'I reckon it's about as good as you'd expect after half a night asleep on the beach in a force four gale.'

'Damn, is it all curly?'

He's biting back his smile. 'I didn't say that.'

'Shit.' He doesn't have to. I can already feel it's exploded from smooth and glossy, into totally wild. I bundle it up in a twist on top of my head as best I can.

'I reckon windswept and sand blasted suits you.'

One thing is clear. 'I can't go to Jaggers to meet Jess looking a mess like this.'

That brings out a full-blown laugh. 'It's four a.m. Aren't we going home?'

I laugh at that idea. 'Jess will party until the morning. But what's she doing with Bart? Wasn't she hell bent on avoiding him?'

Considering he's intent on rushing off, Kip still hasn't got up yet. 'They're on a challenge. Jess is going to drink Bart under the table apparently.' He lets out a weary sigh.

'Heaven help us there then.' No-one takes Jess on and has any brain cells left to remember it with.

Kip shrugs. 'You know he flew in specially?'

There has to be something I'm missing here. 'Half way round the world to drink three-for-two *Sex on the beach* cocktails and end up rat arsed under a purple plastic chair?' I sniff. 'Maybe we can skip Jaggers?' Whatever's going on, we're hours too late to join in.

Kip finally sticks his feet into his shoes, springs to his feet, and offers me his hand. 'I can work with that.'

I put his jacket into his hand, and scramble to my feet on my own. As I pull the blanket around me, I stifle a yawn. 'In that case, next stop is Brides by the Sea, Kipling.'

I'm not sure if it's the wine drinking, my stiff neck, the unscheduled soul-baring we might accidentally have done, or the sheer delayed shock-horror at waking up next to Kip. But by the time we've bounced back into town in Kip's beaten up Landy, my brain's throbbing and my head feels fit to explode. And just when the day – or rather the night – can't get any more strange, we see a figure weaving up the mews. A sudden flash of silver on the feet is the giveaway.

'Oh my giddy aunt, it's Jess.' No doubt on her way home, to her house a few doors along the mews from the shop.

Kip slams the Landy to a halt, and slides back the window. 'Morning Jess, what happened to Uncle Bart?'

Jess rolls her eyes. 'He lost, of course. Don't worry, I poured him into a taxi. Who'd have thought he'd be such a light-weight?'

Which explains Jess's early homecoming.

I fling open the Landy door, and see it's a million miles to the ground. No wonder the Landy motto is 'one life, live it.' I take mine in my hands, and hurl myself all the way down onto the cobbles. 'See you later, Jess,' I say, as I pick myself up. No point saying 'in the morning' when it already is.

'Ditto.' Kip rakes his fingers through his hair, and despite his sunken cheeks and exhausted pallor, as he slams off up the mews, his face breaks into a grin.

I'm left open mouthed, remembering all the stuff I should have thanked him for and haven't. I really hate being this much in debt to a Penryn.

Chapter 32

Wednesday, 28th June
In the kitchen at Brides by the Sea: The morning after the
night before

'If I'd had more sleep last night, it wouldn't have been such a shock to wake up to.'

Poppy and I are in the tiny attic kitchen, and she's whizzing around, whipping up an instant emergency rescue to the shock I just had when I woke this morning after three hours' sleep, and looked at my phone. Only this is a lot more than a hangover cure. This is full-blown after-shock resuscitation.

'Having to deal with Nicole's early appointment can't have helped either.' Poppy frowns as she pulls a bowl down from the shelf, and the icing sugar rises in a cloud as it falls through the sieve. 'Leave this to me. There are plain cupcakes at the ready. I prescribe something very pink and very sweet to go on top.'

She adds soft butter, a couple of drops of colouring, dribbles in the strawberry puree she just mashed, and gets to work with her hand mixer. A few minutes later she's scooping

272

butter cream into her piping bag. I watch mesmerised, sucking back the drool as extra-pink buttercream curls out to land on top of cupcakes in red spotty cases.

Then she slices a strawberry into four, and pops the pieces on top. 'Just when it feels like Facebook can read our minds, they stuff up massively.' Poppy's tirade against Facebook is heartfelt and personal. That was how she found out her ex had cheated on her at a stag party the week after he'd proposed to her. 'But this has to be effing Facebook blunder of the year.'

'I'm fine with people giving their Chihuahuas their own Facebook identities. But unborn children?' Flicking onto my phone first thing and finding Facebook suggesting I might like to be Facebook friends with Thom's pre-natal child's ultra sound picture almost made me swallow my tongue. Apparently, we have three mutual friends. Lucky for me I was saved from choking entirely by my mouth being drier than the Sahara. 'Seeing my ex and his new wife in X ray, waving baby scan pictures isn't the best start to a Wednesday.'

Poppy squeezes me into a hug, then hands me a cupcake. I peel back the paper, and sink my teeth into the sponge. A second later I'm transported to my happy place as the strawberry icing melts onto my tongue. 'Blissful,' I mumble, and pop in a couple of strawberry slices too.

There's a clatter of footsteps on the stairs, and a moment later Jess bursts in. 'Not that bloody Face-place again? Don't worry, Lily, you'll soon feel better when you've had some fizz.' As she pats me on the shoulder, squeezes down the side of the table, and pulls up a stool, she's waving a bottle.

Poppy hands me another cupcake, and grabs the Prosecco. 'Great, I'll pop that in the fridge for later.'

As I take a huge bite of my next cupcake, I'm so glad this happened when I was here with the kind of friends who swoop in to help. Who understand the problems without long explanations. Who get that my heart feels like it's been wrenched out of my chest and trampled on, even though it shouldn't. As I look out of the tiny porthole window at the sun glistening on the water out in the bay, for a second it's like this is where I belong. Which probably means I caught myself on a vulnerable day, given how badly I want to move on.

'I'm supposed to be over Thom, I am over Thom.' I'm wailing through the crumbs. 'But some ridiculous part of me still minds that's not me having a twelve-week scan. What the jeez is that about?'

There's a low voice on the landing, and a knock on the open door. 'Lily? Sorry, I didn't mean to interrupt ...'

Damn. Kip crashing into the teensy kitchen at any time would be unthinkable. Given Poppy's here it's worse still. But catching me in mid rant about Thom's baby makes me want to expire on the spot.

I make my smile extra-large. 'Perfect timing, Kip, as always. Welcome to the matchbox.' If he heard my tirade, there's nothing I can do, other than pretend he didn't. Despite his eyes locking onto the cupcake plate, there's no way I'm about to offer Poppy's baking to the guy who's sworn to take her and Rafe down. However desperate I am to take his mind off my expectant ex. 'What the hell are you doing up here when you could be home playing swing ball?'

He pulls his hand out from behind his back. 'Your bag? You left it in the Landy last night.'

How embarrassing is that? 'Great. Thanks for bringing it back.' I take my black clutch from him. I'm mortified that I hadn't even noticed yet, given my phone was in my pocket. I'm aware I should be sounding more grateful. 'And thanks for yesterday's lift.' With any luck that will flag it as being before midnight, for Poppy's benefit.

He laughs. 'You're welcome. Although dawn drop offs are more Bart's thing than mine.'

As she dives in, and snatches her opportunity with both hands, there's a gleam in Jess's eye. 'And how *is* Uncle Bart this morning?' Despite Bart rubbing her up like sandpaper on sunburn, judging by her purr, she's raring for a re-match.

Kip pulls a face. 'Surprisingly bouncy, all things considered. I just dropped him at the airport.'

Jess lets out a strangled moan. 'He's flying out so soon?' To say she looks crestfallen is an understatement.

Kip's shrug is apologetic. 'You know Bart. He's perpetually on his way to somewhere else.'

If Jess is opening and closing her mouth without sound, it's probably because she's too proud to chase this one.

I jump in to ask the question for her. 'So when's he expected back?' Let's face it, someone has to bring these Penryns to account.

Kip's forehead wrinkles. 'Actually he isn't.' Then his frown eases. 'But these days he's on a plane for any excuse. No doubt he'll want to muscle in when we do the night photos by the lake.'

Jess picks him straight up. 'We'll get onto that immediately then. Won't we, Lily?' Her nostrils only flare and quiver like this when she's nailing her most important deals.

'Is later today okay to measure up and make notes, Kip?' I'd hoped to put it off until next week, but given Jess's forward thrust, that's more than my life's worth. 'Thanks again for returning my bag. I'll see you at the Manor later then.'

That's meant to be his signal to leave, but he doesn't move, because his gaze is still locked on the plate on the table. I cough. How else can I show him the door?

Poppy's lips are twitching. 'Would you like some cupcakes, Kip? I could do you a takeaway box. I promise not to poison them.'

Kip brightens visibly, and he does one of those stomach wrenching swallows. 'Great. Thanks.' He tugs his fingers through his hair. 'Oh, and there's a marigold out too.'

Ten out of ten to Poppy for the takeaway suggestion. Moments afterwards, he's trotting down the stairs with his boxful of goodies, and I'm turning on Poppy.

'Apart from getting rid of him, what exactly are you playing at, gifting the opposition cupcakes?'

She wrinkles her nose. 'He was practically drooling on the floor.' Then she lets out a long sigh. 'Okay, they were mostly for him bringing my bestie home safely at six in the morning.'

I'm straight onto her for that one. 'Six? It was four at the latest.'

'So he can't be all bad.' She sends me a super-significant nod, and grins. 'I know he's going all out to wreck our busi-ness. But if we fight head to head he'll win every time, simply because of what's there at the Manor. If Rafe and I are going to have any chance at all, we need a less direct approach.'

'If we're coming at this by stealth, cupcakes were a great start, Pops.' I say, aware I've made a complete U-turn. 'Yay, I'll see what else I can come up with.' Given we've decided on the non-fighting route, me punching her on the fist probably isn't that appropriate. For now I'm trying to forget last night's insight into why Kip is so driven. This morning for the first time I know so many more reasons he might be impossible to beat.

Jess is only seconds behind. 'Me too. It'll give me immense pleasure putting that jumped-up globe-trotting pretender in his place. Leave it with me.' It doesn't take a mind reader to know she's talking about Uncle Bart. And somehow Jess's intervention feels a lot more personal than just wedding wars. But we'll see.

My immediate idea is to feed Kip so many cupcakes he can't leave the office because he won't fit through the door. Which may not be guaranteed to work, but whatever. At least we've got a new strategy. With luck, and a tonne of women's wiles, we might just pull this off. Despite my niggling doubts, Daisy Hill Farm Weddings may yet come out on top.

Chapter 33

Monday, 10th July

At Rose Hill Manor: Shooting in the dark

It turns out that when Kip says illumination, he's not just thinking big. He's thinking enormous. Which is every bit in line with what's at stake here for him. Jess's eyes almost pop out of her head when she sees how much the first warehouse order comes to, and we've barely begun. Luckily he calls in some guys from the estate, who are so obliging they could almost be Chas's firemen friends. They run around banging in poles, climb up and down ladders fixing cables and wires, and hump around lanterns and jars. Not to mention candles by the ton.

With Kip's own personal surrogate emergency service on the job, progress is fast. As soon as I wave my arms, the job in my head is done. I explain about a meandering path down to the lake, with candle jars on sticks, and white bunting strung between, and next thing I know, it's there. Ditto tall flat faced glass lanterns, up lighters for the box trees, jam jars bobbing on strings between branches in the bushes, and lanterns running along the length of the jetty, to make the most of night time reflections in the lake.

I'm pretty determined Kip's not going to have anything like the illuminated tree at the farm. But in the end, I cave and do him his own version – believe me, the guy could whine for England. And after days of rushing around, a forecast for fine weather coincides with Jules the photographer having a free evening, so Kip decides we're finally ready for some night photos.

'Okay, guys, we'll start as soon as the light begins to fade.' Jules is already jumping around with his cameras and his tripods. As I arrive, and wander out into the gardens, the candles have already been lit, and he sends me a wave. 'We'll keep moving so we get every view from dusk to darkness.'

For once it's a relief to arrive at the Manor and not hear Kip's death metal blaring out across the lake. As Kip jogs over I can't help smiling because he's changed out of his jeans and saggy T-shirt, into a crisp white shirt and very formal suit trousers.

'So what do we do now?' I ask, as he hands me a bottle of chilled vanilla coke.

He takes a swig of his own, and takes time to swallow. 'We gasp at all the amazing lanterns as it gets dark. Jules and I worked out the best views. And once they're done ...'

As he pauses again, I can't help finishing his sentence. 'We get to go home?' It's a no brainer. I haven't quite caught up after my practically sleepless night on the beach yet. My eyes are so tired, they're scratching like they're full of sand.

He waggles his bottle at me. 'Wrong answer, Water Lily. As

if.' He seems to find that funny. 'No, Bart's flown in, and we're going to do some extra special shots.'

It seems like no time since Bart was 'flying out'. Although I've felt every second, because Jess has been uncharacteristically tetchy ever since. 'Where's he coming in from?' It's hard to keep track.

'St Kitts this time.' Kip shakes his head. 'Commuting to the Caribbean's not ideal. But he wanted to be here when we lit up the island.'

'Why put lights out there?' I may have asked this before. Stating the obvious, but it's in the middle of the lake. And it's not as if guests visit it.

'The jetty's just like the one on the shore here, but the angle's much more photogenic.' Kip gives a guilty frown. 'When I mentioned it earlier you seemed reluctant to go. So I improvised. This way you only have to go there once.'

You can hardly blame me for being island-averse. My last visit was when I was eighteen and got stuck there with Quinn. I flick out my phone to take my mind off that, and find Immie on Instagram, cosying up to a Rottweiler. When I read the caption, I let out an accidental whoop.

'And?' Sometimes Kip's so nosey.

My fault for screaming I suppose. Flashing my screen his way will be the fastest way to close him down. 'Immie's auditioning ring bearers. Slightly on the premature side, given she still hasn't got rings. Or a dress come to that. So far we've had Henrietta the hen from the farm office, Snowball the pony, one of Rafe's baby calves, Jet the dog, and the miniature Daxi from the Goose and Duck.' With so many cute animal pictures, her follower numbers just made an exponential leap. And a great move, given Nicole's seriously lagging. And this time Nicole can't retaliate on the cuteness front, because she's definitely not a pet person. I doubt she'd be seen within a mile of a calf, let alone kiss its nose.

Kip pulls his own phone out of his pocket. Luckily it's wafer thin, given his smart trousers aren't exactly a loose fit. 'Some for you here, Water Lily. From the garden. The marigolds and the cornflowers have come into bloom, and the zinnias are electric.'

'You took photos of the flowers?' I scrunch up my nose, not quite understanding why. He's more like a proud dad showing off his kids, than a disinterested house owner who shoved his garden onto a stranger. It's true they're coming out by the hour. When I peeped into there on my way here I could hardly believe how many more flowers there were than yesterday.

His lips twitch. 'They're perfect for the Rose Hill Manor Weddings blog.' So Mr Do-it-all's got one of those too. And that explains the picture-fest.

'Wow, you've got every aspect covered now.' No doubt he whipped it into shape in the spare seconds between lantern lighting and rowing personnel across to stage-set his fake jetty shots.

Despite his smug smile, he shrugs. 'If you're doing a job there's no point stopping half way.' Although that's really not in the usual Penryn spirit of exerting the least effort possible, and trading off the backs of other people. 'I had to get the outside up and running in time for tonight's visit from the award assessors.'

My jaw drops so far, my chin's practically grading the gravel on the path. Then when Jules comes sweeping past, clicking his camera, I pick it up quickly. No way can I risk getting snapped with saggy jowls. Especially if the assessors are on their way. And crap to how that came out of nowhere, too.

Kip carries on seamlessly. 'Bart's meeting them in town first for a spot of hospitality, and bringing them out after dinner.' He can't hide how triumphant his grin is. 'Charm offensives are his speciality.' Although isn't wining and dining them dangerously close to bribery? Just saying.

I'm choking into my tissue with the shock. Jess, for one, would hardly agree Bart is big on the charm part. 'So what am *I* here for?' It suddenly strikes me that his casual 'Why not drop by and see the candles alight while you're checking the garden?' invitation is nothing of the kind. This is Team Penryn precision planning.

Kip looks at me. 'As our in-house stylist, you're here to add gravitas to our case with the assessors. Obviously.'

What a load of bull. 'Wonderful choice of weighty intellect there, Kip.' I try to keep my eyes from hitting the sky. With my five GCSE's and a BTech, I barely know what the word means. I can't decide if it's good they're clutching at straws, or bad they're pulling every trick in the book.

The way Kip's straight on my case, he might be a mind reader. 'Jess demanded a huge fee for you to show up this evening. So I'd think twice before you get into that little pink car of yours and Gucci off up the road.'

Dammit. So much for a fast getaway. 'Fine.' I grin through

gritted teeth. 'I'll bite my tongue and visualise the deposit for my dream flat instead.'

Now it's Kip's turn to look disgusted. He's still shaking his head when we see headlights coming in the distance, behind the wall to the lane. Before we know it, there are voices coming through the house. From the snatches of conversation, Uncle Bart's in full flow, explaining the inside tour's for another day. As they wander out the strings of lights above are being pulled into arcs by the evening breeze. And there's another familiar voice.

'Jess, you're here too?' As she wafts into view I take in the floatiest silk shirt I've ever seen her in. So this has to be some important operation.

Bart beams. 'All our big guns are with us this evening, Lily. Rose Hill Manor's wedding team is out in force.'

I'm waiting for Jess to leap in, put him right, strangle him, and maybe push him in the lake while she's at it. But instead she lets out a purr that's big enough to have come from a tiger.

'Absolutely. Brides by the Sea couldn't be happier to be on board.' She leans over and flicks an invisible speck off Bart's collarless cheesecloth shirt. 'Is it time for the boats?' Someone should tell her. The word hypocrite springs to mind. Or turn-coat. Last time they talked nautically, she called him Captain Pugwash. This time she's eyeing him like he's Johnny Depp on the dessert menu. And before you pull me up on that, I'm not overstating the drool.

It's almost dark as we make our way down to the shore. But the loops of white bunting flapping in the breeze, and

283

the hanging candles, guide us down the field towards the jetty, where the reflections of the lanterns are shining in the glossy black water of the lake.

'Lovely.' The two assessors are murmuring as we walk. 'Completely spectacular.'

When we get there, there are three boats waiting, complete with an oarsman for Jules and the assessors. Which leaves Bart to row Jess, and me with Kip. If I didn't know how far it was from bitter experience, I'd probably opt to swim.

I have to say rowing out to the island at Rose Hill Manor wasn't what I'd planned on doing again ever. Especially not with a damned Penryn brother. But at least the inkiness of the night stops the sense of déjà vu as I scramble down, and wobble onto the plank seat. And Kip's boat handling skills are as good as you'd expect for a guy who spent every summer on the water here as a kid.

We're half way across, rowing towards the jetty lights with long smooth strokes, when the soft splash of the oars stops, and I sense Kip sitting up in the shadows opposite me.

'Is the cabin still on the island then?' The silence seems the ideal time to drop in my question. Not that I'd have brought it up if we weren't on our way. But now we are, it's better to 'fess up in advance that I've been here before, rather than in front of an audience. It was a true Swallows and Amazon's retreat back then. A picturesque wooden building, and a veranda with a view across the water. If I hadn't been trapped there, I might have wanted to stay forever.

'It's still the same, only a bit more faded.' He hesitates. 'You came out here with Quinn, didn't you? Getting stranded on the island was that bad boy's signature chat up tactic. You were the only one of his captives to swim away, though.' He's so matter of fact, talking as if it were ten days ago, not ten years or more.

'You remember?' Damn. And all this time I thought I'd got away with anonymity.

His voice is strangely soft in the darkness. 'As if I'd forget. I was the one who hauled you out when you nearly drowned. Although you were probably too far gone to notice.'

'I wasn't *that* bad.' It's a token protest. In the seconds before those strong hands wrenched me onto the beach, I felt like I'd swallowed so much of the lake, I wasn't going to make it back to shore. 'With six of you, I never knew who actually came in for me. Apart from knowing for sure it wasn't Quinn.' But maybe if Kip was the brother who rescued me, that explains why he seemed so horribly familiar when he pulled me out of the pond at the Sams' wedding party. Thankfully it's dark enough to hide that I'm withering with embarrassment at the other end of the boat.

'Poor Quinn.' Kip blows out a long breath. 'Not that I'm excusing him, but losing our mum as teenagers hit us all hard. Short term seductions were Quinn's way of dealing with the pain.'

I can't help raising my eyes to the stars. 'That's a rich person's euphemism if ever I heard one.' Since when was a one night stand called that? If I'm sounding unsympathetic, it's only because I landed on the receiving end.

Kip sighs again. 'Okay, I admit Quinn would try to sleep with every hot girl he met. He still does. But when you're hurt at that kind of impressionable age, the grief doesn't go away.'

'So you're telling me this is why you're all serial shaggers?' My voice soaring in indignation is on behalf of every woman they've messed around, not just me.

Kip leaps straight in to contradict me. 'Not at all. Our mum was knocked down and killed outright walking my younger brother to school. The shock was why we were all crazy in our different ways.' The low laugh from the other end of the boat has a bitter note. 'I never want pain like that again. But my own way of coping is to make damned sure I never let anyone close. And I'm completely honest about that.'

So maybe it isn't fair to take it out on Kip, especially when he's explained so openly. As for the pangs of sympathy that are twisting my stomach, if I don't close those down as fast as I can he'll only exploit them.

'Thanks for telling me. I'm pleased you've found a less destructive way of coping than Quinn did. And I'm sorry about your mum. When I lost my dad it felt like my heart had been ripped out of my chest. All I wanted to do was howl.' Damn. I've no idea why that slipped out.

'You too? Shit, I'm sorry, I had no idea.' His voice in the darkness is soft and unexpectedly comforting.

'He was struck by lightning up on the golf course. He was up there after he got the news I'd split with Thom. Which makes it my fault. If he hadn't been so upset, he'd have been at home.' If I'm over-sharing, I can't help it. It's a strange place to let this out for the first time.

Kip's sigh is loud enough to travel the length of the boat. 'You can't blame yourself, Water Lily. They were accidents.'

My voice is small and scratchy. 'If I hadn't stuffed up my marriage, I'd still have my dad.'

He sighs again. 'You have to let the bad stuff go. You can't live your life holding on to regrets. That ache inside never goes away though, does it?'

'Nope.' I shake my head, swallowing the sour saliva out of my mouth.

As Kip goes on, his voice has lightened. 'Although on the up side, if your mum hadn't been getting married to David, you wouldn't have forced me to get my act together here. I'd never have got as far as bringing award assessors out to an illuminated island. Or be in a boat in the dark with you, come to that.' His tone is weirdly wistful.

'I'd kind of hoped everyone had forgotten about me being on the island years ago.' Hopefully this will take us back to where we began.

'Why else did you think you got your nickname?' Kip picks up the oars, and the boat begins to slide through the water again.

'Maybe because of the pond weed at the Goose and Duck?' That was what I'd pinned my hopes on up to now. And thankfully it's a long way away from the subject of lost parents.

He laughs. 'Pulling you out of the water's becoming a habit, Water Lily.'

'You do realise in that case I may have to call you Cake-face, Kipling.' Very fitting too, given his tongue was on the floor when he saw Poppy's baking the other day.

He's straight back at me. 'Try that too often, you might find yourself back in the lake again.'

As we ease towards the glowing lanterns on the jetty, I catch sight of the veranda beyond, lit up with a hundred swinging jars and tea lights. For some reason, completely not to do with Kip, I'm imagining a bride – definitely not me, okay? – being rowed across the lake by her new husband. 'Wouldn't this make the most amazing wedding night hideaway?' Despite the dodgy memories, there's something awesome about crossing the water at night. And the yellow flames swaying in the darkness are beyond magical.

Kip laughs. 'Damn. You have all the best ideas – which is obviously why we pay you so much.'

By the time we disembark, and I've checked the boat's properly tied up, the others are already up by the cabin, getting stuck into the fizz. And Kip opting for proper champagne instead of plain old Prosecco is another sign of how seriously they're taking this particular visit from the assessors.

Jules puts down his glass of Bolly and picks up his camera again. 'Okay, raise your glasses everyone, we'll have a few relaxed shots of the candlelight party mood by the cabin.'

Although I'm not that happy about being used as a photo opportunity, given I'm apparently being paid, I grab an empty glass and wave it to show willing.

Jules is staring at Jess. 'Time for you to work your magic, sweetie? Then we'll move on to our iconic jetty shots.'

I watch as Jess whips a cloud of billowing fabric out of her bag. 'What are you doing?'

She shushes me. 'One second, I'm about to make you into a night-time bride.' A few deft twists, and she cinches the fabric around the waist of my T-shirt dress. 'We need something bigger than a normal wedding dress to show up here.

'Me? As a bride?' It comes out as a squawk. What's more, apparently, it's a rhetorical question, as I'm suddenly the one with yards of white chiffon flapping round my legs.

She's tugging at my pony tail. 'Quick, let down your hair, and you're done.' Her finger lands on my lips as she talks under her breath. 'They're being generous enough to make it worth your while jumping in the lake, although I doubt they'll ask you to do that. They only want a couple of shots, so think of your savings balance and play along.'

I'm so indignant, I can't help protest. 'But what if I don't want …?' My personal space is filled with the heady scent of body spray, as Jules swoops in.

He's got his best 'bride calming' voice on. 'We simply need figures, sweetie. Shadows in the darkness. The merest hint of a bride and groom to give scale.'

How had I missed that part? 'There's a groom?' It's a shriek, as my stomach plummets. Of course there's a damned groom. Why else would Kip be rowing a boat in pin stripe trousers?

The groom in question has already made his way down to the water's edge, where he's idly kicking the stones, gazing out at the reflections. Hands in his pockets, white sleeves rolled up to his elbows. As I catch a glimpse of the shadows on his face, the pit of my stomach squishes. For a second he looks so overwhelmingly alone, I have this inexplicable urge to wrap my arms around him. Pull him into a hug, and never let go. It might only last a nano second, but it leaves me open mouthed with horror. Then he spins around, and thankfully his snarky smile blasts it to wherever it came from. But I can't forget it almost came too late. I'd have been way stronger without him sharing his back story on the way over.

A second later, Kip's there, taking my hand, leading me towards the jetty, spinning me to face him as Jules directs us. And even though the air was warm five minutes ago, my arms are pebbling with goosebumps.

'Okay, shake out your hair, Lily, chin up.'

Jess is out on the jetty with us, tweaking, and tutting. Stepping back between poses. As for my outfit, it feels like the times I used to dress up in net curtains in the garden with Poppy when we were kids. Which neatly side steps any agonising comparisons with my own real thing. Although I do allow myself a teensy bit of fantasy to replace the awful Kip with someone more suitable. Anyone else will do. But when I try a mental photoshop to superimpose Fred's easy smile on Kip's head, for some reason I can't get it to stick.

Instead I try another tactic, ignore that my nose is on a level with Kip's neck, and concentrate on the way the collar-bones at the base of his throat are shining in the moonlight. Also not a great idea, as I end up with another seismic shiver. As for me personally, this island is a disaster every time I set foot on it, I should have known better than to come. What's the good of doing a double knot to stop the boat escaping, then ending up as a bridal picture?

'I hope you know I'll get you back for this, Kip.' I'm hissing at him as he drags me along the jetty.

He seems to find it funny. 'I'll look forward to that.'

Jules is still bouncing around us. 'Okay, foreheads together for one last shot.'

I'm not letting up on my grumbling. 'However much the pay cheque is, some things are not worth the money.' Our faces are so close Kip's heat is radiating onto my cheek, and I'm breathing in the scent of his skin.

'Okay, relax. It's a wrap.'

I sag with relief, and as I wobble Kip grabs me. For a dizzy second the world stands still, and I could swear he's going to come in and slide his lips over mine. As I hold my breath, my mouth waters. It has to be the same total disgust reflex you get when you eat sour worms.

Then he lets me go, turns me away from him, and puts his hands on my shoulders. 'No falling off the jetty, Water Lily. You're definitely not contracted for sub-aqua shots.'

And damn that I feel short changed as he marches me all the way back to land.

As we wander back to join the others, Kip homes straight in on the assessors. 'Our other special news is that in addition to our sumptuous bridal suite we'll also be offering the extra option of island hideaway wedding nights in the cabin. In summer, mostly. But with log fires it would work in winter too.' Talk about making it up as he goes along.

Bart's so taken aback, his eyebrows shoot up faster than a moon rocket. 'Well that's a brain wave ... on our part. It'll make us totally unique in the area, if not the country.' From the speed he picks it up and runs with it, the guy is a true pro.

'Absolutely. Fantastic.' The assessors are exchanging significant glances. 'That takes a winning venue into a different league entirely.'

Damn, damn, damn. Damn. If I wasn't in the middle of

being unwrapped by Jess, I would literally kick myself. All my fault again. Anyone would think I was trying to sabotage Rafe and Poppy, not going all out to save them.

I'm grinding my teeth, because I'm *so* furious. With myself for being so thoughtless. And with Kip for being such a flagrant bloody opportunist. Turning my throwaway comment into a main attraction in five seconds flat takes gall. 'Well, much as I hate to break up the party, now you've got all your iconic images, I'd like a lift back to my life please. Before anyone hijacks any more of my random thoughts and turns them into award winning features. If that's okay with you, Kip?'

Bart smooths in. 'Great, our work's all done here. Thanks for a wonderful evening. Everyone back to the boats then?'

There's a rush for the jetty, and it's only when we get there that I look back, and see Bart and Jess aren't with us. They're still up on the veranda. What's worse, he's holding out a chair for Jess, and she's about to sit down on it.

I storm back up the beach. 'Aren't you two coming?'

Bart wrinkles his face. 'Jess and I have a couple of old scores to settle. And there's champagne to finish too. We'll be along as soon as we're done.'

I stare at Jess. This woman needs a reality check, and fast. 'You know there's a long history of Penryns getting stuck on this island with women?'

Jess is biting back her smile. 'Don't worry, Lily, I can look after myself. I eat wimps like Bart for breakfast on a daily basis. You know that.' The glare she turns on Bart is fierce enough to roast him.

Bart scowls. 'You don't say. Along with your old-lady constipation Bran Buds, no doubt.'

And then a second later they both erupt into laughter. Which is completely inexplicable.

'Great.' I sniff. 'Pleased to hear it. Just don't be surprised to find the boat gone when you get back to the jetty, okay?'

The high pitched squealing that follows me down to the water reminds me of … For a second my heart stops in mid beat. Because, despite all of Jess and Bart's snarling, the giggling I can hear now is just like David and my mum. Which can't be right at all. And is probably only down to Bart's extreme jet lag. Maybe the cabin pressure messed with his vocal chords. And Jess quaffing Bolly at the speed of light. But when I scramble into the boat with Kip, and look back at the jetty as he rows away, I have the strangest feeling that their boat is already drifting out into the darkness.

Chapter 34

Monday, 10th July
At Rose Hill Manor: Candle power and happy dances

Back on the shore at the Manor, we've wandered back up the lantern lit path to the house, watched Jules head off into the darkness, and said some suitably grovelling 'goodbyes' to the assessors. They'll be back again for a more thorough daytime inspection, although the mind boggles at what sweeteners slash corruption slash enticements Bart will dream up for that one. And then they'll be negotiating a drop-in at a real live wedding too. They actually turned out to be nice, even if I could have done with them being less damned impressed by the Manor.

As we move towards the house, I'm longing to leave. At least now they're gone, I can stop what actually amounts to paid fawning, and get back into character. As myself. So watch out Kip.

'I'd better be getting off. If that's okay?' At the last minute, I remember the clock might still be running.

'Before you go, I've got something to show you.'

Ooops, still working after all then. 'Great.' Why does this not surprise me? When did Kip not want his pound of flesh? 'I'll tell my eyelid props they need to hang on in there for another half hour then.'

'You remember our first wedding? With Vee?' He pushes his way into the half light of the ballroom. 'I spent some of the tip on a vinyl player upgrade.' Only a guy would find this urgent, when it's almost midnight.

I can't help but grin. 'A typically laddish purchase.' And waaaaaaaahhhh to my instant stab of disappointment. I mean, get real. Who'd have wanted to go on a mini break with Kip, even if he had suggested it? Certainly not me.

He frowns as he eases open the sets of double doors facing onto the terrace. 'You can't underestimate the customer appreciation a top flight turntable will bring. Attention to detail, and all that, hey?' That could have been a half wink, but it was more of a face scrunch. 'Would you like a listen?' He's taking that as a given, because the lights on the deck flick on.

It's half past eleven at night. I'm knackered. I'd rather jump in a vat of boiling oil. 'Okay, but let's make it short.'

'One track.' He's already sliding a record out of its sleeve, and onto the deck. 'I thought we could make the most of the warm evening and have a dance outside.'

As soon as I've picked my jaw up off the floor, I let out a squawk. 'A dance?' I'm playing for time, wondering why the hell I didn't dismiss it out of hand. Why a tiny part of me is wondering how it would feel to have those tanned hands spinning me round. 'Totally not.' Thank Wednesday my sensible-woman-self jumped in and took control there.

His brows knit. 'The two of us are here, and we've got a candlelit terrace all to ourselves. It's a shame not to make the most of the new deck.' Of course. That's what it's about. He stops as he adjusts the stylus arm. 'Every guy who went to boarding school can dance. It's the main thing they teach you. Don't worry, I'll show you how.'

I bite back my amusement. 'And every girl who grew up in Rose Hill went to Jilly's dancing classes in the village hall from being able to walk until we were teenagers. So there'll be no problems on the dance moves.' We learned everything from break dancing to the Viennese Waltz. 'Sorry, it's still a "no" from me. I'll stick to listening.' As I head back outside, I'm expecting to have my eardrums blasted by some heavy metal band. But the opening bars of the track that come floating out are something way softer.

'*These Foolish Things?*' I'm only querying as he follows me out, because it's such an unlikely choice. Although it's maybe not without implication. Me being a fool? I'm with him on that. But I have to give it to him, it's a perfect choice for that dance we're not having.

'*Remind me of you* ... Girly enough?' He rakes his fingers through his hair. 'Seriously though, has it occurred to you, if you let go and enjoyed yourself more, you might get more out of life?'

I'm almost choking, because I can't believe what I'm hearing. 'And has it occurred to you to butt out?' As I stare up at him, I'm almost growling with rage.

He gives a sniff. 'When you open your eyes that wide, I can see they're brown, even in the dark. Although I knew that already.'

296

'So? Yours are brown too.' Well, grey-brown, anyway. And thank Tuesday for that. We're back to our usual thing. Trading insults. At least he can't say anything that derogatory about mine, if his are the same colour.

That's the thing about Kip. He never backs off. 'You know two brown eyed people will always have a brown eyed child.'

Crap. The last response I was ready for. Although it's an improvement on telling me how to run my life. Then the penny drops, and suddenly I know where he's coming from.

'In the kitchen the other day. You heard didn't you?' I haven't exactly had time to dwell on it, thanks to the size of Kip's ideas on candle power. But he has to be talking about my reaction to Thom having a baby.

'I'm sorry. I couldn't avoid it. An ex starting a family can't be the easiest.' He gives a shrug. 'I hate to think of you hurting.'

I sigh. 'When I found out, I felt like I'd been stabbed in the chest.' And who knows why I'm sharing this, with Kip of all people. Apart from him sympathising. 'But after the shock, deep down I know it shouldn't matter. It's a part of my life that's over. In a while I'll mind less.'

He's rubbing the stubble on his chin. 'On the beach the other night you claimed you were happy as you are, but I'm not so sure. If you were, you'd be more comfortable in your own skin.'

Excuse me? I agreed to one track, not psychoanalysis. 'Like you are, you mean?'

He misses the irony. 'Exactly.'

'You don't get any less arrogant, do you?' There's no point me stinting on the truth.

He ignores that, and carries on. 'But you can't deny you're hardly optimistic.'

I pull the corners of my mouth down. 'I've had stuff in my life.'

The wrinkles across his nose say he's not buying that. 'You aren't alone there. But it's easy to get stuck in a miserable mindset. Maybe you need to dance more. Be like the song. Let your heart find wings. Put some effort into finding your happy side again – and I don't just mean listening to Adele.'

Quoting song lyrics now? How corny can you get? 'Okay Mr Perfect, in future I promise I'll try to be more like you.'

From his frown that's not the reply he's looking for. 'But all this talk about moving – you're great at your job, even though I might have implied you wouldn't be. If you'd only settle and give it a chance, your career might be the missing piece that makes you happy.' Now he's making me sound like a jigsaw.

'That's the thing. The job might be working out, but it's in a place where everyone knows I failed.' It all goes back to Thom. Or to me. When I got engaged, I was so damned excited. You can't blame some people for being pleased I fell flat on my face. 'I'll have a better chance of reconnecting with this mythical happy person you keep going on about once I move away again.'

As he considers that, the light catches the indentations in his cheeks. 'Moving on won't cure your sense of failure. That needs to come from inside. You need to learn to believe in what you *can* do, not what you can't.'

I've heard that before. 'And you need to put on weight. You're getting gaunter by the day.' Get rid of those unnerving hollows in his cheeks.

He's right back at me. 'Ditto. Didn't you used to have curves?'

There's a shout from the shadows. 'Okay, hold it there. Great shot, guys.'

'Jules?' Crap. I thought he'd gone home. Damn lucky he didn't catch us dancing.

He skips up out of the shadows. 'Just re-working, now it's completely dark.'

So all Kip's concerned conversation about my happiness suddenly makes sense. It was simply diversion tactics, until Jules got all the shots he needed, complete with convincing 'figures' on the terrace.

I turn to Kip. 'Well thanks for manipulating me into yet another photo opportunity I didn't agree to.'

He opens his mouth to protest, but there's really no point.

There's another thing I need to tackle him on before I go. 'And for the record, I saw you'd untied Jess and Bart's boat earlier.'

Kip's eyes narrow. 'Jules is being spontaneous. Probably not a concept you're familiar with.' However vulnerable he sounded before, he's back to being mocking now. 'As for letting the boat go, that's ridiculous. Why would I do that?'

It's as inexplicable to me as it is to him. 'How the hell do I know? Because you're genetically programmed to do it? Because Bart asked you to?' To be honest, I expected an admission, not a flat denial. I'm distantly aware that the track is over. 'Am I done here?'

He flinches as the questions fly at him. 'Absolutely. You're free to go.'

I march off the terrace, and I'm still stamping when I get back to Gucci. But the strange thing is, when I let myself into Brides by the Sea half an hour later, and check the diary for the morning, I find that Jess has re-arranged every single appointment for herself. And there's a note saying she's not expected in until after lunch.

Chapter 35

Thursday, 13th July
In the Style File at Brides by the Sea: Tea from the dark
ages

'If I can't have the hot tub, the least Kip can do is throw in the horse and carriage.'

Three days later, Nicole's stabbing the air with a long silver finger nail. As I take another leap backwards to avoid getting my cheek lacerated, I catapult into the *Crazy in love* board, send it flying, then hit the wall.

I drag in a deep breath, and rub my elbow as I pick up the sign. How did collecting key fobs get this complicated? 'The carriage was never on offer, Nicole.' More fool Kip for putting up a picture of Sera's sister arriving at her Christmas wedding in one. He should know Nicole watches that blog like a hungry sea hawk.

Nicole's Christian Louboutin platform crashes down on the stone floor of the basement. 'There's no point telling me the horse has gone AWOL, because I've seen him on Immie's Instagram posts.'

Which should be another problem entirely. But might turn out to be the crux of the matter. It's no coincidence that as Immie's Instagram follower numbers have pulled away from Nicole's due to her pet posts, Nicole's becoming more and more insufferable.

'Snowball's living up at the farm, and he's part of the Daisy Hill petting section for now, so he's definitely *not* available for carriage work on *your* wedding day.' This has to be the fiftieth time I've explained this to her in the last week. I don't bother mentioning that Immie's getting married at the farm the same day, because I think Nicole's only too aware of that. 'And only weeks away from your summer wedding is very short notice to find another available horse and carriage.' Although, heaven knows, I've put in the hours ringing around for what, in reality, would only be a ride from the back of the house to the front.

Nicole's mouth is a tight line of Chanel Mighty pink. 'In that case, we'd better talk about the island at Rose Hill Manor instead.' Once she gets her teeth into something she's like a Staffie who won't let go. Except this time – excuse the mixed metaphors – she's relocated her jaws to a bigger fish altogether.

'As far as I know, that's not available for weddings either.' If my insides feel like someone just sat on them, we all know why.

Nicole's first smile of the morning is triumphant. As she folds her arms, her bray of a laugh is a mix of scorn and triumph. 'Well *I* know differently. That's damn well advertised as "available for weddings" on the Manor's new blog too.'

I scurry across to my laptop and as I bring it up on the screen my gulp is large enough to swallow a lantern. 'Exclusive

Island Wedding Night Retreat. You're completely right, Nicole.' There's no escaping the words splashed across the screen. 'But I don't think it's up and running *yet*.'

In this mood Nicole will argue about anything. 'It has to be, someone's already had their picture taken there. Moonlight on the jetty and everything.' She gives a sniff of triumph. 'It's all over Pinterest.'

Worse and worse. I scroll down the screen, and sure enough Kip and I pop into view, all loved up, apparently canoodling on the water's edge. As I ram my fist in my mouth to stifle my scream, there's an iron hand closing round my gut. 'It'll be a publicity shoot, Nicole, not a real wedding. Rule number one, don't believe everything you see on the internet. I mean who gets married in a dress like that?'

Nicole leans to peer over my shoulder. 'What are you talking about, that bride looks amazing.'

Not so much from where I'm standing. 'No, I definitely reckon they've worked wonders with three miles of muslin, and the power of photoshop.' I'm about to suggest she zooms in, but remember just in time that getting recognised by her would be the last straw. What's more, I need to look at whatever pictures Kip's hurled into the world without the distraction of Nicole's Black Opium cloud all around me.

'Did someone mention pictures of the island?' It's Jess, and her clattering footfalls are echoing as she leaps her way down the stairs. If we needed proof that she has an extra bounce in her step lately, it's this. Better still, if anyone has the knowledge to put Nicole right on this, it's Jess.

'What can we tell Nicole about the cabin? I'm not sure

she'd like the accommodation for her wedding night, even if it were available.' Hopefully Jess will pick up on my desperate expression.

As Jess pushes back her uncharacteristically dishevelled bob, she's definitely breathy. 'Island life is definitely more for "famous five" types than super-glamourous women like you, Nicole.'

I jump in to back up Jess. 'It's very rough and ready, way less upmarket than glamping in a tipi.' According to Poppy, the issue of the wedding night in a tipi was where Nicole's differences with Chas first erupted. Which is why it's ridiculous she should be seizing on this now.

Jess is back in there. 'Truly Nicole, you'd hate the cabin. The sofa's threadbare, the bed's lumpy and the kitchen's from the dark ages. I promise, you'd expire on the spot if you had to drink morning tea coming from that blackened kettle. You'll be way happier in your Bridal Suite four poster. Isn't Kip throwing in a complimentary minibar too?'

Good on Jess for going the extra mile to sound so convincing. Detail like that, you'd almost believe she was talking from experience.

We're saved from Nicole's reply when Poppy appears in the doorway.

'Brilliant, just the woman I'm looking for.' She's peeping from behind a stack of cake boxes. 'I've got your hen party cupcake order here, Nicole.'

Nicole dives into her bright orange Gucci bag, and comes out waving her phone. 'Hold it there, Poppy, I need pictures.' She takes photos of Poppy and the cake boxes from every possible angle then slips her phone away, and holds up a finger until she's sure she's got everyone's attention. 'And guess where we're going for my hen party? We're only heading off for a weekend at Hadley Hall – Bath's most totally mega-luxurious spa hotel. I'll be posting to Instagram minute by minute, if you want to drool.' Note she didn't wait to be asked, or pause for our guesses. As for the pictures, stand by your vomit emoticons.

Jess's eyebrows rise in surprise. 'So you know where you're going?'

Nicole wrinkles her nose. 'Unless there are diamonds involved, surprises are a no-no for me – I've organised every delicious minute personally.' She narrows one eye as she takes the boxes from Poppy. 'Is Immie having her hen party soon too?'

Nicole never asks about other people, because it's always all about her. Which is why she has to be fishing here.

I smile. 'Immie's is tomorrow. It's a top-secret destination.' No way am I giving Nicole the satisfaction of the comparison. To everyone's shock, the only hen party Immie would consent to was a day trip to the zoo with Poppy, Cate and I, which Cate's missing because she's away. I blame bird flu for the unenthusiastic hens. My mum insisted on low key too. Lunch at the Harbourside Hotel, with Jenny and two other friends. They were home by four – in the afternoon, not the morning. Whatever happened to wild fowls?

Nicole's scowling. 'Well if that's the best you can tell me, I'll leave you to your dreary little lives and head off for my fun.'

Jess ignores that side swipe, and beams instead. 'Fabulous. We'll make sure we follow every treatment on Instabook.' Considering Nicole's style spend Jess can hardly do anything else. She waves Nicole off up the stairs, then she's back. 'Which reminds me, I need you two girls to teach me how to skip.'

Poppy frowns. 'Have you bought a Fitbit or something?'

I pull a face. 'Sorry, you'll have to count me out, I get the rope tangled every time.'

Jess wrinkles her forehead. 'Not that kind of skipping. I mean the kind you do on your laptop, when you talk to someone far away.'

Suddenly I'm with her. 'You mean Skyping? To somewhere like …' I'm taking a wild guess here. '… the Caribbean?' It couldn't be more obvious.

'Got it in one, Lily.' Jess almost looks relieved. 'Bart's off again. He's going to source us a line of silk shirts which will be perfect for beach weddings while he's there.'

'You're trusting the king of crinkle with your groomswear?' My voice is high with disbelief. I can hardly see Hawaiian brights fitting in at Brides by the Sea.

Jess beams. 'That's why I'll need to check them on screen. It's good to try new lines, and Bart's assured me this bargain buy is too good to miss.' His name is slipping out with a surprising ease and familiarity. But then Jess will always go the extra mile for a great deal.

I open my mouth to warn her about the unreliability of Penryns and their promises. Then I change my mind, and close it again. Let's face it, some life lessons have to be learned the hard way. And we're only talking a few shirts, after all.

Poppy puts a hand on Jess's arm. 'Come over here, we'll give you a quick introduction to Skype on Lily's laptop, then we'll set yours up later.' As she taps the keyboard, my screen flickers back to life, showing the Manor's blog in all its glory. Poppy lets out a long groan. 'Wedding nights on the island? So soon?' Her face is chalk pale as she sinks onto the chair. She scrolls down, squinting at the screen. 'And you still look beautiful, Lily, even if you are wearing a curtain and making out with the opposition.'

'It must be the camera angle, there was absolutely no snogging going on, I promise you.' And dammit if I'm coming out in a hot sweat at that thought.

Poppy sighs. 'Only teasing.'

I pull down the corners of my mouth. 'As for the rest, there's no stopping Kip. The damned guy's super-charged.'

As Poppy hugs her stomach her cheeks have a green tinge. 'I'm so anxious, I feel sick all the time. Fred's almost finished the barn now, but every booking the Manor grabs is one less for us.' She shakes her head. 'And we don't stand a chance of getting the *Wedding Venue of the Year Award* now we're up against this.'

Jess sniffs. 'Don't give up yet, Poppy. I might not be able to skip ...'

'Skype!' Poppy and I chorus.

'Whatever.' Jess rolls her eyes. 'But believe me, I'm working my socks off behind the scenes. It's classified information. But take it from me, we won't be letting those damned pirates win without a damned good fight.'

As I look at Poppy, all hunched and miserable, I only hope

she's right. As I turn back to the doorway, and catch sight of my mum my stomach does the same kind of nose dive it used to do when she came into school unexpectedly. Usually to complain. Very loudly.

'Barbara, how can we help today?' Jess, tweaking the peonies in jugs on the pink table, jumps in to cover for my dumbstruck silence.

My mum's abandoned her gym-wear again, and she's dressed as her old self, in a turquoise silk tunic, covered in red roses the size of flower buckets. 'Dahling, I was hoping you'd have scented candles. Jenny said bamboo and bergamot are particularly soothing.'

I'm hissing at her. 'Shit, Mum, this isn't the supermarket homeware aisle.' We've got a thousand candles, I'm just not sure any are scented.

Jess swoops across to the table drawer. 'Scented candles to relax our brides? What a fabulous idea. Let's put those on our order list, Lily.' She presses two candles in glasses into my mum's hands. 'These are some samples, Barbara. Lavender and vanilla. They have excellent calming properties.'

My mum doesn't pause for breath. 'And three bottles of Rescue Remedy, please.'

Excuse me while I die of embarrassment. 'As available in The Wellbeing Store, right next door to Iron Maidens, the cleaners, Mum.'

Jess's eyebrows shoot upwards. 'Another brides' necessity for our order list, Lily.' She dips into another drawer. 'In the meantime, I'll let you have one of my own personal emergency bottles, Barbara.'

My mum rattles on. 'This *is* what they recommend for brides in a panic?'

Meanwhile, my brain is doing the maths, and my spirits are suddenly soaring. 'You haven't had a fight with David?' Just as I thought time was running out, she's going to come to her senses.

As she turns to me her expression is pained. 'Not *that* kind of stress, silly.'

My excitement fades. 'So what's the trouble?'

From the endless breath she draws in, she's building to something big here. 'Your brother Zac's not coming to the wedding. How *awful* is that?' Her face crumples. 'Oh dear.' Note she's reminding me who Zac is.

Given an over-night visit for Dad's funeral is the most he's managed in ten years, it's hardly a surprise he's running out on her big day.

'He does practically run the world, Mum. It must be hard for him to get time off at short notice.' Not that I'd usually make excuses for her golden boy. But there's more than one down side to rushing into this wedding.

'But he's supposed to be giving me away.' Her voice is almost a wail.

Poppy's shaking her head. 'Don't worry, Barbara, women often do it these days. Lily will be fine to take his place, won't you?' Poppy smiles at me.

I give a shrug. 'I suppose I could.' If I'm hanging back it's because I'm very much my mum's second favourite child. I can see why she'd be upset at the substitution. What's more, the irony of actually giving her away isn't lost on me. Due to the embarrassment factor, I've been trying to disown her for most of my life. Although now it comes to it, I'm not that happy that it's David I'll be passing her on to.

My mum's fanning herself with her fingers. 'Wonderful, dahling. Jenny said you'd be perfect for the job. And so you will, as long as you have your hair curly.'

At times I can't believe where she's coming from. 'My what?'

She's frowning. 'Well I hardly want to be given away by someone whose hair's so poker straight we don't even look like we're related.' She turns to Jess. 'Her curls were always her best asset, even as a toddler. Please tell her she'll look a thousand times better with waves on the day.'

Waaaaahhhhhhhhhhhhhh. Appealing to my boss is below the belt.

'Great, well that's settled then.' Somehow I'm managing to beam at my mum. 'So if that's everything, and there's no charge, shall I see you out?' Before she gets any worse.

She lets out a sigh. 'It's not everything. We need to discuss your outfit.'

Damn. 'For your wedding?' As if it could be anything else. 'I thought I'd wear a very nice LBD.' Not that I've got around to buying it yet. But on a need to know basis, that bit can stay quiet. 'With a matching jacket. Obviously.' That part's the real sweetener. My mum's spent her entire life trying to persuade me into one. It should be enough to send her off happy.

She frowns. 'What's that in English? Because the thing is, Lily, if you turn up in your usual dowdy style, looking *years* older than you are, it's going to be very ageing for me. Especially now you're centre stage giving me away.'

If I'm blinking wildly, and opening and closing my mouth, it's due to the shock. And if we're talking Rescue Remedy, I could do with an intravenous dose please. With an added adrenalin shot to start my heart beating again.

Poppy's screwing her face up in horror behind my mum's back. 'LBD is a little black dress, Barbara. As worn by *everyone* young. It'll be perfect. She won't look a day over twenty-five.'

'Black?' My mum's shriek couldn't have been louder if Poppy had said I was going to be giving her away naked. 'Absolutely not.'

Poppy isn't backing off. 'If we get the seamstress to make it really short, she might even pass for twenty.'

Now it's my mum's turn to blink. 'If you're deliberately trying to upset me here, you're doing a damned good job.' She's fanning her face, and she flops down into the chair that Jess shoves behind her.

Jess switches into her soothing purr. 'Would you like some sweet tea, Barbara? Or some Prosecco?'

Poppy joins in. 'Or gin might be good? Or a cupcake? Or even Rescue Remedy?'

As my mum dives into her bag for a hanky, I notice it's the same pink Gucci model as Nicole's second best one.

She runs her hand through her sandy blonde hair and blows her nose loudly. 'Actually, all I need is for Lily to wear something bright. White with red roses would be good. John Lewis have several suitable outfits.'

'Alright. Fine.' As for me looking like a blooming country garden, I suppose it's only one day in my life.

'And the jacket and accessories would work in cerise.' Me

311

giving in appears to have calmed her faster than an entire tumbler of Jess's gin, because she's already standing up and heading for the stairs. 'I'll send you the links.'

I'm shaking my head, staring at Jess and Poppy as her lilac courts clatter up the staircase. 'Sorry, but I'm not sure I'll ever get used to my mum being computer literate.' And feeling like I just got run over by a lorry doesn't begin to describe it.

Poppy's biting her lip. 'Shit, Lily, I can't believe we just let you get railroaded into a bright pink jacket.'

Jess's nostrils are flaring. 'Barbara's quite a force to be reckoned with.'

'Did I really agree to *matching* accessories?' My voice is a squeak.

Jess is frowning. 'We need to help you learn to stand up for yourself, Lily.'

Poppy squeezes my arm. 'When we were younger we used to laugh at what a nightmare she was. But no-one has the right to put you down like that at any time. And really not at our age. Even if they are getting married.'

I wrinkle my nose as I think. 'I suppose I'm used to it. It's easier to let it go.' She'll never change. And before her wedding is hardly the ideal time to challenge her on a lifetime of put downs. If anything, this is a timely reminder of why I need to get away. Although as I look around the lovely basement, which is getting more beautiful with every delivery, I'm suddenly very sad that I'll be giving it up.

Still, there's lots to do before I think about that. Starting with Immie's hen outing.

Chapter 36

'Shit-a-doodle, my selfie with the meerkats has had a hundred and seventy likes in half an hour.' Immie waggles her fists as she cheers, then yanks her bright pink bride-to-be sash back into place. 'Who'd have thought the zoo would be so popular?'

As we make our way around the enclosures next morning, I'm not sure which she is enjoying most – the animals or the Instagram attention. But her phone is beeping so often, it's like being out with a robot. Albeit a robot with a veil fluttering behind her in the breeze, attached to a diamanté headband perched at a wild angle. All rounded off with a dick-stick straw sticking out of her can of Diet Coke. Which is her one concession to cutting back on the calories in the interests of becoming a slimline bride.

I can't help smiling at her enthusiasm. 'You puckering up, trying to look like that haughty giraffe is way more fun than Nicole getting exfoliated with a salt scrub. Not that it's a

313

competition.' Except we all know it is, and we all love that Immie's smashing it. I know Immie wanted to back pedal on the hen party props, but we couldn't let her walk round completely unmarked. It was thanks to the veil that the head keeper chose her to help lead the elephants when they went out on their morning ramble round the zoo.

Poppy laughs as she throws down her bag on a bench in the dappled shade of a birch tree overlooking the monkey enclosure. 'Nicole's made it hard for herself. It's a huge challenge to make a selfie in a mud wrap look interesting. And steam room shots are bound to be blurry.' She hands us a sandwich each. 'A spa weekend might be fabulous, but the photo opportunities are limited. Whereas the zoo is fun all round.'

Immie pulls back the paper and takes a massive bite of her ham salad baguette. 'I'd hate doing normal hen party stuff. I can't see me making flower crowns, *or* being wrapped in algae. And if we'd gone out on the town my aunties would only have got rat arsed.'

Bear in mind this is Immie talking, and she can drink for England before she falls over. But Immie's aunties are the stuff of legends. And not always in a good way. As a measure of their lairiness, the stripagram they ordered for Immie's gran's eightieth was so scared, he legged it while he still had his clothes on. That was the other minor technical problem which stopped us organising a hen night pub crawl – between them Immie's female relations are banned from most of the bars in St Aidan.

Immie wrinkles up her nose. 'They're one reason we kept the numbers small for the wedding. Them, and Chas still owing the equivalent of the GDP of a small country from when he *didn't* get married to Nicole.'

Poppy winces. 'I didn't know it was *that* much.'

Immie shrugs. 'Poor guy. He'd planned to pay it off over a lifetime. And it *was* a hell of a party.' She gives a throaty laugh, and rubs her nose with her perspex engagement ring. 'It's lucky I don't want a big show, because the finances are on lockdown.'

'So you're sticking with your purple ring then?' My mum still hasn't got an engagement ring, not that I've seen anyway. Probably because David hasn't got any cash of his own to buy one for her either.

Immie grins. 'I couldn't give up on this ring now. And we're having simple wedding bands, so I can clean in mine without worrying.' She's counting off on her fingers. 'Then Poppy's doing the cake as our present. Rafe let me have the venue as my bonus for the next ten years. The Goose and Duck are doing the food and kegs at cost, in return for me doing extra glass collecting. Also for the next ten years. The hen do was £15 entry plus petrol and the picnic. Lily's designed us minimalist flowers.'

When Immie and I talked about that, we settled on single roses in tumblers along the top table. Although at the time, I had no idea it was because their cash was so limited.

Immie wiggles her eyebrows. 'All that's left now is the dress, although there's approximately 50p to buy it with. And we all know how well that search is going.'

Poppy's forehead wrinkles. 'Is that why you won't try them on?'

Immie gives a cough. 'Those first few appointments, I had no idea how much in debt Chas was. But I couldn't bring myself to try any because I was scared I'd look crap. And now, every time I start to think about the dress, I feel like I'm about to vomit.'

Poppy stares at her untouched ham sandwich. 'Exactly how I feel when I think about the Manor, then.'

'Immie, that's awful.' I stretch out and give her a hug. Brides usually shop for their dresses a year ahead of the wedding, not two weeks. And besides the times she made it to the shop, Immie has wriggled out of at least half a dozen other appointments, and blown our cover on every attempt to trick her into dress trying.

Poppy purses her lips, and goes in for a hug from her side. 'As a last resort, you'd look fab in jeans and an *I'm getting married at Daisy Hill Farm* T-shirt.'

Immie's face scrunches up. 'Chas wouldn't mind. He says he loves me, and that's all that matters. I think he'd happily marry me in my cleaning pinny. And I'd be the same if it weren't for ...' She breaks off, but this time it's not to take a bite of sandwich. Instead she's frowning into the distance.

'Immie, you're looking so much like a constipated camel there, it's worthy of a selfie.' Poppy lets out a giggle.

I'll have one guess what's making her scowl like that. 'You aren't worried about Nicole, are you?'

Immie's sigh is huge. 'I can't help it. She was Chas's first choice, she's going to look a million dollars on her day. However hard I try, I'm not like her.' Immie's bottom lip comes out. 'I can't do all that lace and beady shit. And you saw what happened when I tried to walk in high heels.'

Poppy smiles at the recollection. 'Yes, you instantly got a

hundred followers on Instagram. We love you because you *can't* do those things, Immie. Nicole might have a flawless complexion, Barbie's body, and a mouth that could have come from a toothpaste ad. But she's not funny or warm or real or down to earth. She doesn't crease us up with her swearing and her dirty laugh, and haul us out of trouble at a moment's notice with no thought for her chipped nails.'

I throw in another thought. 'If I were Chas, I know who I'd rather have found at the bottom of the fireman's pole, when I slid down it to propose.'

Immie sniffs. 'I don't mind about Nicole having a super expensive wedding, while we're relying on freebies from friends.' Her gruff voice has disappeared to a squeak. 'I just don't want to let Chas down, by turning up looking like a gorilla's backside, that's all.'

Poppy rolls her eyes at me over Immie's spiky hair. 'As if. Now we know what the problem is, we hens will find you the perfect dress. Won't we, Lily?' She gives me a sharp poke behind Immie's shoulders.

'Of course. Absolutely. Leave this to us. The hens are on the case.' Although how the hell we're going to pull this particular proverbial rabbit out of this particular proverbial hat is anyone's guess.

Immie sniffs loudly. 'Thanks guys. You've no idea what a relief that is.' She grabs her hen's veil, dabs at her eyes, then lets out a squawk as she sees the black mascara smears on the lace. 'Waaaaaaaahhhh, now I've got panda eyes.'

I swoop in with my hanky, and wipe away the worst smudges. 'All good again.'

Immie stares at the remains of her baguette. 'If I can forget about the dress, I'm starting to regret opting for a dry hen party. Is there a bar round here?'

I grin as I swing my rucksack down. 'The best hens always travel with Prosecco.' Believe me, I thought she'd never ask. A second later, I'm twisting off the cork, and filling up the plastic flutes.

Chapter 37

At Daisy Hill Farm Barn: Over exposure and dripping hugs

As I drive up to Daisy Hill Farm two days later, the blue and white striped marquee under construction in the wedding meadow should be getting my full attention. The fabulous tea dance wedding for a couple called Shell and Nigel, with pianos, vintage china, decorated garden sheds, and a hundred miles of bunting is one of the days Poppy and I have been looking forward to most all summer. But somehow, since Immie's hen party, all we've been able to concentrate on is the massive question mark of what she's going to wear to get married.

So even as I've been taking delivery of a hundred stripy deck chairs, and an entire period pub interior, not to mention stacks of vintage suitcases, packing crates, and enough potted palms to fill Kew Gardens, my mind has been on Immie. And Poppy, busy with her monster order for cakes for two hundred and fifty afternoon teas, has been the same. Five and a half months on from getting engaged, Immie still hasn't tried on

319

one wedding dress. So with the wedding less than two weeks away, we've decided on a radical change of strategy. And as soon as this is sorted, we'll be full speed ahead on the tea dance.

'If we're resorting to ambush, it's only because we're desperate.' I'm justifying what we're about to do to Immie, as Poppy and I hurry up the courtyard at Daisy Hill Farm. We're heading towards the newly converted wedding barn where Immie is assessing the final clean.

'Bringing the dresses to the bride, rather than the other way around, was a brainwave of yours.' Poppy wiggles her eyebrows at me mischievously. 'Lucky we could call on the big guns too.'

She's talking about Sera the dress designer, who's back from another long weekend in Bristol with her lovely guy, Johnny. She's waiting in the car, primed to follow with the dresses in approximately six minutes. This time we've been rigorous with our pre-selection. We've pared it down to three styles, meticulously chosen with Immie in mind.

As we approach the huge glazed doors across the newly laid stone flags of the courtyard, I'm wide eyed, because the old farm barn with its holes to the hayloft has changed so much since I was last here.

Poppy nods at the planters either side of the door. 'When the bay trees arrive it's a sign it's almost done.' She's playing down how much hard work she's put in.

'It's looking so pretty,' I say. The new window frames are painted pale grey to tie in with the rest of the farm buildings, and the mellow stonework has been newly pointed. As I catch sight of a familiar truck parked in the distance, I catch my breath. 'Is Fred here?'

Poppy laughs. 'Only twenty-four hours a day. He's had a big push to get it finished ahead of schedule, so he can move onto another job in town. It's great to get it done, but we could do without the final bill coming a month early.' Which explains why he hasn't been up at the Manor so often lately.

I sense her tension. 'Cash flow problems?'

She blows out a breath. 'I was hoping if the farm was up for an award, the publicity might bring in some extra bookings to cover it. But the way the Manor's performing, they'll run away with it.'

I scrunch up my face. 'When Kip started out he was a joke. So how did he get himself together so fast?' Not that I think about him often. But when I do my heart sinks on Poppy's behalf.

There are furrows in Poppy's forehead. 'There's no limit to what guys can achieve when they're super-motivated. A bit like Fred. Watch out, hot naked flesh alert, here he comes now ...' Sure enough, he's coming towards the barn doors as we speak.

I wrinkle my nose at Poppy. 'So much tanned torso? At ten in the morning?' As he walks out into the sun, and I take in his six-pack sliding down into his low-slung jeans, I can't help smiling. 'Hey Fred, lovely to see you. Just here to admire the progress.' I'm sticking to our cover story here. Although as far as Fred goes, a little less over-exposure would be preferable this early in the day.

'And you too, Lily.' He hovers on the step for long enough for me to get the full benefit of his gleaming pecs. Then he swoops in for a peck on the cheek, and stays a fraction too long for comfort. 'Not long now until that date you promised me.'

'What did I promise?' With so much rippling muscle crushed up against my elbow, I'm not entirely clear what he's talking about.

He flips back his mop of sandy hair, and laughs. 'My boyfriend six-month probationary period's over in two weeks. Shall I book us that trip to the top of the Empire State building?'

Shucks. As breathing spaces go, that one *flew* by. 'Sorry, Fred, but the wedding season comes before Central Park every time. I've heard Manhattan's fab in late Autumn.' By which time, fingers crossed, I'll be on my way somewhere else. As I add a monster grin to make sure it's clear I'm joking rather than leading him on, I sense Poppy moving towards the open door. 'Are you coming in, Fred?'

He hesitates to rub his biceps, then glances at his watch. 'Wish I could, but my guys are fresh out of wood stain. I'll have to catch you later.' One quick arm squeeze, and he's dashing off up the yard. As he gets to his truck he flings his checked shirt through the open door, and turns back to call down the yard. 'By the way, I might have found someone for your mum's house, Lily. Great news eh?' He gives a double thumbs up as he disappears into the cab. Then the door slams, and a second later he's roaring past us in a dust cloud.

Poppy's squinting at me, biting on the grit in the air. 'That guy's an eternal optimist. Worry about Heavenly Heights selling when it happens.' Her pat on my arm is very welcome. 'Come on in and see what we've been doing with the wedding barn.'

I know my mum's house might go any day. Or it might not sell for months. So it's probably best not to think about it. Especially as I'll need every ounce of concentration for the task ahead. As I follow Poppy into the barn I'm expecting it to be as dark and agricultural as it used to be. But instead the sun is flooding in through glazed sections in the roof, and bouncing off the newly whitewashed walls.

I gaze up at the huge trusses crossing below the sloping ceilings and nod at Poppy. 'It's gorgeous. So rustic, and full of character. And a fabulous place to get married and have a party.' And perfect the way it opens out onto its very own hay meadow at the back.

Poppy's smile is proud. 'It's been a lot of work, but it's even better than we imagined. And our first wedding here is six weeks from now, so we've plenty of breathing space.' As we look out across the field, there's a crash, as Immie staggers into view through a door at the end.

She drops her clipboard and pen, and swipes the sweat off her forehead with her T-shirt sleeve. 'You do know Fred only stripped off when he saw you coming up the yard, Lily. Classic peacock behaviour. Talk about a dominant male doing a come-and-get-me mating display.' As she stamps towards us her high heeled Doc Martens are clomping on the rough-hewn floor boards. She grins, and thumps me on the shoulder. 'Recovered from your hen party hang over?'

It's great she's brought the subject up. 'Actually there's one more hen party surprise for you.' I whip a silk scarf out of my pocket, and hand it to Poppy.

Poppy takes the baton. 'But for this bit we need to pop a blindfold on you.'

'What the eff? You can't hijack me when I'm sorting out my sparkle clean.' Immie's protesting loudly as Poppy pulls the scarf around her eyes, and ties a knot behind her head.

I catch a glimpse of Sera outside the barn doors, dress covers draped over her arms, and wave her in. 'We're not *going* anywhere. But we *are* going to have a little game.'

'We're going to try out the Bride's Dressing Room.' Poppy leads Immie gently to the end of the barn, and through into a lovely room with a mirror and make-up shelf all along one wall, and velvet chairs as comfy as the mother-of-the-bride ones at the shop, softened by a pile of patchwork cushions.

Sera hooks the dresses onto the folding screen, next to a full-length mirror in a chunky wood frame. Then she hitches up her shorts, pushes back her mass of blonde hair, and touches Immie's hand. 'Hi Immie, Sera here. If you'd just slip off your jeans and top, we're going to play "try on the wedding dress".'

'You're what?' Immie's voice is close to a howl.

Poppy's patting her shoulder. 'Calm down. We've brought three dresses from the shop. You don't have to look. All you have to do is to let us put you into them, okay?'

Immie's sputtering. 'But I can't afford a dress from Brides by the Sea ...'

Sera's smiling. 'Remember that ceiling Chas and his friends put up at the Manor for Alice's wedding? Without your help that day, I seriously doubt she'd *ever* have managed to get married. I'll owe you forever for that. So I've brought some of my special designs for you to try, Immie. I'm more than happy for you to get married in any of them.' As soon as Sera heard about Immie's problems, she chose two dresses from her studio, and worked up a third from scratch.

Immie's almost wailing as her Doc Martens go flying and she pulls off her jeans. 'That's *so* great, Sera. But wedding dresses are meant for skinny chips, not big round potatoes.'

'Where do fries come in?' Poppy's frowning, even though we all know Immie would have them for every meal.

Immie stops for a breath. 'Those sodding vegetable body shapes. I hoped I might be an apple, or even a carrot, but I Googled it last week, and I'm definitely a spud. I can't possibly look at dresses.' Poor Immie. She's got such a block about this.

Sera smiles. 'As I see it, you've got fabulous shoulders, great boobs, and hips so narrow, most women would swap you in a heartbeat.'

'That's the whole idea of the blindfold.' I jump in to explain. 'We'll do the choosing, and you'll only see yourself when you're completely beautiful.' It's not ideal, but it's our only chance of getting her into a dress this side of the registrars arriving.

Poppy dips into a box. 'And we have shoes. Try these for size Cinderella.'

Immie gives a grunt as she feels the shoe Poppy hands her.

'You're putting me in Doccie heels like the ones I just took off?'

She's right of course. What she can't see is that these are the cream version. A last-minute compromise of style, comfort, and health and safety.

I laugh. 'On balance we decided you mightn't make it through the day alive if you wore Christian Louboutins.'

Sera's already slipped off the first cover, and she's holding out a slinky satin slip. 'Slide into this, then there's a chiffon overdress, and we can mix and match on the sash.'

'No peeping.' Poppy's beside Immie, tweaking the fabric into place, pulling a narrow ribbon under her boobs. 'Right, stay still.'

The three of us stand back, and take in the transformation. If we don't speak straight away, it's because we're stunned.

I nod at Sera. 'Fabulous. I'd be happy to get married looking like that.' Momentarily forgetting that I wouldn't be doing the marrying bit, but whatever. Not that we're saying this out loud, but the simple lines of the sheer fabric falling over the satin, from the high waist are wonderfully flattering.

Poppy chimes in. 'Me too.'

Sera chews her nail. 'The over dress is reversible. Shall we try it the other way around, with the plunge at the back?'

Immie makes a loud groan. 'Stuff that. Seriously, I can't get married in a dress that could be back to front. That's non-negotiable.'

So much for thinking out loud. 'Okay, moving on,' we chorus.

By the time Poppy's pulled the first dress off over Immie's

head, Sera's ready with the next. This one is more tailored and sophisticated, and fits like it was made for Immie, with a pencil skirt, and a Bardot neckline.

'Lovely.' When Poppy eases up the zip, and murmurs the word, she's speaking for all of us.

'Even better than the last.' I say. 'Isn't that oyster satin beautiful?'

'Ahem.' Immie clears her throat and slides her hands over her seemingly non-existent hips. 'Excuse me butting in here, but isn't satin a nightmare for messy pups like me? Like I'm already worrying about marks. And one other small point – I can't move my legs.'

I wrinkle my nose. 'I'd happily stay in one spot for a day to look that pretty.' But Immie's right. She has to feel comfortable.

'Okay, last one ...' As Sera takes it down Poppy and I exchange defeated glances. With two flat rejections in as many minutes, why did we think this could ever work? I don't hold out any hope, given the last dress was still on the fabric rolls in the studio yesterday, and Sera's rushed it together overnight. Sera must think it's hopeless too, because she's switched on a running commentary as Immie wiggles into it.

'So this one's got a fitted satin bodice but there's floaty lace over the top, so you don't need to worry about the marks.'

'Yay, I can actually walk.' The slinky lace-covered skirt falls from the low waistline that sits on Immie's neat hips, gently flaring at the floor for walking room. Immie gives a kick, just to prove the point, then puts her hands on her waist. 'Well, how is it?'

Poppy's got her fist on her mouth. 'It couldn't be more perfect. How on earth did you do that, Sera?'

I'm staring, open mouthed. 'It's so clever, Sera. I love the way those tiny beads around the waist catch the light.'

Sera's mouth has stretched into a grin. 'It's made for you, Immie. But it's only beautiful because you are.'

Immie's grabbing at the scarf.

Poppy grasps her hand. 'No, Immie, the plan is you only see this on the wedding day.' We can't risk her getting cold feet and backing out of this. It's not like we have a back-up option.

'Toad bollocks to that, I can't wait until next week.' A second later the scarf is off, and Immie's staring down at herself.

I grab Sera's hand, because I know how much she hates the part where the bride reacts to the dress. Having her work under scrutiny. The risk of rejection, even if it's not personal. I'm squeezing her fingers harder and harder. And the longer the silence goes on, the worse it gets.

Poppy's encouraging Immie. 'Here, you'll get the effect better in the long mirror.' Immie's got her hands over her face now, and she's peering through the cracks between her fingers.

Still no reaction. She must hate it. I'm starting to kick myself, for putting not just Immie through this, but Sera too. For all the fruitless work Sera has done. The shadows under her eyes from sewing late into the night are getting darker as our hearts sink lower with every moment we don't hear anything. I'm almost ready to run and bundle the dresses into the car, when there's a noise like a blocked drain emptying. *Surely it can't be Immie's infamous vomit noise?* Then there's a huge gasp. Then a gulp and a moan as Immie bends forwards. It's only when I hear another snort and a splutter that I look down, and see the drips on the floor that the penny drops. She's crying.

'Tissues, quick. Anyone got any?' Our wonderful hard-boiled, tough-guy Immie is bawling her heart out, and the tears are spurting out in all directions like a tap that's lost its washer. I'm slapping my jeans, but every pocket is empty. 'Don't get tears on the satin, Immie.'

Sera's turned out her pockets too, and she's diving into her bag, throwing the contents over the floor.

Poppy hurls herself at the door, and when she hurtles back she's thrusting a Jay cloth into Immie's hand. 'Sweetie, I'm sorry, we should never have started this without Kleenex. How silly am I bringing you to the brand-new Bride's Room and forgetting the tissues?'

'S'alright.' Immie mops her face with the cloth, and as she blows her nose loudly, her voice is a croak. 'I'll be okay in a bit.' There's another snort. 'So long as I don't look too hard at myself. I just never knew I could feel this good. In a flipping dress, too ...'

'Oh Immie.' Poppy and I are either side of her hugging an arm each. 'You look like yourself. And you look truly amazing.'

Immie rams her fists into her eyes, then stares back in the mirror. 'Unbelievable. Totally un-frigging-believable.' She blows out her cheeks. 'You know, I've always felt bad about my body. And me landing Chas was such a fluke, I always worried that I couldn't measure up.' The sniff she gives has to be because she's thinking of Nicole. 'But for the first time ever, this dress makes me feel good enough. Good enough for Chas. Good enough to be his bride. For the first time in my *entire* life I feel beautiful. And you've no idea how wonderful that is.'

She puts her arms round Sera first, then drags Poppy and me into a group hug that's horribly damp.

As Immie eases her grip, she lets out a growl. 'And you finally got me into effing lace. Who'd have thought I'd damn well love the stuff?' She runs her fingers across the delicate fabric. 'Jeez, are those diamonds down there?'

Poppy grins. 'We thought you'd like one or two ...' Meaning 'eat your heart out Nicole'. And let's pray she doesn't decide to reject them.

I'm rubbing my eyes with my T-shirt sleeve, and laughing, from sheer relief. 'It's official. You're Brides by the Sea's most difficult bride yet.' But somehow she's my best bride ever.

Sera chimes in. 'It's the hard ones that are *so* worth the work, every time. Look at you ...'

'As I've said before, all our brides are beautiful. But it'll be a long time before a bride makes me prouder than you, Immie.' Just because of the challenge. And the protest. And her total transformation into a woman who finally believes in her own worth. And listen to me, talking like I'm staying forever, when I'll be moving on before I know it.

Sometimes once you crack the toughest problems, afterwards it's hard to see why it was ever difficult. That's what it's like as Immie swishes around, grinning at herself in the mirror, lifting her skirts to nod happily at her cream Doccie's. So now it's full steam ahead to this weekend's vintage wedding.

Then we'll be flat out getting ready for Immie's and Nicole's the weekend after, then on to my mum's after that.

And now we've sorted this dress, we're pretty much invincible. The rest should be easy-peasy in comparison.

Chapter 38

Thursday, 10th August
At Daisy Hill Farm: Be careful what you wish for

'So I hear Nicole's getting her hot tub at the Manor after all, then?'

With my hood up and two days to go to Immie and Nicole's weddings, the first clue I have that Poppy's come up behind me in the courtyard at the farm, is when she taps me on the shoulder as I'm opening the store door.

Months ago, when Nicole stole the wedding date from under my mum's nose, and I wished it would rain for Nicole's wedding day, it was a mean, throwaway thought. Now I'm so involved, and with Immie's wedding on the same day, wet weather is the last thing I want. So when the long, hot, scorching summer finally breaks in a clattering thunderstorm soon after the vintage tea dance wedding, and it's still raining what seems like weeks later, we're all wandering round with faces as long as wet weddings inside our cagoules. As for me, it's not just the agonising guilt and the drips running off my nose that are depressing. With sluicing rain and a whipping wind, however long I spend with the hair straighteners, my hair resorts to its natural state. Within seconds of stepping outside, it's 'goodbye smooth gloss, hello crazy curls'. Although before seven in the morning, at Daisy Hill Farm, the Thursday before the double wedding, I wasn't exactly expecting to be seen. I'm here to meet a man in a van, because there's a barn full of props that need to be taken over to the Manor.

'It's the first I've heard of a hot tub lately,' I say to Poppy. 'Kip finally gave in then?'

Poppy laughs. 'No, Nicole bullied Fred into loaning her one. Here he comes now, no doubt he'll give you all the gory details.' She wiggles her eyebrows, which is totally unnecessary.

'Details? About what?' Immie's head pops out of the laundry with an expectant gleam in her eye. As for me thinking I'd be here on my own, how wrong was that?

Fred is coming down from the wedding barn, hands in his Barbour pockets. From the swagger in his step, he's particularly pleased with his installation. 'Someone asking about hot tubs? We certainly did pop a super-deluxe version onto the terrace at the Manor late last night. Just for the weekend.' He grins and holds his hands out to catch the falling drops. 'Perfect weather for it too. There's nothing like a warm soak in the rain.' Somehow his puppy-dog optimism is infectious.

I smile. 'At least the rain means you get a few days off from the garden.' With the heat the last week, the flowers have been wilting.

He frowns at me. 'What have gardens got to do with anything?'

'Nice try, Fred. I'm talking about the non-stop watering ... with the hose ... at the Manor ...' I give him a teasing stare.

Immie's leaning on the door post. 'For frigg's sake, Fred, when are you going to come clean about ...'

As a bashed up Landrover screeches to a halt lower down the yard, Fred literally leaps on the spot. 'Another time, Immie. Right now, I'm off. Laters, guys.' The second after, he's dashed away up the cobbles, and dodged out of view.

In the country, there are so many scrubby four by fours they're interchangeable. But as I squint at the figure leaping down from this latest one, the scuffed paintwork is strangely familiar. 'Is that ... *Kip?*' This is the last place in the world he should be.

'Looks like he's in a hurry too.' Immie chortles. 'He's hurtling towards us like he's an Olympic sprinter.'

'If he's hoping for more of Poppy's cupcakes he can forget it.' Just saying. There's nothing else round here worth running that fast for.

As he skids to a halt, he's pale and breathless. 'Lily, thank jeez you're here.'

Funny, I didn't have Kip down as a drama queen. But given their history, and that I'll be on my way to the Manor the minute van man arrives, he's bang out of order rampaging round on Rafe and Poppy's territory. 'This better be important, Kip.'

He blinks away his disgust as he rakes his fingers through his hair. 'There's a flood at the Manor, Lily. Most of the ground floor's under water.' He must be shaken, or he'd have jumped on me for my 'important' crack.

'Crap. What happened?' As my insides turn to jelly, I'm ashamed for doubting him. My mind races. 'Rain? Shit, has the lake overflowed?'

He drags in a breath. 'Nope. The guys who installed the hot tub late yesterday accidentally opened a valve to a dead pipe, and I went to bed without noticing. It ran all night until I got up at six, which is a hell of a lot of water. And this one's down to me.'

Flipping out his phone, he flicks through some pictures.

'Oh my.' I groan as I take in the sodden sofas, with water lapping round the legs, papers floating by the fireplace. I resist the urge to comment about the floating gnome, but only because the ballroom looks like an extension of the lake, with watermarks leaching up the plasterwork. There are more pictures of antique tables under plastic by the front door, and I do a double take as I see what they're next to.

'What's Jess's car doing there?' Okay, given the scale of the disaster, it's totally not important. But it's too weird not to ask.

Kip blows out his cheeks. 'Bart's back.'

'Not more of those damned Caribbean shirts?' Why Jess is so set on pursuing this particular line is a mystery.

A flicker crosses Kip's face before he scrunches it up. 'Something like that. She went back to the shop to see an early bride, and left Bart with the insurance guys.'

No doubt when you have a stately home, the loss adjusters will zoom out straight away.

Now the immediate shock has subsided, my mind's buzzing with a thousand and one practical questions. 'So what are the chances of Nicole's wedding going ahead?' As I wait for the answer I hardly dare move. I've got half a hectare of white hydrangeas arriving from the wholesalers, and that's just the start.

'Honestly?' Kip raises his eyebrows. 'Absolutely zero. But given it's clean water, your mum might be luckier.'

Now I'm the one blowing. 'And does Nicole know?'

Kip looks at his phone. 'It's seven now. I'll ring her before eight.'

There's a new question flashing into my head. 'So why have you come to find *me*?' Unless he's simply come to stop the delivery of the props, the news for my mum could have waited. And surely it's his place to break this to Nicole and Miles? Like now would be good.

Kip sniffs. 'I'm up shit creek, Water Lily. It's obvious you're the first one I'd to turn to. You're the one with all the ideas, tons of friends, and I know you'll come through for me. I'm responsible for a wedding party, with no place to hold it. If anyone can pull me out of this, it's going to be you.'

Which makes a change. Twice in the past he's been the one dragging me to safety. I'm not sure *anyone* ever asked *me* to rescue them before. Although, seriously, I need to stop feeling flattered and get to grips with the practicalities.

'Your usual answer to a problem is to hurl cash at it. That's not going to work this time.' Although even as I say it, there's a glimmer of an idea in my mind.

Kip closes his eyes. 'Too right.'

'Although Poppy does happen to have a brand-new wedding barn ...' Poppy's been listening intently, and as I meet her eye

I'm very aware why she refused to take Nicole's booking six months ago. 'But Immie and Chas have signed up for exclusive use of the whole farm here, for their wedding in the house. And given Chas is Nicole's ex-fiancée, you can see why they wouldn't want to compromise their privacy.'

Poppy shakes her head. 'Knowing Nicole and Miles, I'm not sure they'd go for anything as rustic as the barn anyway.'

Kip perks up visibly. 'The insurance guys seemed to think we can still use the bedrooms at the Manor. And we have to keep the ceremonies in the same places, even if the Winter Garden's damp. So it's only the reception space we're looking for. And Nicole's numbers aren't huge.'

The more I'm talking, the more my idea of getting Poppy and Immie an instant cash boost seems like bad judgement. 'In which case maybe your best bet is to ring around and try for some last-minute marquees, Kip, or another vacant venue.'

Immie gives a loud cough. 'Hash tag bride waving. I am *here*. ' She does her jazz hands. 'Surely Chas and me are the ones you should be asking about this?'

Poppy frowns. 'I think we've already all made the decision *not* to make any changes, Immie.'

Immie screws up her face. 'Remember last year, all Nicole wanted was to get married in the farmhouse? And this time round the farmhouse was her first choice too.' She pulls down the corners of her mouth.

I can't help laughing at Kip's wounded expression. 'Sorry to break it to you, Kip, but for Nicole the Manor was a consolation prize.' Only I wouldn't be making fun of him if I didn't have the feeling we were about to haul him off his proverbial cliff edge.

Immie carries on. 'Chas and I are having this fabulous wedding, but it's only thanks to some whopping favours. The farmhouse is lovely, but when push comes to shove, we chose it so it would be different from when Chas didn't marry Nicole. It wouldn't matter to me if I had to marry Chas in a cardboard box. What's important for us is getting married in front of all our friends, then having a great party. And that doesn't *have* to be in the house.'

As I swallow back the lump in my throat, I can see Poppy scraping the corner of her eye.

Immie gives a gruff laugh. 'There was a time when I felt like second best beside Nicole. But I don't any more. I got the man, my dress is ace, and I beat her on Instagram too.'

Kip's eyes are like hubcaps. 'Really?'

'Too right mate.' Immie wiggles her phone at him. 'I'll have to check with Chas obviously. But speaking for myself, a party in the wedding barn would be more than perfect for us. Add in bunting and fairy lights, and we'd be ecstatic.'

Kip eyeballs me. 'Fairy lights we can help with. Are there still some in the coach house, Lily?'

I nod. 'Just a few hundred boxes. I'm guessing we can call on the firemen again to put them up.'

Kip's giving me a 'look' for that quip. 'As for flowers, we've got masses in our mixed borders in the walled garden haven't we, Lily? Perfect for a rustic setting.'

'Absolutely. Although you do realise you're stealing all my lines here?' And since when was he tuned into me well enough to do that? 'This is so good of you, Immie.' I grin at her.

'If it means Nicole gets the day she wants, I'm happy to help. There's no way Chas and I could enjoy our wedding party knowing Nicole and Miles had lost their day.' She slides back into the building. 'Give me a minute.'

With Immie out of the way, it's time for the straight talking. I channel Jess in my mind set, then launch.

'So I'd need to help decorate the barn for Immie, in which case Nicole may need to give up some of my time. But I'll do the Winter Garden at the Manor for the ceremony as planned, and transfer her ballroom scheme across to the farmhouse as best I can.' I'm still talking in the conditional tense. It's certainly not a done deal, given Nicole doesn't even know about it yet.

Kip's straight in there. 'Obviously, I'll pay any extra fees for you ... at triple rate.'

Nice one. Only what Jess would have asked for. 'And you'll have to look after the farmhouse wedding yourself, because the rest of us will be busy with Immie's.'

'Agreed.' He nods.

I give him a stern look. 'And most of all, you'll have to promise to use every last ounce of your charm and manly wiles to keep Nicole happy.'

Kip's grin is the width of the courtyard. At least. 'That's the first time you've admitted I've got any.'

Dammit. I walked into that. 'Watch it, Cake-face. Nicole's the only one it works on. And we're only here because you stuffed up big time, remember.' If I'm lashing out, it's because of that accidental and misguided slip. Although a tiny part of me can't help feeling Kip's quietly taking the rap here for someone else's cock up. I know when they were dishing out integrity, the Penryns missed out altogether. But it seems like Kip got hold of some after all.

'And we'll obviously pay you too, Poppy. Would double the full price of our venue be suitable? And we'll pay for Immie and Chas's new venue too.'

And dammit again, this time because he pre-empted my 'this is going to cost you' line. Even though I know Poppy would hate me making demands for cash, and profiting out of people's misfortune.

I'm straight back at him. 'Triple,' I snap, thinking of how Jess would play this. At least this should go some way to helping Poppy's cash flow troubles, and paying off Immie's extra hours.

'Great.' Kip says. From his squishy smile he's still basking in my charm blunder. 'Thanks, Lily. Thanks all of you. I owe you all for this. Big time.' Let's face it, he *should* be whooping. We've seriously saved his ass here. For a rival he's enjoying fabulous concessions.

Poppy chips in. 'Well all this, and we're still standing in the rain. Talking of cakes ...' She pauses to give me a 'what the hell?' look for earlier. 'How about we settle the details over tea and ginger muffins?' I only hope she's doing the thing where you keep your friends close, and your enemies closer. As for the ginger, the stress from the Manor's onslaught has sent her off chocolate. How awful is that? And particularly ironic given her choice of breakfast guest.

But before we have the chance to stampede to the kitchen, Immie reappears, beaming. 'It's official, Chas is on board. Go ahead. Call Nicole.'

And by the time we finally finish hugging Immie, Kip is on his way to the office phone. But we already know what Nicole's going to say.

Chapter 39

Saturday, 12th August
At Daisy Hill Farm on the double wedding day: Pearls and pigs

The next two days go down as the busiest of my life. But the great thing is, there's so much to do, that even though Immie's a close friend, for some reason this time round I'm not brooding about how it was all those years ago, getting ready for my own wedding. There's simply no time to feel sad. Maybe I've got Kip to thank for that. His first contribution to the flood clean-up is to revert to type. The way the walls are reverberating so hard with heavy rock, you'd think loud music had drying properties. There's too much noise from Iron Maiden to leave any space in my head for thinking. On the plus side, he does his best to dry out the tiled floor of the Winter Garden and helps me in with the ten foot trees Nicole ordered to go along the aisle. Then he sends his estate guys up step ladders to wire the hundreds of white flowers into the branches, and drape the diamanté strings from tree to tree. If my hydrangea blooms in shiny tubs are wilting due to an overdose of Deep Purple, for one time only, I'll let it go.

'I promise, if it's the last thing I do, I'll make this place ready for your mum,' Kip says as he staggers past me with a stack of chairs. So much for Penryns running out on responsibility. This one is ready to take on the problems of the whole world single handed.

I still have my entourage of helpers when I arrive at the farm, along with everything that's not going into the ballroom. There are enough trees for the orangery and the terrace too. Where, for the record, it's still raining. The diamanté strings are thrashing around in the wind, but they're a perfect addition to the walled garden with its neat lawn, and pretty border of tangled plants and climbing roses. Jess is back at the shop, overseeing the glittering of Nicole's roses, and table arrangements adorned with as many dangling diamonds as a Kardashian's jewellery box. Meanwhile I'm in the house, overseeing the table stylings, and pulling together the thousand finishing touches that Nicole has spent six months deliberating over. This isn't so much a wedding as a work of art.

Over the top? Unreservedly. Bling? By the shedload. After all, she's walking down the aisle to *Diamonds Are Forever*. And somehow it couldn't be a better fit for Nicole and her gem encrusted lifestyle. At the Manor the accessories would have been fabulous. But when everything arrives, and it's set against the backdrop of the simple lime wash and vintage details of the farmhouse, it's astonishing.

'Flaming toad bums, posh, or what?' Immie says when she

clomps in to inspect the orangery on her way to her wedding-morning make-up session. But Poppy and I can tell from the glow in her cheeks that she loves it.

The irony is – and there's going to be plenty of it today – that Immie and Chas are going to be the first ones to enjoy the sparkle, because they're having their ceremony here at eleven. An early slot, chosen to give maximum party time. And fingers crossed, they should be finished and away up to the barn for when Nicole and Miles and their guests come on from their one o'clock Winter Garden ceremony and photos.

I catch up with Immie getting ready after I've set out the masses of jugs and jars of flowers in the barn. Gathered by the armful from the walled garden at dusk yesterday, by Kip and me. There's just enough time for me to change out of my jeans into my navy broderie anglaise shift, and gulp down a glass of bucks fizz, before we're hurrying off down the court-yard, with Immie in her wedding dress.

As I carry her tiny rosebud posy, and Poppy carries her bag, Immie's between us, an arm linked through each of ours, hands holding up her skirt.

'I know you're not bridesmaids, but you've got to stay with me.' She's striding out in her Doccies, as if she's off to do the laundry. 'For eff sake, Morg, are the ring bearers ready?' She calls back to her son, Morgan, who's a few paces behind us, folding up the umbrella, because by some twist of fate the rain's stopped. After so many wet days, if you want evidence for karma, the rain stopping at this moment has to be it.

He rolls his eyes. 'Take a chill pill, Mum. Rafe's got them outside the garden, next to Nicole's caterer's vans.'

Who incidentally are waiting in the wings, and coming back into the farmhouse as soon as Chas and Immie leave. Complicated? Just a bit.

I'd almost forgotten. 'Ring bearers? Which did you decide on?' After all those Instagram posts, I can't believe I don't know.

Immie gives a chuckle. 'You'll see soon enough. I'd have had Henrietta the hen if it hadn't been for the bird flu scare. Believe me, these ones will look brill next to all those diamonds though.'

'So long as they behave they'll be lovely.' Poppy's OMG eyebrow wiggle over Immie's head tells me it's not a given. That's the trouble. When you involve animals, anything could happen.

As we arrive at the garden gate, Immie pauses to spike up her hair, and lets out a small squeal. 'I can't believe it's happening so fast. Where the hell did this morning go?'

'Four hours drinking lager, and having your make up done.' Poppy laughs. 'Worth every second. You've got contours and eyebrows to die for.' As far as we know, Immie didn't exceed her self-imposed five-can limit.

Immie thumps me on the arm as we go down the side of the house. 'It's only thanks to you and your sodding blindfold that I'm not here in my jeans, Lily.' She lets out a belly laugh, blows up her non-existent fringe, flaps her fingers in front of her face, and starts to hyperventilate. 'Toad bollocks, this really is it. I need to pinch myself to suspend my disbelief. Who'd have thought I'd ever get such a hottie? I truly am actually going to get to marry frigging wonderful Chas.'

'You totally are.' Poppy and I sniff, and exchange teary glances.

Half way across the grass Immie digs her heels in, and as she stops we both jolt into her. 'Omigod, I feel sick.'

Poppy groans, and rubs her stomach. 'Me too.'

I glance at my watch and realise it's down to me to get Immie the last ten yards to the door. 'Two minutes past eleven. Fashionably late, but still early enough to keep the registrars happy.' I tug on her arm, propelling her forwards. 'Come on, Immie, Chas is waiting for you. Let's do this.' I break into the nearest thing to a run I can manage in my second highest Miss KG heels.

As we dip under the swinging diamond strands hanging from the terrace trees, and reach the orangery doors I catch a glimpse of Chas way up front, raking his fingers through his sandy hair. Frowning, but fabulous in his navy suit.

'Ready to go?' Sometimes you just have to get on with it. Pressing the posy into Immie's hands, I pull her to me for the briefest of hugs, turn her into the doorway, aim between the first two trees on the aisle, and give her a huge push. Then I throw Morgan in after her.

As he catches up and grasps her arm, she starts to move her legs.

'Perfect or what?' I whisper to Poppy as Elvis starts singing the first few words of *Burning Love*, and the sun breaks through the clouds. As Poppy and I creep into the back row of chairs in the orangery, I catch a glimpse of Rafe being pulled across the grass, hanging onto two leads.

'Pigs?' I gasp. Cream with black spots, the size of small dogs. 'Oh my, Jules is going to have a field day.'

Poppy's grin is rueful. 'They were piglets when Immie chose them, but they grew.'

And dangling from each of their necks is a ring box.

Chapter 40

Saturday, 12th August
At Daisy Hill Farm on the double wedding day: Regal
dressing and secret agents

'Not saying you should go anywhere, but just to let you know Nicole and Miles' first guests are arriving.' Poppy whisks two vol au vents from the tray the landlady of the Goose and Duck is carrying as she passes, and puts one into my hand.

'I'll wander down soon. Miles seemed very grateful when he popped in earlier for a preview. But he doesn't have Nicole's appetite for complaining.' I bite on the delicious asparagus and cheese, and lick the pastry flakes off my fingers. 'I don't know how you stand the stress of a wedding every week.' What's more, if Kip's thinking of doing a wedding a day, he has to be bonkers. Or maybe hooked on the adrenalin rush? Which would explain how on task and wedding-attentive he's been lately.

You know those days when there's so much going on, and the stakes are so high, you're too stiff to breathe? And it's

348

about much more than your feet being scrunched into heels that you can't wait to take off. The kind of day when there's not even time to fantasise about how it's going to feel much later when you finally slide your feet into pumps. That's me, now.

'Bart's in charge back at the Manor, Kip's trouble shooting here. And your mum and David were in the courtyard.' This is Poppy bringing me up to speed. We're sunning ourselves with the guests, under flapping flowery bunting in the meadow behind the barn, as Immie and Chas work their way around hand in hand, swigging cans of beer, and saying their 'hellos'.

'It's weird Mum and Nicole ending up at each other's weddings.' I say. 'They were so fighty the day they met in Kip's office.' Although they're scarily alike. And it runs a lot deeper than their Mighty pink lipstick.

Poppy's grin is mischievous. 'They've bonded over the Manor. Plus they both adore you of course.'

'How was she looking?' It's a question I always ask about my mum, and I brace myself for the answer.

Poppy wrinkles her nose. 'Queenly, in an easy to spot in a crowd kind of way. Typical Barbara. Lime suit, orange hat, and grenadine pink accessories.' As expected. The bigger the occasion, the brighter the palette.

'A bit like a hurricane cocktail, then,' I say. 'Or a parrot.' Poppy and I are alcohol free, due to our responsibility levels, but for the first time ever I could do with a stress-busting drink. As I swig my Coke ruefully, I'm looking at the ring bearers in their pen in the corner of the field. 'Weren't the pigs good?'

Poppy laughs. 'Those last two words aren't often in the same sentence. Especially with the adolescent ones. Immie goes the extra mile for Daisy Hill every time. Photogenic ring-bearing pigs will be excellent publicity for us.' She pats my arm as someone waves her inside. 'Back in a minute.'

As I watch the pigs cross the field, at first I'm thinking their pen must be huge. It's only as they break into a trot, and nip around the corner of the barn, that I remember the escaping sheep.

'Shit. The pigs are out.' I bash the nearest guest on the shoulder but they look at me blankly. 'Tell Poppy,' I add, wildly.

I can't hang around. I'm not a farmer, but if there are loose pigs, with two wedding parties going on, I have to go after them. By the time I've nipped round the side of the barn, the pigs are out in the courtyard, sniffing the air. I'm willing them to turn left, up towards the fields but they turn down hill instead. As they amble past the holiday cottages I stay close to the stone walls, stalking them. I watch as they stop by the front door of the last cottage, stick their snouts into a plant pot, and root.

'Nice piggies, stay where you are.' If I talk loud enough I'm hoping someone will hear me. Come to help. Anyone would do. So many people, and they're all either in the barn, or out in the meadow.

As the plant pot clatters over, spilling soil across the cobbles, the pigs skitter away, and I totter after them.

'Shit. Wait for me. Please don't go near the farmhouse.' I'm wailing as we all pick up speed. As for these two rampaging through Nicole's reception ... 'Stop. Please stop.'

We whizz past the laundry, our store, the farm office. As we draw level with the door to Poppy's kitchen, we're breaking into a run. Running? Me? I avoid it for an entire lifetime, and end up doing it twice in one day. Hurtling along in heels, panting from sheer panic. Miss KG's were never designed to travel at this speed. And neither was I.

'Stop.' It's a random howl in case there's anyone in Poppy's part of the house. We're belting on down the yard, and I catch a flash of my mum's chartreuse plumage in the group of arriving guests milling in front of the farmhouse. And oh my god, the door to the farmhouse is wide open.

'Waaaaaaaaaaaaaaaahhhhh!' As I open my mouth and let out a scream, I catch sight of a familiar face. 'Fred, stop the pigs, head them off ...'

As eight trotters clatter towards him, Fred leaps backwards, hits the wall, and as he disappears over it the pigs veer off, straight towards the open door.

There's no time to be gobsmacked at Fred's total fail, because in my head I'm already seeing fifty chairs meticulously spaced around the tables, in the reception room with the grand piano. Each carefully chosen chair with a bow, tweaked to Nicole's exact specification. Hand-tied rose posies secured a measured distance up from the seats. Not to mention dangling linen cloths at pig height, every table laid to silver service standards, with plates, cutlery, glasses and table centres. Worse still, there's the wedding cake Poppy's been slaving over all week. Five towering silver-leafed tiers, a cascade of roses and diamonds, and at least a sackful of edible glitter. All balanced on a narrow pedestal table. One push of a piggy snout would be enough to send it flying. In my head the cake's already exploding into a million pieces as it crashes, and the pigs are snuffling up the crumbs from the polished oak floor.

Then a bright green figure darts out of the crowd. It's my mum, and she's yelling like a banshee, clapping her hands. 'Daviiiiiiiiid ... here ... now ... please ...'

What happens next is like something from a Bond film, over dubbed with me screaming in one long howl. As the action slips into slow motion the pigs are galloping, stiff legged, towards the house, scattering the startled guests as they charge. They're a couple of metres from the building, when two guys in tuxes come storming out of the doorway, like secret agents without the guns. Jackets flying, they hurl themselves horizontally through the air, landing face down on top of a pig each. As they rugby tackle the porkers to the ground, Rafe comes rushing down the yard too. It's only when the guys stand up, and begin to manhandle their captives across the cobbles that I realise they aren't crack spies at all.

'David?' If I'm blinking wildly it's because I'm gobsmacked. 'And Kip?' Somehow I've stopped howling, and we've flipped back to normal speed too.

'We heard your mum calling.' David says. 'It's always best to come when she asks.'

Fred, back on the right side of the wall, runs up and makes a grab for a pig. 'I've got this, I can take it from here.'

Kip raises an eyebrow. 'Leave it to the professionals, mate.' He grins as he catches my eye. 'On Her Majesty's Secret Service or what?'

'Nice work guys,' I say. Even though that's seriously understating what they just did, we all know I'm being ironic. Frigging genius wouldn't begin to cover it.

David's shrug is diffident. 'Barbara's the one you need to thank. She gave us the alarm call.' And other than a scuffed shoe, and a couple of mud marks on their shirts, they're still box-fresh and Bond-cool as they push the pigs into a nearby stable, and saunter back to wait for the bride and groom.

So much so that when Mr and Mrs Ferrara's white Rolls purrs in a couple of minutes later, Nicole's none the wiser. As the door opens there's a huge waft of Lady Million, then as a familiar jewel-studded sandal appears, there's a shriek.

'Lileeeeeeeee!'

A second later, my face is being rammed into a chestful of diamonds, as I'm engulfed in one of Nicole's most massive hugs ever.

'Haven't things worked out perfectly? I always wanted to have my wedding here. Thank you sooooooo much. And have you seen my ring?' A sparkling circle arrives next to my nose.

'More diamonds? *All* the way round? Ooooooooh, fabulous. How brilliant is that?' By now I know to super-size my reaction.

As she eases her grip her gaze falls on the spangly heart hanging on the farmhouse front door, and her fingers begin to flap. 'Omigod, the heart wreath! It isn't vertical! What *were*

353

you thinking? I can't arrive at my wedding breakfast with a wonky door decoration. Somebody sort it! Quick!'

As she claps her hands Kip and I take a moment to exchange heartfelt grimaces. Then he dashes off to do as he's told, and we both move on with our day.

Chapter 41

Saturday, 12th August
At Daisy Hill Farm on the double wedding day: A moment
in the dark

'I can't begin to thank you for today, Water Lily.'

At midnight on Immie's wedding day, after three days with no sleep, a chat with Kip is not top of my list of priorities. Especially not in the darkest corner of the courtyard. And he's either dead on his feet, or been hitting the Prosecco, because his voice has gone so low and sincere, it's almost emotional.

'Maybe you could start by being less of a jerk?' Hopefully my half-joke will brush away that he's veering scarily close to sentimental. Although even as I say it, I know it's unfair. I can't quite put my finger on when it happened, but somewhere down the line his rich-kid get-right-up-your-nose arrogance melted away. And got replaced by ... *Shit. Please tell me I wasn't about to think the words 'something way more subtle and attractive'.* 'What are you doing up here anyway? Haven't you got your own wedding to look after?'

He wrinkles his nose. 'Just checking you hadn't got into difficulties catching any more bouquets.'

A likely story. He'll be scoping out the opposition's new venue while he's got the chance. 'No danger today. Immie didn't throw hers.' No, I didn't have her down as a softie either. But the rosebuds will dry beautifully. And she swears she's going to keep them for her grandchildren. So watch this space on that one.

'I wanted to see your flowers too. They look amazing, especially against the backdrop of the barn.' Since when did Kip enthuse about flowers?

My chest is pumping up with pride. 'Those cottage garden varieties are perfect for a country setting,' I say, even though I shouldn't take *all* the credit, when someone else did the bulk of the watering on those borders.

'Definitely worth the walk up from the house.' Despite the shadows, Kip's broad smile is visible. 'And I also came to flag up that the award assessors dropped in earlier.'

Now he tells me. I wince. 'Of all the days.' And if for a fleeting second the curve of his lips is making my stomach squish, it's only because I'm entirely knackered, and my feet are killing me, okay?

Kip gives a 'nothing to do with me' shrug. 'The assessors should have seen the Ferraras at the Manor. Don't worry, they loved it here, and I put in a good word for Rafe and Poppy.'

'That was big of you.' What I said earlier about him not being a knobhead? Forget it. 'Although this double wedding has made me see how different your venues are.'

'And?' His eyes narrow. 'When you do that frown, there's usually something profound and brilliant on the way.'

I sigh, because now's really not the time for a marketing discussion. 'This far you've both been competing for the same couples, and each getting half the bookings.' Which is hopeless for everyone. 'But the Manor's so unique, I reckon you should be pitching it a lot further up the market. Charge way more, have fewer events. Less work for a better return.' And give Poppy and Rafe their customers back. I can't understand why a lazy-bum Penryn hasn't worked this out already.

Kip's banging his hand on his head. 'This is exactly why I need you as my stylist. Yet another one you've hit out of the ballpark. Why didn't I think of that?'

I laugh. 'Probably because you've been too busy placating Nicole.'

'I did have time out to pull Fred up the meadow, and settle an old score just now.'

I can't believe what I'm hearing. 'You had time to play tug of war?' Seems like I sneaked into Poppy's kitchen for a tea revival at exactly the wrong moment. Or maybe the right one.

Kip's sidestepping my question. 'It's ironic you missed it. Fred only challenged me to impress you. Turns out he's all bulk, no strength.' No need to ask who came out of that one best. Which might explain why Kip's grin refuses to go away.

I'm not going to rise to that any further. 'In case you've forgotten, you're in charge of a wedding party, Kip.'

He smiles. 'Which has moved back to the Manor, for champagne in the hot tub ...' He pauses to share his wide-eyed 'what the hell' head shake. '... as overseen by Bart, with help from Jess. Where no doubt I'll catch up with them very soon. Meanwhile, I'm snatching my first breather of the day, which believe me, is exceedingly well earned.'

I'm sounding stern. 'Professional wedding coordinators only get a break once the guests leave for *home*.' As for what Jess is doing there helping, well, shall I just say that Kip's staffing arrangements are getting more and more unorthodox?

He's got his wheedling voice on. 'You're such a party pooper, Water Lily. That glitterball's too good for us to miss. Come and dance. Just one track. *Then* I'll leave.'

Rolling my gaze upwards, I catch sight of the half moon, shining between the stars. 'Totally not appropriate.' He's out of order, on every side. Although it's a relief to know he hasn't nailed the perfect venue manager act after all. As for the glitterball, that was a gigantic last-minute brainwave from Blue Watch. Strange I'm even considering dancing, let alone tempted. Gritting my teeth, I put my hands on my hips. Then point my finger firmly towards the farmhouse, and Rose Hill Manor beyond. 'Go, Kipling. I mean it. Right now.' Hopefully that's convincing enough for both of us.

As he hesitates, and narrows his eyes, my heart rate picks up. Then he swallows, and as he hitches his breath, my knees feel like they're chocolate that melted. Then a play punch lands on my arm, pins me back to the wall, and knocks me back to reality.

'Okay, you win, Lily flower. ' He turns, puts his hands in

his jacket pockets, and turns down the yard. 'If you're insisting I go, I'll have to catch you in the morning then.'

I watch his moon shadow bobbing on the cobbles until he disappears into the darkness. And when he's completely gone, I'm disgusted to find the night feels horribly empty.

Chapter 42

Monday, 11th September
In the garden at Rose Hill Manor: Clashing colours and
cutting back

'So, what's popping?'

It's the Monday before Barbara and David's wedding. It's David – and the answer to his question is his head if I did what I'm tempted to do and slam it in the door to the walled garden at the Manor as he sticks it through. Even if he saved Nicole's day, and her wedding cake, by wrestling half of the bacon brothers into submission, I'm still dying on his behalf every time he uses that phrase. Why the hell can't he manage a plain and simple 'hi' like everyone else does?

To bring you up to date, the Ferraras are honeymooning on a yacht in Monte Carlo. As boats go, apparently theirs is so big it barely fits into the harbour. Not that we're jealous, but Nicole would like us to spread the word. More locally, Chas and Immie have almost recovered from their wedding party hangovers. And three weeks on from the flood, thanks to a workforce who've slaved non-stop, the Manor is almost back to how it was. Give or take a few sofas, currently in transit. Which is why my mum and David have dropped by to check on progress.

'Dahling, at last … we've *finally* found you.' As my mum skips past David, and down the grassy path, I can't help but colour match her pedal pushers to the acid yellow African marigolds that came up in the border by mistake. 'Kip gave us our tour, and assured us everything's hunky dory back at the house, then he *very* kindly brought us on here.'

I pick up my scissors and move my garden trug across to the cosmos border. 'I knew you'd be fine with Kip. I've been catching up on some tidying.' I don't have to admit I was ducking out of their tour. With flowers bursting out in every corner, on sunny days it's so idyllic here, I can't stay away. I'm here whenever I can fit it in. And often when I can't.

'We barely see you these days, dahling.' My mum consistently forgets the rest of the world doesn't enjoy three six five days a year leisure time.

I wrinkle my nose. 'There's a lot on at work.' It's true. Not only are there future bookings coming in, but lots of brides come down to the Style File for inspiration and one off orders. And since the double wedding day, we've also done a beach wedding party, a hipster wedding, and a Wild West reception in the fields at the farm.

As I look up from my dead heading, I see Kip wandering in too, chatting to David. 'Am I getting three for the price of two today?'

'I thought your mum would like to see how her flowers are doing,' Kip says. He's got no idea she won't.

Given I was supposed to be meeting them all back at the house for coffee, it's my guess he's had enough of my mum for one morning, and is handing her on, A.S.A.P. But obviously no-one's told him she avoids gardens like the plague due to the dirt, unless she's visiting the washing line. Although lately, thanks to her fixation with Fred, I've noticed she'll go out to check the wood store too.

My mum frowns. 'I'm not so much of a garden person. Seeing the flowers when they're in the bouquet at the wedding will be absolutely soon enough for me. Although now I'm here, I do want to talk about your "plus one" for next weekend, Lily.'

I'm so shocked I drop my scissors and they stab my foot as they land. Bending down to rub my toe gives me time to regroup. 'There's nothing to discuss. I'm coming as "me, myself and I". Strictly speaking that's me "plus two".'

She's straight back at me. 'Absolutely not. It's all arranged. Fred's agreed to go with you.'

'What?' I let out an indignant shriek. And not only because of her massive interference. I'm thinking back to suspicious log spills, falling carnations, non-scheduled muck deliveries, and escaping sheep. Not to mention hot tub floods. 'I know he's been very helpful in the garden, but that doesn't mean I have to pair up with him.' It's completely unfair to send him the wrong messages too.

Her expression changes. 'I can't see Fred gardening, dahling. He doesn't know one end of a spade from another.' Which only shows how little she knows Fred.

I shake my head in exasperation, then remember what

Poppy and Jess told me. I need to stand up for myself here. 'I refuse to go to your wedding paired up with Fred. End of. Okay?' Calm and quiet. Easy as. Although from my mum's thunderous eyes, it's anything but.

Her lips are like a pink zinnia as they pinch together tightly. 'You've had six months to make yourself attractive enough to land a man. Anyone would do. Yet you're happy to ruin my big day, just because you can't damn well be bothered to put in the effort.'

David's suddenly at her shoulder. 'That's a bit strong, Barbs. Lily's great as she is. Not everyone wants to be a couple.'

My mouth's open ready to tell him to butt out, but I shut it again. He's only trying to help.

Kip's brow wrinkles. 'Lily's hot. But she doesn't currently have room for a man in her life. For the record, Barbara, she's turned me down more than once.'

My mum's jaw drops. '*You* offered?' Her voice is squeaky with shock.

Now it's my turn to frown. 'When exactly?' I might be shooting myself in the foot here, but I suspect he's bullshitting big time. On every front.

Kip shrugs. 'On the lane when you were taking selfies with the wedding venue sign. The night the assessors came. Again at Immie's wedding.' As his eyes light up with wickedness, I know there's something worse coming. 'We even spent a night together. You surely haven't forgotten that already, Water Lily?'

David's beaming. 'Didn't I tell you, Barbs?'

Kip goes on. 'I'll be more than happy to partner Lily at

your wedding. No strings, for one day only, if she wants it in the small print. But that has to be *her* decision.'

I narrow my eyes at Kip. 'Thanks, I'll get back to you on that. And the rest.' I'm not sure if this has made it better or worse.

My mum's voice is a growl. 'You'd better say "yes", Lily. I refuse to let you unbalance my photos and be a single embarrassment in front of all my friends.' Although seriously, with attitudes like this it's a wonder she's got any friends at all. 'Ready to go, David?'

Given David's wearing his athletics shorts, you couldn't blame him for running a mile when she snaps at him like that. He gives her a long suffering smile. 'Aren't you forgetting why we came, Barbs?'

My mum's mouth is a perfect 'O', as her cheeks blanch. 'Right. Of course.' It's almost a croak. 'It's the house. We've had an offer.'

'Crap.' My stomach implodes. I've been rushing around so much, somehow I'd almost forgotten. It takes a minute to get my voice to come out again. 'And will you accept?'

My mum draws herself up to her full five foot four. 'I expect we will.'

Crap again then. 'Well that's just great. I hope you'll be very happy obliterating every trace of Dad, and moving on to your spanky new flat with your shiny new toy boy.' It's like a boil's been lanced, and the poison's gushing out. And now it's started, there's nothing I can do to stop it. 'It's your life, Mum. You're old enough. Feel free to go ahead and fuck it up.'

As the 'f' word resounds off the garden walls, and the age barb hits home, my mum clasps her hands to her chest, and sinks against the delphinium stakes. 'I can't believe you're being so selfish, Lily. Your father would be *so* ashamed of you. And your language.'

I'm growling inside. 'Leave *my* dad out of this. And stop turning this back on to me, when you're the most self-centred person in the world.'

As I'm getting louder, my mum's turning more steely. 'I don't know how you can be so manipulative, Lily. It's been all about you ever since the day I got engaged. We've tried to ignore how difficult and obstructive you've been, but this time you've gone too far.'

My voice rises to a roar, because I know how unfair that is. 'That's rich, coming from the queen of the guilt trip.' I must have some restraint left, because so far I've left out the 'Bridezilla' word. Even though she totally has been.

Her cheeks are red and blotchy. 'No one's forcing you to be present next weekend, Lily. In fact, I'm officially uninviting you. With attitudes like yours I don't want you there when I get married. You'll only spoil that too.'

Kip's eyes are wide with disbelief. 'How about we all calm down and have a drink? I know Lily needs to start standing up for herself, but maybe now's not the moment. Anyone for coffee? Or brandy maybe?' Nice try, mate.

I drop my trug and throw down my gloves. 'Not for me, thanks. I've got somewhere else to be.' Like anywhere in the world would be preferable to here.

As I belt out of the garden and back to Gucci I'm kicking

myself. I'd truly promised myself I wouldn't make a squeak before the wedding. For once Kip's completely right about the timing. And now we've just had world war three. There are some arguments you can't ever come back from. I think this is one of them.

Chapter 43

In the Style File at Brides by the Sea: Short change and the housing market

'I've brought you some sweet peas.' It's David, and he's dropped a bundle of newspaper on the counter. 'We grew them at your mum's.'

Given how much my mum hates dirt, I seriously doubt she had anything to do with them. As for what happened yesterday at the Manor, it seems like it's so huge, we're actually blanking it from our memories because we can't cope with it.

'Lovely.' It's a knee jerk reaction, with a completely fake matching smile to hide that my heart is squishing to nothing in my chest. Dad loved his sweet peas. We're years down the line, but for the first time ever, it hits me he's never going to grow another. And this is one of those moments that bursts from nowhere. Then pole-axes you. When my chin eventually stops wobbling, I lift up a crumpled page, and peer in at the pastel petals. As the scent wafts up my nostrils, I see I was right first time. Whoever grew these, lovely is the perfect word for them.

David's leaning towards me, a pained frown on his face. 'She said yours didn't grow, so I was coming to say you can have some from us if you want. Although I think there are other flowers she likes better. But now it might not matter anyway.'

It has to be the longest sentence he's ever managed. Probably because I usually cut him off way shorter.

'Thanks. I didn't know you gardened. Didn't you live in a bedsit?'

His frown deepens. 'Temporarily. When my wife died I rushed into moving out of our home, because it was too painful to stay where we'd lived. We had one of the big houses on the St Aidan cliff road, with a huge garden, and views across the bay. Too big for two, let alone one.'

'I see ... I mean, I'm sorry.' I'm ashamed to admit I've never really looked beyond the jeans and my hasty assumptions. A grieving widower living on what's locally known as 'millionaire's row' was the last thing I imagined he'd be. So much for me writing him off as a gold digger.

He winces. 'That's why I'm worried about your mum. I'm sure that's why she flipped out at the Manor yesterday. Selling the family home is a major step for both of you. I don't need to move again. I've had my new start moving in with her. I think she should reconsider the move.'

I'm picking myself up off the floor here. 'But what about the penthouse?'

David's sniff is dismissive. 'It's glitzy, but it's not really us.

We'd be far better off staying at your mum's.' If what he says is true, Rock Quay would probably be small change to him.

'She's already got an offer though.' It sticks in my throat as I say it.

His frown deepens. 'You know she's never worn the engagement ring we chose.'

Weren't we talking about house sales? 'She hasn't?' I've never seen a ring at all.

He lets out a long sigh. 'And after her blow out with you, now we've had our first argument too.' Somehow he's skipping bits.

I'm not sure I want to hear this. Although part of me still thinks I should be whooping to think my mum's finally coming to her senses. Even if we aren't speaking. 'You had a fight because she won't wear the ring?'

His stare is bemused. 'Not exactly. The thing is, she's always criticising you. And she shouldn't have spoken to you as she did yesterday. But when I suggested she needed to back off and break the habit, she went ballistic.'

I'm chomping on my lip because I can't believe what I'm hearing. 'You told her *that*?'

His expression is panicked. 'Her criticism comes from a good place. She does it because she loves you. But for now I'm on my way back to my bedsit.' He nods at the flowers. 'I picked those before it happened.'

'Shit.' I'm opening and closing my mouth, rearranging my sweet pea package, because I can't think what else to add. People talk about surprises coming out of left field, but this is so shocking, it could have come from outer space.

He hitches up his jeans and lets out another defeated sigh. 'I'm just checking in to say your mum's a wonderful woman. She lit up my life when I was in a very dark place. I don't want to lose her, but I'd hate to push her into something she's not ready for. Like a house move. Or marriage. So I've been in touch with Kip to put things on hold. And I'm giving her some space. Time to think it over.' As he squeezes my upper arm for a second, his hand is trembling. 'Thanks for listening, Lily. I'll leave it with you.'

A second later he's left, and he's running up the stairs.

Five days to go, and reading between the lines my mum's wedding just hit the buffers. Can I help to sort my mum out in time? That's not going to be easy when we're not even talking.

Chapter 44

Wednesday, 13th September
In the garden at Rose Hill Manor: Lavender flowers and
empty seats

'Kip, what are *you* doing here? Whatever happened to
swing ball?'

I know it's his walled garden. It's just I've never actually
come and found him in it before.

He puts down the spade he's holding. 'Straight back at you.
It's only five. Why aren't you at the shop?'

Good point well made. But since David dropped by with
his sweet peas and his wedding bombshell yesterday, my
mind hasn't exactly been on the job. There's nothing like a
couple of hours pottering among the flowers to calm you
down. So, pushed by Poppy, I made a fast getaway, and here
I am at the Manor. As I hear the bees buzzing on the daisies,
the invisible tourniquet pulled tight around my head loosens.
I wander across to my corner of the garden, run my hand
across the feathery leaves of a border of dill, and nip away

a couple of seed heads in a vibrant patch of orange and yellow marigolds.

'Poppy sent me home early with a box of goodies.' She saw me tugging my hair and pacing, and came to the rescue. As I hold up my swag I can't help laughing as his expression brightens.

'Cupcakes?' Tongue hanging out doesn't begin to cover it. Kip jumps down from the raised border by the wall where he's standing, and saunters across to the love seat. Installed especially for picturesque bride and groom photo opportunities.

I nod. 'Glad to see your confectionery antennae are in perfect working order.' I'm relieved when he pushes a trailing nasturtium out of the way, and sits on the wall opposite, leaving the pretty cream painted bench under the climbing rose free for me.

I settle myself in, take a second to admire how the pink cosmos go perfectly with the smoky purple cat mint flowers either side of me, and hand him the box. 'Raspberry and vanilla, or lemon. They're leftovers.'

'I can live with that. Still with the "I do" stickers on too.' He smiles and takes one of each. 'I was planting some lavender, I hope that's okay?'

Planting? I hide that I'm surprised. 'You don't have to ask me for permission. It is your garden, after all.' As I take a bite of sponge, and the raspberry icing melts into my mouth, the day immediately gets better.

He brushes the crumbs off his top lip. 'I'd rather think of it as our garden. Would you like some water with these?'

I watch him swing off to the shed, and emerge with two glasses. Then as he turns on the outside tap, goes straight to the end of the hose a couple of borders away, and fills them, I'm puzzled by his ease.

He hands me my glass. 'Something wrong?'

I pull down the corner of my mouth. 'Only how at home you look. Considering how rarely you're in here.'

He shrugs that off. 'My mum loved lavender. As boys, when we were home from school, she bought us to the Manor a lot more often than our London house. And this walled garden was her favourite place of all. While we ran wild, she spent her time here. When Bart and Quinn insisted I should come back to Rose Hill, I have to admit it was the memories of this garden that drew me back, not the thought of weddings.' He pulls a wry face. 'But I think you guessed that.'

I sigh. 'Immie texted earlier, to say my mum's back in her pyjamas again.' Kip's up to speed with my mum's wedding cancellation.

He blows out his cheeks. 'I know your mum isn't easy. But deep down she's very proud of you. You should have heard her singing your praises at Nicole's wedding. The trouble is, she never tells you.'

I roll my eyes. 'I was always closer to my dad. My mum and I are so unalike, we always found it hard to get on.'

Kip's frown is as perplexed as I feel. 'My dad was shit, but I still hang onto him. It's thanks to him I landed up here, but that one's for another time.' He puts his fingers together. 'Family's about much more than how well you get on. When I messed up, mine forgave me. Even though you disapproved, look how hard you've fought for your mum's wedding. The way you've kicked my ass into gear, so she'd have the best day possible. You may have your differences. But when it comes to the important stuff, you've got each other's backs.'

I bite my lip, because he does have a point. 'Maybe.' I'm just not sure what to do about it.

He rolls down the case on his second cupcake. 'It was all down to your mum that we caught those pigs before they turned Nicole's wedding upside down. We all owe her for that, if nothing else.' He takes a bite and pauses to chew. 'What I'm saying is, you've only got one mum, so it would be really good if you could find a way to make up with her. Especially as she needs you. I suspect you're the only one who can help her with her current problem.' I think what he's really saying is, I'm damned lucky to have my mum, when he hasn't got his anymore. And as with so many other things, he's right, of course.

'She did save us all with the pigs.' I'm rocking backwards and forwards on the slatted seat.

His eyes are grave as he rubs his thumb on his chin. 'Whatever else is going on, I think you're the main reason she's hesitating over the wedding, Water Lily. Maybe you need to find a way to let her move on. If you set her free, you might set yourself free too. And you can't do that without talking to her.'

I'm thinking hard. Staring into the tangled mass of flowers in the border letting the words sink in. Suddenly, along the path, something extra orange catches my eye.

As I let out a wail, my agonising over my mum is suddenly eclipsed. 'Kip, please tell me that isn't a gnome over there?'

Kip's face crumples. 'He's only here temporarily, taking refuge from the builders. Since they invaded the house, I've been hanging out here even more, too.'

'*Even* more? More than *what*?' And suddenly, I'm thinking. Anyone who can go straight to the hose end has to have left it there. As the proverbial penny finally drops to wherever it goes to, I'm kicking myself for being so blind all these months. 'It's damn well been you all along, hasn't it? The digging, the watering. This whole damned beautiful garden grew because you've been here caring for it.' All this time I thought it was Fred. How crap am I?

His grin is sheepish. 'I can't think why you'd say that.'

'Digging holes for lavender plants? Of course it's been you.'

Kip dodges the empty cupcake box as it flies across the path. 'It's down to both of us. It wouldn't have happened without you, Lily. Just like I'd never have learned what to do at weddings if you hadn't pushed me as hard as you did. I was so pleased when I found you wanted to grow things here, I couldn't resist helping. But I didn't want to get in your way and I thought if you knew it was me you'd ask me to stop.'

I'm running my fingers through my hair. 'I feel like such an idiot. Immie was always trying to tell me.' As for Fred taking full credit, that fits too. 'All these months, and three days from the end of my flower growing challenge, I find out.'

He's suddenly serious. 'We *can* carry on, can't we? For next year, we'll get the flowers up on a website. We can do it together properly, as a joint venture.'

'But I'm supposed to be leaving town.' In three days' time, I'll finally be free to go.

His voice rises. 'But you *have* to stay. Look at your success with the shop, and the styling. If you make a fresh start with your mum, why move away?'

As I look around the garden, I feel a strange pull. 'It's an odd thing. For the first time in my life I'm good at things. It's as if these last few months I've actually reconnected with who I really am. Bringing the garden to life here has put me back in touch with the little girl I used to be, when I gardened with my dad all those years ago. As I grew up I was desperate to work with flowers because flowers make me happy. Somewhere along the line in Bath I'd lost sight of that. It's as if recalling that has made me remember who I am, and what I should be doing. And I'm doing things I love again. These flowers. The styling. People are turning to me for help. But the most amazing thing is, I don't feel defined by my failed marriage any more. It's like I've become a whole new person. I'm so different from the broken one who arrived here on Valentine's Day.' When I came I was all on my own, and determined to be strong and independent and run away to continue licking my wounds. But surrounded by friends, I've found a whole different strength.

Kip's smile is the kind that makes your stomach squelch. 'I've got a hell of a lot to thank you for here, and I don't just mean in the garden. You haul me out of trouble every time. You're the one with all the good ideas. No-one's ever been there for me like that before, Water Lily. Sorry to sound selfish, but I really don't want you to go.'

'Great.' I'm trying to work out how to stop the fluttering in my chest when I look at him. It's like rose petal confetti in the wind. 'It's important for you too, Kip. You need to find out what you like doing. Whatever those dreams of yours are, life's too short not to chase them. You owe it to yourself to do something you enjoy. I know you want to prove yourself with the wedding business, but you shouldn't only do things to please your family.'

Kip gives a wry smile. 'You're sounding very profound suddenly.'

If my cheeks are hot, it's because I've probably overstepped the mark here. Telling Kip how to run his life, when it's none of my business. If I'm out of line, it's only because I think he deserves to be happy.

I go back to what he was saying. 'You do know you'll come to the end of my wedding knowledge very soon. If you carry on your current exponential learning curve, I predict that'll happen sometime around three forty five tomorrow afternoon.' What's more, for the first time, I know I can trust him too. And omigod, and what the hell? But who'd have thought I'd ever get to say that about a Penryn?

He pushes himself up to standing, and gives me a nudge on the arm. 'Now go and see your mum and make things right. Truly, I haven't worked my ass off to get the house dried out only to have her cancel on us.'

As my eyes lock on the square of tanned thigh behind the rip in his jeans, I know he's right. It's just hard. 'What am I going to say?'

There are those lovely creases in his cheeks again as his

hand lands on my shoulder. 'Just go. Once you get there, I promise you'll find the words.'

As I jump into Gucci, and zoom along the lane towards Heavenly Heights, I only hope he's right.

Chapter 45

'What the heck happened to Trevor?'
      It wasn't what I planned to say as an ice breaker.
But as my mum opens her door a crack, the gap next to the
orange begonia where the gnome should be standing is so
gaping, I can't let it go.

My pumps are off ready, so I drop them on the shoe rack
behind the door, and follow her saggy fawn jogging bottoms
into the lounge. As she turns and sinks onto a sofa, my heart
sinks too. Her cheeks are as washed-out as her leisure suit,
and without her foundation and popping pink lips, she's aged
twenty years. Worse still, I'm in my gardening capris, and she
hasn't made me sit on a throw.

'The gnome's gone.' Her voice is flat as she pulls her cardie
round her. 'The For Sale board too. And I cancelled the cake,
and gave the wedding dress to the Cats Protection shop.' She's

also ripped the wallpaper off an entire feature wall, but for now, that's the least of my worries.

As I pull out a rug, and edge onto a chair, I'm struggling to catch up. 'So what happened?' This might be what I've secretly been hoping for the last six months, but now it's real it couldn't be more horrible.

She pulls a tissue from up her sleeve. 'David and I argued. I've made so many mistakes, and rushing into getting married was only one of them. I was such a fool to think I could ever carry off sequins.' She dabs at the corner of her eye. 'But I've been thinking a lot. The last few days I'm finally facing up to everything I should have considered months ago. You're right, I have been very selfish. The way we got engaged, we weren't right to spring it on you like that. We were just so excited, we didn't think.'

I'm not sure I've ever heard my mum admit to being wrong before. 'I suppose you were in love ...' At the time I was so shocked, I wasn't exactly sympathetic.

She blots her nose. 'It's okay, I've put it behind me.'

I'm biting my lip because she's so deflated. 'But you look like you did when Dad died.'

She clutches her shoulders. 'Actually that's what I feel like. It's as if the last five years never happened at all.'

'I'm so sorry if I caused this. I didn't mean to.' When I accidentally lost it the other day, I had no idea this would be the outcome.

My mum drags in a breath. 'It's better that it happened now. And I'm glad I listened to how you felt.'

I owe it to her to try to explain. I'm thinking back to the

night in the boat with Kip. 'I think the house is so important to me because if it hadn't been for him trying to deal with my divorce news, Dad wouldn't have died. Worse still, the last thing he knew before he died was what a mess I'd made of my life. And as much as I try, I find it hard to move on from that. All I want to do is cling on to the past when I was happier.'

My mum leans forward. 'But it wasn't like that.'

I've no idea how she can forget something this important. 'He was up on the golf course the afternoon I rang and told you about me and Thom. He always went up there when he wanted space to think.'

My mum's face wrinkles. 'I'm so sorry. He never knew about you and Thom, Lily. You rang me in the morning, and I spent all day trying to pluck up courage to ring him. But I couldn't find the words to tell him. I was going to break it to him when he got home.' Her voice cracks. 'But he never came.' She hesitates. 'Sorry, I should have said before. There was so much chaos. It never occurred to me you'd think that.'

'I never thought to ask.' In the weeks after, my mum was so dazed, she could hardly speak at all. And when she seemed to be moving forward, I never wanted to remind her. I'm sighing, because the stone of guilt I've carried round in my chest for five years has just been lifted. 'It was an awful time. But thanks for telling me. It makes it hurt a tiny bit less.' I reach across and clasp her wrist.

She pats my hand. 'You've got no idea how awful it was being on my own, even after the shock wore off. I was so lonely. When you lose your partner it never stops hurting. You never get used to it. You just learn better ways to carry the ache around with you.' She's rubbing her hands. 'I'll never be able to replace your dad. I wasn't looking to. It's just somehow David and I clicked. We both knew what the other was going through. We supported each other. And then when we realised maybe life was going to be worth living again, we got a bit carried away. But I've come to my senses again.'

I'm not completely sure that's a good thing. 'David came to see me. He said you lit up his life.' I have to tell her. When he said it he sounded so sincere.

'He told me that too.' She gives a wistful smile, before she goes on. 'I loved your dad. But the thing was, you and Zac were so clever, I often felt like you were all laughing at me.'

'Oh Mum, that's awful.' It was how we were. The family dynamic. We never really stopped to think.

She pulls a face. 'I know I always embarrassed you. I couldn't help feeling I was left out, that you were only putting up with me. And maybe that made me extra critical.'

'Dad and I were close because we enjoyed the same things.' I can see why she might have felt excluded.

My mum's looking seriously thoughtful. 'The thing is with David, for the first time in my life I felt as though he liked me for me. As I am. He didn't want me to change. Except to be nicer to you, and go with him to the gym, of course. But the things I've done lately, like the computer classes and the dating, I didn't feel like anyone was looking down on me.'

'That's so good, Mum.' Maybe for the first time in my life, I'm looking at her as a person too. Not just as my rather annoying mum. 'And look at you with your spinning and your fitness, and all your new interests. You're like a whole new version of yourself.'

A watery smile comes after her next nose blow. 'If your dad came back and saw me, I think he might be surprised.' Her smile strengthens. 'Quite a lot of the time I surprise myself. I'm not saying I'm glad. Just that in the end it wasn't as bad as I thought it was going to be at first.' She rubs her eye. 'David will never be your dad. But he makes me feel very loved and very special in a different way altogether.'

My eyes are filling with tears. 'I'm so glad we talked.' The warmth inside me is something I haven't felt. Possibly ever. 'You know I never saw your new engagement ring. Have you got one?'

Her eyes fill with tears too. 'It's still in its box. When it came to it, I couldn't possibly wear it. So much is *so* hard when you're trying to move on. You try to embrace new things, but sometimes it's too painful to let go of the past.'

'It's difficult.' I can hardly believe what she's saying. Or that I've got her so wrong. That I couldn't see past her exuberance to see how much she was still hurting underneath.

She swallows loudly. 'A while after I met David I took off the rings your dad gave me, and I've been wearing them on a chain around my neck. But somehow I could never bear to wear the new ring on my finger at the same time.'

My mouth's stretching into a wail I can't stop. 'I do miss Dad so much.'

'Me too.' My mum buries her face in my shoulder, and we have a long and very wet hug. It's a while later when we both let go, go back to our seats, and sniff at each other again.

'You know your dad and I never argued.' She's staring out at the garden, and David's row of pink and blue sweet peas along the fence. They're a different variety from Dad's. The blooms are smaller. And the foliage isn't so bushy. Which is kind of how it should be.

It's good to bring up their lack of arguing. 'I'm not sure how healthy that was. Dad sometimes gave in to you just to get an easy life.' All the time, really, but I'm not going to say that. So it's no surprise the row with David has knocked her sideways. 'Arguments can let you resolve issues though. Like with us, I didn't mean all the nasty things I said the other day. But without it we wouldn't have talked. And I'd still like it if you'd stop going on about me getting a boyfriend.'

She's putting her fingers together, looking down as she speaks. 'I'd hate you to end up being as lonely and unhappy as I felt. But I appreciate you're an adult, it's your decision. David's convinced me you wouldn't be on your own if that wasn't the way you wanted it. In the same way bright pink lipstick isn't for everyone.'

It's so great she's the one to bring this up. 'Definitely not me, okay? The same with Phase Eight clothes. They're great on you, but I'm not ready for them yet.'

'Understood.' Her meek nod is very unlike her. 'I only wanted to help, because you always looked so miserable. But you've changed. You smile a lot more now.'

I shrug, and give a grin. 'I'm not sure if it's work, or the garden. But I think these last few months here I learned how to be properly happy again. By reconnecting with the person I was before I met Thom, it's as if I'm starting again. Letting my bad times go. That feels good.'

And finally I can get onto the decorative devastation.

'So what's with the wall? I thought you liked your geometrics.'

My mum rolls her eyes at the half stripped paper. 'That's the funny thing. My whole life in this house, I've been obsessed with redecorating. But since I've been with David, we're so busy doing other things, I barely notice the paper, let alone have time to change it.'

'Although you will have to do something with that.' Given she's pulled off the top layer of paper, and there's bare plaster peeping through in places too.

She gives an exasperated blow. 'It was a mad moment. I could always put the same pattern back on again.'

'Or maybe you could let David choose?' It's a radical suggestion, given how things stand. When she doesn't shout me down, I carry on. 'I do think you should think carefully about marrying David. It sounds to me like it could be what you want. After talking to you both about how you feel, I do think it's right for you.' Is this really me saying this? Who'd have thought it, but yes, it damn well is. 'You make each other happy. And you really are too young to be on your own for the rest of your life. Especially if you love him.'

'You really think so?' My mum's voice is small.

As I nod, I'm biting back the tears. 'Yes, I really do.'

My mum leans forward, and her voice drops to a confidential whisper. 'You do realise he's only six months younger than me? He's just very fit ...' There's a gleam in her eye as she wiggles her eyebrows. 'And *exceptionally* well toned. It's not just his buttocks either.'

I've got my hands over my ears. 'Please stop there, that's way too much information.'

'So changing the subject ...' My mum's sitting up again, waiting for me to take my hands off my ears, suddenly much more perky. 'About the house ...' Brave woman for getting on to this. 'I'm not blaming Fred, but Rock Quay was more his idea than ours.'

I drag in a breath. 'Fred can be very persuasive.' As I know too well, resisting him is like standing up to a tank assault. He's also very driven in pursuit of his own goals.

My mum nods in agreement. 'When the offer came on this place, I hated the idea of anyone else living here. But as David said before we argued, if we did want to move onto something smaller eventually, you and Kip could always live here.'

I wrinkle up my nose. 'What's Kip got to do with this? He's got his own mansion.' Although I do owe him hugely for making me come round for this chat. Who'd have thought he'd be so wise? Or perceptive.

My mum's inscrutable smile is back. And I've never been so pleased to see it. 'I've absolutely no idea where David got the idea from. You'll have to ask him about that.'

'Talking of whom ...' I'm staring at my mum's leisure suit, really not understanding how she ever came to own anything so beige. 'If you go upstairs, have a shower, and get your lippy on, I could give David a ring, and suggest he pops over?'

'Lovely idea, dahling.' She's beaming as she scurries out of the room. 'If there's going to be some make up sex, I'd better find my Fitbit.'

Okay, I know. We've come a long way in the last hour. But this is real life, not a fantasy world. There are still going to be times I need my vomit bag. On the upside, it turns out David's a lot more than just a fab pig catcher. When I ring him and suggest he might like to come over and marry my mum after all he just says, 'Brill.' When I suggest he might like to bring five rolls of geometric paper, and his wallpapering scissors, and pick up a gnome on the way, he says 'Gotcha. Give me thirty, I'll be there.'

For the first time ever, I forget to wince. When it comes to it, my mum would have to look a long way to find anyone who loved her more. And I'm so happy I can finally see that.

Chapter 46

'All ready then?'

It's a silly question to ask your mum when she's one room away from her wedding. But we descend into nervous whispering as we come down the stairs from where she's been changing in the Bridal Suite at Rose Hill Manor. As we pause for Jules to take pictures at the bottom of the broad oak staircase, my mum turns to me.

'How ever did we think we'd fit in wallpapering?' She's right. Compressing a week's worth of wedding preps into two days has been manic. Especially given the arrival of my brother Zac, who jetted in late Thursday night. Weddings are fraught enough. A prodigal making an unannounced return when the emotional cauldron is already bubbling over is plain mean. Just saying. While it's brill he turned up, at the same time my poor mum lost hours of valuable run-up time due to apoplectic shock.

'Decorating in wedding week was always a crazy idea.' I

stoop to adjust the back of her skirt, where the hem ripples onto the floor in the subtlest hint of a train. 'Your dress is perfect though, the satin's gorgeous, it's moving with you.' Jess and Sera really came through for her with this at zero notice.

She smiles down at the silky shadows of her skirt. 'In the end it does feel classier than the sequins.'

They persuaded her into the simplest style in cream, with a pale grey edging to the flattering off the shoulder neckline. With the satin skimming her curves and falling like waves, she looks truly amazing.

She puts her hand on mine. 'You're the surprise though. I *knew* deep cherry would work for your jacket. Against your dark waves it couldn't be better.' Okay. It's only one teensy raw silk shrug. Somehow once it was my decision, I was happy to go with it. And yes, I gave in on the giant rose print bodycon too. Thanks to the curls I feel like Crystal from the old cartoon *Crystal Tipps and Alistair*, but whatever. It's for one day only. Although hopefully the colour's way more burgundy than the bubblegum she first flagged up. And thank heavens next-day delivery has finally reached Cornwall.

Her fingers close even more tightly around mine as we catch a view of the sun sparking off the lake beyond the terrace, then pause for a second to gasp at Poppy's cake. Three smooth white tiers, with a glorious cascade of ivory roses. Then as we cross the lounge we glimpse the waiting ballroom.

'It's beautiful, dahling. All beautiful. You've worked *so* hard for us.' My mum's dream turned out to be cream roses, candles and lanterns, and masses of eucalyptus. That's what we've given her in the Winter Garden too, which is where we're heading now for the ceremony. And if Kip's gnome has been sneaked back in to nestle by the double doors into the ball-room, I'm not going to be the one to complain.

By the last sofa there's a tug on my hand. My mum comes to a halt, and dips into her bag. 'Just a minute ...'

For a moment I'm worried that she's got cold feet, and she's about to turn and run. But she's too engrossed for that. As she holds something out to me, her hand's shaking. 'I want you to have these, Lily. It came to me the other day after we'd talked. I'm giving you the rings from last time. You're the perfect person to look after them for all of us.'

I hold out my hand, and the chain dangles onto my palm. As my fingers close around the wedding ring and engagement ring I've seen on her finger all my life, the lump in my throat swells to the size of a melon. 'I promise I'll keep them safe.' I fumble through my tears to put the chain around my neck.

She gently closes the fastening, and pats my skin. 'I know you will. That's good.' Then she dips into her bag, pulls out a ring, slips it onto her right hand for now, and holds it out for me to see. 'White gold this time. Not quite as blingy as Nicole's.'

'It's lovely.' A small solitaire, in the simplest setting.

She fastens her bag, and as she spreads her fingers, the diamond catches the light. 'It looks very new.'

I smile. 'Exactly right for a new woman, making a new beginning.' I clasp her hand. 'I'm very proud of you, Mum. What you're doing is *so* brave.'

My mum smiles, and squeezes back. 'Thank you. Right,

now that's done, I really am all set. Look, the boys are waiting for us.'

Over by the door to the Winter Garden the two dark heads with wavy hair are almost identical. Zac's shorter, and stockier, hands in pockets. Kip's all cheekbones and stubble shadows, holding tight to my mum's posy, which he insisted on bringing down for us. Probably just to prove what a perfect wedding host he's become.

Zac offers his arm. 'Ready then, Mom?' His transatlantic twang is a new shock each time he opens his mouth.

My mum hesitates. 'Actually, it's lovely of you to offer, but you go on in. We've got this sorted.'

Zac's forehead wrinkles. 'But I've just flown six thousand miles to give you away.'

I don't think my mum has ever refused him anything in his life.

She purses her lips. 'When you said you couldn't come, I asked Lily. She's done so much to make this wedding happen, we'll stay with that. You'll get your turn with the speeches.' As Zac raises his eyebrows and obediently disappears through the doors, my mum smiles. 'It feels right, Lily. You're the one who's been here for me. You're the one whose permission I want most.'

I scrunch her into the biggest hug I dare, given she's wearing cream satin, and my tears are streaming so fast they're dripping off the end of my chin.

'Your flowers, Barbara.' As Kip holds them out I let her go, and his face creases into a concerned smile. One small handful. Zinnias and marigolds, nasturtiums, fennel. Cosmos and cornflowers. A lavender sprig from the plant Kip bought last week. And sweet peas from David. All bound with trailing cream and grey ribbons.

My mum gazes down at them. 'They're lovely. Thank you for growing them. Both of you.' She sniffs as she looks at them, and when she looks up again she's smiling. 'I'm so pleased you came back, Lily.'

I wrinkle my nose. 'Me too.'

Who would have thought growing one small bunch of flowers would have taken so much agony and effort? Or, in the end, make me fall in love with gardening all over again? And better still, make me love my mum so much?

As I hold out my arm for her to take, Kip nods at someone through the door. The first haunting notes from the piano drift up towards the high ceiling sound very familiar, but I can't place them. 'What is it?' I whisper.

Kip mouths back. 'It's Rafe, playing *The Glasgow Love Theme* – the *Love Actually* music, from the bit where the girl falls in the lake.'

Beyond Kip's ironic would-you-believe-it glance I catch a glimpse of David at the front of the Winter Garden. He puts up his hand, grins at me, and we make the hang loose sign at each other before he dips out of sight.

Then as my mum and I begin to walk, Kip leans in closer and hisses in my ear. 'Good luck, Water Lily. I'd say you've smashed this one.' And for a nano second I'm regretting that I gave in on the outfit, but not the plus one.

The fittingly poignant music is only the start, and it shows me how much these two *have* thought about what they're doing. But even though I'm crying so hard I lose count of the tissues I go through over the next half hour, as my mum and David say their vows and sign the register, the scent of Kip's aftershave stays with me all the way.

Chapter 47

Saturday, 16th September
At Rose Hill Manor: Splash and dash

'Surviving, Water Lily?'

By the time Kip finds me tucked away in a quiet corner of the terrace, on the evening of my mum's wedding day, the swinging lights above our heads are bright against the darkening sky.

'I'm blending in,' I say. Not that he'll notice, but the roses on my dress carry on seamlessly from the scented ones tumbling down from the pergola. As the breathy September breeze brings out my goosebumps I pull my cashmere cardie closer. This is the first and last time I'm venturing out dressed like a garden, okay? Straight after the speeches I bundled the jacket into the office filing cabinet and pulled on the cardie I'm far more comfortable wearing.

He narrows his eyes. 'Did I miss the bouquet throwing?' You see what I mean when I say he's nailing his wedding game?

I laugh. 'My newly considerate mum very thoughtfully

decided to skip that part, seeing as I'm practically the only single female here.'

The worst thing about wonderful wedding days is how fast they fly by. My mum's has been a blur of tears, drinking, hysterical laughter, and delicious food. Prawn cocktail, goat's cheese tart, duck à l'orange. Trifle, lemon meringue pie, Eton Mess, profiteroles, banoffee pie. And although I was throwing down Prosecco like there's no tomorrow, thanks to the pudding table, the alcohol's had no effect at all. I was completely steady in my highest Miss KG heels, as I chatted mainly to my mum's bestie, Jenny, and Zac's charming American girlfriend, Angel. Short for Angelina. Although when it came to the seventies disco where everyone is still going wild now, all I can say is I'm damned grateful there are bows holding the shoes on my feet.

Kip hands me a bottle. 'I brought you a Fentimans. I thought we might ...'

He hesitates for long enough for my stomach to do a somer-sault, then a second later, another voice slices through the night air.

'Lily, just the woman, where have you been hiding all day?' It's Fred, swinging into view around a pergola post.

A second later Kip crashes down beside me on the wooden bench. 'Anything we can help you with, Fred?'

Fred's broad smile falters momentarily. 'I've got a fabulous suite on the first floor. The dancing's practically over, how about we go up for coffee and brandy before bed, Lily?'

I'm opening my mouth to ask how the hell he blagged that particular bedroom, but Kip jumps in first.

'Lily's with me today.' His arm slides along the seat behind me. 'And tonight too. So we'll catch you in the morning.' He laughs. 'That's if we decide to bother with breakfast.'

We both know he's only faking it to get rid of Fred, but it still sends my heart rate off the scale.

Fred's face folds into a scowl. 'And what about the date you owe me, Lily? You're not getting out of it that easily.'

I can feel Kip's spine going rigid beside me, but I get in first. 'Bollocks, Fred. I don't *owe* you anything. As for dates, they won't be happening. Not tonight. Or any other time come to that.' After standing up to my mum, Fred's a walkover.

Kip wades in. 'So if that's everything, maybe you can leave us to our lemonade?'

'Fizzy pop?' Fred's jeering as he backs away. 'Very rock and roll. And don't forget the condoms, Lily. These Penryns like to put it around, you know. You don't want to catch anything nasty.'

'Great.' Even if Fred's drunk, I'm reeling at the bitterness of that jibe. 'Does he have a problem with you?' It feels like a massive understatement.

Kip gives a sigh. 'It's mutual. That lowlife regularly gave Quinn a kicking, because he resented the fact that we had money and he didn't.' He gives a low laugh. 'Bart gave him a break, and let him rent some land. Ironic how things change. Now he's rolling in it, and we're broke.'

'Very funny.' I say, smiling at Kip's joke, and kind of hoping he won't take his arm away. And then I remember the logs across the road on that first open day. 'The escaping sheep, the garden, the flood and the rest ... Is that why he did it all?'

Kip blows out his cheeks. 'Who knows? Maybe he's just loyal to Rafe. Or competing for you. He'd certainly like to see me fail. Whatever, it's best to rise above it.' Given the list his long sigh seems justified. 'Enough about that. What are we doing next?'

I laugh. 'I was planning to go to my single person's room, up on the top floor.' I flinch as his fingers accidentally brush my shoulder.

He tilts his head on one side. 'Which coincidentally happens to be right next to my very own top floor single room. Or we could forget all about being sad singletons, and row out to the island. Sit on the beach and watch the dawn come up.' As he rubs me on the arm I shiver. 'It was fun last time we did it.'

As I lean sideways, the warmth of his body is solid against mine. 'That's the most tempting offer I've had in years.' Although it's meant to sound jokey it's the complete truth. 'Only one catch though. You're in charge of a wedding. Like I told you at Nicole's, you can't run out until it's over.'

He gives a low laugh. 'Which is why I have two guys from the estate manning the office. They'll call if I'm needed.' He dangles a slim black box in front of me.

If my voice is a squeak it's because I'm stunned. 'When did you get a pager?' Or overnight stand-ins for that matter.

He grins. 'We're trialling the system. Here at the Manor we take our responsibilities very seriously.' He nudges my leg with his. 'And someone's got to blow out the candles on the island. It might as well be us.'

I let that last one go, because he has excelled himself here.

This is Kip at the top of his wedding game. And if he's looking seriously edible due to my Prosecco goggles, for one night only I'm not going to fight it. Although, who am I kidding? My stomach's been squishing for weeks at the sight of his sexy sharp cheekbones and the shadows underneath them. Not to mention those tanned wrists.

'Are you okay in those shoes?'

'Fine.' If I go two floors up to find better ones he might change his mind.

'Shall we go then?' Him leading me by the hand seems completely natural. 'Is this your maximum speed, Water Lily? Not that there's any hurry ... But we were hoping to get there *before* sunrise ...'

Half way down the field, I undo my bows, kick off my shoes and dangle them from my fingers. When we reach the jetty the planks are smooth under the soles of my feet. After the prickles and bumps of the meadow, I'm exceedingly happy to roll into a boat.

'Definitely no getting stranded this time,' Kip's joking as he takes the oars, and pushes us off into water where the half moon's reflection is shimmering off the surface ripples.

But however much I'm the one who's drummed the responsibility into him, getting stuck here wouldn't be so bad. Not tonight. Given the quality company.

He rows a long way out without talking. As I trail my finger over the side of the boat the water's cool on my fingertips and I finally break into the gentle swish of the oars through the water. 'So what about those dreams you never told me about. Is there time to tell me tonight?'

I hear him let out a low laugh. 'It's as good a time as any. When you asked me that night on the beach, I'd have given a different answer from the one I'd give now. Losing a company is a shock at the time. But in the long term, there's a lot to learn from it.'

I never pushed it that night on the beach. 'But what went wrong? How did you come to make one decision to send it to the wall?' Now I know Kip better, it feels the right time to ask.

'That part wasn't actually me, it was my dad. He was taken in, ploughed everything we had and more, into an offer that was too good to refuse. But the catch was, what he was buying into didn't exist. By the time I found out, the deal was done, there was no going back. It was too late. We'd lost the lot.'

Shit. 'But I thought you said it was your fault?'

Kip sniffs. 'I'll always feel I was to blame. I should have kept a closer eye on Dad, should have seen what he was doing, and put a stop to it. Maybe I wasn't concentrating as much as I should have been.'

'You sound like you're being hard on yourself.'

'Only because I should be. Someone like Fred would say, "easy come, easy go". I'd done nothing to earn any of what I was enjoying in that company. I simply walked into it as a birthright. There were fast cars, prestigious offices, fabulous homes in London. But they all went. The personal equity I'd built up in my own house paid the last of the creditors, and bought the smallest flat imaginable for my dad. When you asked me before, all I wanted at the time was to get it all back. Go back to what we were. But somehow I don't feel that anymore.'

Even if it was handed to him on a plate, my chest is still aching for what he lost. 'I had no idea that's what you'd come from.'

'I left Dad with a pension, and I rocked up here with a promise from Bart that I could use the house until I was back on my feet again, and a fledgling idea from Quinn about doing weddings. The brothers promised to keep me going until I turned a profit. But the night I arrived I had enough capital to buy supper at the pub, the Landy, and an advertising hoarding.' Kip's voice is grim.

'Oh my frigging giddy aunt, how awful.' My gasp doesn't begin to cover it. No wonder he looked desperate. Driven. Like he had no idea. All of the above. Although he did a damn good job of covering it up with his arrogant act.

His voice is grave. 'There are times when your life derails, but the knack is to pick yourself up and keep on going. To learn to be happy again. It's not about making money, that's not what matters. I'd done it once after my mum died, so I knew I could do it again. And Bart was here for me too. Luckily he's taken the Caribbean side of the business from strength to strength.'

'So you want something different now?'

'My aims have changed, because I have. Let's just say, the guy I am now would have been straight onto that mistake, before it even happened. Somehow you taught me to give attention to detail, to focus. Taught me to care about what I'm doing, in a way I didn't before. And the upside is that I really enjoy what I'm doing now, in a way I never enjoyed working for Penryn Trading.'

'Well that's all good.' At least it is for Kip.

'I suspect making me do weddings might have been Quinn's punishment. My penance. I was certainly appalled by it at first.' Kip's low laugh ripples into the darkness. 'If that was the case, it backfired. In the best way possible.'

I'm smiling in the dark as I remember how Kip used to be. 'You were spectacularly clueless about brides and grooms when you arrived. Although the Manor was so amazing, it saved you every time.'

Kip draws in a breath. 'If I'd been as tuned into the business as I am now, I'd have saved the company. Knowing that means I can hold my head up again. I've got my self respect back. And having lost a huge chunk of what I took for granted, I damn well appreciate what's left. I've learned so much the last few months. About myself, about what's important to me. Building the basis of a great business here at the Manor is only a tiny part of the good that's come out of it. Although I never thought I'd say it, I can't think of anything I'd rather be doing than my job here. And you can't put a value on that. Maybe with a rethink on the three six five, along the lines you mentioned. Thanks again for that.'

My smile splits into a grin. 'You're welcome.'

He clears his throat. 'So in answer to your first question, I suppose we dream about what we think will make us happy. And in my case, that's the life I've got. Exactly as it is. Meaning I really don't want you to move on, because you have to admit, we do make a cracking team. But six months ago, who'd have thought I'd be saying that?'

Every part of that sends shivers through my ribcage. 'Don't

they say "real life starts where your comfort zone ends"?' I'm gripping the boat sides to stop my voice wavering. The trouble is, comfort zones aren't called that for nothing. They're great places to hang out simply *because* they're so cosy.

Kip's low laugh comes over the silky swish of the water. 'I think that's been true for both of us. We both washed up here, and were pushed into doing stuff we'd never done before. And in a strange way, we've got rather good at it. Probably largely due to you. How unexpected is that?'

Now it's my turn to laugh, because he sounds so pleased with himself. 'You think?' Although once I do, he's right again. Damn him. 'With your styling demands, and your garden, you pushed me out of my comfort zone as much as I pushed you.' What's more we've almost reached our destination. The lights along the jetty shining out over the water are coming closer.

Kip takes a few minutes to slide the boat in close. 'Surprising, but damned satisfying. I'd say we've done so well, we deserve a beach toast of our own. We'll grab some champagne from the cabin.' He leaps ashore, thuds onto the boards, and ties the boat up. 'As soon as you've checked the knot we'll be on our way.'

As he guides me off the plank walkway, there's a tiny part of me hoping that maybe we'll get into the kitchen, and he'll bump into me. That somehow, somewhere in the shadows, my mouth will find his. As I imagine how he might taste, I swallow hard, and clench my thighs as I get a hugely unfamiliar kick in the pit of my stomach.

'Ouch.' A small stone sticking into the base of my foot

yanks me back to real life. And of all of Kip's nightmare playlist, this really isn't the moment for *Orgasm Addict* to start buzzing through my head.

'Just for the record, when Quinn saw the wedding publicity pictures of us on the blog, he rang me and relinquished his claim.'

'What?' I'm squeaking because I can't believe he's talking about me.

He laughs. 'Just our ethics code that stopped us killing each other, remember.'

I shake my head. 'Boys' crap, you mean? I'm entirely disgusted you shared that.' But at the same time, I'm secretly quite pleased he did. Even if it's only come up because we're on the jetty again.

As we make our way onto the verandah, Kip pulls a battery lamp out of the shadows, and pushes the cabin door open. 'Lumos,' he says, as he strikes a match, and lights some candles above the empty fireplace.

As he hands me a candlestick, and disappears into the next room, I can make out a chair cover very like my dress fabric. 'Hey, look, I match the sofa.'

Kip's laugh is low as he comes back, bottle under his arm and glasses in hand. 'I'd say that's one excellent reason not to let your mum choose your clothes.'

Maybe my outfit dilemmas haven't stayed as private as I intended. For some reason I begin to giggle. It starts as a tiddler, then as Kip joins in it grows. Then I slap him, and he gives me a gentle cuff, which only makes us both explode more.

When our gasping and screaming laughter eventually subsides he nudges me. 'You look awesome in that dress.' He puts our candlesticks onto a table, then spins me round to face him.

'Thanks.' I lock my eyes on the dusky triangle of skin where his shirt collar opens, and try to ignore that my insides just left the building. 'You're not looking so shabby yourself.' I shiver as he traces his finger along my forehead, and pushes my hair out of my eyes.

His voice is low and husky as his face comes towards mine. 'Do you realise I've spent the entire day wanting to grab you.'

My eyes are closing and I'm tilting my face upwards, when a huge clatter makes us jolt. Then freeze. As we spin round, the open doorway behind us lights up.

Kip purses his lips as I gasp. As we creep forwards my heart is bouncing off my chest wall, and not in the good way it was five seconds ago. As we peer into the room, there's enough light to make out a bed.

There's a growl as the cover shifts. 'Bastard barnacles, what the frigate are you doing in *our* cabin?'

Kip lets out an astonished whoop as a weathered face pops up. 'Bart?'

And as a tousled head comes into view beside him there's another squawk. 'Lily? Is that you?'

My gulp is so huge, I almost inhale the eiderdown. It takes me a second to respond. 'Jess?'

Kip's laughing. 'What the hell are you two doing *here* of all places?'

Bart grunts. 'I'd have thought that was obvious.'

Kip's shaking his head and grinning. 'What, sex on the beach? Again?'

Bart gives a snort of protest. 'We're hiding from the revellers. There's only so many Bay City Rollers songs a man can take.'

The surprise seems to be the location, not his choice of bed partner. I have to ask, if only because I'm so far behind. 'Are you on board with this, Jess?' Last time I heard she hated Bart.

As Jess yanks the covers up to her chin she recovers her decorum. 'Don't worry, it's all in the plan, Lily.' She shoots me a wink. 'I'm taking one for the team here. Remember that?'

My gaping mouth is stretching into a grin the width of St Aidan Bay. 'Nice work, Jess.' We never did know the details. But whatever the reasoning behind her about-turn, she sounds like she's having a great time.

'Well, sorry for disturbing your island idyll, guys.' This is Kip, finally sounding repentant. 'We won't tell a soul, will we, Lily?' He gives me a jab in the ribs.

I get the picture. 'Absolutely not.'

There's a creak from the bed as Bart shifts on the pillows. 'No worries. As of tomorrow, there's no more skulking around. We've decided to go public. Haven't we Jess?' He gives her the same kind of poke Kip just gave me.

Jess raises an eyebrow. 'If you say so.'

'Congratulations! High fives to that.' Kip dives back out of the door, and comes back with the bottle and glasses. 'In which case we'll leave the champers with you.'

It's only as Kip and I are blowing out the lights on the jetty as we leave that we notice their boat pulled up a lot further along the beach. If they hadn't got here first, I can't help thinking it might have been us in that bed. But somehow the moment's gone.

'I did not see that coming,' I say. As we hurry into our boat, the wind is chillier, and there are clouds scudding across the moon.

'They were teenage sweethearts. It's the worst kind of unfinished business.' Kip wrinkles his nose. He begins to row, and with his long swift strokes, and a following wind, we cross the water in no time.

'How about watching the sunrise from this side?' As he ties up the boat against the jetty, and yanks me ashore with one easy pull, there's drizzle in the air.

I open my mouth to reply, but a beep comes from Kip's pocket.

He gives a rueful grin as he pulls out the pager. 'Whose idea was this? Damn, it's urgent.'

I throw down my shoes, wriggle my feet into them. By the time I've done up my bows the raindrops are getting bigger. 'In that case, Kipling, it's "laters".' I reach up on tip toe, and as I drop a kiss on his cheek my mouth waters. 'Thanks for a wonderful day.'

And a second later, despite my four and a half inch heels, I'm running towards the house.

Chapter 48

Sunday, 17th September
At Rose Hill Manor: Here and there, home and away

'Who turned the tap on?' I'm groaning, and looking at the sky as the first massive raindrops fall.

It's mid afternoon next day by the time all the guests have left. As my mum and David finally get to leave the Manor themselves, they've already made approximately a million trips back and forth to Heavenly Heights ferrying suitcases, dress covers, flowers, the cake, and all their presents. After a wet night, the sun broke through again at breakfast. But as they run to get in the car for the last time, the clouds turn smoky grey, and within seconds the rain is hammering and bouncing up off the gravel.

'Just a second, dahling.' My mum hurries into the passenger seat, and as David winds down her window, she flips down the sun visor for running repairs to her make up.

'Excuse me, I am getting soaked here.' Just saying. I'd expected a flash over of Chanel Mighty, not a full facial.

'All done.' She beams. 'Ready for one last selfie of the three of us?'

I lean backwards through the car window, and make a 'hang loose' sign behind our heads as she holds out her phone.

'Cheese everyone.' She shouts. And then it really is over.

'Umbrella coming.' It's Kip. He pulls me in beside him under a big brolly from the office, but as we stand grinning in at the car window I'm already dripping.

'Thank you both. For everything.' My mum's voice is breaking, and there's a clash of hands and faces as we do our last goodbye touches.

Eventually I step back, dragging Kip with me. 'Right. I'll see you up at yours very soon.' Given it'll probably be all of half an hour before I arrive with even more flowers, we might be going over-board on the goodbyes. I stand flapping both my hands like mad as the tyres scrunch on the gravel. They do a circuit of the car park, and it's only as they pick up speed and come around for a second time that I catch a blur of colour at my mum's open window. A nano second later, a missile is flying through the air towards us, and suddenly Kip and I are both clamping my mum's posy to my chest.

'Jeez.' As I untangle the ribbons from my fingers, and rearrange the crumpled petals, I can still hear my mum's laugh echoing along the drive.

Kip gives a low cough as he extracts his hand. 'Sorry for the grope. Most inappropriate. '

'Any time,' I say. Then kick myself for the slip and smile very brightly to cover it up. 'No worries.'

'Catching two bouquets in a row,' he says. 'There has to be a subliminal message in there somewhere.' With that deadpan expression he has to be teasing.

I ignore him, and move on swiftly. 'So that's that then.' My mum's was the last of this season's weddings. So unless there are some late Christmas bookings, we're done here for a while.

Kip blows out his cheeks. 'Not quite. There's one thing more. In the ballroom.'

'And?' It's empty, and as we arrive, I'm mainly checking to see my soaked shirt has only gone blotchy, and not completely see through.

He sighs. 'I just wanted to dance with you now everyone's gone. That's all.'

I close my eyes and swallow. Try to find a reason not to have his hand on my waist, and my eyes locked on his throat. I was hoping that the Prosecco goggles would have worn off this morning, but if anything they've got worse. There's something insanely sexy about Kip, even the pale and wrecked version.

'Okay.' My eyes are as wide as his because I gave in so easily. But sometimes the fastest way is to get things over. Resisting could take forever. A dance will take no time. Four short minutes, and I'll be free to get back to my life again.

He walks across to the music decks. 'So that idea you had ... your vision for taking the Manor up-market ... we're going to run with it ... go for six mega exclusive weddings a year.'

'Brilliant.' Mentally I'm punching the air. I can't wait to see Poppy's face when I tell her. I'm bouncing already. 'And what are we dancing to?' I'm bracing my ear drums for an assault from The Foo Fighters, or Motorhead.

'I was going to go for *Somewhere only we know*, then I remembered this.' As he flicks on the music a laid back guitar twangs across the ballroom.

A smile creeps across my face. '*Say Hello and Wave Goodbye?* Good choice.' I love this song.

He shrugs as he walks towards me. 'I've heard you play it sometimes roaring up the drive. It's kind of fitting. And the best thing is, it's nine minutes long.'

In an effort to stay in control, I hold up my hands and look businesslike. 'So what kind of dance? A two step? Or we could try some Salsa moves?' Both ridiculous given the tempo, but whatever.

He takes my fingers, then slides his hands around my back. 'Let's keep it simple.' As he draws me against his body we begin to sway.

As dances go, we're practically stationary. But I shake back my damp hair, and close my eyes. As our bodies fuse into a single plank of warmth, I breathe him in. The feel of him is all the sweeter for having waited. If this is delayed gratification, I'm happy to take it. His hands glancing across the skin where my top ends are light, and deliciously tingly. Shiveringly unfamiliar, for someone I know so well. And as the muscles of his back are flexing under my fingertips, I'm loving the strength of him. I could so easily take this man to bed, and tear off his clothes, and have achingly amazing sex with him. Not something I'd imagined I'd ever do again. Not that we're going to. But after so long, that one simple thought sets me free for the rest of my life. Not that Kip will feel the same, given his aversion for getting close to anyone. But dancing has to mean something. As for the hormone rush telling me to forget bed, and jump him here and now, against the wall, I need to shut that down right now.

I yank my mind to a cleaner place. 'Six weddings a year. So how will that work?'

Kip's voice resonates close to my ear. 'Better for Bart and Jess, now he's moving back to the Manor full time.'

Crikey. 'Permanently? As in three six five?' The way I'm hearing their names together, it's like they're already a well-established couple. 'Whatever happened to transatlantic commuting?'

Kip pulls down the corners of his mouth. 'The power of love and all that. I guess he's smitten with Jess, and she's based very firmly here. Bart's been on his own for a long time, so if he's got a chance to be happy he deserves to grab it.'

Was this what Jess meant by her top secret plan? Who'd have thought Bart would ever find a reason to settle down. In Rose Hill of all places.

'So remind me why we're dancing?' At two in the afternoon, it's a bit random, even for Kip. And maybe there's a tiny part of me hoping I'll draw him off the fence about where he stands with me.

His sigh is almost a whisper. 'It could be our last chance.'

My insides drop faster than the lift in the Empire State building. Whatever answer I was expecting, it wasn't that. 'So where exactly do you fit into the new-look Rose Hill Manor?'

Kip gives a snort. 'I won't be sticking round playing gooseberry if that's what you mean.' His laugh is almost bitter. 'Bart has work for me in St Kitts. So that's where I'll be heading.'

My voice almost disappears. 'The Caribbean?' That's seriously far away. My stomach feels like a banana that's been stamped on. 'And the garden?' I'm guessing that's our flower growing out the window.

'You'll still be able to use the garden. But I won't be here to help.' Kip's pulling his fingers through the damp strands of my hair. 'I'm so sorry. This wasn't how it was meant to be. Bart only fully decided this morning. It's unexpected for all of us, but the Manor *is* his home. I was damn lucky to get to use it when I did.'

I drag in a breath. 'It's weird how love turns life upside down.' It did for my mum, and now it has for Kip. I'm also thinking about how much I've come to depend on everything at the Manor being the way it is. And how shattered I'll be if Kip's not here, hanging around the office. Messing around at his swing ball, with his torn jeans and his awful music.

There are deep shadows under his eyes. 'Just when I felt like I'd finally found what I was good at, and was here forever, my lucky break dematerialised.' He purses his lips. 'All the more reason for you to stay and make the most of yours, Water Lily. At least tell me you'll do that.'

'I'll think about it.' And I do mean that. 'But what about all next year's bookings here?' I'm remembering the chart in the office. Some months there were so many reserved stickers it looked like Kip had nailed his Vegas dream.

Kip gives another long sigh. 'Bart will look after those.' His forehead crinkles. 'There maybe aren't *quite* as many bookings as there are stickers on the office wall.'

My voice rises. 'Kip?' When I think of how worried they

made Poppy. And how desperate we were to fight back. And how damned determined Jess was to go all the way for us.

He gives an inscrutable shrug. 'So maybe I made a few up, after Bart shoved the prices sky high. It's a well-known sales trick, to encourage people to make up their minds.' His frown deepens. 'You didn't seriously think ...?'

'It doesn't matter.' There's nothing we can change now. And who'd have thought I'd finally be so gutted to see Kip taken down. Like this, and so suddenly.

'We don't have much time, Water Lily.' As his mouth finds mine, the kiss he drags me into is sweet and hot. After a long time, I break away to stop the world spinning, and he shakes his head. 'I'm sorry. This is such a mess.'

'When do you leave?' All I can hear in the background is bloody David Gray. *Say hello and wave goodbye.* When Kip said it was fitting, I never thought he meant like this.

Kip's voice is bleak. 'I fly out tomorrow.'

As his face dips back towards me, some primal self-preservation instinct kicks in. And instead of desperately burying my mouth in his, I'm pushing him away.

'I was hoping ...' he begins.

But I'm already half way across the ballroom, running blindly towards the double doors. Hoping? Hoping for a Penryn one-night-stand before he left, probably. And dammit if I'm being a hypocrite, given I was contemplating the same. But the big difference was I wasn't going to sleep with him, then get the hell out of here.

As I bump my way through the lounge, the blue sofas are blurring. By the time I dash to the office to grab my bag, and rush out of the front door, my tears are flooding down my cheeks, but the deluge of rain washes them away. As I dive into Gucci, the sobs are wracking my body.

'Bloody Penryns breaking hearts and leaving town. Nothing new there.' But as I rage through my tears I'm not just crying for me. I'm crying for Kip too. Because he was so close to nailing his dream. And now it's gone.

Chapter 49

September, October, November...

W ho'd have thought one guy disappearing over the horizon would make you feel so crap, when mostly you didn't like them anyway. Although his last piece of wisdom stays with me. Sorry, this is Kip I'm talking about – no surprise there then. He texted me before he left to point out we'd never had that mini break. How ridiculous was that? I didn't text back. But whenever I close my eyes, it's his face I see. And try as I might, I can't stop replaying those last few moments in the ballroom.

'I can't understand why you and Kip aren't skipping,' Jess says one day.

No idea how the heck she knows we aren't. Skyping, I mean. It's a sign that I'm not quite myself yet when I can't be bothered to correct her. As for Jess, the harder she is on Bart, the more besotted with her he becomes. And it's also become obvious that her commitment to the team isn't temporary. She's playing the long game here. Committed even.

'When I asked you to work on the styling, I knew you'd

be amazing, but I had no idea it would take off so well,' she says another day. Jules has made us some picture boards from photographs of the weddings we've worked on, and we're hanging them on the back wall in the basement. 'At the start I lured you in by saying it was temporary. But I'd love you to stay. The way it's going we could buy the shop next door. We could extend along the street.' This is Jess. She can't help her ambition running away with her.

In the end, I don't throw away my own chance to make a success of my career, and leave St Aidan. Instead I delete my job application files, and settle down to grow the styling department at Brides by the Sea. As for Kip, I know I'm the one in the wrong here. I had no right to be in love with him, when he never promised me anything, and certainly never encouraged me. All he did was help me learn how to be myself. Gave me that push to be properly happy. And I was so pleased when I thought I'd cracked it. I had no idea it would only work when he was there.

The Daisy Hill Farm End-of-Season Wedding Fair brings in a rush of wedding bookings, as well as lots of future styling bookings. Although despite the changes at the Manor, and the bookings now coming out of her ears, Poppy's anxiety sickness still refuses to go away. When Immie and I finally persuade her to pee on a pregnancy test stick, it takes ten goes before she believes what's been staring us all in the face for months. Luckily Rafe's delighted. Then before we know it, a late October frost turns the nasturtiums in the walled garden to slimy mush overnight. And it's time for the Venue Awards evening.

Chapter 50

Tuesday, 21st November
The Awards Reception at The Harbourside Hotel:
Corkscrews and pure genius

'I promise there'll be a surprise if you come, Lily.'

This is Poppy, trying to overcome my last minute cold feet about the Awards Gala Night. I'm almost ready, but making the final move, and pulling my dusky grey crushed velvet dress over my head suddenly feels like too much effort.

'What kind of surprise? Popping candy chocolate gateau ... Gourmet donuts ...' Since September I only go out when bribed by ever more elaborate confectionery.

As Poppy scrunches up her face, she isn't giving anything away. 'Something like that. Or better, even.' She wiggles her eyebrows, and gives her tummy a rub.

I'm warming to the idea of leaving the flat. 'Pecan and crackle toffee cake?' Let's face it, that's the ultimate. 'And you definitely aren't looking fat, Pops, however much you're complaining you've grown out of all your clothes.'

Despite the minor hold up, we reach the polished foyer of the hotel in time for the start. The room where the reception is being held is bathed in pink light, and most guests are already seated around wide circular tables, underneath glitzy chandeliers. As Poppy guides us through to ours, I'm puzzled to see Jess and Bart sitting with Rafe, Immie, Chas, and Jules.

I whisper in her ear as we get there. 'Is there a mistake in the seating? Just because we all come from Rose Hill, doesn't mean we want to sit together.' Let's face it, we're still daggers drawn when it comes to the awards.

Poppy laughs. 'It's fine. Jess has been building bridges.'

If this is the surprise, to be honest, it's more of a shock. Although the conflicts at the table are less than they could be as we make our way through the three-course dinner, because Bart seems more preoccupied with checking his phone than with chatting. We've devoured our pâté, wolfed our chicken Valentino stuffed with mozzarella and red peppers, and everyone except Poppy has knocked back a lot of wine. We're well into our key lime pie, when he finally puts his phone away.

As he heads off to schmooze the various sponsors, Jess leans across to us. 'Don't mind Bart, he's a teensy bit preoccupied. But while he's gone, just for the record ...' She narrows her eyes so far they're almost shut. 'The night Jules took photos, and Bart and I got stuck on the island, I was the one who let the boat go.'

'No.' As Immie, Poppy and I gasp, then exchange glances, our faces are screwing into frowns of disbelief.

Jess's grin is wide. 'It was a fast forward way of landing the man. All part of our fabulous plan. But I didn't want you to think it was down to him.' As timing goes, Jess's is brilliant.

There's no chance to ask any more, because the speeches begin and roll seamlessly through beginning with the different categories of tourist attractions, and hotel awards. As the compere finally gets to the section we've all been waiting for Bart slides back into his seat, and gives Jess a thumbs up.

The compere holds up the mike. 'So now to the award for Cornwall's Best Wedding Venue ...'

Rafe and Poppy are clutching each other's hands, Chas has his arm slung over Immie's shoulder. We're pursing our lips, and holding our breaths as the compere fumbles with a gold envelope.

Then as he says the words 'And the award goes to Weddings at Daisy Hill Farm ...' we all erupt into the hugest cheer of the evening. As Poppy and Rafe wiggle their way to claim the shimmering crystal heart trophy the compere is holding aloft, Immie is roaring. And I'm screaming like a proverbial banshee, and crying at the same time, because I know how much anguish Rafe and Poppy have gone through during the last nine months. After photos and a thousand handshakes, as they make their way back towards us their eyes are shining.

'Tossing toad arse, bleeding brilliant, woman ... and man.' Immie stops flapping her hands in front of her face, and hauls them into a hug. Then she passes them along to me for my squeeze, then I pass them on to Jess.

As the applause dies down, I can't help noticing Bart's still cheering, and he gets up to give Rafe an individual slap of congratulation on the shoulder. So, he's not so sore about the Manor losing out, or else being in love has made him into a spectacular good sport.

As we all sit quietly cooing over the trophy, the compere begins again. 'In fact there were so many high-quality entries in this category, the assessors decided to create an ultimate category, namely the Castle and Country House Wedding Venues.'

For once in her life Jess loses her cool, and her voice is all squeaky. 'Which is where Bart comes in ...' She moves seamlessly into a loud whoop, that sounds most unlike herself.

As the compere pauses I take in Bart's ear-to-ear beam, and I hiss at Poppy, 'Did you know about this? Is this the surprise?'

She's grinning as she mouths back. 'Wait and see.'

'And the winner in the super-category for Best Castle and Country House Wedding Venue, is ...' There's another dramatic pause. '... Rose Hill Manor.'

'Well done, Bart.' We're all yelling, and waving and cheering, and waiting for him to get up. But he's just sitting there clapping along with us.

And then from nowhere, a tall slim figure in a tux hurries in through the door. As I take in the dark wavy hair and the gaunt face, I have to shut my eyes. Simply because I can't believe what I'm seeing. *It can't be ... Kip?* When I look again, his face has creased into the biggest smile in the world, and those smoky eyes are crinkling straight at me.

As he comes within reach, he holds out his hand to me. 'Come on, Water Lily. This one's as much yours as it is mine.' For a second he swoops in and kisses my cheek, then he's pulled me to my feet, and we're running towards the stage.

I'm crying so hard, I'm wiping tears and slobber all over Kip's lapels as he wedges me under his arm to accept his award, but no-one seems to mind or notice.

His voice is low in my ear as he crushes me into a bear hug. 'It's so good to see you, Water Lily, hell, I've missed you.' It's so much of a blur, I barely seem to be moving my legs, but he's swept me off my feet, and carried me back to the table.

'My, you must be strong,' I say, as he deftly drops me back onto my seat.

He laughs. 'All without dinner too. I almost didn't make it because the flight was delayed.'

As Bart takes the shimmering crystal heart in his hands he's laughing too. 'I spent the entire meal tracking you with my app. Apologies for that everyone.' He dips in to his pocket. 'Hanky, Lily?'

My face couldn't be any wetter if I'd been dipped in the lake. I take the hanky, and scrub my cheeks. I'm still sniffing and gulping, but I have to speak. 'I'm so happy to see you, Kip.' I'm wailing at Poppy. 'It's the best surprise ever.'

Poppy smiles, and does an eyebrow wiggle. 'That's not quite everything.'

I give her an appalled frown. 'You're not having twins? Is that the rest?'

She closes her eyes. 'You tell her Kip.'

'Well I hope you'll be pleased, Water Lily ...' He hesitates, as if he's nervous. 'I'm coming back for good. With the baby on the way, Rafe and Poppy need help with the Daisy Hill Farm weddings, and they've offered me the job of wedding manager at the farm. And together we'll look after the six super-weddings at the Manor too. How cool is that?'

'Pure genius. You get to do your dream job after all.' I can't help flapping my hands with excitement. We've spent so long doing it with Nicole, I think it's catching. 'That's *so* brilliant.' After he's given me another hug and as big a snog as is decent given we're in a reception with chandeliers I frown, and laugh at Poppy. 'You do know about his terrible taste in music?'

Poppy smiles back. 'He has mentioned it. Although Rafe thought it wasn't so bad.'

Scanning the circle of smiling faces around the table, as they watch my reaction there's not even a mild trace of surprise. I turn on them. 'So you all knew, and no-one said a word?'

Immie gives a loud guffaw. 'You know what the Rose Hill grape vine's like. The whole village is in on it.'

Chas joins in with an incredulous head shake. 'Everyone down the Goose and Duck have known for months. It's a dead cert you and Kip will be moving up to Heavenly Heights the minute Barbara and David find a suitable place to move on to. And in the meantime, Rafe's got a cottage with your names on.'

'Jeez, thanks, Rafe,' I say. How embarrassing is this? 'I don't even know if I want to live at Heavenly Heights. Have you seen the parallelograms on the wallpaper there?' But when I catch Kip's eye I can see he doesn't mind at all.

Rafe gives a smug smile. 'You could have a cottage at the farm. But it's one of those times when there's no point fighting the will of the village.'

Poppy's laughing too. 'The moment you caught Sam's bouquet, you were done for.'

I screw up my face. 'But that wasn't me. It was Jess.'

This time it's Bart's turn to beam. 'And we all know how that worked out.'

Jess is protesting loudly. 'You definitely caught those flowers first, Lily. My luck is rebound luck.' Her laugh is husky. 'Not that I'm implying Bart's inferior, but he is a bit of a pirate.' Although as he's a pirate with a country house with a lake, not to mention properties in Antigua and Klosters, it could be worse.

Kip's nodding. 'I was there when that bouquet got caught. Sorry, but the flowers hit you first, Water Lily. Given they came at you like a rocket, I'd say your single days had to be numbered.' He's squeezing my fingers tight, and he comes in close to my ear. 'Fancy a walk on the beach, so I can say "hello" properly?'

I grin, because it's November, and the wind's blowing a howler around the bay. And yet even if it's freezing, and guaranteed to turn my hair to corkscrews in three seconds flat, I can't think of anything I'd like better. 'We could sit out and watch the dawn breaking? For old time's sake.'

Kip looks alarmed. 'Hell no. When I've booked us a double

room upstairs, with a queen-sized bed, there's no way we're sitting on the sand like singles.' He gives me another nudge. 'Your mum wouldn't hear of it.'

Which just about covers everything except for one massive outstanding question.

Chapter 51

Tuesday, 21st November
On the beach: Rising tides and last words

By the time we've come down a hundred steps from the hotel and we're stomping along the sand, battling into a head wind, I've got Kip's parka zipped on top of my own coat. I'm *so* happy to see him, but I'm wearing so many layers, groping's simply not practical. What's more the sand's blowing horizontally into every snog.

'My teeth are gritty,' I'm yelling into the wind, from the beach by the far end of the bay, watching the lights around the coast twinkle in the blackness.

'Mine too. We won't stay long.' Kip shouts, as he opens his overcoat and pulls me inside it. 'I wanted to bring you here to tell you I love you, that's all. I think I already loved you that other night on the beach, I just didn't recognise the feeling. And I wanted to tell you the day in the ballroom when we were dancing, but you ran away from me.'

As I shiver against him, and listen to the sound of the waves skidding up the beach, my knees turn to hot syrup. 'I love you too, Kip. It's so weird. Just like in all the songs, isn't it?' As soon as I say it, and remember the kind of racket he likes, I rethink that. 'Maybe not the songs you listen to. But now I'm in love, I know I wasn't ever before.' I don't even need to mention last time. It's simply not important any more.

'It's a first for me too. But you know that already. Although I did fall a tiny bit in love with a girl I pulled out of the lake a long, long time ago. But she never knew.'

Hearing that brings a lump into my throat. 'I had the strangest sense I already knew you when you dragged me out of the pond on Valentine's Day. And I suppose I did. But about my question. You said you never wanted to get close to anyone after your mum died.'

There's a low rumble in his throat. 'I never intended to. But you were there every day, and I fell in love with you because I couldn't not. That day in the ballroom, when you ran I wanted to come after you. I didn't because I had nothing to offer you. But the second I went away I knew I couldn't live my life without you.'

And there's that too. 'I'm so sorry the way things happened. I never dreamed Bart would send you to Antigua.'

He laughs. 'It worked out. The pain of being apart from you totally made me see without any doubt that I had to be with you. If Poppy and Rafe hadn't offered me the job at the farm, I'd have had to find some other way of getting back. It's non-negotiable. You know that don't you? And as from now, the details aren't important, so long as we're together.'

I grin. 'You need to watch out Cake-face, or you'll end up with migraine wallpaper, and gnomes on the porch.'

He laughs back. 'I won't mind. I'm very adaptable. Apart from wanting to go back to the hotel. To take you to bed. Like right now would be good?'

As a wave comes in, we skip up the sand. 'Lucky for you the tide's coming in. So, we're definitely watching the dawn come up from the balcony, Kipling.' We both gaze upwards at the black velvet sky, pricked with stars.

'Whatever you say, Water Lily.' He laughs, then he turns and pulls me up the beach.

Acknowledgements

A big thank you...

To my wonderful editor Charlotte Ledger, who is talented, brilliant, supportive and lovely – all at the same time. This series belongs to both of us. And I love it more with every book. To Kimberley Young and the team at HarperCollins for three fabulous covers and all round expertise and support. To my lovely agent, Amanda Preston, for being so generous with her time and wisdom, and adding so much support and inspiration.

To Debbie Johnson and Zara Stoneley, and my brilliant writing friends across the world. To the fabulous book bloggers, who spread the word.

A special shout out and thank you to the most fabulous wedding-related people we've met over the last couple of years ... To Emily Bridal of Sheffield, whose shop and dresses are simply fab. Emily came up with the most amazing wedding dresses for both my girls. I literally get tears in my eyes every time I think of how beautiful she made them as brides. To Jenn Edwards and Natalie Manlove, and the Jenn Edwards Wedding Hair and Make-up Team, who travel nationwide, making women into the most beautiful versions of themselves. Jenn and Natty gave me hair and make-up that made me feel like Sera on the day of Alice's wedding. I *so* love it when real life and fiction get mixed up. To Melanie Brunt from Drop Dead Gorgeous Sheffield for fab nail and beauty treatments and expertise. I'll remember my bright pink gel nails forever. Thanks, and huge admiration go to brave and super-talented photographers Jon Dennis from S6 Photography, Sally from Sally T Photography, and Hannah from CameraHannah. Coming on to the sweet part, thanks to Ashleigh Marsh at Oh No! Delicious, for cakes so astonishing they take your breath away. And thanks to amazing cake baker, Caroline Tranter for bringing the cakes in the books to life, and for letting us use her fab pictures. To High Street Bride guru, Samantha Birch for sharing her insider knowledge. To Losehill House Hotel, near Edale, and West Mill, in Derby, for two wedding days that could not have been more wonderful. Two very different venues, both spectacular, each perfect in their own way.

Big hugs, to India and Richard, for their amazing wedding, which is where this series began. And more hugs and good luck to Anna and Jamie whose very own Sequins and Snowflakes wedding in February was the happiest of days ... complete with surprise snow the day before that almost sent this mother-of-the-bride over the edge! To my entire family, for cheering me on all the way. To my wonderful dad, and my lovely mum, who has been so courageous since she's been on her own. To Max for being the man about our house and bringing me cake. To Caroline for making the cake. And big love to my own hero, Phil ... You know all the down sides of living with a writer and still hang on in there every day. Thank you for never letting me give up.

Favourite Summer
Cocktails from Brides by the Sea

In case you'd like to try a taste of Brides by the Sea at home, it's become a bit of a tradition to include a few recipes at the end of the book. So here's how to make some of the fab drinks featured in. Don't stress too much about the quantities – at Brides by the Sea it's much more about sloshing it in and having a good time. As Jess would say, LET THE FUN BEGIN...

IDEAS FOR PIMPING YOUR PROSECCO...

RASPBERRY PROSECCO BELLINI

This low-calorie Prosecco Bellini is made with one part raspberry liqueur, a sprig of basil, and four parts premium Prosecco. Quantities depend on your choice of glass size.

Perfect served in champagne flutes. Add the Prosecco to the raspberry liqueur and watch the red liqueur float upwards. Fabulous with fresh raspberries floating on top.

FORAGERS' FIZZ

This country-hedgerow cocktail is made using sloe gin, and Prosecco. Go easy on the gin, or you might end up accidentally falling in the village pond! Not something Jess would ever say ... One part sloe gin to four parts Prosecco is a good mix to begin with but slosh it in according to your taste. Floating blackberries add a fitting rustic finish.

Looks lovely in pretty glasses. If you're feeling extra fancy, use a mini peg to fix some hedgerow flowers to the outside of the glass edge to decorate.

HIBISCUS PROSECCO

For the most simple version of this, simply place a hibiscus flower in the bottom of a glass along with one teaspoon of the syrup the flower comes in and top up with Prosecco. Completely delish, totally summery, with a touch of the exotic. Add a splash of vodka for an extra kick. To make it even prettier, choose pink Prosecco.

RASPBERRY BASIL AND LIMONCELLO PROSECCO

For this totally delectable drink, take a dash of limoncello, a splash of vodka (optional) and top up with Prosecco. To finish, float basil leaves, lemon wedges and raspberries. Great served in highball glasses. Garnish with a lemon wheel on the glass edge if you're in a fancy mood. Stir in a teaspoon of fine sugar if you're feeling extra sweet.

AND NOW FOR SOME FUN ROMANTIC COCKTAILS...

... as served at the Valentine's Day wedding party in the book. As with every Brides by the Sea drink, if you love the taste, they're fab all year round too.

KISS ON THE LIPS COCKTAIL

Easy going and fruity, this cocktail is great to help you stay hydrated. For an alcohol-free version, use peach cordial instead of the schnapps.

11/2 oz peach schnapps
5oz frozen mango
1 tablespoon grenadine
Cherry and pineapple to garnish

Blend the schnapps and frozen mango together until smooth. Put the grenadine in a glass, then add the mango and peach mixture. Top with pineapple and a cherry. Pretty and delish.

THE LOVE BITE COCKTAIL

To create the layers in this cocktail, add each ingredient very slowly and smoothly, over the back of an up-turned teaspoon. It may take practice but the result is impressive.

1oz cherry liqueur
1oz orange liqueur
1oz cream

Pour in the cherry liqueur, layer in the orange liqueur. Then top with cream, and serve.

SCARLETT O'HARA COCKTAIL

Who could resist a cocktail with a name like this, and a colour to match?

1 1/2 oz Southern Comfort
Cranberry juice
Wedges of lime

Fill a tall glass with ice and squeeze the juice from a lime wedge over the ice cubes. Add Southern Comfort. Top up with cranberry juice and stir. Garnish with a lime wedge. Enjoy!

SEX ON THE DRIVEWAY COCKTAIL

It would be a shame to miss out this naughty bright blue drink with the raunchy name. It's a variation on the Sex on the Beach cocktail, the old favourite at Jaggers bar. Perfect for summer parties, it's sweet, fruity and easy to make. It does have a lot of vodka in, so watch out ... Too many might sneak up on you.

1oz peach schnapps
1oz Curacao
2oz vodka
6oz lemonade
Crushed ice

Place the crushed ice in a glass. Add the alcohol, then top up with lemonade.

Cheers!

Love Jane xx